REVOLUTION

PIET HEIN WOKKE

REVOLUTION

XOWOX PUBLISHING

2016
First Edition
by Xowox Publishing BV
Vinkenstraat 150b
1013 JW Amsterdam

Typeset in Great Britain
Printed in the UK by CPI Group (UK) Ltd, Croydon cro 4yy

ISBN 978-90-826190-0-3

MIX
Paper from
responsible sources
FSC
www.fsc.org
FSC® C013604

TO MY BROTHER

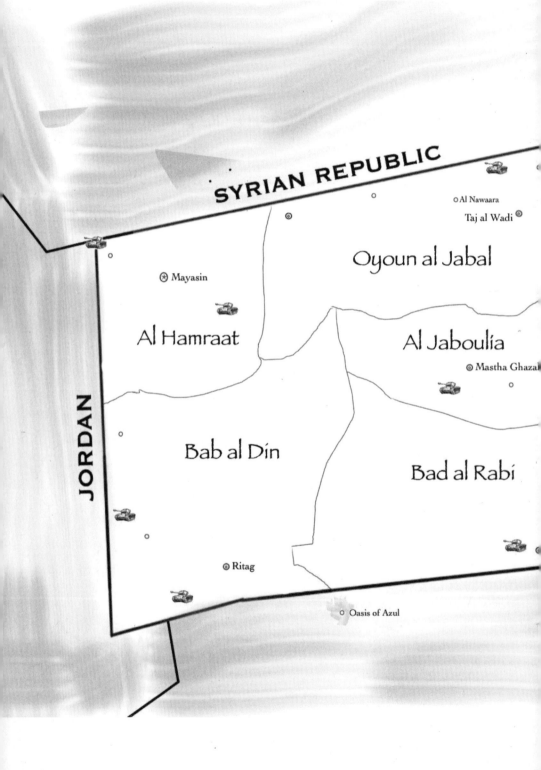

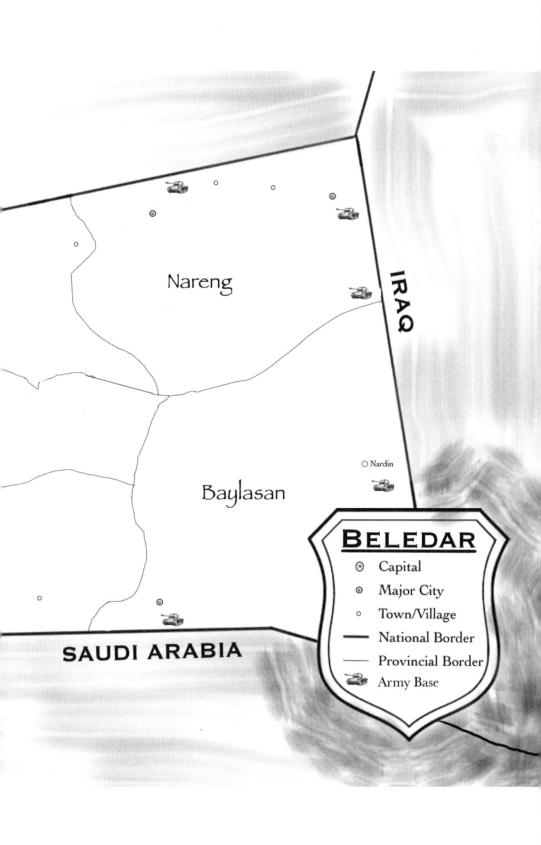

PROLOGUE:

PRINCE JALAL
Oxford

27 April 1932 A.D.

Jalal is working on a letter to his father, Emir Hussein of Beledar, when the door opens and his manservant announces Lord Richard Rockingham.

'Care to buy me a drink, old boy?' are the first words out of his friend's mouth after the servant lets him pass.

'Hello to you too,' he says as Richard makes straight for the whisky tray. 'Please, help yourself.'

'Thank you, that was my plan exactly,' his friend answers, ignoring the sarcasm. 'Want one?'

'I'd rather have one at the Randolph.'

'Only if you're buying.'

'Why? I thought you were one of the few people in Oxford who had both a title and money?' Perhaps the Depression has made things worse, but it appears to Jalal that if there is one group that has not flourished as a result of the British 'democracy,' it is the old aristocracy. In fact, he has decided that once he inherits the throne from his father, he is going to use the exact same mechanism to break the power of the Beledarian lords.

Richard sits down in the comfortable chesterfield in the corner of the room and sighs deeply. 'I am, or at least I'm going to be when my father dies. But a couple of sharks have had the rather unfortunate idea to send information about my personal credit—or lack of it—to my father; can't say the old man is very pleased. He has promised to gamble the whole estate away unless I economise.'

'I feel for you.'

'You should.' Richard again ignores the sarcasm. 'Are you game?'

Jalal looks at his friend and grins. The Rockinghams are one of the richest families in England and appear immune to the Depression; it's funny that this doesn't stop the marquis from cutting off his son's credit.

'Why not.'

'Excellent!' Richard beams, but he does not get up. 'You know, the other day I read a book about the Middle East, and I started to wonder. Are you a Mohammedan?'

'I am a Muslim,' Jalal corrects him. He does not care much for the term 'Middle East' either, but there is no use explaining why it's demeaning to a young man who's convinced that London is the centre of the world.

His friend frowns. 'What's wrong with Mohammedan?'

'Listen, do you want to go out, or do you want a history lecture?' Jalal says, pretending to be annoyed.

'I think I'll go for the lecture,' Richard replies, and he makes another move for the whisky carafe. Jalal is quicker, though, and puts it out of reach.

'Suit yourself. I'm going out.'

Before he reaches the door, Richard is next to him. 'Of course, you could educate me while we're walking.'

'Or you could buy another book.'

'That's not the same. Besides, I doubt that the author of my book really knew what he was talking about.'

'Why's that?' Jalal asks as they step outside. For a second he stops, closes his eyes, and takes a deep breath. He hated being sent to England, but there is nothing like a beautiful spring day in Oxford.

'For one, he referred to your people as Mohammedans, and I have just learned that I should be using the term Muslim.'

Jalal opens his eyes again and looks at his friend. Normally, it is Richard educating him; it feels good that it's the other way around for a change.

'It's wrong, because when you call us Mohammedans, you imply that we worship Muhammad, like you worship Christ,' he says as they start to walk.

'I imply no such thing. I imply that you are followers of Mohammed, just like we are followers of Christ.'

'Perhaps, yet while following Christ is central to your religion, in mine what matters most is that we submit ourselves to God.'

'Is that the same with Sunnis as with the Shi'a?'

'Yes, it is.'

'Then what's the difference? According to my book, they've been fighting each other pretty much since the day Mohammed died.'

'That's because the main difference between Sunnis and Shi'a is whom they believe to be the true successor of *Muhammad*.'

'Like Catholics believe the pope to be the highest religious authority on earth, Protestants the bible, and we English the king?'

Jalal laughs. 'Something like that, yes.'

'And they are still fighting over that today?' Richard sounds sincerely intrigued.

'Do people ever really fight over religion?' Jalal looks at his friend. 'Or do they use religion to fight?'

'Shepherds use religion to fight; sheep fight over religion,' his friend answers. And then, in a lighter tone, Richard asks, 'And you? Are you a Sunni or a Shi'a?'

'I am a Sunni.'

'And what does that mean? Do you follow the pope or the Quran?'

'We follow the Ulama—I think in English you would call them scholars. They are men who spend most of their lives studying the Quran, commentaries on Muhammad's life and each other's interpretations of those commentaries. Moreover, they are judges and lawmakers at the same time.'

They have just entered the Randolph Hotel, and Jalal wants to explain to his friend that in spite of these scholars, not all Sunnis believe the same things, but the sight of the most beautiful woman in the world distracts him. She has auburn hair, hazel eyes, a smooth face, and full lips that are emphasised by a dark red lipstick. A pastel green dress, emerald earrings, and an emerald necklace make her appearance perfect.

'Yes, she is without a doubt the Lady Helen of our time,' Richard, who has caught him staring, whispers in his ear.

'Who is she?' he whispers back without taking his eyes of her.

'She is Mademoiselle Anna Christina Marceau, daughter of Monsieur Philippe Marceau, a French banker who is said to own half of Paris.'

Jalal considers some words the barrister, Mr Jinnah, spoke to him during the summer: '*There are two powers in this world. One is the sword and the other the pen. There is great competition and rivalry between the two. However, there is a third power that is stronger than both: that of a woman.*'

Mr Jinnah was right; Jalal would gladly burn down Beledar for this woman. It's a pity that his father already has great plans for his marriage partners. A Raslan, an Ismat, a Kalaldeh—he will marry a daughter of every lord in the realm, and preferably also a Saudi, an Iraqi, and a Jordanian princess, for the sole purpose of bringing stability to the realm. His father has even threatened Jalal that if he accidentally were to marry an English woman, he would not be allowed back into Beledar.

But then she smiles. Didn't Richard just tell him she was French?

'I want her,' he mutters.

'Join the queue. She is rich and beautiful; you'll be competing with every nobleman in the country.'

'I am a prince.'

'So is the Duke of Kent,' his friend drily replies.

'You're not being very helpful. Will I be competing with you too?'

'I don't need the money. Besides, women like that only cause trouble.'

Jalal lays his hand on his friend's shoulder. 'My life will be full of trouble no matter what. I might as well have the woman too. Now let's go and have a drink.'

But Richard does not move. 'You do realise she is a feminist?'

Jalal frowns and turns to his friend. 'What does that mean?'

'It means that if just a tiny part of my book about your world is true, she'll never accept the laws of those scholars of yours.'

'Then I will change them.'

Richard smiles. 'I appreciate your spirit, but in that case I advise you to beware of the sheep.'

Part I

ABDULLAH

CHAPTER ONE

Mayasin

Month of Separation 23, 1361 A.H. (4 September 1942 A.D.)

'Mister! Mister!'

Abdullah is walking backwards in front of two English officers, trying to get their attention. Every day, after returning their shoeboxes to Mr Darwish's store, he and Ghulam go deeper into the city. They go to Alhawtah and try to get as near as they can to the Mayasin Palace Hotel, the grandest hotel in the city, where they try to make a little more money.

'Mister! Mister! You buy cigarettes?'

He holds the packet out in front of him, but one of the officers responds by smiling, shaking his head, and showing the pack he is keeping in his own pocket. He has a very red head; like most Englishmen, he is not used to the Beledarian sun.

'American! Good quality! Good price!' Abdullah says, but the man shakes his head again.

Not taking no for an answer, Abdullah puts the packet back in his tunic and takes out a bottle.

'Arak?'

The officers speak to each other, but they use many words he doesn't understand. Even if he had known the words, they would still be speaking too fast for him. By the gesture one of the officers makes, and the look on his face, it appears he is explaining to the other what arak is, but Abdullah isn't sure.

'This arak, real good!'

Both men laugh, and the red man asks, 'How much?'

'Ten,' he replies.

The men laugh again. 'One,' the red man counters.

'Eight,' Abdullah says. Had he known the English word for nine he would have said nine. He could use his hands, but then he would have to put the bottle away and during his short time as a street trader, he has learned it is vital that customers are able to keep their eyes on the prize at all moments.

'Two.'

'Seven,' he counters immediately. Experience has also taught him that in the beginning of a negotiation it is best to come with counteroffers quickly. That way you can get your buyer invested before he knows what's happening.

'Two and sixpence.'

This is going too well. They've added a coin worth half a shilling to their offer. He makes a mental note that he has to learn to pronounce the name of the coin himself so that he can use it in future negotiations. If he can add a couple more pennies, he can buy some food for himself and still have enough left to pass on to his mother. It is time for some theatrics.

'I like you! King George, Vera Lynn, very good!' he says. 'I like England, and I like you, so five. Special price for you: five!'

The men look at each other, before the red man responds, 'Three.'

Maybe Abdullah will buy a pastry for himself at Pervaíz's cafe. He can almost taste it. Silently he thanks God and tells himself to remain cool while pretending to be physically hurt. 'Three is too cheap! I lose money, and no food for me!' He pauses a moment for effect, then sighs very deeply. 'Because Vera Lynn, four. Only for you. Four!'

'Three and sixpence.'

'You ruin me!' he replies, shaking his head.

Is it wise to repeat his offer? If he takes this, he can buy a pastry, and his mother will never suspect that he did not pass on all the money. But if he makes another half shilling, he can take home real goat meat. What a surprise that will be for his mother! And for his little brother, Samir, who loves goat meat, but never gets it. If Abdullah succeeds, he can make him so happy!

Will these men kill the deal over half a shilling? They are officers in an army that controls half of the world. They do not care about half a shilling more or less. And if they do pull back, it will not be a complete disaster. In less than a week the Month of Burning will start, and although Abdullah hates it when he is not allowed to eat and drink between sunrise and sunset, he vividly remembers how generous everyone was the previous year.

'I have baby sister; she must eat or she dead. Four!' he repeats, his heart racing.

The soldier glances at his colleague, who shrugs and once again speaks words Abdullah does not understand. Then the officer looks back at him and says, 'Okay.'

Abdullah, who has been walking backwards the entire time, stops so abruptly he almost falls over. After receiving the shillings, he hands them the bottle.

'Thank you,' he wants to say, but before the words have left his mouth, the two soldiers are walking again. He falls down to his knees and thanks God instead. His mother is going to be so proud!

He gets up and starts to walk, wondering how he can learn more English words. Trading will be easier if he gains a better grasp of the infidels' language. He doesn't just have to learn the half a shilling word; he has to learn all the words.

Submerged in his thoughts, he does not watch where he is going and bumps into a policeman. This is not good news, and the rat immediately grabs his arm.

'You know it's illegal to beg here, right?'

'I wasn't begging, sir. I was selling something.'

'Really?' There is something in the voice of this policeman that Abdullah does not like.

'Yes, sir. I sold two English officers a bottle of arak. If God wills it, go ask them.'

'Why would I, when I know all about lying vagabonds like you?'

'Because they will tell you that I'm not lying,' Abdullah snaps, following it up with a slightly late 'sir.'

Ten yards away from him, his friend Ghulam is slowly making his retreat. The boy catches his eye and shakes his head, indicating that Abdullah should keep his calm, but with the great injustice that seems to be coming his way, that is not easy.

The rat brings his face very close to Abdullah's. Clearly, this man does not mind a little arak himself.

'Maybe you did not lie about that, but how in the name of God did you get a bottle of arak in the first place? Did you steal it?'

'No, sir.'

Abdullah tries to free himself, but his effort is unsuccessful. Instead, the policeman pulls him even closer.

'Admit you stole it!'

'I didn't steal it, sir.'

Clap!

Tears roll down his face. Abdullah doesn't mind the pain; it is his anger and the fear of losing his money that causes him to cry, and he hates the rat even more for it.

Some of the people who pass by give them a short, inquisitive stare, but nobody intervenes on his behalf or pauses to watch what will happen. In 1361 Mayasin, few people have problems with police officers slapping the boys that swarm the streets. Someone will have to raise the boys, and often it's not going to be their fathers.

'Do you know what happens to thieves?' The rat is now seriously hurting his arm.

'Yes, sir.'

Officially, thieves get their hands chopped off, but in reality that hardly ever happens. Ghulam was once picked up from the street and accused of stealing. They took him to a dark hole and dumped him back on the streets two days later with a scar that would mark him forever. But what worried Abdullah even more than his friend's scar was the fact that after Ghulam was released, he started to tell everyone who would listen that there was no God. Abdullah does not want to become insane like his friend.

'Where did you steal the bottle?'

The rat is now shaking him. Out of the corner of his eye, Abdullah sees Ghulam returning with a stone in his hand. Silently, he thanks God, while he replies, 'I didn't.'

The rat raises his hand again, and at that exact moment Ghulam's stone hits him in the face. The man screams in pain, and his grip loosens.

'Thanks be to God!' Abdullah exclaims as he pulls loose his arm, turns around, and runs.

He has caught the rat by surprise, and for a second the man is in doubt about whom he should follow. When he comes back to his senses, Abdullah hears him shout, 'Stop him!', but he is already a dozen yards away.

If the rat catches him, he will also be punished for the stone Ghulam has thrown; he'll be lucky if all he loses is his hand. He runs as fast as he can. He sees a corner and turns, and then goes straight around the next.

'Stop him! In the name of God, stop him!'

The sound is getting more distant. Another corner and another street. He looks over his shoulder; he's lost the rat. He slows his pace, and suddenly a man swings an arm around his chest. Abdullah looks up: a new rat.

God, what did I do!? This is not his lucky day, after all.

'Why are you running, boy?'

'I was just playing with my friend, sir.'

The policeman gives him an intense stare, and Abdullah knows the man doesn't believe him. 'You stole something, didn't you?'

He shakes his head. 'No, sir.'

'Empty your pockets.'

Abdullah sighs and grudgingly does as he is told. Out come the cigarettes, the shillings, and a handful of pennies from his morning's labour.

'Where did you get that money?'

'I shine shoes in the morning, and this afternoon I sold a bottle of arak to an English soldier, sir.'

'Where did you shine shoes?'

'The business district, sir.'

The majority of men in Mayasin wear traditional garments, but in the business district, following the example of the English businessmen who visit the city, most self-respecting businessmen have exchanged their long white robes and sandals for dark suits and black leather shoes.

'And where do you get your gear?'

'Mr Darwish's shop, sir. At the edge of Juban and Dhamar.'

'I know Mr Darwish's store,' the rat sneers, apparently offended that Abdullah felt the need to clarify the location. 'Did you pay taxes on your sale?'

'I bought the arak with my own money, sir.'

'I understand, but you do know that when you sell something, you have to pay taxes?'

'What do you mean?' Abdullah has never heard about taxes.

Clap!

The second slap in fifteen minutes, yet this time he has no trouble controlling his tears; he had not been focused. 'What do you mean, *sir*?'

'Everyone who makes money in this country pays a little bit of that money to the emir. This money is called *tax*. When you do not pay taxes, you commit a crime. In our situation, you are the merchant and I'm representing the emir, so you pay your taxes to me. If you don't pay your taxes voluntarily, you go to jail. However, considering you didn't know this and that I am a God-fearing man, this time I will let you get away with a small fine.'

Outrageous! Why does the emir get his money? He has not worked for it, and besides, the emir has money enough; one only needs to look at his palace to see how rich he is. Abdullah feels his blood rising again, but if he does not get away soon, paying taxes and a fine will be the least of his troubles. He nods, and as calmly as he can, he replies, 'Thank you, sir.'

The rat takes his arm from Abdullah's shoulder and waves it. 'Your fine is five shillings. Pay me, and we forget all about it.'

Five shillings! Abdullah sighs before realising this is going to be a problem. 'Sir, I do not have five shillings. I have four and some pennies.'

'All right.' The policeman actually manages to sound gracious. 'I am in a good mood today, so I will let you go if you give me three. However, you must swear by the Quran that the next time you sell something and you are on my streets, you will come to find me, and you'll give me one quarter of your revenues. Do you swear it?'

'I swear it, sir.'

He hands over the shillings and wants to set off again, but there is a new arm on his shoulder. He is too late!

'Nadir! You've caught him! Thanks be to God!'

Abdullah turns his head. The first rat has appeared again, breathing heavily.

'Rizq,' says the officer to whom he's just paid his taxes. 'What are you doing here?'

'I followed him.' Rizq is now standing next to them, still panting, and points at Abdullah. 'He stole a bottle of arak and then he ordered his friend to throw a stone at me. We need to take him to the prison; they will know what to do with him.'

'This boy is a tax-paying citizen. You accuse him of theft and abusing an officer of the law. Do you have proof?'

'Look at my face!' There is a bruise where Ghulam's rock has hit him.

'But you just said that he didn't throw the rock, did you not?'

'I said he ordered his friend to throw the rock.'

Nadir raises his eyebrows. 'Can you prove that? Maybe it was just some kid who didn't like your face and figured he'd brighten it up a bit!'

'Are you calling me a liar?'

'I am saying you are as wise as a baboon born without a head; it is written.'

If Abdullah wasn't scared and angry, he could not have stopped himself from laughing. As it is, he has no problem controlling himself, which, he realises, is probably a good thing.

'You're the son of a donkey!' There is a foul look on Rizq's face, but it does not intimidate Nadir. On the contrary, Nadir takes a step toward the other rat. They are so close now that their noses almost touch.

'I would be very careful if I were you,' Nadir says. 'You are on my street.'

Rizq snorts and steps back, taking his hand off Abdullah's shoulder before almost pricking his finger in the boy's eye.

'You are lucky today, piece of filth. God willing, someday soon we will meet again, and that day Nadir won't be here to protect you. I will be looking forward to that!'

Then he laughs, a high sound that makes Abdullah shiver.

'It was God's will that we met today,' Nadir says to Abdullah when Rizq is out of earshot. 'This street is mine, and on my streets you can sell anything you want, if you remember your oath. Forget your oath, and I will personally deliver you to Rizq. Do you understand?'

'Yes, sir.' Abdullah bows his head.

'Until the next time then,' Nadir replies, and Abdullah walks away. He has had enough of this day, and while normally he hates being home, right now there is nothing he wants more than to curl up in his blanket against the wall and close his eyes until darkness has come and gone.

CHAPTER TWO

Mayasin

Month of Burning 27, 1361 A.H. (7 October 1942)

A sound wakes Abdullah, and he instantly opens his eyes. The sun is not up yet. *God is praised.* His little brother is curled up against him, and after he has taken a little time to let his eyes adjust to the dark, he gives Samir a soft push and he slowly gets up. He takes a look at his brother. After last night's dinner, Samir will certainly wake up hungry, but he won't get any food before the sun goes down. Abdullah shakes his head. There's nothing he can do about it.

He moves aside the thin curtain that separates his family's room from the next and steps through. From here, his door to freedom is only four steps away, yet he must take them with care. The women who live in this room are all whores, and if he wakes one of them, he will not escape a beating—he knows that from experience. Fortunately, most evenings they drink, and they are not easily woken this time of morning.

One step.

Two.

Three.

Four. He is at the door. He opens it as quietly as he can, yet he cannot avoid it making a loud shriek. Startled, he looks at the women on the floor, but not one of them moves. He exhales deeply, steps through the door, and closes it behind him.

The street is still deserted, and Abdullah cannot see a light in any of the houses. Again, he silently praises God before starting to make his way through Kobajjeb as rapidly as he can. Thousands of stars light his path, but even without the stars Abdullah can easily find his way through the chaotic slum. Here he has lived his ten or eleven years, and he knows every house, every alley, and every ditch.

In winter, Kobajjeb is a not a bad area. The rain regularly washes the dirt away, and early in the morning the streets smell like a mixture of smothering charcoal and sweet perfume. But it's not yet winter. The Month of Burning feels even warmer than it did last year, and this morning, all Abdullah can smell is shit. He tries to ignore it and starts to run, and when he finally passes through the old gate that marks the start of the Juban quarter, the smell is gone. He stops, closes his eyes, and takes a deep breath.

After the sewer system here was finished, the emir banned all horses and camels from entering the city. In Juban, where most of the merchants live, the people were livid. The Emir's Guard and even Lord Tali'a himself had come into Juban to keep them from revolting. But then summer had come, and the absence of the smell of shit had really quieted the people down.

Another deep breath. *Please God, when the emir starts building sewers again, let them be in Juban.*

Abdullah opens his eyes again, and now he can see a light in one of the houses. He must hurry. Mr Darwish's store is on the edge of Juban and Dhamar—the fancy part of town—and that is still a long way. He sets off, doubling his pace, and every fifty yards he looks at the sky. The sun still seems far away, yet all around him people are waking up.

The sun still isn't up when he reaches the store. Before he enters, he takes a moment to catch his breath. He is soaked in sweat, but he does not care. He has made it; that's all that matters. Inside the store, there are shoes everywhere: on shelves, in and on boxes on the floor, and hanging on clotheslines throughout the store. Abdullah makes his way through them, and in a little room in the back he finds the shoe vendor eating his breakfast. Thank God he is on time.

Mr Darwish looks up and smiles. 'May peace be upon you.'

'And may peace be upon you too,' Abdullah answers.

'How are you, Abdullah?' the old man asks.

'I am good, thanks be to God,' he replies. 'And you, Mr Darwish?'

'All circumstances considered, I am very good—thanks be to God.'

He sighs. *All circumstances considered.* Mr Darwish uses the same phrase every morning. The first morning that Abdullah came here, he had asked for an explanation. '*Old age brings a man more than wisdom. If God grants you the gift of aged wisdom, you will know what I mean,*' was the answer.

But Mr Darwish ate meat every day, and he had twice been to Mecca. Abdullah cannot think of a way that the old man's circumstances could be better, and instead of repeating his question for another meaningless answer, today he simply asks, 'May I get the box myself, Mr Darwish?'

The old man nods, and Abdullah descends into a small basement, where he collects a black shoeshine box. After checking that everything is complete, he goes back upstairs.

'Have you had breakfast?' Mr Darwish asks. Abdullah shakes his head, and the shoe vendor continues, 'Would you like something?'

Of course he would; he hasn't run through the city for nothing! He looks longingly at the food as he replies, 'No, thank you, sir.'

'Are you sure?' the old man asks. 'I have far more than I can eat, and you must eat too. It will not be much longer before the sun comes up.'

'I am sure, sir,' Abdullah says without taking his eyes of the food.

'But I have pita bread and yoghurt with garlic and lemon, and it tastes extraordinarily good! In the name of God, take some.'

Abdullah has seen the bread and the yoghurt. There is not much left, but definitely enough for him. This time he looks up at Mr Darwish and answers, 'If it is that good, then it would be rude of me not to try some.'

Mr Darwish takes two large pieces of pita bread, dips them regally into the bowl of yoghurt, and smiles as he hands them over to the boy.

Thank you, sir, Abdullah wants to say, but he has already crammed one of the pieces into his mouth, and he is temporarily unable to speak. Mr Darwish was not lying. The yoghurt does taste extraordinarily good. The moment the first piece of bread is gone he continues with the second, and only after he has used his tongue to remove the last bread crumbs from behind his teeth, he says, 'Thank you, sir.'

Mr Darwish nods. 'Would you like some more?'

'No, thank you, sir.' Abdullah shakes his head to emphasise his words, but his gaze does not leave the bread.

'Are you sure? You have to admit that it is very good,' the old man says.

Abdullah looks up and smiles. 'All right, a little more.'

The old man dips two more pieces of bread into the bowl just as Abdullah notices a weak light coming in through the window. His eyes widen, and he tries to hide the fact that he has noticed the light, but he cannot avoid giving away that something is wrong. Mr Darwish looks at the window. He is still holding the bread. What will the old man do?

'This bread has already touched the yoghurt,' Mr Darwish says. 'Therefore I can no longer save it, but it would be a terrible sin to throw such food away. Please, help me avoid that sin.'

Is Mr Darwish really telling him that he can eat when the sun is already up during the Month of Burning? Abdullah does not really care about sinning, but he does not want to lose the old man's respect. 'Mr Darwish, I want to help you, but would I not be committing a terrible sin then as well?'

'Not a terrible sin, Abdullah. You would be committing a very small sin to prevent me from committing a very big one. In the name of God, I cannot think of anything more honourable.'

Abdullah takes the bread with a smile. He is pretty sure Mr Darwish made up the story about saving him from a bigger sin, but he is very grateful for it. Before he has stepped out of the door, he has finished the other two pieces.

He is still hungry, but the bread has strengthened him, and he makes his way to the business district as quickly as he can. There is one great advantage of walking through the city this early in the morning: he does not have to worry about Rizq. The past weeks he has been looking over his shoulder constantly, but eventually he has decided that the rat probably won't be on the street this early. Now he mostly worries when he makes his way from Mr Darwish's store to Nadir's streets in the afternoon and on his way home. He has agreed with Ghulam that they will always make those journeys together.

His favourite pitch, right in front of a small coffeehouse, is still free, and Pervaíz, the owner of the coffeehouse, has already set up a couple of chairs in front of his shop. The first time Abdullah set up his little shoebox here, Perváiz was reluctant to lend him a chair. Considering he had once been young and poor himself, he eventually decided to acquiesce, and God had rewarded him for his kindness; most men who sit down to have their shoes shined appreciate some coffee while waiting for the boys to finish. Upon learning that the boys are actually good for business, he now puts a couple of chairs outside every morning and welcomes the boys heartily.

Abdullah does not know anyone who hates the Month of Burning more than Perváiz, and hoping for some coffee, he goes inside to greet him. 'Good morning!'

'Morning of light,' the young man replies. If he is in a bad mood, he does not show it, and he offers Abdullah what he has come in for.

Abdullah takes the small, hot cup and carefully drinks the sweet nectar. Early morning is the best time for business, and it won't be long now before his customers start to arrive. Most men have their shoes shined right before they come into the office—they do it to impress their colleagues and clients, but shining them at home is not very useful; twenty minutes on the streets of Mayasin are enough to make any shoe dusty.

'Good morning,' he says to two men who walk past him, but they take no notice of the boy and go straight into the coffeehouse. He has better luck with the next duo.

'Good morning.' They pause their step. 'Those shoes certainly could use a little polish, gentlemen. Please, if God wants it, sit down.'

He gestures at the chairs, but the men hesitate. 'Are you alone?' asks the older gentleman.

'Yes. Don't worry, though, God willing, I work very fast.'

'Ah, we've got time,' the older man says, and then, to the man next to him, he orders, 'Please, sit down.'

But the younger man does not move. 'In the name of God,' he replies, 'you go first.'

'No,' says the older, 'I can wait. You go.'

'Really, I insist,' the younger man says, and only after repeated invitations from both parties is it decided that the older man will sit down first.

'Maybe you could get some coffee for us?' the old man asks Abdullah while taking his seat behind the shoebox; the boy nods and sticks his head around the door of the coffee shop.

'Perva íz, two coffees!' Afraid that another boy might steal one of his clients, Abdullah goes straight to work.

'May peace be upon you, gentlemen.' After a couple of minutes, Perva íz comes outside with a small tray, a coffeepot, and two cups. 'How are you today?'

A little absentmindedly, the old man replies, 'May peace be upon you, too.' The younger man simply ignores the enthusiastic coffee shop owner.

Perva íz does not mind; he is used to being ignored. He has started a coffeehouse here to make money, not small talk. Smiling broadly, he asks, 'If God wills it, perhaps you would also like something to eat? I have some very nice sweet rolls with fresh cream cheese.'

The younger man shakes his head, but his older companion replies, 'I'll have a roll, but a small one.' He raises his eyebrows and continues, 'It's the Month of Burning, after all.'

Perva íz's smile grows even broader. 'I know all about it.' He bows and leaves them, returning a moment later with a roll that's anything but small.

'In the name of God, I do not understand why you are spitting on the pillars of the faith,' the younger man reproaches the old man. 'Three more days and the Month of Burning is over, and you can eat anything you want, whenever you want. Why do you not wait?'

'Othman, I give much money to the poor, I pray five times a day, and I do not drink alcohol. God does not mind if I eat a little roll and drink some coffee while the sun is up,' the older man answers.

Abdullah is working on the man's shoes, but his ears are wide open.

'If God doesn't mind, then why is honouring the Month of Burning one of the pillars of our faith?' Othman asks.

'Because this way, people who cannot afford to give money to the poor can still honour God. If they honour the Month of Burning, they know that they are just as important to God as the people who have much to give.'

'Are you saying that the pillars of Islam are a menu a Muslim can choose from, rather than a duty for every Muslim?'

Abdullah glances at Othman and wonders if it is the suit that allows him to speak to his elders in this way.

'In a way, I suppose they are. My mother, she can no longer get out of bed for morning prayers, and when it is time for the evening prayer, she is already in bed. Does this make her a bad person in God's eyes?'

'But your mother cannot help it. You can!'

'Who says I can? I am a big man, and if I want to get through the day, my stomach'—the old man rubs his belly—'needs more than what my wives give me for breakfast. I have suffered for twenty-six days, and I cannot suffer anymore. Now, if you worry about your soul, then I will worry about mine.'

Othman shakes his head in dismay, yet he does not argue. Instead, he changes the subject. 'I have heard that the emir will die soon and that Prince Jalal will succeed him.'

Abdullah did not miss the venom in Othman's voice, but apparently the older man has. Gravely, he replies, 'That is good. I have heard that during his exile, Prince Jalal has worked to prepare the British king for our independence. And there are many good stories about him from the front. He will make a good emir.'

Again, Othman shakes his head in dismay, and this time he does argue. 'The emir's brother, Prince Sharif, should be the next emir. Unlike Jalal, everyone knows that he is a good Muslim. He has fought for us against the Turks, and he is openly against the English. Prince Jalal is out fighting with the English, and he is married to a French whore!'

The older man sighs. 'You are talking about the wife of the prince. The prince who is risking his life in a war so that the British will finally give us freedom. You reproach me for eating a little roll and ordering some coffee when you dare to use language like this during the holiest of months.'

'I speak only the truth.'

'You speak gossip, and that is worse than any other sin during the Month of Burning. It's written. The princess may be French, but she has converted to Islam, and she has taken the name of the Prophet's favourite wife. If anything does not have a place during Ramadan, it is talk like this. However, I think I will make a deal with you, young Othman. If you stop this talk, I will stop eating my roll.'

Abdullah looks at the roll. The older man has taken only three small bites. *Please God, make Othman say yes.*

Othman nods, albeit very slowly, like he feels obliged to the old man but does not really want to make the deal. But then he says, 'The prince *is* risking his life for our independence.'

And with that, the conversation changes to business, and Abdullah loses interest.

While the old man may have said that the fasting rule was mostly meant for boys like him, Abdullah does not care. He is sure that God will not blame him for finishing the roll the old man is going to leave behind. Pervaíz cannot sell it again, and, as Mr Darwish said, it would be a dreadful sin to throw it away.

When the men leave, they give him a big tip—it is the Month of Burning, after all—and the moment they have gone around the corner, he takes the bread. As he is eating it, a boy with a scar on his face from his hairline to his chin approaches. It is Ghulam. Abdullah will not eat the entire roll, after all; he will save half for his friend. The one advantage of not believing in God is that his friend does not feel the least bit guilty when he eats during the day.

CHAPTER THREE

Mayasin

Month of Pregnancy 18, 1361 A.H. (28 October 1942 A.D.)

Abdullah is walking through the streets again. Since the Feast of Breaking the Fast, food is becoming more expensive by the day. To make matters even worse, last night his mother pulled him aside and told him that the money from Ramadan would not last them much longer. That is why Abdullah is not in Nadir's streets; he cannot spare the taxes.

Working in Rizq's streets is dangerous, but he is the only boy working here, and he is having a fantastic day. Normally, he only has one bottle of arak on him, but today his supply seems endless. He has already sold two bottles at great prices, and he has a good feeling about selling a third as well. At the end of this day, he will have over fifty shillings!

A couple more days like this and his family will never have to worry again. Even better, they will be able to move into a real house—a house in Juban! They will no longer have to live with the whores, and he will never have to make his way through the smell of shit again. Why didn't he think of doing this earlier?

It doesn't matter. He just has to make the most of his luck now that God is at his side. He sees another red Englishman and strides towards him.

'Mister! Mister!' The Englishman looks at him. His eyes are too black for an Englishman, and the man's face isn't red at all. In fact, the man is not an Englishman; he is a Beledarian. He is even wearing a tunic! How could Abdullah have missed that?

The man grins, showing a mouth with at least three teeth missing, and Abdullah's eyes turn wide. He is not just any Beledarian; he is Rizq.

Abdullah takes a step back, but he's too late. Rizq has grabbed his shoulder, and he is not going to let go. With his other hand, the rat presses a dagger against Abdullah's cheek; the curved blade is so sharp that it effortlessly breaks his skin. He wants to scream, but no sound comes out of his mouth. He looks around for help, but he is no longer on the street; he is in the dark room where the rats took Ghulam. There are no people here, only ghosts. And Nadir.

'This is what happens when you do not pay your taxes,' the rat hisses.

Abdullah shakes his head. It's a mistake; it's all a terrible mistake! He closes his eyes to protect them from the dagger and silently prays for redemption. *Please God, Most Merciful God, I promise that I will always be good! I will be the best Muslim that walks this Earth, but, please, You have to save me!*

'Abdullah, run!' Ghulam's voice; God has heard him!

He feels Rizq's grip loosening, and when he opens his eyes, he sees that Ghulam has hit the rat in the face again, while Nadir and the ghosts have disappeared. He wrenches himself free and starts to run.

'Stop him!' Rizq shouts. 'Stop him!'

There are only red Englishmen around who cannot understand the rat. Rizq is never going to catch up, and Abdullah is almost safe. *God is praised.*

But then he trips and falls into a ravine. Why hadn't he been on the lookout for the ravines, if they are so dangerous? As he is falling, he sighs. It does not matter; it won't be long before he'll be in Paradise.

In fact, he is already on the ground, and all he has to do now is die. But there is a blanket covering him, and he feels a shock of relief flow through his body. Was it all just a dream?

Very carefully, he opens an eye and looks to his side. There is his brother. He opens his other eye. This isn't the first time he's had a dream like this; since he met Rizq, he's dreamt about running into the rat at least three times a week. Every dream was different, but they always ended with him tripping and dying, sometimes in the ravine, sometimes by Rizq's dagger.

He sighs and feels his stomach aching. He looks at the window and sees weak light shining through. Time to get some breakfast at Mr Darwish's store.

Abdullah is sitting in the shade of the shoe store. What's taking Ghulam so long? Maybe he should leave without him. But what if he runs into Rizq? *Next time, Nadir will not be there to protect you.* He shivers. Money is worthless if he cannot bring it home to his mother.

'Abdullah! Abdullah!' In the distance he sees Ghulam running in his direction, and he jumps up. What's wrong? His friend never runs anywhere, unless he's being chased by a rat. He narrows his eyes; it doesn't appear that anyone is chasing Ghulam. 'Have you heard?'

'Heard what?' Abdullah asks when Ghulam has reached him.

Breathing heavily, his friend answers, 'The emir is dead!'

That's it? Why is his friend so excited about that? Absent-mindedly, he replies, 'May God bless him and grant him peace.'

His friend does not notice his lack of interest. 'Let's go tell Mr Darwish!'

'Sure.'

'We knew that it was going to happen someday,' the old man says upon hearing the news, 'but I will not deny that I had hoped that he would hang on for a couple of years more. Do you know if the prince is back in the capital?'

'Prince Jalal arrived back yesterday. This morning, Lord Tali'a had the entire Emir's Guard in the palace swear fealty to him. His uncles and cousins have all made it clear that they will accept him as heir to Emir Hussein, yet, according to my cousin, the atmosphere in the palace is exceptionally tense.'

Ghulam's cousin, Zahaar, is a member of the Emir's Guard, and while Abdullah has never met him, his friend speaks of him like he is second only to Lord Tali'a himself.

The old shoe vendor shakes his head and sits down on his small stool. Suddenly, he looks a decade older than he did when Abdullah returned his shoebox, not very long ago.

'What's wrong, Mr Darwish?' Abdullah asks.

'Hussein Amin was a good emir. Prince Jalal . . .' He pauses and looks at Abdullah. 'Kings and emirs, they don't come and go quietly. It is a good sign that Lord Tali'a has made the Emir's Guard swear an oath, but they are not the only force in this city.'

Abdullah frowns, yet before he can say anything, Ghulam asks, 'What do you mean?'

'The emir sent Prince Jalal to England when he was fifteen years old; he only returned three years ago. He has a French wife, and there are questions about his faith.' The old man shakes his head again. 'Many people will perceive him as vulnerable, and a vulnerable prince is a target. In a country where a prince is a target, people like us are . . . *expendable.*'

'But didn't the prince do a lot of work when he was in England to procure our independence?' Abdullah asks. He doesn't quite understand what Mr Darwish is saying, but he feels like his question makes a valuable addition to the conversation.

'Some people say that he did, yet we are still a British protectorate. Others, they say that he is actually trying to keep it that way.'

'What do you think?' Ghulam asks.

The old man shrugs. 'Only God has the answer to questions like this. However, Prince Jalal is a descendant of Muhammad, and, therefore, I think that we should have faith in him. Come again tomorrow, and I will have breakfast and maybe some more answers. But for now, I think I would like to be left alone for a little while.'

Moments later, they are outside again and Abdullah says to Ghulam, 'I cannot believe that Mr Darwish was so shocked! I mean, what is it the emir does? He sits in his palace and takes our money. What does it matter who the emir is?'

'He is afraid that there'll be a war about the succession . . .'

'But we are already in a war!' Abdullah blurts out, suddenly thinking about his father who is, or, according to his mother, *was* fighting it.

'That war is far away. Mr Darwish fears a war right here, in these streets. I have read in a book that most wars are fought after kings die.'

Abdullah tugs at his earlobe and looks to his side. 'Where did you learn to read?'

'There are many places in this city where you can learn things, if you know where to look.'

Abdullah frowns. There are schools for the more fortunate boys, but he has never noticed any places where kids like him or

Ghulam can learn how to read. Then again, even if he knew where they were, he still would not have the time. He has an entire family to take care of.

Ghulam does not have such problems. He is a good kid, but, in a way, his friend is fortunate that all of his brothers and sisters are dead. His father is in the army too, and his mother takes care of herself, while his cousin gives him food and money from time to time. Perhaps . . .

'Ghulam, do you hear much from your father?'

'Of course! He says that war is tough but that we will win because we have the English on our side.'

'And you write back?' His friend nods. 'Do you think you could ask him if my father is still alive?'

'Sure I can. What's his name?'

Abdullah takes a moment to think about that before answering. 'Saíd.'

Ghulam nods. 'And what is his father's name?'

He takes another moment to think before realising that he has no idea. 'I would have to ask my mother.' But his mother had told him ages ago he must presume his father to be dead and give up all hope. 'Is it really necessary that you know that?'

His friend scratches his head. 'Not really. I can ask my father to find out if Saíd, the father of Abdullah, is still alive. My father is an officer, so if anyone can do it, it is him.'

Abdullah smiles and says, 'Thank you.'

'No problem. Now, let's go to the palace and see what's going on,' Ghulam says.

'Yes! No . . .' For a second there, Abdullah had forgotten that if he wanted to ensure his family's safety, he could not waste any more time with trivial things. 'If I don't bring home money, my family will not eat, and there won't be any foreigners at the palace square to whom we can sell.'

Ghulam nods and lays a hand on Abdullah's shoulder. 'There is a way to make more money than you could ever imagine.'

'What is it?'

His friend smiles. 'It is a secret, and you have to swear by the Quran that you will not tell anyone else.'

'I thought you didn't believe in God.'

'I don't, but you do.'

CHAPTER FOUR

Mayasin

Month of Pregnancy 27, 1361 A.H. (6 November 1942 A.D.)

'Cigarettes?' An Englishwoman on his streets is a rare sight, and this isn't just any woman. This is a lady, and she completely ignores him. He puts the cigarettes back into his tunic and takes out the bottle.

'Arak?' She keeps on walking like he does not exist, but Abdullah's stomach is hurting, and he is not in the mood to give up easily. This woman must have money, lots of it, and if she's out here she must want something.

'Scarf?'

Still nothing.

'Jewels? Tea set?' Sometimes he guides English soldiers to places where they can buy gifts for their girlfriends. It is a trick Nadir taught him. If he brings customers to stores or market stalls, he can ask for a commission.

'Real Beledarian. Good quality, good price. All you want, I know where.' They have almost reached the end of Nadir's streets, and the woman stops just in time. Abdullah hates paying taxes, but running into Rizq again will be even worse.

And it's not all bad on Nadir's streets. There are a couple of good stores and many rich people, like this lady. She says something, but she speaks so fast that he does not understand any of her words. He looks at her questioningly. She repeats herself, slower this time.

'I am . . . for . . . people here . . . you know where I . . . get?'

He was right: she does want something!

'I get everything, but don't understand,' he replies.

She points at her feet. Does she need lotion? Or maybe shoes? She is already wearing very nice shoes, not suited for the streets of Mayasin, but very nice; nicer than the ones they make here.

He is wearing sandals himself, and he points at the sole of his sandal, demonstratively avoiding his foot, to make sure he has not misinterpreted. The lady gives him two thumbs up and smiles. He frowns, but she is not calling him a piece of filth; it's the kind of thumbs up the English soldiers use when they say that something is good.

'Okay!' He beams and wants to start walking immediately. There is a shoe store nearby, on one of Nadir's streets. But then he reconsiders. He has found a lady who wants shoes; why not bring her to Mr Darwish? It's the least he can do for all the food and advice the old man has given him the past year.

It's also a risk, though. If he runs into Rizq . . . but surely the rat won't dare touch him when he's with this lady.

'I know best place; it's short walk. Follow me.'

Every twenty metres, he looks over his shoulder to see if she is still there, and every time, slightly to his own surprise, he finds that she is. More importantly, he does not see Rizq anywhere. Yet something is not right. Everywhere he looks, he sees men standing together in closed little groups, talking in hushed voices.

'Is it much farther?' the lady asks.

Abdullah turns to face her but does not stop walking. He knows this question, but because he is distracted, it takes a couple of moments for him to process it. He keeps walking backwards without slowing his pace—he is well practiced in this by now—and repeats her question in his head.

'Not far,' he finally answers. 'Five minutes, maximum.'

This is his standard reply to the question, regardless of whether it is actually two minutes or fifteen. He has never had a particularly good sense of time, but five minutes is an acceptable distance for everyone. More importantly, after people have been on the way for five minutes, few want to turn back for just five minutes more. Sometimes they ask often, and en route he has to tell them five minutes three or four times.

The lady isn't difficult; she says nothing and just follows him until some time later—maybe five minutes, maybe fifteen—they find the old man sitting in front of his store.

'Peace be upon you, Abdullah.'

'And upon you be peace, Mr Darwish. In the name of God, I have brought a customer to you.'

Mr Darwish looks up and says to the woman, 'Peace be upon you.'

'And may peace be upon you,' the lady answers. No more Arabic follows; it is probably the only phrase she knows. Instead, she explains what she wants in English, and Abdullah notices that Mr Darwish understands next to nothing. Nonetheless, the old man goes inside and comes back with a large stack of boxes.

He opens them one by one, but every time the lady just shakes her head. When she has rejected all the boxes, Mr Darwish makes a gesture with his hands, which seems to mean, 'If it's not any of these shoes, I give up.'

The lady points at Abdullah's feet. Why would she do that? Would she want his sandals? He looks again at all the footwear lying around in front of the store. There are only shoes and boots, no sandals.

'Mr Darwish,' he says, 'I believe the lady wants sandals.'

Mr Darwish gives him a puzzled look before he says, 'That woman does not want sandals. Why would she want sandals?'

'Mr Darwish, can't we try?'

The old man sighs, but he does go back inside. When he returns and opens the first box to show a pair of sandals, the lady joyfully claps her hands. It is not the lucky pair yet, but now they are getting somewhere. Fifteen minutes later, they are off again, the lady carrying a small box with a pair of red sandals.

Abdullah is delighted. He has assisted a great English lady in acquiring her sandals, while helping Mr Darwish at the same time. Some days, life is beautiful.

Then a taxi passes by, and the lady raises her hand. She says something in Arabic that, with a little goodwill, might be interpreted as 'thank you' and hands him a shilling. Just like that she is gone, and the next thing he knows, he is standing there by himself, watching the taxi drive off.

He turns back to Mr Darwish, who is still standing in front of the store, smiling broadly and holding the lady's money in his hand.

'God is praised,' the old man says; the lady had not negotiated about the price, paying thereby the price of three pairs of shoes for one pair of sandals.

Abdullah smiles back. He is sure Mr Darwish will give him a very good commission, perhaps even enough to take care of his family for a week.

He has considered Ghulam's way to make more money for a brief moment, but he hopes that he'll never have to succumb to that. Better to be a little hungry and disappoint his mother than to challenge God.

All of a sudden, Mr Darwish's smile changes to a forced grimace. His eyes get bigger, and he starts moving around clumsily.

'Mr Darwish?' Abdullah says.

The shoe vendor does not reply. He grabs his left arm, coughs violently a couple of times, takes a few uncoordinated steps, and falls over.

'Mr Darwish!?' Abdullah screams. 'Mr Darwish!'

He runs over to the old man; his eyes are open and he is taking quick, shallow breaths, each one weaker than the previous one. Abdullah shakes him, but there is no reaction.

'Help!' he shouts. 'In the name of God, help!'

A man runs over to them. 'Get out of the way,' he says.

Abdullah gets up and takes two steps back. The man looks up at him. 'What happened?'

'I don't know.' He feels tears forming in his eyes. 'One moment he was laughing and the next he fell down.'

The man pounds on the old man's chest, and Abdullah turns around; he does not dare to watch.

'God, please God, most merciful God,' he prays out loud as he looks at the sky to find the direction of Mecca. 'Greatest God, Most Merciful God, please help my friend.'

There is a hand on his shoulder; it is the man. 'God has helped him much during his life, my young friend. This man had been granted many years, but every road must end somewhere. His has ended here.'

'No!' Abdullah shouts. 'No!'

He turns back to Mr Darwish and puts his head on his chest, which rapidly gets moist with his tears. For a moment, he feels the hand on his shoulder again.

He looks up. The man is gone, and in front of him is the scarred face of Ghulam. There is no emotion in his friend's eyes; he is simply staring at him and the dead shoe vendor.

'What should we do?' he asks his friend.

'We need to go. Soon, rats will come; you never know if they might blame us for his death.'

'But Mr Darwish needs to be buried, in the name of God.'

'That is the responsibility of his family, not us.'

'But we are his family, we, the boys who come to his store!'

'No, we are not. Many boys came before us, and had he not died here today, many would come after us as well.'

Is that so? Abdullah realises he knows nothing about Mr Darwish's own family. In fact, he doesn't even know if the old man has any family. Is he married? *Was* he married? Did he have sons of his own?

'Come on,' Ghulam pulls his arm back, 'old men die every day. Wisest thing now is to get away.'

Abdullah raises himself and looks at the old man. 'Goodbye, Mr Darwish, may God bless you and grant you peace.'

Then he bows his head and closes his eyes a moment. When he opens them, he notices Ghulam has bent down next to Mr Darwish and is, unobtrusively, removing the money from his hand. 'You cannot do that!'

'Why not? You need money, you told me so yourself. Mr Darwish doesn't need it anymore; not where he's going.' His friend puts it in his own pocket and walks away.

Abdullah looks around again. No one has seen Ghulam take the money. He runs after him. At least half of the money is his.

'What happened?'

'I don't know,' Abdullah answers, and he feels his eyes getting wet again. 'He had just made a very good sale, and he seemed very happy, and then he just fell down. There was a man, and I thought that he would help him, but he couldn't.'

Ghulam shakes his head. 'Strange days.'

'How do you mean?'

'I just met with my cousin. He told me that last night the emir's wife was walking through the palace half-naked. And then very early this morning, Lord Tali'a arrested the emir's uncles, his cousins, and his uncles' wives. At this very moment they are all locked in the dungeons under the palace.'

'Why?' Abdullah thinks back to the young man named Othman who had claimed that the emir's wife was a French whore and the emir's uncle the true heir to Beledar.

'My cousin says that they are traitors; that they were planning to poison the emir.'

'Why would the emir's uncle want to do that?'

Ghulam shakes his head. 'Sometimes you are as dumb as a statue. Prince Sharif wants to be emir, of course. With Jalal gone, he would only have Prince Faisal to stand in his way, but everyone knows that Prince Faisal isn't right in the head.'

Abdullah frowns. 'Did your cousin also happen to say something about whether or not the emir is going to take care of food? I don't know what it's like in the palace, but it seems to me that he should be worrying about more pressing issues than arresting his uncles.'

As they reach a split in the road, his friend stops walking and turns to him. In a near whisper, Ghulam replies, 'As a matter of fact, the emir's wife, Princess Aisha, has charmed King Farouk of Egypt into opening the Egyptian grain warehouses for us during the ceremony where Jalal was crowned emir. They don't know when it will arrive, but they believe that Prince Sharif was waiting for that moment to poison the emir.'

'*If* it will arrive,' Abdullah says. He does not like that their fate appears to have been put in the hands of a woman. What's more, many people are saying that the scarcity in food is the punishment for the emir's behaviour, and while his friend may not believe in God, to Abdullah this sounds totally reasonable.

Ghulam snorts, and with a sharp tongue he answers, 'If my cousin says that grain will arrive from Egypt, then grain will arrive from Egypt; it's written.'

CHAPTER FIVE

Mayasin

Month of Truce 9, 1361 A.H. (17 November 1942 A.D.)

Mr Darwish has been gone for two weeks, and Abdullah's life has become much more difficult. The money he'd made shining shoes might have been negligible, but it was better than nothing and without the pieces of pita bread as breakfast and the leftover pastry rolls from Pervaíz in the morning, he walks the streets hungry every day.

He also goes to bed hungry. Yesterday, his mother served him soup made of rats caught by his brother. Gaunt rats, for that matter, and, according to his little brother, the last ones in Kobajjeb. If he does not make any money today, there won't be anything at all in the soup tonight.

An English officer comes around the corner, and Abdullah rushes toward him while taking the pack of cigarettes from his tunic. The man shakes his head when he shows it to him.

'Arak?' He presents the bottle. Once more, the man shakes his head.

'Present for wife? Jewels? Very cheap.'

No.

'Scarf? Real Beledarian.'

No.

'Tea set? Very beautiful!'

No.

No. No. No. Abdullah sighs; he does not have a choice. 'You want—what was the word again? *'Girlfriend?'* He stretches the word and makes a funny face, just like Ghulam has shown him.

'*Try to seduce them,*' his friend had said. To his astonishment, it works. While the man does not reply, Abdullah can see that he has caught his attention.

'You want girlfriend now? Tonight? Tomorrow?' The man stops, and he continues. 'I know where. Good price. I show you. For you, *special*—he stretches this word too—price.'

'Do you know the Mayasin Palace Hotel?' the man asks.

He nods. Everyone knows the Mayasin Palace Hotel.

'Meet me outside, tonight, ten thirty.'

He nods again. 'Yes, sir. I will be there.'

The fact that this man is staying in the Second Palace is good news. He has money, and Siraj will get a good price for his girls, which means a good commission for Abdullah. However, it also presents a problem: rats do not want to see boys like him anywhere near the place. Nadir will have to arrange for protection, and this will make Abdullah's share smaller. He sighs. Better a smaller share than an adventure that ends in a dark hole.

That evening as Abdullah waits outside the hotel, it starts to rain and turns cold. He shivers; he is still dressed for warm weather, and he is quickly freezing. He wonders if this weather is a sign from God that he should not be here. He does not know the Quran well, but he does know that God does not approve of selling girls to infidels.

But it's more the emir's fault than his. He is sure that God will understand that he has to eat, and that food from Egypt that Ghulam was talking about is still nowhere to be seen.

Two men come out of the hotel. They look around, scanning the street. Is one of them his man? He isn't sure; darkness and rain cloud his vision.

He leaves his hiding place and moves closer to find out. It does not take long for the men to spot him.

'Boy,' one says. He recognises the voice. It is the man from the afternoon. 'Is two a problem?'

'No problem,' he replies. Siraj has girls enough; two is better than one. 'Two is good, special price.'

'Is it far?' the other man asks, obviously annoyed by the rain. The men are unlucky. Even in winter God rarely sends this kind of weather to Mayasin, and again Abdullah wonders if it isn't an omen, yet he hides his anxiety when he replies.

'Not far. Five minutes. Follow me.'

He starts to walk and looks over his shoulder. The men are following him. He steps up his pace and looks over his shoulder again, but the men hardly seem to notice; they are much taller than him and have no trouble keeping up. After some time, the man asks, 'Is it much farther?'

Abdullah turns around. 'Not much farther. Five minutes.'

'You said "five minutes" ten minutes ago. Look, there's a taxi, why don't we just take that?' And the man raises his arm.

'No!' For a second Abdullah panics. If they take a taxi, the chauffeur will receive all the commission. What terrible luck that exactly at this moment a taxi passes by; the chances are almost zero. 'No taxi! Very dangerous! Maybe police! Police not good!'

'Taxis aren't police,' the man says as the taxi pulls over next to them.

'This Mayasin, here taxi maybe police!' Abdullah repeats. 'Very dangerous! Two minutes!'

The man sighs, and the other man says something to him that Abdullah can't hear. Just as the chauffeur opens the door, the man gestures that he isn't needed. 'Sorry, my mistake!'

'*Screw you and the sow that gave birth to you!*' Abdullah hears the taxi chauffeur grunt, but it is in Arabic, so the men do not understand. This was definitely not a police officer.

'Two minutes, you said?'

'Follow me.' Abdullah sets off again, walking as fast as he can. Was the taxi another sign from God? Should he turn back? He shakes his head to no one in particular; it's too late now.

A little more than five minutes later, they arrive at Siraj's House of Dreams, and the pimp himself is standing in the door opening, smoking a cigarette.

'Come, gentlemen, and welcome to Siraj's House of Dreams!'

The men follow him inside, and Abdullah hesitates. Ghulam had instructed him to wait in front of the door until the clients were done, but it is cold and raining. He steps inside after the men and suddenly finds himself in the most beautiful room he has ever set foot in.

It is painted golden and pink, and behind a marble mantelpiece is a nice, warm fire. In front of the fire there are two colourfully clothed sofas, and sitting on the sofas are six girls. They are scantily clad, but all of them have their faces covered by dark veils, only showing their eyes. It is clear that they are nothing like the women living in Abdullah's house; these girls are young, and their bodies are beautiful.

There is also music: Vera Lynn! Siraj plays it to make his clients long for home and the sweet arms of their wives, whom they can temporarily replace here with one of his girls—or at least that is what Ghulam has told Abdullah. Abdullah has often used Vera

Lynn's name to connect with customers, but he has never heard her sing; it is the most beautiful music he has ever heard.

'Would you like some brandy, gentlemen?' Without waiting for their answer, the pimp picks up a bottle, fills two crystal brandy glasses, and presents them to the men. 'Please, sit down.'

He flicks his fingers, and the girls move to make room for the men. 'Now, perhaps you would like some dancing? Naturally, all my girls are trained in the ancient art of belly dancing. We can do it here, or maybe in private?'

Abdullah admires the hustler's English. In the last year he has learned to speak a decent bit of English himself, but he cannot do it like Siraj. When the hustler speaks, the words flow with the melodies of the music.

'Maybe first another brandy,' the impatient man says. He has already finished his glass. 'And give the boy a glass too.'

'Not for me, sir. It is . . .' Abdullah wants to say forbidden, but before he can say another word, Siraj squeezes his cheek so hard, it hurts.

'He believes it is too generous of you!' the hustler says, 'but he is raised on the streets and he does not know it is most impolite to refuse. Of course, he will have a brandy. He will have two, three; as many as he can take before he falls down!'

The men laugh loudly, and Siraj flicks his fingers again at the girls. 'The boy too,' he says in Arabic.

One of the girls gets up, and as she pours Abdullah a glass of the golden liquor, she looks sensually into his eyes. Now that she is so close, he can see through her veil. Her eyelashes and eyelids are painted dark green up to her temples, like she is wearing a mask, and her lips are coloured to match.

The glass in Abdullah's hand is heavier than it looks, and the brandy does not smell bad. Abdullah knows that he cannot drink it—it is forbidden—but when Siraj lays a hand on his shoulder, he realises that he does not have a choice.

In Arabic, in a most friendly tone, the pimp says, 'You are in my house, and if God wants it, here you will drink everything my guests buy for you, at the same speed they are drinking. If you do not, I will cut the price of the drinks from your commission, and I promise you that at my prices, you will be paying me.

'On the other hand, for every drink that you do take, I will pay you a quarter of its price. Now, act like you are particularly looking forward to brandy.'

Siraj removes his hand and smiles at the gentlemen; Abdullah follows suit. Just to be here makes him a sinner. How much worse can it get if he plays his part? The gentlemen raise their glasses at him, and, while saying a silent prayer, he raises his glass and takes a sip.

The brandy burns in his throat, but when the pain is gone he also feels warmer inside.

From the sofa, two girls stand up, and they climb onto the small platform set against the wall. Abdullah looks at them as they start to move sensually and in harmony. The men have already taken another large gulp, and he tries to catch up while keeping his eyes on the platform. It is sinful to enjoy this, he knows, yet he can do nothing but watch. They squirm over the floor and over each other; while they do so, they look at him!

The brandy girl comes again, and he quickly finishes his glass— too quickly. For a second, he feels like the brandy is going to burn through his gullet. Then the pain disappears, and as the girl refills his glass, her smile is unmistakable.

Two new girls stand up, carrying swords. As they start to dance, they balance the swords on their faces and their bellies. Suddenly, the girls start fighting. They slash at each other, their movements remaining completely in rhythm with the music, and soon the veils come off, just like the few items of clothing they are wearing. Abdullah thanks God when both girls leave the stage unharmed.

He has never before thought about girls, but these creatures light a fire in him. He wants to feel if their skin is as soft as it looks; he wants to smell them and discover if their odour is as sweet as they look, and he wants them to keep on dancing so that he can keep on looking at them.

Another brandy arrives, and this time there is no pain as he downs what's left in his glass. While the naked girls cover themselves with sarongs, a new girl steps onto the platform. In her hands she carries a wicker basket, which she opens and puts on the front of the stage. Abdullah tries to see what's in it, but his angle isn't right.

Then, the sound of a flute floats into the room from the gramophone, and the girl starts to move. The notes from the flute grow higher-pitched, and two serpents rise. They glide through the air, matching the tone of the flute, and they keep going up and up. The girl spreads her arms, and each of the snakes makes its way onto one of them before they start to glide over her body. Abdullah looks away. He does not like snakes, and the way they slither over the girl's body makes him feel sick.

Suddenly, there is a loud cry, and he looks at the platform again. The girl has fallen to the ground, shaking; the other girls start to scream.

'The snake! The snake!' one of the men shouts before taking out his gun and shooting it. The crack hurts Abdullah's ears, and he realises that he needs to get away before the rats come.

He stands up, but only now does he realise that the room around him is spinning. In fact, he feels like he is in a dream. This couldn't really be happening.

More cracks. What are they shooting at?

Abdullah takes a step in the direction of the stage and sees the girl; there is a large, bleeding hole in the upper side of her left thigh, while the rest of her body is covered in snake blood.

This is too much for him. He walks toward the door, and the moment he has stepped through it, he starts to throw up.

He is so tired, and the fact that the world around him is spinning does not make it easier for him to get away. *Thank God at least the rain has stopped.* He sits down and closes his eyes.

When he wakes, it is light, and the door to Siraj's House of Dreams is bolted.

CHAPTER SIX

Mayasin

Month of Truce 12, 1361 A.H. (20 November 1942)

Abdullah had hoped the rain that came down on Mayasin three days ago had signalled the start of winter, but instead, summer has returned. In fact, it is so hot that Abdullah has decided to find a place in the shade of what was until recently Mr Darwish's store, instead of wasting his energy scavenging through the streets. It is there that Ghulam finds him.

'I have been looking for you,' the boy says. 'You need to come with me.'

Abdullah looks at his friend. 'Why? What's out there for us?'

'Work. Well-paid. At Siraj's House of Dreams.'

Abdullah hadn't been able to re-enter the house after waking up in front of the door, but the hustler had been true to his word, and Abdullah had found his commission in his tunic. If Siraj is offering well-paid work, the hustler will not be lying—not that there is much for sale at the moment, but only the emir can do something about that. Besides, if Abdullah takes on the work, he might meet the girls again.

He follows his friend. 'What do we have to do?'

'There was a girl there; she was bitten by snake.'

'I know,' Abdullah says. 'I was there.'

'You were there! How did it happen?'

Abdullah's doesn't much like his friend's enthusiasm. Witnessing the girl getting bitten was awful. 'Trust me, you didn't miss anything. Do you know how she is doing?'

'She is dead.'

'Dead?' he exclaims.

'It was a dangerous snake,' Ghulam drily answers.

Abdullah takes a few moments to digest this before asking, 'What do we have to do?'

'Siraj wants the body out of his house as soon as possible. He is afraid her smell will attract the attention of the wrong kind of rat.'

'The wrong kind of rat?'

'A member of the Emir's Guard.'

'Why does he call you? Isn't this more a job for Nadir or one of the other rats?'

Selling girls is illegal, but many police officers, including Nadir, are on Siraj's payroll.

Ghulam shakes his head. 'All of Siraj's rats work in the good streets. They have their hands full protecting the shops and stalls that are still selling food. Lord al-Rikabi has promised to hang any rat that leaves his area, excuse or no excuse.'

This isn't too surprising. At the moment shops with food don't just need protection from thieves and vagrants; they need protection from everyone except the wealthiest people in the city.

'What about the doctor, or the servants of the doctor?'

Again Ghulam shakes his head. 'No doctor. Best for Siraj not to spread the word too much that he is letting poisonous snakes dance with naked girls for the entertainment of foreigners.'

Abdullah shakes his head. Without a doctor, the girl never stood a chance. He can't believe Siraj just let her die like that, but afraid that Ghulam might find someone else for the job, he does not bring it up.

When they reach the House of Dreams, Ghulam goes around and lets Abdullah in through the back. Abdullah does not see any of the girls as his friend leads him to a room filled with books. Ghulam fumbles a little with a wooden panel, and a secret door opens, revealing a completely bare room where the snake girl is lying on the floor, everything but her face covered by a blanket.

Amazingly enough, the look on her face does not show the nasty circumstances of her death. Her face is pale, yet it is still very pretty, even prettier than he remembers it. While it almost appears like she is simply taking a peaceful nap, the smell is awful. Siraj would have done better to bring them in earlier.

'Here.' Ghulam hands him a saw.

'What do I do with it?'

'We can't remove the body like this; it is too heavy!'

He removes the sheet, and now Abdullah can really see the consequence of the bite. Within three days, the girl's entire leg has almost completely rotted away. It is the most disgusting thing he has ever seen, and he turns around and pukes.

Someone is clapping his hands. He looks up and sees Siraj.

'I see you have brought the puking boy!' he says sarcastically to Ghulam.

'He is my friend, and he can do the work.'

'It's no problem with me, as long as this time he cleans up his own mess; if God wants it. I have enough problems with the people working for me already, like this one.' The hustler gestures at the girl lying dead on the floor. 'Those men shot my snakes, and I have no idea where to get new ones!'

'You want to get new snakes?' Abdullah asks incredulously.

'Of course! Did you not see how aroused those men were by the act? But trained snakes are expensive; I can buy three girls for the price of one snake. Ha!' And the hustler turns around and disappears again.

'Can you believe that?' Abdullah asks Ghulam.

'I can't believe you puked in Siraj's house, twice,' his friend answers.

'Last time it was outside, in front of his door. They had given me brandy, and then the snake bit this girl.'

Ghulam shakes his head in dismay and replies, 'We'd better get to work.'

Cutting a body into pieces is harder work than it might seem, especially when the saws are blunt, but eventually they succeed. They wrap the limbs in cloth, and as unobtrusively as they can, they take the pieces outside. Abdullah looks at what he and Ghulam are carrying and considers what they have left behind. He doesn't know where they're going, but wherever it is, they will have to walk three times; he does not like it.

'Come on,' his friend says, and he silently follows.

About ten minutes later, they arrive at a building that looks a lot like the house Abdullah lives in, although this one may be even more derelict. Inside, a small fire is burning, but it's not there to keep out the cold; the smell of burned meat is everywhere.

'Who are you?' one of the men near the fire asks.

'We come to sell,' Ghulam says.

'What do you have?'

'Meat.' He throws the bag on the floor; Abdullah follows his example.

The man walks over to them, grabs one of the bags, looks inside, and smells.

'This meat is bad.'

'It will be better when you cook it.'

'It is also illegal. Do you know what happens when a rat catches you cooking this?'

'I don't suppose it will be much worse than when he takes a closer look at what you've got on that fire right now.'

The man laughs, and the other people around the fire follow his example.

'Tell me,' the man says, 'why shouldn't we just throw you and your friend there on the fire?'

Abdullah takes a step back, but Ghulam is not intimidated. 'We don't have any meat; we're just bones and skin. This one, on the other hand, was well fed.'

'All right. Two shillings for everything,' the man says.

Ghulam shakes his head. 'Eleven, six up front.'

'Four, after,' the man counters.

'Nine, five up front.'

'You're crazy,' the man says. 'Five, one up front.'

But Ghulam holds his ground. 'Eight, four up front.'

'Six, two up front.'

'Seven, four up front.'

The man sighs. 'Three.'

'Four, or in the name of God, we take this meat and go to the guys around the corner.'

The man turns to the small group of people around the fire, and after a short deliberation, he says, 'You have a deal,' and he hands over four shillings to Ghulam.

Ghulam smiles. 'If God wants it, we're going to collect the rest.'

'You'd better return soon, or in the name of God, we will find you!'

Outside, Abdullah asks, 'Are people really doing this around the corner too?'

Ghulam shrugs. 'These guys aren't the only ones in the city, that's for sure. If we go around enough corners, we're bound to find more people interested in buying.'

Abdullah shakes his head. Somehow, everything that has any relation to Siraj is against the rules of God. However, at the moment money is just money, and if he gets enough of it, maybe he can buy something in the expensive stores. Eventually, anything is better than nothing.

They run back to the House of Dreams, and within fifteen minutes the second shipment is delivered, but their third trip proves a little more problematic.

'Emir's Guard!' Ghulam hisses when he turns a corner, and he instantly takes a couple steps back. 'It's good that they can't see what we're carrying!'

'They can't see it, no,' Abdullah says, absolutely not comforted by this remark, 'but I am sure they can smell it.'

Ghulam looks at him. 'What is the Emir's Guard doing here anyway?'

'I have no idea. I don't believe there is anything of importance left to guard here.' Suddenly he has an idea. 'What if Lord Tali'a has ordered them to go after the men-eaters?'

'That would not be good.'

'What do we do?' he asks.

'Well, we're standing in the sun with body parts in our hands that smell worse every minute we wait; I suggest you act casual.'

Ghulam starts to walk again, and Abdullah has no choice but to follow. On their short journey to the derelict house, they meet at least a dozen guards, and each time Abdullah passes one, he thinks he sees him staring.

But it's all in his imagination. To the guards, two children aren't all that interesting, even when they're carrying cloths that smell like there are rotting corpses inside.

56

The moment they open the door to the house, Ghulam throws in his bag. Then he takes Abdullah's bag from him and throws it in too.

'Let's go!' he commands and walks away from the house again.

Abdullah follows, but once his friend slows his pace, he gives him a push. 'What are you doing? They still owe us three more shillings!'

'They will never give them to us. Who are we going to tell that we have been swindled while we were selling human limbs? In fact, it is more likely that they would have tried to kidnap us for when their other meat runs out; better not to give them any chance.'

They walk on, and pondering Ghulam's words, Abdullah doesn't notice the lorries in the streets. His friend is right, as usual, yet it is still a disappointment. One and a half shillings, tax-free, is not money he wants to let go.

At the House of Dreams there is still the unhappy prospect of the floor that needs to be cleaned, and his puke is by no means the dirtiest thing there. It takes about an hour of intense scrubbing until they are finally done, and Siraj, who has been casually watching them for the last ten minutes, throws ten shillings on the floor.

For Abdullah, that makes seven shillings for the day, more than three times as much as he had hoped to earn when he left home that morning, yet he cannot shake his depression as he and Ghulam walk away. How much food will all this money buy him, and will the expensive stores even let him in?

On the street they pass more guards, but Abdullah doesn't notice. Maybe it's the hunger, or maybe it's just tiredness, but one thing is certain: he has started to hallucinate. Across the street from them he sees a small market stall, amply filled with food. And not far away there is another one.

'I think I'm seeing things,' Ghulam says.

At least Abdullah isn't the only one. 'Me too.'

As they walk on, they pass more stalls, and at each stall there are more people than at the previous one. Suddenly a thought strikes him. 'Do you think that maybe all those guards could be on the streets to organise that food?'

'There's only one way to find out.' Ghulam walks to the nearest stall, and Abdullah follows him. He can smell the freshly baked bread, and he sees people walking away with it. This cannot be a dream! When one of the men behind the stalls finally looks down at him and he asks for three loaves of bread, the man answers, 'Two loaves maximum per person.'

They are so cheap that if the prices do not change, he will have enough money for weeks! As he walks home, he eats a whole loaf by himself, thanking God and Emir Jalal with every bite he takes. Clearly the men who blamed the emir for the shortages were wrong, while Ghulam's cousin was right. After all, since the Emir's Guard brought the food to the people, surely the new emir had arranged it.

CHAPTER SEVEN

Mayasin

Month of Truce 12-13, 1361 A.H. (20-21 November 1942)

For the first time in months, Abdullah walks through the city with a full stomach. Ghulam is not with him, yet tonight he does not fear Rizq. After all, he is far from alone. All across the city, people are celebrating and singing songs in honour of the emir. There are lights everywhere, and the ecstatic mood of the people is reflected in the foreign soldiers, who have all suddenly appeared from their caves to join in the celebrations.

It would be the perfect night to make money, but Abdullah does not feel like working. He does not need to, and he deserves a night off. He doesn't notice the men as he passes them, and when they call him, he doesn't look back. In fact, he doesn't even hear them call.

'Boy! Boy!' they call again, and this time he does hear them, but since he hasn't tried to make contact with anyone, it merely makes him wonder what strange kind of boy is ignoring the foreigners when they are so obviously calling him. Only when he feels a hand on his shoulder does he turn around. In front of him is one of the two men who were with him when the snake girl got bitten.

59

'It's you! George, it's him!' The impatient man is there too. 'We were looking for you. We have been trying to find that whorehouse, but it seems to have disappeared.'

There are too many noises, and the man is talking too fast for him to understand.

'What?' Abdullah asks loudly. 'More slow!'

The man repeats himself, and this time Abdullah catches most of what he says. 'You want to go to House of Dreams?'

The man nods.

He considers this a moment. Earlier that day, he vowed never to go back there; it is a bad place. On the other hand, if he never returns, he will never see the girls again, and no one will give him any brandy. The headache afterward was bad, yet he also remembers how happy the drink had made him, how far away his problems had seemed.

The man sees him hesitate and decides to press the issue. 'You'll be well compensated,' he says and shows the boy an English bank note.

Abdullah does not have much experience with notes, but he knows the least valuable one is worth ten shillings. This man is going to give him ten shillings, and that will be excluding Siraj's commission, *and* Abdullah is going to see the girls. What harm can one more time do? God will surely understand.

'The money first,' he says, and the man hands him the note. Abdullah beams. He now has over sixteen shillings in his pocket. That's more than he has ever had before.

'All right. We go!'

Siraj receives them heartily, even Abdullah, showing all the charm that was missing that afternoon. 'Ah, my good friends, I am so pleased that you have returned. I was afraid that after the last time, maybe you had grown scared!'

'Not scared, just lost,' the impatient man says. 'This city is a little more difficult to navigate than it seems. Fortunately, we ran into our young friend again.'

Siraj grins. 'Ah, yes! Our young friend is a man of many talents, but I think he is mostly back for the brandy! What do you think?'

'I think he deserves one, and I think that we deserve one too!'

'Of course! Come inside!' He steps aside to let Abdullah and the men enter. It's much busier than last time; Abdullah counts nine men and a dozen girls. The pimp lays his hands on the shoulders of the officers. 'Fatima! Brandy for these gentlemen; we drink to the emir!'

There is the brandy girl again, not wearing a veil today. She cannot be much older than Abdullah, and her face is heavily painted. In the eyes of Abdullah, she is the most beautiful piece of art ever created.

Slowly, he sips the brandy and looks at the stage. There is just one girl dancing tonight. There are no swords and no snakes. He looks to the men at his side. They have already finished their first glass, and, remembering Siraj's threat, he rapidly kills his own. The burning pain in his throat makes him wonder how the men can possibly drink so fast.

'Do you want a cigarette?' the impatient man asks.

He accepts it. He has never smoked before, but everyone has to start someday. All men smoke, and now that he is drinking brandy and spending time in the company of half-naked girls, he is a man too.

Perhaps it is because his throat has been slightly numbed by the brandy, but the first drag does not make Abdullah cough. In fact, he likes the taste. He wonders how this is possible when men who smoke always stink.

They are joined by a couple girls who only show interest in the Englishmen, but since they're close enough for Abdullah to smell them, their presence makes him happy even without their attention.

'Is everything all right?' Siraj comes to ask.

'We were thinking of taking these two girls someplace a little more private.'

'Of course, of course!' Siraj says, grinning.

The men get up, each of them holding hands with a girl, but before they've made it halfway through the room, the impatient man stops to shout at Siraj. 'And you can give the boy another brandy, on my tab!'

'Of course! As much brandy for the boy as he wants, or at least as he can drink!' Siraj personally refills Abdullah's glass while he says, 'And since the gentleman is paying for it, I suggest you drink a lot!'

Abdullah smiles. That sounds like an excellent plan. He drinks a third and a fourth before getting up to find a bathroom. Just like the last time, the room has started to spin, but he finds his way. When he arrives back at the bar, Fatima is there to pour him some more brandy.

She smiles at him, and for a second he fears that he might drown in her painted eyes, but then he understands that she is actually longing for him.

And he wants her too. She smells fantastic! He doesn't want to touch any of the other girls; he had never wanted to touch any of the other girls. This girl is the only reason he is here.

He reaches his hand out and puts it on her naked hip, but smiling, she instantly takes it off. Her hand is stronger and her grip harder and more resolute than he expected, and he wonders why she does that when it's clear she also likes him. Maybe she isn't allowed to touch him, since he didn't bring money.

He has another brandy, and then he realises that he *has* brought money; quite a lot, actually. On the other side of the room he sees Siraj and walks over to him. It's not far, but the sofa that's in between them is acting very annoying, actively blocking his passage. Why doesn't it stay where it is?

He smiles to himself. A spinning room and a moving sofa; this place is magical.

When he finally reaches Siraj, the hustler is talking to a man with a moustache, probably negotiating over some girl, and Abdullah can't follow. Why did he move over here again? He looks at the girls, yet he can't remember. What's more, he suddenly feels terribly tired; perhaps he should just go home.

'Ah, Abdullah.' Siraj smiles. 'Just the man we were talking about.'

The hustler grabs him by the shoulders, pulls him close, and turns back to the moustached man. 'You are saying that this is more to your liking than my beautiful girls?'

'Is that a problem?' the man asks. Of course Abdullah is more to his liking. He has brought the English gentlemen here, after all, hasn't he? And what's more, he is a good Muslim boy, unlike these sinful girls who are all whores, except maybe for the brandy girl.

That's it! That is why he has moved over here. He must not forget it again.

Siraj sighs and shakes his head. 'There are places where you can get this kind of thing, and I will gladly help you find one, but this is not one of them.'

'I thought this was a house of dreams.'

There is disappointment in the man's voice, Abdullah is certain of it, but he cannot understand what it is about.

'This is Siraj's House of Dreams, but if I give you your dream, tomorrow it will belong to someone else.' Siraj waves his hand at the room and continues. 'Please, have another brandy and take any girl you fancy.'

'What about the girl serving the drinks?'

The hustler bows head and repeats, 'Any girl you fancy.'

A smirk appears on the man's face.

'No wait, I money!' Abdullah intervenes in English.

He takes the money from his tunic, but someone bumps into him, and it falls to the ground. People are laughing at him, but he doesn't care. He must prevent the man from buying his girl; he must get his money. He bends down to pick it up.

A sharp pain in his ear stops him. Someone has grabbed him and is dragging him away from his money. He looks up: Siraj.

'Wait! I have money for the girl,' he tries to say.

Siraj does not respond; there's fire shooting out of his eyes. The pain in Abdullah's ear is so bad that all he can do is follow, and before he knows it, he is outside.

'Go home, and do not come anywhere near here again tonight!' the hustler scowls.

Before Abdullah realises what has happened, Siraj has disappeared and Abdullah is outside, alone. He wants to go back in, but when he pushes the door, it doesn't move. He bangs his fists on the door; no one answers.

Fine! If Siraj wants him to go home, he will go home. He stands up and starts to walk. He will not come back again!

Except maybe to get his money. So much money, and it is all on the floor. Is that why Siraj has thrown him out, so that he can have Abdullah's money?

It does seem like that.

Or is the hustler afraid that his serving girl is in love with Abdullah? Siraj sold the girl to the fat Englishman with the moustache. Abdullah shakes his head. God will punish Siraj! Or perhaps . . .

'I told you we would meet again . . .' That icy voice. It's the voice that haunts his dreams. Probably, this is a dream as well. It does feel like a dream. Everything is vague, and even the stars in the sky are moving.

He looks up. Rizq! He smiles. If this is a dream, then Siraj has not really sold the girl to the moustached man.

'Don't you have anything to say?' the rat hisses.

He does. He wants to say that he can take this rat. It is his dream, and he is done with people hunting him in his dreams. He takes a step forward, but when he opens his mouth he is attacked from the core of his gullet, and instead of words, a thick orange vomit comes out.

The force is so violent that he falls to his knees, and when he tries to catch his breath, the smell that is now coming from the ground makes him puke again.

And again.

And then he looks up. Rizq is still there with an evil grin on his face. What if this time he is not dreaming? What if his nightmare has turned into reality?

'Please God, wake me now!' he says.

'God can't hear you.' Rizq spits on him. 'God can't save you either!'

He must flee. He gets up and tries to run away, but before he's made it ten yards, he trips. Of course he trips.

He feels the rat's hand in his hair, pulling him up. It hurts, but not as much as when Siraj dragged him through his House of Dreams by his ear. He tries to get away, but Rizq is much too strong, and despite all his efforts, the rat is pulling him closer.

If he doesn't think of something soon, he'll die just like in his dream. Rizq will put the dagger to his face, and he will kill him very slowly.

The dagger.

It's his only chance. He takes a deep breath and lets Rizq pull him close. 'Now, you and me are going to have some fun,' the rat whispers in his ear.

Abdullah doesn't listen. *Please God, let the curve be moderate and the point as sharp as a pin.*

He reaches behind him for the dagger, and before Rizq has realised what's happening, it's already out of its sheath. The rat lets go of his hair just as Abdullah brings the dagger down. Rizq groans and lashes at him with his fist, hitting Abdullah on the back of his head.

He falls forward, but he doesn't feel any pain. Through some miracle he's held on to the dagger. He jumps up and runs at Rizq again. The rat hits him, right on the nose, and he goes down again.

But he doesn't stay down. He can see blood coming from the policeman's leg. Shoulder first, with his full weight behind him, he jumps at the rat, and the moment he feels his shoulder touch Rizq's body, he thrusts with the knife.

The blade goes through the rat's flesh as though it was cutting through stewed goat meat, but then Rizq hits him again, and he loses his grip and falls backwards.

If Rizq regains his strength now, Abdullah is lost. He looks at the rat, who pulls the dagger out of his stomach. Abdullah knows he should get up, but he can only move his eyes, and he uses them to follow the rat, who is slowly coming closer. If Ghulam were here, his friend could attack the rat from behind and finish him once and for all. But Abdullah is alone with the rat, sent outside by Siraj to be murdered.

'You thought you could take on Rizq?'

The rat stands over him now and laughs sinisterly, but then the laugh turns into a cough, and Abdullah can see blood coming out of Rizq's mouth. The cough turns more violent, and the blood paints red stains on Abdullah's tunic, first a few, then many.

The rat goes down on one knee, and Abdullah can hear him breathing quickly and heavily. The arm holding the knife goes up, but before Rizq can bring it down, another coughing attack over-takes the policeman.

Abdullah can taste his blood. He should do something. Hit the man; kick him. Yet he still can't move. He closes his eyes and prays.

God, forgive me. Protect my family.

He does not get further.

'Goodbye,' the rat hisses, but the word turns into another cough, and then Abdullah feels the heavy man falling on top of him. He opens his eyes again, sees the rat is not moving, and can't believe the danger is gone.

Using all of his strength, he pulls himself from under the policeman and crawls up. He kicks against the body that is now lying on the street. It doesn't move. He kicks harder. It still doesn't move.

He feels a tear running down his face. It's over. Never again will he have to live in fear of this man waiting in the shadows.

The tears flow freely now, and he starts to walk away. Never again will he be haunted by this nightmare.

His body is aching; it doesn't matter. He's finally free.

But he is covered in blood, and if people see him like this, they'll know. They'll know that he's a murderer. They'll know that he's murdered a policeman!

He must ignore the pain in his body and get away from here. He starts to walk as fast as his legs allow him. He needs to get home, but where is home? He knows this city so well, yet at the moment he doesn't have a clue where he is or where he's going.

There are still people in the streets. What are they doing here at this hour? Are they staring at him?

He looks at the road and walks even faster. The pain in his leg grows stronger; the pain in his back too. And his head feels like he has just found himself on the wrong end of a severe beating.

'Abdullah, Abdullah,' he hears voices hissing. 'Abdullah, come to us!'

The people that were on the streets earlier have turned into ghosts. Why has God sent ghosts to come and get him? Why would He care about a man like Rizq? Abdullah starts to run. He has always known ghosts existed, yet he had never thought that one day they would be coming for him.

'Abdullah, Abdullah!'

Minutes go by—or are they hours?—and the ghosts are closing in. They are everywhere, laughing at him, shouting. He trips, and suddenly he's at the mercy of the ghosts. He needs to fight them now, or they will possess him.

'There is no God but God, and Muhammad is His messenger!' he shouts. It feels great, and it holds off the ghosts, but what if he wakes the people? 'There is no God but God, and Muhammad is His messenger.'

He gets up, muttering the words over and over again. The lights that were everywhere earlier in the evening have disappeared with the people, and so have the stars. In fact, nights in Beledar do not get much darker than this.

He wants to shout the creed again. Anything to make more noise than the ghosts around him, but he does not dare risk it. Even if the ghosts do not betray him, one look at him and people will know what he's done.

The sound of a door opening startles him, and he starts to run again. What can he do? Where can he go? Where is he? He looks around, and then, right in front of him at the other side of the square of Hussein the Great, he sees the magnificent Green Mosque. The ghosts will not dare to follow him there!

A boy like Abdullah isn't welcome there either, but it cannot be a coincidence that God has led him here. Using his last bits of strength, he makes for the great doors as rapidly as he can.

They are locked.

Unbelievable. Here he is, covered in blood in the fanciest area of Mayasin, and God keeps the doors to His house closed.

'Greatest God, most Merciful God, I beg You: open Your doors to me now,' he calls with his last breath as he bangs on the doors.

Nothing happens. He kicks the doors; they don't give an inch.

He turns around. He needs to find shelter, a place to hide from the ghosts. But he has no strength left. This is the end of the road, and all he can do is sit down against the doors.

God, it was an accident, and I did not have a choice. Forgive me.

There they come. Rizq is with them, and Siraj. Another yard, and they both change into Mr Darwish. It hurts to see how disappointed the old man looks.

Why did he have to run here? Why did he not run home?

It was because of the brandy. The brandy disoriented him. Devil's drink.

Well, at least he will not have to run anymore. He closes his eyes and lies down. There is a man bending over him. He opens one eye.

'Father . . .'

CHAPTER EIGHT

Mayasin

Month of Truce 13, 1361 A.H. (21 November 1942 A.D.)

Abdullah is lying on something soft, and under his head is the softest pillow he has ever felt. He opens his eyes and looks around. He is on a real bed in a small room. On the walls there are beautiful paintings of letters he cannot read. On the floor there are thousands of very small, coloured stones that form beautiful patterns. Next to his bed is a stool with a tunic laid out on it, and he realises that he is naked.

Gradually, the events of the previous night come back to him, but they don't make sense. If he is in Paradise, then why did God send ghosts to get him? Maybe the ghosts brought him here. It's definitely more likely than God punishing him for what he did to Rizq.

He gets up and puts on the tunic. It's whiter than anything he has ever worn and smells like flowers. He walks to the door, and when he opens it, he has to blink a couple times to fully take in what he is seeing. He's in an enormous, magnificent hall, shining in a green light. He has never seen anything like this; he must be in Paradise!

And in the middle of the hall there's a big man with a great beard.

He creeps toward the man, and when he has almost reached him, the man turns and says, 'Welcome, my son.'

'Are you God?' Abdullah asks.

The man smiles and shakes his head. 'I am Muhammad al-Rubaie. I am a scholar, and many days I act as a reverend. What is your name?'

Abdullah frowns. 'My name is Abdullah. Why do they need scholars in Paradise?'

'They don't,' the man answers. 'Is your name just Abdullah?'

He nods.

'Then what is your father's name?'

In his head, he hears his mother sneering, '*Saíd!*' and he answers, 'My father's name is Saíd. Or it was Saíd. But perhaps here it is Saíd. Do you know my father?'

The man shakes his head. 'I do not, Abdullah son of Saíd. But tell me, what brings you to the Green Mosque?'

The Green Mosque? Is he in the Green Mosque? Of course, that makes more sense than Paradise . . . He says, 'I am lost.'

'You mean you *were* lost,' Mr al-Rubaie replies in a friendly tone. 'One who has found his way to the house of God is never lost.'

INTERMISSION:

EMIR JALAL
Mayasin

Month of Pilgrimage 2, 1361 A.H. (10 December 1942 A.D.)

Jalal looks at the women who are on their knees in his office. They are the only two wives of his father that have outlived the former emir, but neither of them is his mother. And why they are begging for the lives of traitors, he does not understand—even if they are his uncles. His father's wives should support him and they should have warned him. Instead, it was Richard who set the ball rolling.

'*Now is the winter of our discontent, made glorious by this sun of York; and all the clouds that lour'd upon our house, in the deep bosom of the ocean buried.*' His friend quoted Shakespeare's Richard III after his father's funeral to warn him, and Lord Tali'a confirmed his uncles' betrayal.

'In the name of God, they are your family!' one of the women pleads for the sixth time. 'And it's the Month of Pilgrimage, according to some scholars the holiest of all months. God will reward you if you show forgiveness.'

Maybe God will reward him, but Anna Christina certainly won't. His wife had converted to Islam; she had learned Arabic; she had even changed her beautiful name to the name of the

72

Prophet's favourite wife. Yet while he was out fighting a war, his uncles, his cousins, and their wives spent two years treating her like *persona non grata*, and she still hates them for it.

'I can't. They were plotting to kill me, my wife, my daughter. I cannot grant them forgiveness,' he replies.

'Lord Tali'a *says* they were plotting to kill you,' the woman counters, 'but where is the proof? If there was proof, you could show it to us.'

Jalal sighs. The woman has a point here. Signed confessions, Lord Tali'a has promised him, yet so far no admission of guilt has found him. Apparently a month of torture hasn't been able to break his uncles; does this mean that they are not guilty?

If only Aisha had given him a son instead of a daughter as his first child. If he dies today, who will succeed him? Both Lord Raslan and Lord Kalaldeh have taken one of his aunts as one of their wives. What if Lord Tali'a is secretly working with either of them? Without his uncles, the commander of the Emir's Guard will decide the next emir, or he could even take the throne for himself.

'I will go,' he says. 'I'll go and find Lord Tali'a right now, and I will see if he has the confessions. If he doesn't, I will release everyone.'

'God is praised!' the women shout in harmony as they throw themselves right at his feet. 'God is praised!'

Naturally, Lord Tali'a is nowhere to be found, so Jalal decides to pay his uncles a visit in the dungeons and ask them, man to man, if they were plotting to betray him.

'He won't tell you much,' the guard says as he opens the cell.

'Why not?'

'We have cut out his tongue.' It is the voice of Lord Tali'a, who has suddenly appeared behind Jalal, yet he does not turn to look at the commander of the Emir's Guard and keeps his stare fixed on his uncle.

'What did you do that for?' Jalal has a strong urge to ask about the confessions, but he does not feel like listening to excuses.

'Because one should never allow a snake to talk too much. Have you not read the Bible, Your Grace?'

'As a matter of fact, I haven't.' He is surprised that Lord Tali'a, as pious a Muslim as he has ever known, has.

'It says that if you listen too long to a snake, you will be banned from Paradise.'

On a better day, Jalal would have thought this remark an interesting conversation starter, but not today. He carefully studies his uncle. There isn't much left of the once-proud man. Prince Sharif, the big man who used to have his own Italian tailor—a present from Mussolini—and wore only the most beautiful suits, appears much smaller in the dirty, ragged nightshirt hanging loosely around him. There are deep bags under his eyes, and Jalal notices that the man no longer has any fingernails. He wonders what he would see if his uncle were to take off his nightshirt.

'Perhaps you should talk to your other uncle,' he hears Lord Tali'a say.

Jalal turns around. He won't get much out of Sharif, and the man stinks like shit—literally. Faisal is in the opposite cell, and while his eldest uncle does not look quite as bad as his brother, he smells pretty much the same.

'Uncle Faisal, may peace be upon you.'

'And may peace be upon you, Your Highness.'

'I have heard that you were planning for something other than peace to be upon me.'

'Highness, it's all lies. In the name of God, you have to believe me. It's all lies,' Prince Faisal says, but the man is very difficult to understand.

Jalal sits down on a small stool a guard hands him. 'You don't look particularly well.'

His uncle sort of smiles. Although the prince still has his tongue, Jalal can now see that they have taken his teeth, probably without any anaesthetic. Luckily for the prince, there had not been many left to take.

'Every night, every half hour, they wake me,' Prince Faisal says. 'In the morning, they come to take some part of my body. They feed me mouldy bread and brown water, hoping that I will die, but I hold on. I hold on because I know that one day, God willing, my emir will come and rescue me. And here you are.'

'Why should I rescue you?'

'Because I am innocent! I swear it by the Quran; all of it is lies!'

'Are you saying that Lord Tali'a is a liar?'

'Yes!' Prince Faisal looks up, eyes big, and then looks down again. 'No. Not Lord Tali'a, he's a good Muslim.'

Then his uncle looks up again, his eyes even bigger, but Jalal isn't sure if they actually see him. 'My enemies! My enemies have planned this. *Our* enemies!'

Suddenly, his uncle's head moves skittishly to the left, as though the man fears some kind of danger from there, but there is only a stone wall.

'If it was your enemies who have come up with these lies, why did you sign the confession?' Jalal asks.

His uncle turns his eyes back to him. 'I did not sign a confession!' There is another violent turn of his head. 'Or maybe I did, a long time ago. Maybe they made me! They told me that they would make me a eunuch if I did not sign. Majesty, I am a man, I cannot live as a eunuch!'

So there are confessions.

'You had nothing to do with any complot?'

Uncle Faisal violently shakes his head. 'Never, Majesty. Upon the Prophet, may God bless him and grant him peace, I swear: never!'

Jalal nods. 'Really, Faisal, it's okay. It's almost over now. You can tell me.'

'I swear . . . in the name of God . . . there was never any complot against you. All that Sharif and I wanted was to secure the future of the realm, in the name of God. The boy, Highness, he is too young. He is not from here; his wife is not from here. She is French. Remember the French? We did not see them when we fought the Turks, yet they claimed half the Arab lands after our victory. The boy, Highness, he wants crazy things, and the lords, they see him as an insult . . .' Prince Faisal hesitates.

'The lords see the boy as an insult?' Jalal asks.

'Brother, the lords will eat him up. That is what Sharif said. They will eat him up, and when they've finished with him, they will destroy our father's house; it is written. It wasn't your fault. You were sick. You could not see how weak he was, but we saw, and we acted . . .' The prince hesitates again. 'You know, he had to go.'

Jalal stands up. 'Don't worry, Uncle, the boy will go.'

'No, wait!' Suddenly there is terror in his uncle's voice. 'In the name of God, I did not mean that! It is not real; it is a trick!'

Without casting another look at his uncle, he walks out of the cell. 'Hang them, in the name of God,' he says as he passes the commander.

'I'm not done with them,' Lord Tali'a replies.

Emir Jalal stops and turns. 'Hang them all. My uncles, their wives, my cousins, I want them hanged before nightfall!'

'They will hang, Your Grace, if God wants it.'

And Jalal turns again and walks away, forgetting to ask about the confessions. Somewhere, a part of him had hoped that he was wrong; that Richard and Lord Tali'a had been wrong; that he had allowed his family to be tortured for nothing.

He is still unsure about Lord Tali'a's loyalty, but the man has not lied about the uncles. Instead of helping to build the most powerful country in the region, they decided to remove him. *Close relatives, they are like scorpions.*

Part II

KHALID

CHAPTER ONE

Al Nawaara

Month of Burning 17, 1362 A.H. (16 September 1943 A.D.)

There are men shouting outside the classroom, and even though Khalid is curious about this disruption of the normal tranquillity, he doesn't move. Next to him, his brother almost jumps up, but one look at the teacher makes Aadhil reconsider too. Not all boys are that wise; a few move toward the small window. Before they've come anywhere near it, Mr Nouri's bamboo stick has found them.

In general, the teacher does not discriminate where he hits the boys, and at this particular moment their faces seem to be most convenient. It takes just two hits and a couple of loud screams to get the four boys back on the floor.

'Mr Khalid Khan,' the teacher says as if nothing has happened, 'what is significant about the last pilgrimage?'

Khalid knows that he knows this, but it is much too warm in the classroom, and he is horribly hungry. Normally, he eats whenever he gets the chance, but for some reason God has forbidden eating when the sun is up during the Month of Burning; at moments like this, he really hates Him. He stares at the teacher and tells himself to focus. When Mr Nouri is teaching the boys about arithmetic or language, the man does not mind when they get answers wrong. However, this question is about the Prophet, and if Khalid gets it wrong here, he will be the next to fall victim to the teacher's stick.

Was it the trip where the Prophet's favourite wife Aisha was left behind? When a foot soldier returned her to Medina?

The teacher takes a step closer.

There were allegations that Aisha had stayed behind on purpose so that she could be alone with the soldier. The Prophet had gone to Ali for advice on the matter, and his son-in-law had told him that he should just divorce her. Muhammad hadn't followed up on his advice, but the rift it had caused between Ali and Aisha was never resolved.

It was a significant event, but it had happened before the last pilgrimage.

'Mr Khan, we haven't got all day.' The teacher takes another step closer and is now less than a yard away from Khalid.

The last pilgrimage . . . It must have something to do with Ali. The teacher always starts his religious lessons with Ali, Hassan, and Hussein—men he appears to regard as just as important as the Prophet himself. Of course!

Khalid answers, 'After the last pilgrimage, the Prophet—may God bless him and grant him peace—called the community together and told them that every man who accepted him as his leader should also accept Ali.'

Mr Nouri stares at him, but Khalid is not intimidated; he knows that his answer is correct.

'So he effectively named Ali his successor?'

Khalid nods and loudly replies, 'Yes, sir.'

'But Ali did not succeed him, did he?'

'No, sir!'

'Who did?'

'Abu Bakr, sir. The Prophet's father-in-law.'

There are men in the village who believe that this was as it should be; that Muhammad's successor needs to be elected, but these men are not real Muslims. Vividly, Khalid remembers the teacher explaining this on the day he first arrived at school.

'And when Ali was finally elected to his rightful position as Successor, he would not accept the title. What title did he take?'

Mr Nouri is still looking at him, and while Khalid knows the answer to the question too, he now faces a different dilemma. He has already answered three questions correctly; if he answers this one as well, his classmates might punish him for it. However, this too is an important question, and if he gets it wrong, Mr Nouri will hit him.

'Well, Mr Khan?'

He takes a deep breath. The teacher's stick is an absolute certainty, but most of the children in the class fear Aadhil. As long as his brother stands by him, they will not dare hurt him. Besides, he does not like to look stupid.

'He took the title *Commander of the Faithful* like Omar had done, and the title of *Reverend*, to show that he would lead the faithful in prayers.'

'Very good, Mr Khan.'

The teacher takes his eyes off him, and he gets a nod from his brother. For a moment he feels proud of himself, but when he looks around he sees that the rest of the boys are clearly less impressed. He hopes he is right about their fear of Aadhil.

'Mr Mohid Ali.' At least the teacher has stepped past him. 'Today, when we pray, who acts as reverend?'

'You, sir.' Khalid hears the boy answer without sounding very confident.

'And why me?'

'Because you are a *guardian*, sir.'

'And what if I wasn't here? What if only you and the youngest Mr Khan were here?'

'What then, sir?'

There are a couple of smothered laughs in the classroom, and Khalid can hear the stick zoom through the air and touch down.

'Aargh!'

'Do we think we are funny, Mr Ali?'

'No, sir.'

'Let's try again then. If you and Mr Khalid Khan were in this room together, and you heard the call for prayer, who would be reverend?'

'Me, sir.' Khalid closes his eyes. It's obvious what the teacher's next question will be, and there is so much uncertainty in Mohid's voice that he is bound to get it wrong.

'And why is that?'

'Because I am older.'

'Stretch out your arm,' the teacher commands. Khalid hears Mohid breathing heavily behind him, and while he does not dare to look back, he can imagine the fear in his classmate's eyes. The stick zooms through the air again, and Mohid's scream sends a chill through the room.

'No, Mr Ali,' Mr Nouri says calmly. 'The one who knows most about Islam is the one who acts as reverend, and, in this case, that is obviously young Mr Khan.'

Khalid sighs. Why did the teacher involve him? Mohid has many friends, and even if they might have been willing to let his streak of good answers go, they will definitely try to repay him for the pain that has been dealt to Mohid by Mr Nouri. If not today, then tomorrow or the day after.

'Now.' Oblivious to this dynamic, the teacher continues with the lesson, but for the moment his lust for blood is satisfied.

'Mr Naíb, let's move on to arithmetic. If God wants it, explain to me . . .'

Khalid will never learn what the teacher wants Mr Naíb to explain, because the door opens and a man he has never seen before bursts through it.

'One of the caravans has been attacked!'

A wave of outrage rolls through the classroom, and Khalid's brother, Aadhil, jumps to his feet and taps him on the shoulder, gesturing that he should pack up their things. The teacher notices.

'Mr Khan the elder, what exactly is your plan here?'

'Our father and our brothers are travelling with a caravan!' Aadhil yells.

'Perhaps they were even with the caravan that was attacked.' The teacher looks incisively at his brother. 'But what are you going to do about it?'

'If it is my family, God willing, I will kill whoever attacked them.' Khalid's brother sounds ready to fight, and despite the fact that he is only eleven years old, not one of the boys in the class is laughing.

Mr Nouri, however, is less impressed. He takes a couple steps until he's between the door and Aadhil. 'Mr Khan, I promise you that the last thing anybody wants right now is for a child to get in the way of men. Sit down, and we will talk no more about it.'

'I will not sit down! I'm going to see if my family is okay, and if they're not at our house, in the name of God I swear that I'm going to look for them. Khalid!'

Hesitantly, Khalid gets to his feet too. This is not a good situation. If he decides to follow his brother, one day soon the teacher will punish him for it, and the whipping will be one he won't forget for the rest of his life. But without his brother to protect him, neither will he forget the beating he'll receive from Mohid's friends.

'Young Khans, I will give you one final warning . . .'

Aadhil does not wait for Mr Nouri to finish his warning. He throws his notebook at the teacher's head and himself after it, taking Mr Nouri completely by surprise.

'Khalid!' his brother urges him from the doorway. Khalid looks around and takes a deep breath. It's clear what the best choice is. He picks up his bag and runs after his brother, making sure to stay out of reach of Mr Nouri's stick.

Khalid does his best to keep up with his brother, but being almost two years his junior, he quickly loses sight of him and gives up running. His legs are too weak, anyway, and he is in desperate need of water.

What has he done, and what will his mother say? In the short term he's made the right choice, he is pretty sure about that, but he has not yet considered the long-term effect.

Aadhil never liked school in the first place and is always saying that he will go and work with his father and their half-brothers the moment he can carry his weight, but Mother will not allow it. Recently, a real secondary school has opened in Taj al Wadi, and their mother is determined that her children will attend it.

And now Aadhil has attacked the teacher and they have run away from school! Carefully, he approaches the house. Before he can see them, he can hear his mother yelling at his brother. From the sound of it, she is not happy at all.

He is nearly at the door when his little sister Shiya catches sight of him. She points at him, and her eyes light up as she teasingly sings, 'You . . . are . . . in trouble . . .'

He points his finger back at her and gives her a semi-serious angry look that makes her giggle, and she runs away. Khalid is sure that Aadhil would have punished her if she acted the same way toward him, but God will not approve if he takes out his fear of Mother on his little sister.

He takes a couple more steps toward the house, and now he can hear exactly what is being said inside.

'You are an ungrateful pig! I do everything for you! I wash, I clean, I get you into school, I make sure that you get the best future, and what do you do? You run away! You besmirch your father's good name! You are even worse than a pig . . .'

Khalid looks in through the doorway. His mother is standing with her back to him, but his brother notices him. Using his head Aadhil gestures to him to get away, to save himself, but Khalid takes a deep breath and steps inside.

'As I told you, the teacher allowed us to go home after he heard that the caravan was attacked.' Aadhil looks at his mother defiantly and continues. 'He knew that I was now the man in the house, and he understood that. It is my duty to go out and find them.'

Clap!

With the back of her hand, Mrs Khan hits her son in the face, and he falls from his chair. Khalid takes this as a sign.

'It is true, Mother. The teacher let us go home to search for Father—and Nourad and Saifan.'

For a woman with a bad limp, his mother turns around astonishingly fast.

Clap!

Khalid too collapses from the force of his mother's hand. As he feels his cheek burning and wonders how quickly it will redden, his mother starts laughing sarcastically. 'Only dumb little boys can come up with an idea like that. You ran away from class, and if God wants it, I am going to take you back right now!'

'No!' Aadhil screams, and Khalid feels a deep admiration for his brother. 'I want to go and look for Father!'

'Listen, boy . . .' his mother says as she raises her hand again. Instinctively, Aadhil raises his arms to protect his face, and Mrs Khan, seeing that she can't give him a straight hit this way, lowers her arm and gives him a lethal stare instead. 'At this very moment, there are people looking for the caravan. They don't want you with them, so right now you have two choices: either you are going back to school, or in the name of God, I will make you understand what real pain is!'

It is not an idle threat, Khalid is sure of it, and, when his brother looks at him, he gestures that he must choose the school option. After all, they can let themselves get beaten up by their mother any day of the week, but no matter how hard she beats them, after the beating she will still send them back.

'Daughter of Muhammad, may peace be upon you,' the teacher says as his mother opens the door to the classroom, her two sons behind her.

'And may peace be upon you too,' she replies. 'I believe you have lost two students during the course of the day. In the name of God, I have come to return them to you.'

'I am sorry, Mrs Khan, but your sons attacked me. It is impossible for your children to return to this school.'

Khalid looks at Aadhil. His brother's eyes are open wide and he's unsure if this is because Aadhil is scared of his mother's reaction to his attack on Mr Nouri or because he has just heard that they have been expelled. Perhaps he is simply thinking about the beating they'll receive when they arrive home.

'And why did my sons attack you?' he hears his mother ask.

'They wanted to leave the classroom to go and search for their father.'

'You do not believe that it is the duty of any boy to search for his family when they have been attacked in the desert? God does not want my sons to avenge their father and brothers because they are too young?'

Mr Nouri shakes his head in dismay. 'I do not believe that it would help anyone if, as a reaction to the attack on the caravan, nine- and eleven-year-old boys get themselves lost in the desert as well. Besides, we do not even know if it is indeed your husband's caravan that was attacked. God is Merciful, and perhaps your husband was not even near the attack.'

'God is Merciful, that is true. But He does not favour cowards, and perhaps my husband is lying somewhere in the desert at this very moment, bereft of water and shelter, waiting for someone to find him. How will my sons live with themselves if, one day, they find out that they could have saved him? What apology can they make to God?'

'Daughter of Muhammad, the sun is too strong, and if your boys go out there, they will not survive. They deserve punishment, but if it is true that you have already lost a husband and two sons today, do not risk your other sons as well. Let me punish them, and after that I will consider taking the younger one back.'

'Mr Nouri,' Khalid watches as his mother fights her limp to erect herself, 'God will protect my boys from the desert, and I will protect them from you.'

Without another word, their mother turns and limps away, and, bewildered, the boys follow.

CHAPTER TWO

The Desert

Month of Burning 17-22, 1362 A.H. (16-21 September, 1943 A.D.)

Khalid and Aadhil have never before attended a village meeting, and after finishing their dinner in record time, they race to the square of Tanvir and arrive an hour before it starts. Khalid does not mind, though; his heart is racing, and he does not want to miss anything.

He grabs his brother's hand and holds it while they observe the village elders and other men of importance pass them and enter the mosque. Their grandfather winks at them, whereas Mr Nouri pretends not to see them. As they wait for the men to come out again, the square gradually grows busier.

The doors of the mosque open. Khalid squeezes Aadhil's hand, and his brother squeezes back. He looks to his right, and Aadhil nods at him, a gesture that slows his heart rate, if only a little. One by one the elders come out, and in the middle of the square they sit down in a circle. Last to come out is the teacher from the Sunni school, a young man with a big, impressive frame. He raises his hands, and immediately the crowd becomes quiet.

'Men of Al Nawaara, this afternoon two stray camels walked into the village. They were alone, and they carried cloths. We believe that this means a caravan has been attacked not far from here. We don't know the location of the attack, but they came from the direction of Mayasin. We are also not sure that the caravan is ours, but this council has decided that it is irrelevant; if it is not one of ours this year, it will be the next—unless we act.'

He pauses, and one of the men in the crowd uses the silence to ask, 'Do you know who the attackers are?'

'It is very unlikely that the raiders came from around here. The last war was less than ten years ago, and we do not believe that any of our neighbours would risk a new one. As for thugs from Taj al Wadi, Lord Tanvir has arrested all vagrants and sent them to the emir to fight side by side with Prince Jalal and the English in the War of the West.

'Ergo, we have come to the conclusion that it could only have been men from the Banu Farud.'

'Who are they?' another man in the crowd asks, although *man* may be too big a word. He is a teenager, no more than ten years older than Khalid.

'They are nomads; they came to the north at the end of spring, and a month ago, a group of them was here in Al Nawaara to trade. Now that the summer is coming to its end, they are returning south.'

'And what are we going to do about it?' It is a woman's voice, and all eyes turn her way. Women are not allowed at village meetings, but this is Mrs al-Tahtawi, the first wife of Khalid's father's main competitor; if it isn't his father's caravan that's been attacked, it most likely is her husband's.

'Mrs al-Tahtawi.' This time it is not the young scholar who speaks, but Lord Raihan, the oldest man in the village. He has stood up and is leaning on his stick. 'I have personally sent my eldest grandson as a delegate to Lord Tanvir and my son to Taj al Wadi to ask for assistance. Other sons have gone to other villages, and together we will send expeditions to find the caravan and to catch up with the Banu Farud and punish the criminals!'

'But it is the Month of Burning, the holiest of all months. God will not forgive us if we violate it by sending men out to fight,' the first man calls.

'In fact,' the young scholar says, 'both Mr Nouri and I completely agree that this is a special circumstance. Not only will God forgive us for taking up arms during a holy month . . . He will punish every man who does not contribute!'

Aadhil lets go of Khalid's hand and takes two steps forward so that everyone can see him. 'Lord Raihan, I can fight!'

Everyone laughs, but in the middle of the circle Khalid sees his grandfather smiling and gazing proudly on his brother. Not wanting to stay behind, he pushes a man aside and steps forward too.

'If God wants it, I will fight too!'

There is more laughter, and somewhere in the back a man shouts, 'They can fight! Thanks be to God!'

But then Mr Nouri stands up, and Khalid can feel his heart sinking.

'You can laugh,' the teacher says. 'But these boys are not going anywhere. They will die out there and . . .'

'Mr Nouri,' old Lord Raihan intervenes, 'these boys have just as much right to join our expedition as everyone else. They are young and strong, and if my son would have been out there, I would go too, despite the fact that I am old and weak.'

He takes a step toward the boys, and, unconsciously, Khalid takes a step back. Lord Raihan is much bigger than he had expected, and despite his age, he clearly isn't as weak as he says he is.

'How old are you boys?'

'I am eleven years old, sir,' Aadhil says, 'and my brother is nine.'

Mr Raihan smiles. 'Well, together you are twenty; a great age for a soldier. Now, go and run to your mother and tell her that you will be leaving tomorrow at first light.'

'Yes, sir!' Aadhil salutes, causing even more laughter in the crowd, and runs off, while Khalid waves quickly at their grandfather before following him.

The expedition force from Al Nawaara consists of thirty-three men and six camels that carry water, food, and blankets. Every man, including Khalid and Aadhil, also carries a goatskin of water for himself. Khalid wishes he wasn't though. He cannot drink from it while the sun is up, and it's constantly reminding him how thirsty he is.

The first two days are extremely dull. They break fast before dawn, start to walk, rest during the warmest hours of the day, and then they walk some more. Khalid spends most of his time saying prayers and wondering why they had not gone with one of the expeditions that actually went out to search for the victims, but Aadhil tells him that they are part of the best expedition. Khalid does not know if that is true, but it is probably the most exciting one.

On the third day, the heat, the hunger, and the exertion start to kick in, and Khalid falls into a trance. He is with the patrol, but he isn't really part of it; he's putting one foot in front of the other, but he's not really walking; he hears Aadhil tell stories, but he can't understand what the stories are about, and when Aadhil stops talking and falls into a similar trance, he doesn't notice.

When it's dark, they eat and drink; when the patrol stops, they sleep. Some of the men worry about them and offer the boys a ride on the camels; Aadhil and Khalid decline. Other men offer them water while the sun is up; Aadhil and Khalid refuse. Even if they are not completely conscious, they are members of the patrol, and they know that if they want to earn the respect of the men, they cannot accept privileges.

Thus, they go on, step by step, day by day, more asleep than awake. Until, at the end of the fifth day, they reach the Oasis of Ri-fadh, where the caravan stops to rest. Khalid and Aadhil find themselves a place to sleep, and they do not wake until the sun is high.

With fewer than four dozen houses, the 'village' that is the Oasis of Ri-fadh is much smaller than Khalid expected; Al Nawaara is a metropolis in comparison. He goes to rinse himself in the small lake and unobtrusively waters his mouth. It will be at least five more hours until sunset, but he's sure that God will forgive him this little cheat.

Fifteen minutes later, he sits down with Aadhil and Mr Raihan, Lord Raihan's eldest son and the leader of their caravan.

'Why are we waiting?' he asks Mr Raihan.

'We wait for a great patrol from Taj al Wadi. According to the villagers, they will arrive presently. We are going to team up with them.'

'Won't we fall too far behind the Banu Farud?'

Mr Raihan shakes his head. 'The Banu Farud were here only three days ago, and since they have women and children and many possessions, they travel slowly; it is written. They have to pass every oasis along the way. It will take them three more days to get to the next oasis and from there five more to get to the great oasis of Azul. If God wills it, we can travel to the oasis of Azul directly in six days, and we will wait for the Banu Farud there.'

Aadhil turns to him and says, 'One week, and we will avenge our father and brothers.'

'*If* something has happened to them,' Khalid answers, and again he says a silent prayer.

CHAPTER THREE

Oasis of Azul

Month of Burning 28-29, 1362 A.H. (28-29 September 1943 A.D.)

The sound of female voices wakes Khalid. For a minute he is confused, but then he sees the small houses and the women to whom the voices belong. He jumps up and starts to shake his brother.

'Aadhil, Aadhil, thanks be to God! We are in Azul!'

Grudgingly, his brother opens his eyes. 'Of course we are in Azul; we arrived here last night. If you had not been walking around like a corpse, you would have known.'

'I have not been walking around like a corpse!'

'Yes, you have; don't deny it. We have all seen that you are not exactly the example of vigilance.' Aadhil scowls. 'If all our men are as weak as you, we will not stand a chance against the Banu Farud.'

Khalid snorts and angrily walks away in search of water and something to eat, but then he realises that since the Month of Burning isn't over yet, he's got a long wait ahead of him before he can do something about his empty stomach. His brother was right; if his head had been clear, he would have woken much earlier. From now on, he is going to be an example of vigilance.

At the oasis he finds the men from the patrol and many other men who he, corpse or no corpse, is sure were not with them the previous day. He also finds water, and he rinses himself so that he can make up for the prayers he has missed and drink as much water as he inconspicuously can. After begging for forgiveness and asking for the well-being of his father and brothers, he goes to look for Mr Raihan to ask who the new men are.

'They are the men Lord Tanvir has sent,' Mr Raihan tells him. 'My nephew is with them.'

Khalid smiles. Now the Banu Farud will not stand a chance if it comes to a battle.

Khalid spends most of the day resting; without food and water his body is too weak to do anything else.

The next day, Aadhil and Khalid wake in time for breakfast, and after eating as much as they can, they climb a hill to make sure they will be the first to spot the Banu Farud. The morning creeps past, and just before the sun reaches its highest point, they see dust rise in the distance. The brothers run down the hill to inform the rest of the men.

'You saw only dust?' asks Mr Ensour, a man from their village. 'Then they are still at least six hours away. They won't be here until the sun is on its way down.'

This is ridiculous. They go to find Mr Raihan; he must command the men to get ready for battle.

'Mr Raihan, they are coming! They are coming!' Aadhil shouts the moment they see their leader.

'Young man, they are coming indeed—Mr Ensour has informed me—but, for now, we need to rest. We still have much time, and it is going to be a long night.'

'But what if Mr Ensour is wrong? What if they travel faster?' Khalid counters.

'Mr Ensour is not wrong.'

'But what if he is!' Aadhil is still shouting, even though they are now standing almost next to Mr Raihan. 'We must make haste!'

'In haste there is regret,' Mr Raihan replies calmly. All the men around them are looking at them now, and while Khalid wants to step back, Aadhil does not seem to notice.

'In complacency is regret.' His brother scowls. 'We must act now!'

'Young men,' Mr Raihan's voice has become a little less calm, 'another word, and if God wants it, I will bind you both to a camel.'

The men laugh, and Khalid can see the anger coming out of his brother's ears, but Aadhil does not protest anymore, and the boys return to their hill.

Hours later, when the sun is well on its way down, two men on camels enter the village. Their shock at finding a small army is palpable. They descend and call for the village elders, and while they wait for the elders to arrive, Khalid analyses the men. Both have great, grey beards, both stand very straight, and both are covered in sand. If it weren't for the fact that one of them is very tall and the other very short, they could be brothers.

'We are here!' a man calls, and three old men appear from the back of the village.

After greetings are exchanged, the small man says, 'The rest of our tribe is close behind us, and we come in peace. We need water and a place to let our camels graze.'

'That is not going to happen!' A young, beautifully dressed man, whom Khalid and Aadhil have never seen before, has appeared out of nowhere.

'Who are you?' the tall man asks.

'I am Lord Maher Tanvir, son of Lord Tanvir, governor of the Oyoun al Jabal province and commander of this army.'

The small man sniffs. 'This is Arabia, and Oyoun al Jabal is very far away. Neither you nor your father has any authority here; it is written.'

'He speaks for us!' one of the village elders calls.

'What!' the short man exclaims, clearly surprised and upset. 'When we came here in the spring, we brought many gifts. We were promised that we would be allowed to visit here on our way back too. Besides, it is our ancient right! You cannot stop us from drinking the water, nor can you stop our camels from eating the vegetation. It is written.'

'Perhaps it is, but I am sure that we can stop you. We have the greatest army in the vicinity stationed here,' Lord Maher retorts. 'If you try to force your way to the oasis, you can be sure that if God wants it, we will kill everyone in your tribe—to the last child.'

The anger almost explodes from the men's faces, and for a moment Khalid believes that the small man is going to attack Lord Maher, but the tall man holds him back and asks, 'What do you want?'

'We want the men from your tribe that attacked our caravan.'

The man shakes his head. 'By the Prophet, no man from our tribe has attacked any caravan.'

'You bring us the thugs, and we will allow you to get water. You don't, you will have to fight for it. I have five hundred men, heavily armed. How many do you have?'

Lord Maher is completely calm, and Khalid cannot help but be impressed.

'I already told you, none of our men attacked your caravan.'

'We do not believe you. You want the water? In the name of God, bring us the thugs!'

And with that Lord Maher turns around and walks away. The nomads exchange a brief glance before mounting their camels and ride off.

After dinner, Khalid and Aadhil return to their hill to watch the camp of the Banu Farud, but all they can see are campfires. After watching the stars for a bit, they go to find some people they know.

Inside the village, men are fiddling with their guns and conversation is hushed. No man is asleep.

'We must go and stand watch,' Aadhil says solemnly.

Khalid nods; at the moment his heart is beating way too hard for him to sleep anyway. They walk to the outskirts of the village from fire to fire until they find one where they recognise men from their village.

'Welcome, boys,' Mr Ensour says. 'You can sit down, but do not look into the fire; it will ruin your eyesight.'

'Do you think they are going to attack us tonight?' Aadhil asks.

'That is a question only God has the answer to,' Mr Ensour answers. 'But if they do, know that I have faced worse odds and survived.'

'Maybe you should tell the boys a story about the Great Revolt,' a man whose name Khalid does not know says, and at exactly the same time, he and Aadhil call, 'Yes!'

At home, boys sometimes joked about Khalid's father being a coward because he had not fought, and one day he had gathered all of his courage to ask his old man why he had refrained from fighting. His father had answered that it did not matter whether the king lived in Istanbul, Mayasin, or Mecca; all that mattered was that the king was able to keep the roads safe for traders. What was more, according to his father, no war ever made roads safer.

Khalid is a little ashamed of this, and he is glad that he is now part of a group of men who have fought to free their nation.

'Well, we were young men ourselves back then,' Mr Ensour begins, 'a little older than you, but not much. When Lord Tanvir's father called every man to arms, there was nothing we could do but answer; nothing else we wanted to do for that matter, either.

'In the eyes of the sultan we were outlaws, and they came at us with everything they had. The only battalion that won every battle was the one led by the Emir Hussein and Lord Tali'a. Mind you, they were still Lord Hussein and Captain Tali'a back then, but it hardly mattered. As a direct descendent of Muhammad, we venerated Emir Hussein, and wherever he and Lord Tali'a went, the Turks fled.

'I remember my first meeting with Lord Tali'a like it was yester-day. He came to visit the troops of Lord Tanvir and discuss some of Emir Hussein's plans with him. And guess what . . .'

'What?' Aadhil asks.

'That very day a complete brigade of Turks, thousands of men, arrived to fight us. Here we were, five hundred men from Lord Tanvir, many of them boys, about fifty English boys, and Captain Tali'a with his escort of a dozen heavily armed soldiers.

'Now, Lord Tanvir and the Tommy captain, they were truly shitting themselves. They were sitting together and arguing about how fast they should surrender to the sultan. Lord Tanvir wanted to walk straight out of the meeting with a white flag, while the Tommy captain was asking why they weren't outside already.

'Lord Tali'a listened to them for about three minutes and then—I swear on the Prophet, may God bless him and grant him peace, that what I tell you now is true—he casually stood up, and, without a word, he walked over to the old lord and the captain, grabbed them both by the hair, and smacked their heads together, leaving them bleeding on the floor.

'Any other man would have been arrested and stoned to death before they could have spoken the word "insubordination," but not Lord Tali'a. The English lieutenants squawked in astonishment, while Lord Tanvir's men, his sons included, just sat there and stared at him. Nobody helped the lord and the captain, and like nothing had happened, Lord Tali'a casually walked back to his chair and sat down again, waiting for the Tommy and Lord Tanvir to get up.

'Once they had, he looked around the table and said, "Death, gentlemen, will only bring you to your God. If you are desperate to meet Him, in His name surrender and I am sure the Turks will be very happy to oblige. And if they don't, Lord Hussein will once he has conquered this city back from the sultan.

' "Of course, he won't have to recover this city, because I am going to stay here and hold it. I will arm the vagrants; I will arm the old men; I will arm the poor Christians; and I will arm the Jews. You are all free men, and therefore you are free to go and surrender, but God willing, I will hold this city, even if I have to give a stick to all of your women so that they can fight the battle their husbands are too scared to fight.

' "So, to everyone who is not with me I say, 'stand up and go now,' because if anyone at this table utters the word 'surrender' again, I promise that in God's name I will tear out his eyes with my bare hands, and then I will put them up his asshole. Is that understood?"

'I don't know if anyone dared to look at Lord Tali'a at that moment, since I was very busy staring at the floor. I do know that no one dared to break the silence, and after what felt like an eternity went by, Lord Tali'a just said, "Excellent. Since nobody is protesting, I will take that as a unanimous vow to defend this city to the last man. Now, if God wants it, let us act like adult men and discuss how we are going to keep out the Turks."

'We held the town for five days, and then, thanks be to God, Emir Hussein came with his army and a battalion of Tommies. In the end it was the Turks who were hunted down to the last man.

'When the Emir later asked Lord Tali'a how the men from Taj al Wadi had handled the threat, do you think he told the big man that he literally had to knock some sense into the lord and the English captain?

'No. All Lord Tali'a replied was, "I believe they are disappointed that you came. Most of the men hoped that after their meeting with the Turks they would be in Paradise."

'I heard the English king even gave that Tommy captain a medal for his bravery. They say he is a general now, can you believe that? Ha!'

Khalid looks at his brother, and he knows Aadhil is thinking the same. At home, they sometimes hear their father and brothers speak about great deals they have made, but all these deals are forgotten within days. Twenty-five years later, these men still live in awe of the actions they have witnessed from the emir and Lord Tali'a.

CHAPTER FOUR

Oasis of Azul

Month of Pregnancy 1, 1362 A.H. (30 September 1943 A.D.)

Even before Khalid opens his eyes, he can feel the sun on his face. Why did no one wake him? It's not fair; now he has to go yet another day without food and water. He lifts himself up and sees that the fire is still burning. What's more, he is not the only one who has slept through breakfast this morning. His brother and four other men are lying asleep.

Mr Ensour is not asleep and winks at him when they make eye contact. Khalid snorts. He cannot believe that the man went off to eat without waking them. If the Banu Farud had attacked, would he have let them sleep as well?

He stands up and walks through the village towards the water. He is going to drink as much as he can before his morning prayer, and he is not even going to care if other people notice. If God does not like that, then God should have woken him.

It smells like food, and outside the houses he sees pans hanging about above small fires. Stupid people. Don't they realise they cannot eat any of that stuff for at least ten or eleven hours?

'Boy, you want a taste?' A woman looks at him while holding out a ladle.

He points to the sun and grunts, 'It's too late.'

The woman smiles and answers, 'It's not too late; it's the Feast of Breaking the Fast.'

His eyes open wide. The Feast of Breaking the Fast! He looks around again. Of course! That's why all of these people are preparing food during daylight. Normally he counts the days until the Month of Burning is over, but he has been so worried about the Banu Farud these last couple of days, he has not thought of that at all!

'Praise be unto God!' he calls before accepting the ladle from the woman.

He has no idea what she has given him, but it may just be the best thing he has ever tasted, and after two more ladles, he runs back to his fire and starts to shake his brother.

'Why didn't you wake me earlier?' Aadhil sneers the moment he opens his eyes.

'It's the Feast of Breaking the Fast! It's the Feast of Breaking the Fast!'

Aadhil lifts himself up and turns to Mr Ensour.

'Is this true?'

Mr Ensour smiles and nods, and Aadhil grabs Khalid's shoulders and shakes him back. 'It's the Feast of Breaking the Fast!'

They take food from everyone who wants to share with them, and only when they are sure they cannot eat any more do they sit down against one of the houses, and the moment Khalid closes his eyes, he is asleep. It feels like mere seconds later when Aadhil slaps him awake, yet in those seconds the sun has travelled a great distance.

'They're here! They're here!' his brother shouts.

Khalid jumps up and, together with his brother, runs to the edge of the village, where they see three members of the Banu

Farud approaching. Khalid recognises the tall man and the small man. A very old man is new to the delegation, and, after they have descended from their camels, he is the one who speaks.

'Friends, I am Lord Farud, and I wish we will have peace, in the name of God!' he calls.

Khalid looks at his brother, who whispers, 'This man does not look like a lord at all.'

'That is because he is not a lord,' Khalid whispers back. 'Or at least not a lord like Lord Maher.'

'If he is a lord like the old men in our village, then why does he call himself a lord?'

'He also is not a lord like the old men in our village,' Khalid answers. Back in Al Nawaara, all old men are addressed as 'lord,' even when they don't have armies or other real powers. 'He is a different kind of lord.'

'What different kind of lord is there?' his brother asks. Khalid wants to hear what the men are saying, but he cannot ignore his brother.

'The nomad tribes elect a man from their midst to rule themselves, and that man is called "lord." However, he is not a lord for life. If he favours his own family over his tribe, for example, the tribe will get rid of him.'

'And what do you have to do to be elected?'

'You have to be a brave warrior when you are young, and all through your life you have to behave honourably and hospitably.' For a second Khalid pauses and then adds, 'And you have to be born as a member of the tribe.'

'Oh.' The disappointment in his brother's voice is not lost on Khalid, who felt the same when his grandfather told him about the nomad tribes. Even though the lord of a nomad tribe is not as high a position as lord of a province, it would still have been very honourable and impressive to end up as one.

They turn their attention back to Lord Farud, who says, 'Perhaps there were men among the Banu Farud who have attacked a caravan, but these men are no longer amongst us.'

'You mean they fled?' Lord Maher replies.

'I mean that they had already left us before they attacked your caravan. I swear it by the Prophet, may God bless him and grant him peace. They have not returned to us, and we suspect they have travelled either to Mayasin or Syria.'

'That is not good for you. We have lost eight strong adult men, twenty-seven camels, and at least ten pounds of gold's worth in merchandise. If you want the water, then, in the name of God, that is what you will have to return to us.'

'Lord Maher,' the old nomad answers. He speaks softly, yet all men can hear him. 'We want to compensate you, we really do. We are ashamed that we quarrel with you on the Feast of Breaking the Fast, when we ought to be celebrating together. But what you are suggesting is impossible. In the name of God, maybe we can discuss this in private, lord to lord?'

Lord Farud says this like they are equals, which of course they are not—one only has to look at their outfits to understand their difference in standing—yet Lord Maher smiles gracefully, as though the old nomad is doing him an honour, and with even more grace he stretches out his arm and calls, 'Of course, Lord Farud. Come with me!'

'Thanks be to God,' Lord Farud replies, and he walks forward. The tall man and the short man want to follow, but Mr Raihan blocks them.

'Only the lord.'

'That is unacceptable!' the short man objects. 'I am the general of our tribe and this,' he puts his arm on the shoulder of the man next to him, 'is our judge.'

'Only the lord,' Mr Raihan repeats.

The short man wants to protest again, but an unobtrusive gesture from Lord Farud makes him hold his tongue. 'Friends, would you trust me with the honour of negotiating by myself?'

The moment the lords disappear into a house, Aadhil pokes Khalid and says with a wide grin, 'He is weak; it is written.'

'It is written,' Khalid confirms. If this lord has to ask his men permission to negotiate by himself, he must be weak indeed. He feels his confidence growing and wants to ask Mr Raihan what is going to happen now, but his brother asks him why Lord Farud isn't also the general, if he was once a great warrior.

'The nomad tribes divide the most important positions amongst two or three men so that no man can grow too powerful,' Khalid answers. He is not sure if he is right, but there is little chance his brother will ever find out if he's not; Aadhil prefers making things and fighting over studying.

He wants say more, but he sees Mr Raihan walk past. 'Mr Raihan, what happens now?'

The man pauses and smiles. He looks extremely tired, but thanks be to God, he seems to have forgotten his threat to bind the boys to a camel.

'Right now, Lord Farud is trying to bring down the amount of gold and the number of camels to a reasonable amount, and he will be offering girls and boys, perhaps even a couple of elder men and women, to compensate for the men.'

'Why would the commander accept that?' Aadhil asks.

'Lord Maher does not want war. You must realise that the nomad general was not wrong when he said that Lord Maher has no official power here. We are in Arabia, and these villagers only want peace, but if men from King Abdul-Aziz spot us here,' Mr Raihan shakes his head, 'we may have a problem. Therefore, it is in everybody's best interest to settle this business as quickly and peacefully as possible, and to expedite the process, Lord Farud will offer a little extra gold on the side for Lord Maher and his father; a personal appeaser.'

'But Lord Maher and his father have not lost any men, nor have they lost merchandise. Why should they be getting extra gold?' Aadhil is almost shouting again, and Mr Tanvir grabs him by the shoulders and pulls him away from the men.

'Careful!' he hisses. 'About half of the soldiers here are brought by Lord Maher. Without them, we'd already have been fighting, and there would not be any gold at all.'

'And what about the men from Taj al Wadi? Are they also to be compensated?' Khalid shares his brother's anger, yet he manages to speak calmly.

'They are, but you should not worry. With the compensation for the camels and the extra money for the missing men, God willing, you will be wealthy men. If it was indeed your father's caravan.'

Khalid shakes his head. Being wealthy is stupid. What he wants is a reckoning. But he can sense that Aadhil is almost exploding, and to distract him, he asks, 'Do you think we will ever find the real thugs?'

Mr Tanvir casually shrugs. 'Probably not. They might be anywhere now, but they might also be among the Banu Farud, too important for the rest to give up; only God knows. It doesn't matter, though. Someday the Lord will punish them, and we will punish their families.'

CHAPTER FIVE

The Desert

Month of Pregnancy 3-14, 1362 A.H. (2-13 October 1943 A.D.)

When they left Al Nawaara, it had appeared to be a great adventure. Now, as they make their way home, Khalid walking hand in hand with his brother, he wishes he had stayed in Mr Nouri's classroom.

After Lord Maher and Lord Farud came to an agreement, they had stayed one more night in the village—a sleepless night, yet according to Mr Ensour the real danger is still to come. The Banu Farud can send their soldiers after them, while keeping their women and children safely away. And Khalid can't stop looking over his shoulder, even though all he can see behind him are the heavily armed men from Lord Tanvir. The Oasis of Azul is already out of sight. On all sides they are surrounded by endless stretches of sand.

'Do you think we are already back in Beledar?' he asks Aadhil. For some reason, Khalid feels like they will be safer once they are back in their own country.

'It doesn't matter. There was no one guarding the border on the way to the oasis, and there won't be anyone guarding it on our way home. If the nomads return for the prisoners, no one will stop them.'

The prisoners.

They are not too far from them, five boys, two old men, and seven girls. Together with fourteen camels and an unclear amount of gold, they are the reward for making this godforsaken journey through the desert.

In front of them, one of the men from Taj al Wadi smacks a camel on its ass, and the beast starts to run. The boy who is bound to it falls to the ground, and the camel drags him fifty yards through the sand before it stops. The first time it happened it was funny, and still a little bit funny the second time. But this being the fifth time in fewer hours, Khalid can't even muster a smile.

When they pass the boy, he is still on the ground, and Aadhil stops to help him up.

'Are you all right?'

'I am, thanks be unto God,' the boy answers.

'God is praised,' Aadhil says before continuing. 'I am Aadhil, and this is my brother Khalid.'

'I am Omar,' the boy answers, 'and my brothers are still at the camp, except for one. I don't know where he is.'

'Is that why you are here?' Aadhil asks.

Khalid looks first at his brother and then at the boy. It does not feel good to be fraternising with the enemy. After all, that is what the boy is: their enemy. Omar doesn't really look like their enemy, though; he looks more like the boys from their class.

'My brother has done something bad; something that could start a war. That is why my family has sent me away, to prevent it.'

'Are you not angered by that?'

The boy shakes his head and sounds genuine when he says, 'I get to prevent a war and rescue my tribe. I am proud that my parents have chosen me.'

Aadhil shakes his head and replies, 'You are as dumb as a statue,' but it is meant in good humour, and all three boys laugh before they continue their journey together.

'Where are we going?' Omar asks.

'Al Nawaara,' Aadhil answers. 'Or maybe Taj al Wadi. I am not sure where you . . . I mean the prisoners will be going.'

'Is it nice there?'

'That depends. If you have a mother who is not crazy like our mother, it is nice. And if you don't have to go to school, it is even nicer. Or if you are like my brother,' Aadhil pokes Khalid, 'and you like school, it is nice too.'

'My mother is crazy,' Omar says, 'but I don't know what school is.'

'School is where you sit in a small room with many children and a man tells you all kind of things about the Prophet—may God bless him and grant him peace—history, and numbers.'

'That does not sound too bad.'

'I know, but the man also asks you questions, and when you get the answers wrong, he will hit you with a stick.'

Omar shrugs. 'My mother hits me with a stick all the time. My father does it too.'

'So how did you like living in the tribe?' asks Khalid, whose curiosity finally triumphs over his suspicion.

'I suppose it was all right, but I never liked that we moved around so much. When we went to get water, I'd sometimes meet other boys who stayed in the same place their entire lives. I think I would like that as well when I'm older. Do you think I am going to stay in Al Nawaara for a long time?'

Khalid and Aadhil have no idea what is going to happen to the prisoners, yet Aadhil answers, 'Sure you can; you can stay with us!'

*　　*　　*

His feet are covered in blisters, his knees feel as though there are nails inside them, and his head has become too heavy for his neck. Although the autumn sun hasn't allowed even a tuft of white to settle in the sky, over the last week, thunderclouds have been gathering over Khalid's head. As soon as his head touches the ground, a deep, tiresome sleep falls upon him in which he keeps on walking and walking, haunted by ghosts and nomads. He cannot understand their words, but if they are not there to predict his father's demise, why can't he shake them?

Khalid doesn't know how much farther it is. Both of the old men had died on the second day—they had paused to bury them—and after that he lost count of the days. If only he was as strong as his brother and Omar; they are still walking and talking like they can go on for days, and they don't have problems with ghosts at night.

Lord Maher and his men split from the caravan. They take one third of the gold with them—apart from the gold Lord Maher has received on the side—five of the camels, the two prettiest girls, and two of the boys.

'What is going to happen to them?' Aadhil asks Mr Ensour.

'One of the girls will be added to Lord Maher's harem, the other one to his father's. The boys will serve as slaves.'

Slaves. Khalid knows that there are still slaves in Taj al Wadi, and he has no doubt that slavery will be the fate of the boys that are sent there, but he had not expected Lord Tanvir to use men as slaves as well. According his teacher—or is Mr Nouri his former teacher now?—there is nothing as barbaric and ungodly as slavery, and he is glad that Omar has so far been spared this destiny.

He wonders what would have happened to the old men if they'd made it this far. What use would they have served as slaves?

What about his father? Have the bandits buried him too? Or is he still alive? Are his brothers, Nourad and Saifan, still alive?

It is hard to believe that the brother of Omar might be responsible for his own brothers' death. Omar believes in the same God, he does not want to follow in his father's footsteps when he grows older, he likes a good fight with boys his age, and he laughs at Aadhil's jokes. He is not Khalid's enemy, no more than the girls that they have taken, or the other boys, or the old men.

The caravan stops. He looks at Aadhil and asks, 'What's going on?'

Aadhil shrugs, but behind him he hears Mr Ensour. 'We are approaching the edge of the desert. Look, in the distance you can see the beginning of the green lands.'

Khalid squints and sees Mr Ensour is right: in the distance he can see spots of green. Finally, it will not be much longer.

'But why stop?'

'This is where the men from Taj al Wadi leave us. They travel to the east; we continue to the north.'

But it is not as simple as that, and suddenly people are shouting at the front of the caravan. Khalid, Aadhil, Omar, and Mr Ensour stride forward to find the men from Al Nawaara and the men from Taj al Wadi dividing themselves into two groups. In between them is Mr Raihan and a man Khalid recognises as the leader of the men from Taj al Wadi.

'In the name of God, this is unacceptable!' the man shouts.

'This is fair; it is written,' Mr Raihan answers.

'You . . . your five fathers should have mounted a sheep on the night they mounted your mother!'

Before Khalid realises that the man from Taj al Wadi has just called Mr Raihan's mother a whore, he's pushed to the ground by Mr Ensour. All around him, the men from Al Nawaara ready their rifles and point them at the men from Taj al Wadi.

Mr Raihan turns to his men, raises his hands, and says loudly, 'Do not mind him. He cannot help that his mother is a Jew who gave birth to a pig!'

This insult brings out the rifles on the other side. Khalid glances at his brother, who is also on the ground. He can read in Aadhil's eyes that his brother agrees this is crazy.

'Do you want war?' the man from Taj al Wadi calls. 'We will give you war!'

Khalid looks back at the men in the middle. If any rifle goes off now, they will definitely die.

'I am not afraid to return to God,' Mr Raihan says, 'but we have many young men who deserve more time in this world.'

'Not all of my men are ready for paradise either,' the man from Taj al Wadi replies, calmer now, 'but what you are offering is not fair, and rest assured that I am not afraid.'

'Then we will let you have three camels, two boys, and two girls. No gold!' Mr Raihan calls.

'Still unacceptable! Half the gold, five camels, two boys, and three girls!' the man counters.

Aside from the wind, there is not a single sound around them. Mr Raihan takes a step toward the other man, and even though he almost whispers, Khalid has no problem hearing him. 'The camels are transportable gold; you can have them all. We keep the real gold.'

'Then we'll take all the girls,' the man replies, only a little louder, but his voice rises as he continues. 'There is a house in Taj al Wadi where they can serve our whole community; you don't have such a house in Al Nawaara. If any of your men comes to Taj al Wadi, I swear by the Quran that they will serve him too, free of charge!'

This remark ignites a spark of laughter on both sides, but when Khalid looks back at the girls who are standing six feet behind him, he can see the fear in their eyes.

'In the name of God, you are a tough man to negotiate with, but you have a deal!' Mr Raihan calls to the clear relief of all the men, and he shakes the man's hand. Khalid gets up again, and, as if nothing has happened, the men from Taj al Wadi and the men from Al Nawaara suddenly appear to be best friends, hugging and cheerfully saying goodbye.

But then one of the men from Taj al Wadi is standing with them and pointing at Omar. 'We'll take him.'

Khalid shakes his head, and next to him his brother steps in front of their new friend.

'No. In the name of God, you will not take him!'

A nasty grin forms on the man's face, and Mr Ensour intervenes and says, 'Boys, let the man take him.'

'No!' Aadhil shouts angrily, articulating Khalid's feeling too. If Omar goes to Taj al Wadi, they will turn him into a slave, and he'd rather have a war than let this boy from the Banu Farud become a slave.

'If the boys want to keep their little nomad pig, let them,' the man says. 'We'll simply take the other two boys.'

Khalid sighs. Clearly, the men from Taj al Wadi are not going to fight a war over Omar. And yet the worried look in Mr Ensour's face tells him that all is not okay.

Chapter Six

Al Nawaara

Month of Pregnancy 15, 1362 A.H. (14 October 1943 A.D.)

As the caravan approaches Al Nawaara, Khalid can no longer feel the blisters on his feet or the pain in his knees and back. His heart is pounding, and every other minute he casts a nervous glance at his brother. Sometimes he hears Aadhil mumble what he has prayed for, countless times: 'God, please let them be there.'

Suddenly he can see miniature figures approaching them, and his heart skips a beat. Will his father be amongst them? His brothers? Their progress is painfully slow, and the figures are still at least half an hour away. He looks at his brother, who nods and says confidently, 'They are with them. It was not their caravan that was attacked.'

'How can you be sure?'

'I feel it. It is just . . .' Aadhil hesitates, and when he continues, his voice breaks. 'If God wants it . . . They just can't be . . . You know?'

Khalid does not respond. He knows. If he closes his eyes, he can see his family. His father isn't like his little brother, who died a year ago. Hussein had been small and weak, while his father is, well, perhaps not big and strong, but definitely tough. After all, the old man has survived his mother all these years.

And his big brothers, Nourad and Saifan, they really are big and strong. Surely a band of bandits could not have gotten to them, no matter how ferocious.

The puppets are growing into people, and if his legs would hold him, he would start running. However, even though he presently cannot feel the pain, he knows there is no strength left. This morning, he had so much difficulty getting up that when the caravan paused about two hours ago, he didn't dare to sit down. Now, afraid that his legs will give way and the men will laugh at him, he doesn't dare to run.

It won't be much longer now, though, and in a way he is also pleased that he cannot run. If there is bad news, at least he can continue to hope for a little while longer.

At the front of the caravan he already sees the first villagers; gradually, he can make out their faces. A small person is running past the caravan. It is a girl. In fact, it is his sister Shiya. She has seen them too, and the moment she is in front of them, she jumps at him, almost throwing him to the ground.

Why does she do that? Doesn't she realise that he has just walked across the entire country? If he had the energy, Khalid would scream at her and beat her, but all he can do is hold on to his sister. He can feel Shiya breathing heavily, and the moment she lets him go to move on to his brother, his annoyance disappears and he wishes that she was still in his arms.

Only after she has let his brother go too does she start to talk. 'You made it back! I was so worried! Father was so angry with Mother that she let you go on the expedition, but then Mother said she did not raise cowards, and then they did not speak for days. And . . .'

'Shiya,' Aadhil interrupts his little sister. Despite his brother's fatigue, there is still an air of authority in his voice. 'Father is still alive?'

Shiya nods and jumps up and down. 'Father is alive, and Mr al-Tahtawi is dead and his sons and everyone who was with them is dead. And Mrs al-Tahtawi and her daughters will not stop crying and Mother said I had to bring them food. And . . .'

'And Nourad and Saifan are still alive?' Aadhil interrupts her again.

Shiya smiles. 'Nourad said that you were so stupid to believe that anything could happen to them. That you should have trusted that God would protect them. And . . .'

'And that you should have left the fighting to the grownups!' This time it is a deep, manly voice that interrupts Khalid's sister. He looks up.

'Nourad!'

He takes three large steps toward his older brother and hugs him. Nourad receives him warmheartedly and kisses him on both cheeks.

'We heard you have brought us the brother of one of the thugs,' another voice says.

Saifan!

'If God wants it, we will prepare a little something for him.'

'Yes, this is . . .' Khalid answers as he turns to Omar so that he can introduce him to their brothers, but the nomad boy has disappeared. 'Where did he go?'

Aadhil shrugs. 'I don't know. I swear by the Prophet that he was here just a minute ago!'

'Don't worry about him,' Nourad says. 'I am sure he is somewhere safe.'

Khalid nods, and then he sees his father approaching. Mr Khan calls Khalid and Aadhil heroes, and Khalid swells with pride, forgetting all about Omar.

'Where did Nourad and Saifan go?' Aadhil asks as they make their way to the house with their father and Shiya.

Now it is Khalid's turn to shrug. His thoughts have changed to his mother, and he has just realised that he can't wait to see her. A hug that crushes his bones and lasts a little too long makes him forget that eagerness the moment they arrive at home.

He would like nothing better than to lie down and sleep, but apparently something big is about to happen.

'Go and watch,' his mother says with a meaningful glance at his father. At least they have made up again, or Shiya had simply embellished the whole fight.

'Can I go too?' Shiya asks.

'What? You think I am going to prepare all the food by myself? Let the men watch; we can do the work.'

'Watch what?' Khalid asks.

'You will see,' his father answers, and he leads the way to the river, where a rapidly growing crowd is standing around a small wooden shed, no more than three feet wide on all sides and three feet high, that had not been there when Khalid and Aadhil left.

'Why are all these people here?' Khalid asks his father.

'They are here to watch the prisoner receive his punishment,' Mr Khan answers.

'But Omar did not do anything!' Aadhil says.

'Really? Omar?' His father grabs Aadhil by the shoulder. 'You are calling the prisoner by name?'

Aadhil wrenches himself free, and his face turns dark. 'Why? What is wrong with that?'

'What's wrong is that the nomads could just as easily have taken us,' his father answers. 'Perhaps Omar did not do anything, but his brother killed eight men. Mrs al-Tahtawi has lost her husband and all of her sons, and now one of the thugs is going to lose his brother; that is fair!'

'It's not fair! It's . . .' But before Aadhil can say another word, his father's fist has found his face, and he falls to the ground. 'That's enough! You do not speak that way to your father.'

A man turns around and reaches out a hand to Aadhil. It's Mr Ensour. After helping his brother up, Mr Ensour turns to his father and says, 'Your son has just returned from a long journey. I am sure it was tiredness that made him speak this way, rather than disrespect.'

Mr Khan snorts while he grabs Aadhil's shoulder and pulls him away from Mr Ensour. 'This is a family business, and my son has to learn that his place is to listen.'

Mr Ensour nods, and Khalid looks at his brother. Already, he can see the area around Aadhil's left eye swelling, and his brother's eyes are flaming with even more rage. If only he was as courageous as Aadhil; he would never dare to argue with their father in that way. For a couple of minutes, they stand together silently. To break the silence, he asks, 'Where are Nourad and Saifan?'

His father looks around, and suddenly they hear screams in the distance. Mr Khan's eyes light up. He points to where the screaming is coming from and grimly replies, 'There.'

Khalid follows his father's finger, and indeed, he can see his older brothers approaching, and with a rope they are dragging a small, naked boy behind them. Omar!

His hands and feet are tied together; there's blood all over his face, and once he's closer, Khalid sees bloody streaks on his back. The hot sand makes the wounds even worse, and there is terror in Omar's eyes. Aadhil has seen it too, and he tries to run toward Nourad and Saifan, but his father grabs him by the hair and gives him another smack in the face.

When Saifan and Nourad reach the middle of the square, they let go of their rope. Nourad turns to Omar, who is still screaming, and hisses, 'One more sound and I will cut out your tongue. I swear it by the Quran!'

'Men from Al Nawaara.' The Sunni scholar they had met at the village meeting before their expedition steps forward. He casts a quick glance at Mrs al-Tahtawi, the only woman present, but he does not acknowledge her.

'You all know by now that our expedition has been a success. We have confronted the Banu Farud, and while the bandits have fled, they have compensated us for our losses; Mr al-Tahtawi's family will not spend the rest of their days in poverty, thanks to the brave actions of many of the men here.'

These remarks are greeted by loud cheers, and for a brief moment, even Khalid forgets that Omar is lying in the middle of the square and joins in. Aadhil does not, and an angry look from his brother silences Khalid. When the cheers die out, the scholar continues.

'While the thugs may have fled, this does not mean that they will escape punishment. They will be punished at Lord Tanvir's palace! They will be punished in Taj al Wadi! And they will be punished here! This boy . . .' the scholar gestures to Omar, who is still crying, 'will be punished for the sins of his brother, and all the world will know what we have done to him, so that his brother cannot fail to hear of it!'

More cheers from the crowd, and Khalid can see a satisfied smile on the scholar's face; it is almost like the man crossed the desert himself.

'What are you going to do with him?' someone in the crowd calls.

'We are going to do a little something Mr al-Tahtawi picked up during his journeys through Persia. We are going to scaph him,' Nourad answers.

Khalid looks at his brother and whispers, 'What is scaphing?' but his brother is still too angry to hear him.

'Wait!' Mr Ensour steps forward, and all the men look at him. 'This boy, he does not deserve this fate. Yes, his brother is a criminal, and yes, he needs to be punished, but this boy does not deserve to be scaphed for the crimes committed by another man! He is still a boy.'

'Mr Ensour, you make an honourable suggestion, but this boy's brother will not hear of it if we hang him, nor will the men who think to copy the men from the Banu Farud.' It is old Lord Raihan who has stepped forward and is looking around the crowd as he leans heavily on his stick. 'Men of Al Nawaara, last year the young emir took his father's seat in the great palace in Mayasin, and we have seen the result. We knew that Emir Hussein protected us, but so far Emir Jalal has not shown his hand here, and we do not know if he ever will. We have to protect ourselves, and if we do not set an example, next year every nomad tribe will come here to take what is ours!'

Mr Ensour takes another step toward the middle, and now it's his turn to look around at the crowd.

'Men of Al Nawaara, it is true that the new emir has not yet shown his hand, but we must give him time. If we scaph this boy, not only his brother will hear of it, the emir will hear of it too, and why would he protect villages that scaph innocent boys?'

'Innocent? This boy is as guilty as his tribe! It is written!' Nourad interrupts before a gesture from old Lord Raihan shuts him up.

'Mr Ensour, the new emir is not from here. His wife is not from here. Even if his intentions are good, he cannot protect us if we do not protect ourselves. And if we don't show the nomads, or anyone else who attacks us, for that matter, what the consequences are, next year men will come here to take our camels, our lands, and our daughters; it is written!'

Again the crowd cheers, and as Mr Ensour raises his arms to ask for silence, they start to boo him. Minutes seem to go by before it is quiet enough for Mr Ensour to give it his final try.

'Lord Raihan, God has given you long life to preserve your wisdom for us; it is written. But while your words may be true, this . . .' he gestures to Omar again, 'this is just a boy. Let us put the decision to Mrs al-Tahtawi. She has lost her family; if she has had enough bloodshed, we should honour her wish.'

This remark causes outrage, and Khalid can hear the scholar calling that it is not right, since Mrs al-Tahtawi is a woman, but when Lord Raihan raises his free arm, the crowd instantly turns quiet.

'Mrs al-Tahtawi,' the old man says, 'Mr Ensour is right. You have lost your family. You should decide the fate of this boy.'

Next to him, Khalid can hear his brother breathing. He closes his eyes and prays silently: *Please God, let Mrs al-Tahtawi spare Omar. He has done nothing, and he honours You like I do. Greatest God, most Merciful God, show Your mercy, and I will be your servant forever.*

Minutes appear to go by, and when he hears nothing, he opens his eyes again and gazes at Mrs al-Tahtawi. He can see the hate in her eyes, but there is also something else. Is it doubt? If it is, then there is hope. He turns his eyes to Omar, who has managed to position himself on his knees toward his judge, and Khalid hears his nomad friend pledge. 'Please. In the name of God.'

But Mrs al-Tahtawi's does not look at the boy. Her eyes move from Lord Raihan to Nourad and Saifan, and she says, 'Scaph him.'

Mr Ensour bows his head, but the crowd starts to cheer even louder than before. This is what they have come for. The words also set Saifan and Nourad into action. Together, they pick up Omar and throw him into the shed.

'Two men hold his head!' Nourad calls, and half a dozen men step forward from the crowd. The men who arrive at the shed first take the boy's head and pull it up and back. Next, Nourad takes a funnel and gives it to Saifan, who shoves it down Omar's throat and closes his nose.

'What is that?' asks Khalid, who now sees Nourad holding a container with white fluid.

'Goat milk,' his father answers, 'with honey.'

'And what are they going to do with it?' he asks, but before his father can answer, Nourad starts to pour the fluid into the funnel. When he has emptied almost a third of the container, Omar starts shaking violently, and Nourad shouts, 'In the name of God, hold his head!'

The men tighten their grip, and Nourad continues to pour; the container is almost two-thirds empty when he withdraws it and calls, 'This is it.'

'One!' Nourad and Saifan call.

'Two!' half the crowd calls.

'Three!' Khalid can even hear his father shout.

All three men let go at once and step back as quickly as they can. Omar's head jerks forward violently, and to the amusement of the crowd, he pukes all over himself. Khalid can see his father laughing, but on his own face he feels tears. Swiftly, he wipes them off.

Nourad pushes the boy's head a couple of times, and when he is convinced the boy is truly done puking, he steps into the shed with a large jar of honey in his hand. With a cloth he takes honey from the jar and smears it around the Omar's eyes and nose. He dabs the cloth back in the jar and smears some more in the boy's ears. Finally, he drizzles honey over Omar's penis and ass, turning him slightly with his foot to spread it as much as he can without touching the boy. When he has stepped out of the shed, Nourad takes the container of milk and throws what is left over the boy's head and body.

'Bastards!' Khalid hears Aadhil shouting before his brother once again wrenches himself free from their father and runs away.

Since the excitement is too great for other men to notice, his father lets him go.

When Nourad is finished, Lord Raihan steps forward again.

'Men of Al Nawaara, let it be known that we have decided on the fate of this boy together, and any man who attacks someone from our lands will receive the same fate. However,' Lord Raihan casts a glance at Mr Ensour, 'should any man from our village decide to free, spare, or rescue this boy, he will take his place. I swear that by the Quran, and my sons swear it too.'

On the way back to the house, Nourad and Saifan joke and laugh, but Khalid cannot talk. In honour of him and Aadhil, his mother has prepared the largest goat stew that he has ever seen, yet Aadhil is not there, and he cannot taste the food.

When he retreats to his thin mattress in the room he shares with his brothers, right after dinner, Aadhil still has not returned. Khalid is worried, and he wants to come up with a plan to save Omar, but the moment he closes his eyes, he falls asleep.

Al Nawaara

Month of Pregnancy 16-20, 1362 A.H. (15-19 October 1943 A.D.)

The next morning, Khalid's mother sends him back to school. Not Aadhil, who has returned while Khalid was sleeping. According to his father, Aadhil has forfeited his rights to school.

Khalid has crossed the desert to face the Banu Farud, yet as he makes his way to the little white building, he feels his heart pounding in his chest. How is Mr Nouri going to react? And his fellow students?

He walks through the door, but the teacher does not acknowledge him. As the hours go by, he has to struggle to keep his eyes open, and just as he fears that he's going to lose that battle, Mr Nouri singles him out.

'Mr Khan, a long time ago the Prophet told his followers upon returning from a military campaign, "Today we have returned from the minor jihad to the major jihad." What did he mean by that?'

He takes a deep breath. In a way the question is appropriate; after all, he has just returned from a sort of jihad. He answers, 'He meant that when external enemies are defeated, we return to the struggle that's within ourselves. Our fight to live as good Muslims.'

'And why is this the *major* jihad?'

'Life brings many temptations, and only a man who truly submits to God can withstand them; resisting those temptations is a greater challenge than resisting an army of infidels.'

He remembers the words almost exactly as the teacher had spoken them, long before he and Aadhil went on the expedition, before Omar was thrown into that shed.

Omar.

'And your little expedition against the Banu Farud, would you call that a righteous jihad?'

Khalid looks around. All the eyes of his classmates are upon him. On the way, no one had even used the word *jihad*; is Mr Nouri trying to trick him?

'Well, Mr Khan?'

He has just called it some sort of jihad in his head, but he knows that it actually wasn't. Jihad is fought against infidels, and Omar is not an infidel. He looks around. Even if his fellow students have forgotten the business with Mohid before he ran off, they will certainly be reminded of it when he gives his answer.

'*Never show weakness, and when they attack you, fight until you cannot fight anymore,*' Aadhil had said the morning before he left home. '*Even better if you are the one to throw the first punch; aim for their noses.*'

Easy for his brother to say, but Khalid is not like his brother, and he can see himself lying in a ditch next to the school, bleeding and unable to get up. On the other hand, at this moment Omar is lying in an open shed, bleeding and without any protection from the sun.

'Sir, our expedition had nothing to do with jihad. Our expedition was about protecting the village from future attacks, while jihad is about protecting the faith.'

'Those are very wise words, Mr Khan. Remember them well.'

If his classmates want him, they can come and get him. His mind drifts back to Omar. There must be something he can do. Lord Raihan said men who helped the boy would be punished, but what if he could do it in secret, late at night?

Since it's Gathering Day, the teacher sends the children away early, and slowly, his mind still on Omar, Khalid packs his stuff and walks out of the door. Outside, his fellow students are waiting for him. He takes a deep breath; there are far too many of them to throw the first punch.

'Khalid.' Mohid steps forward. 'What was it like? Did you fight?'

'It was hot,' he says. The boys laugh. 'And there was much walking.'

'We heard you saw Lord Maher,' another boy says. 'Is he as great a warrior as the people say he is?'

He can hardly believe it. He has not done anything, his friend has been sentenced to death, yet all these boys look at him as though he is a hero. It's not fair. It may be better than having to fight them, but it is not fair.

'Tonight, we are going to save Omar,' Aadhil whispers to Khalid after they leave the mosque.

He looks at his brother and whispers back, 'How?'

'I don't know yet, but we will think of something.'

But it is not that easy.

'Where do you think you're going?' their mother asks when they casually try to walk away from home after dinner.

'Friends,' Khalid answers. 'They all want to hear stories about the expedition.'

'You will do no such thing.' Mrs Khan sneers. 'You can tell your stories tomorrow. Tonight, you will go to bed. You look like a couple of ghosts, both of you!'

Khalid can hear his brothers and father laughing at them, and he looks at Aadhil. There is no way they can get away now. They go back inside, and when they are lying next to each other, Aadhil whispers, 'Just pretend to sleep. After Nourad and Saifan go to bed, we will sneak out.'

Khalid nods and closes his eyes, pretending to sleep. When he opens them again, it is light.

Since it is the Sixth Day, Khalid does not have to go to school. Nevertheless, trying to free Omar during the day turns out to be impossible. In fact, Khalid's mother doesn't give them any time to think about their friend, using him and Aadhil as slaves. Khalid is almost pleased when Nourad comes to rescue them from their chores.

'Come on, little brothers, I have a job for you.' Nourad is carrying a half-full container in one hand and a funnel in the other. 'Come on; it will be fun!'

He hands the container to Aadhil and the funnel to Khalid, who looks to his side. His brother's face has turned dark, but Aadhil doesn't protest.

Nourad starts to walk in the direction the river, and through his teeth Aadhil hisses to Khalid, 'Do everything he says and don't let him notice that we want to rescue Omar.'

Khalid nods, but he isn't sure if Aadhil is telling this to him or to himself. So far, Nourad doesn't seem to notice anything; he appears to be perfectly pleased with himself and with them.

'I don't think that our prisoner will look too bad today, but I swear to you, two days from now you will no longer recognise him!'

'Why?' Khalid asks casually. 'What is he going to look like?'

'Don't let me spoil it; come and see two days from now!'

Khalid sees people walking by the shed when they arrive, casting sideways glances—there are many more people at this point of the river than usual—yet no one dares to actually stand next to the shed and stare at the boy.

'Khalid, fill that container with water,' Nourad commands as he points to an empty container next to the shed.

He puts down the funnel and moves toward the container, and only when he picks it up does he notice the smell that is coming from the shed. He does not know what it is, but he has never smelled anything this cruel before.

When he returns with a full container, he glances inside the shed and sees his friend, naked, red, bugs crawling over him, and clearly the cause of the smell. The smell!

He feels his breakfast coming upwards through his stomach, and while he tries to fight it, he cannot, and he vomits over his own feet.

'In the shed, boy!' Nourad calls. 'No problem if you puke, but in the name of God, will you direct it at our prisoner!'

Khalid comes up, and the smell returns to attack him, but he does not want to vomit over his friend, and he is sure that Nourad will grow suspicious if he pukes next to the shed again. It costs him all his power to fight his stomach. Thanks to God, he succeeds.

'If you are not going to vomit over him, hold his head,' Nourad commands, slightly annoyed.

Khalid takes a step forward, and now he gets a really good look at Omar. The bugs are everywhere. One of his eyes is half open but appears to be empty, while the other is swollen so badly that it appears a large red fig is growing on top of it. He is no longer crying.

'The boy is unclean,' he says.

'Of course the boy is unclean! That is why you and Aadhil are going to hold his head and not me.' And then, in a softer tone, 'Grab him by his hair; it will be the least dirty part of him.'

The people who have come to the river to see the prisoner are now staring at them, and Khalid looks at Aadhil. His brother nods; they have no choice.

'It's going to be okay,' Aadhil whispers unobtrusively to Omar when they grab his hair.

'Aadhil?' the prisoner mumbles. The brothers look at each other and glance at Nourad, but he is busy talking with one of the villagers. 'Please. Let me out. God will reward you.'

Khalid looks at Aadhil again. What can they say? If Omar knows that they are here and repeats their names in front of Nourad, their older brother will know who has freed him, if they succeed. Aadhil shakes his head; clearly, he is thinking the same.

But Omar now knows that there are people standing next to him, and he does not give up. 'I will tell you where my brother went, if God wants it. Please, in the name of God, I will tell you everything. I know it.'

'And I know that you are going to be a dead boy, but not too soon!' Nourad's booming voice silences the boy. 'Hold his head!'

Khalid and Aadhil both grab a piece of Omar's hair. He is not protesting, and Nourad hands Aadhil the funnel.

'Put it in his mouth.'

For Khalid he conjures up a cloth.

'Use this to close his nose.'

Nourad takes the container Khalid has filled in the river and starts pouring water into the funnel. When the boy has been force-fed about a quarter of the container, he stops. Omar coughs heavily, but Nourad ignores him and says, 'If we do this twice a day, he will live at least for another week; maybe even two!'

'We can let go?' Aadhil asks, ignoring their eldest brother's happy torture tale.

'Of course!'

Khalid instantly pulls back his hands. The boy is so dirty. On the way back, Omar was their friend, but now that he looks like this, he isn't sure anymore.

'Just one more thing.' Nourad approaches the shed with the container that Aadhil carried from home and pours it over the boy; more goat milk with honey.

'Trust me, boys, two days from now, you will witness something you have never seen before!'

That evening, Khalid tries as hard as he can to stay awake, but neither Nourad or Saifan is making any haste going to bed. He can hear his brothers talking in front of the house, and when he hears Aadhil's snores, he decides to give up the fight as well.

The next night isn't any more successful, but the third night he feels someone pushing against his shoulder. He opens his eyes and sees Aadhil's face in front of him, his brother's finger against his lips.

He nods, indicating that he understands this is the moment, and, as quietly as he can, he gets up and follows his brother outside. It is cold there, much colder than he had expected, but his brother has prepared two blankets for them, and he wraps one around himself.

Aadhil starts to walk, and when they are a safe distance from the house, he says, 'Don't be scared, little brother. No one is going to know that it was us.'

Khalid doubts it, but he knows they have an obligation to Omar. The sky is filled with stars, so there is no need bring a lantern; God is on their side. Even if the villagers decide to punish them for rescuing Omar, He will reward them. They are almost at the river, and he can already smell their friend, but Aadhil does not slow down.

His legs are heavy; he remembers how Nourad promised that they were going to witness something they had never seen before, yet he does not want to witness it. He wants to go back to the house, back to sleep, and forget about Omar.

'Come on,' his brother hisses when he sees him hesitate.

He takes the final steps to reach the shed and then, in the light of the stars, he sees Omar.

The sight of his friend turns his bowels inside out, and everything comes out. For about half a minute, he believes that he's going to choke, but then it stops, and Khalid closes his eyes to regain his composure.

He opens them to find that the light has not deceived him.

Omar's legs are covered in puke —Khalid's puke—but the rest of the boy's body is covered in bugs. Never before has Khalid seen so many of them. They are even nesting inside him; coming out of his butthole, his ears, and his eyes. Khalid hears sounds, but the boy is not crying; ants have eaten away his tear ducts.

'In the name of God, kill me,' the boy mutters. Even in the light of the stars, Khalid can see bugs coming out of his mouth with every word.

'We are here to rescue you!' Aadhil hisses back. He looks at Khalid and repeats, 'We came to rescue you.'

Slowly, the boy shakes his head and grunts, 'Kill me. Please. Kill me.'

'No!' Aadhil hisses again, but Khalid can see in his brother's eyes that Aadhil has lost faith. He wonders whether they are allowed to kill Omar.

God forbids all Muslims from killing other Muslims, and Omar is a Muslim, just like them. On the other hand, they would not really be killing the boy; Lord Raihan, Mrs al-Tahtawi, Nourad and Saifan have done that. Mr Ensour has tried to rescue him; Aadhil has protested. What has Khalid done?

Nothing.

He looks back at his brother and whispers, 'I think we must. He cannot walk, and we definitely cannot carry him!'

'You kill him,' Aadhil hisses.

It is the only option, and to show his brother that he is not scared, he does not hesitate when he asks, 'Do you have a dagger?'

Aadhil shakes his head. He glances at Omar and wonders how he can kill his nomad friend without climbing in the shed and without a dagger. There is no way.

'Please, send me to Paradise.'

How weak his voice is.

'Let's draw straws,' he says to his brother, but Aadhil shakes his head.

'You want to kill him, you kill him.'

Khalid looks back at the bugs. He hates bugs. The ants will bite him for sure. The rest . . . if he goes in there, he will feel like he is going to be covered in bugs for weeks to come. They will be with him whenever his tunic itches and whenever he closes his eyes. But then again, if he does not kill Omar now, the bugs might follow his friend to Paradise.

He looks around. Everything is quiet; the whole village is fast asleep. Perhaps it is actually good that he does not have a dagger. If he uses his hands to kill Omar, no one will know that the boy was murdered. Nourad had said that he might live for two more weeks, yet it is not unrealistic to presume that the bugs have killed him.

He takes off his tunic and carefully, so that he does not make any sound, he climbs into the shed. His feet are covered in bugs even before they have touched the ground. He wants to take a deep breath but reconsiders due to the smell, and instead he says a silent prayer. He bows over the boy and whispers, 'Omar, do you have any last words?'

Almost unnoticeably, Omar nods and then he grunts, 'Thank you.'

And again, a little louder this time, 'Thank you.'

God, Merciful God, forgive me, Khalid prays silently before he closes the Omar's nose with his left hand and Omar's mouth with his right.

The world around him fades away; even the bugs disappear. He is completely connected with his nomad boy until he feels his brother's hand on his shoulder, and he hears Aadhil whispering firmly, 'Khalid, it is done. We have to go. Khalid, we have to go. Khalid. Khalid. Khalid. Khalid. Khalid. Khalid.'

He lets Omar go and observes himself from outside his body. His brother helps him climb out of the shed and guides him to the river. He pushes him in, and the cold water transports him back to his body. He lets Aadhil clothe him and stands dead still while his brother wraps both blankets around him.

Aadhil holds his hand as they silently run back to their house, and when they are back on their thin mattresses, lying side by side, he is still holding Khalid's hand.

Khalid wishes that it was a dream and that they had never left the house; he wishes that he could turn back time, but he knows what he has done, and tears start to roll down his face.

'Sssht,' Aadhil whispers.

One day, God will judge him.

'Sssht,' Aadhil whispers again. He knows that his brother is right; he must not wake up Nourad and Saifan, but he cannot control his sobbing.

He takes a deep breath and starts to pray.

EMIR JALAL
Mayasin

First Month of Spring 17, 1365 A.H. (18 February 1946 A.D.)

Jalal walks into his office to find his wife waiting for him. 'Congratulations, *King* Jalal,' she says.

'And congratulations to you, *Queen* Aisha,' he answers, and he sees her flinch, but within a fraction of a second she has recomposed herself and smiles. He knows his wife still doesn't care much for her new name and would prefer to become Queen Anna Christina, but she knew what she was signing up for when she decided to go down the rabbit hole with him, and let's face it, few women become queens.

'Champagne?' she asks, and he accepts the glass she's holding out.

'How is my son doing?' He looks at her belly; she is five months pregnant now, and it is clearly showing.

'What makes you think it's a son?'

He lights two cigarettes and gives one of them to Anna Christina. 'Nothing, it's just that a boy would make our lives a lot easier. Don't get me wrong, I love our daughter, but I don't see Dunya inheriting the throne anytime soon.'

'I thought we were going to change that?'

'We are, but the War of the West and our struggle for independence were skirmishes compared with the war we'll have to fight to succeed.'

'Perhaps it's time that you enlightened me about that war.' His wife takes a long drag from her cigarette before continuing. 'I appreciate that you have been preoccupied with the War of the West, and with negotiating our independence, but now that's over, and I'd like to know what we're up against.'

Jalal stares at her. Before he married her, he promised that they were going to change Beledar together and that when they were finished, it would be the most modern country in the world. And he is definitely planning to involve her in his plans, but not tonight. Tonight, he just wants to drink and celebrate.

A knock on the door saves him, and the footman says, 'Majesty, Lord Richard Rockingham has been waiting all afternoon to see you. Should I send him in?'

'Of course!' He looks as his wife and says, 'Sorry, dear, but the last time we saw Richard was after my father died. I will enlighten you a different night; tomorrow perhaps.'

She nods. He knew Richard was coming one of these days, yet it is terribly good luck that he has chosen exactly this moment for his visit.

'Jalal, good friend! Or should I call you *Majesty*?' Richard asks as he walks in. 'Do you think you'll make a good king?'

'I think we should let history decide that,' he answers as he hands his friend a glass of champagne.

'Wise idea,' Richard says. 'I think I would make dreadful king. So many responsibilities. Although I do think that I wouldn't do too bad as King of England. Sign some laws, visit some banquets, give some speeches—everyone would love me!'

'How many people need to die before you inherit the British throne?' Jalal asks.

Richard shrugs. 'A couple of hundred.'

'Talking about succession,' Anna Christina interrupts, 'Jalal was just about to tell me about the challenges we're going to face in putting Dunya on top of the line of succession.'

'Really?' Richard says as he sits down. 'A master class in Beledarian politics from the future king of Beledar. Do we have enough champagne here, or shall I call the boy outside to get some more?'

Jalal looks at his wife and his friend and realises that they've got him trapped, but perhaps it's better that Richard is here too. His friend might respond humbly to the prospect of a master class from him, yet he knows that Richard is well up to date regarding the political situation in the entire region. 'If we're going to talk politics, I'm getting a cigar and the whisky. Richard?'

'It's like I've just entered Cockaigne,' his friend says with a big smirk.

'All right. So if we want to get Dunya to the the top of the list of succession, we need to change the way the people of Beledar look at women,' Jalal says after he has moved the whisky tray to the coffee table, lit a large Bolivar, and sat down on the sofa.

'We were going to do that anyway,' Anna Christina adds while looking at Richard. 'Before we got married, we agreed that we were going to make women completely equal to men.'

'That's true,' Jalal says. 'But the problem is with the people and the scholars—I mean the clerics . . .'

'I know what the scholars are,' Richard interrupts him. 'You explained that to me fifteen years ago. They make the law and act as judges at the courts of divine law at the same time.'

'Exactly! Anyway, we have Mr al-Rubaie here in the city on our side, and he's one of the most important scholars in the Arab world. As to the rest . . . Let's just say that the deeper into the country you go, the more conservative they become. Not that the people are much better, though, but considering their lack of education and the kind of nonsense their scholars, guardians, and priests are feeding them, I don't think we can blame then.'

'So? Why don't you name yourself head of your—should I say "church?"—in Beledar and execute any scholar who does not accept that?' Richard asks.

'Because unlike Britain, Beledar is not an island, and if I were to do that, our neighbours would invade us within weeks. No, I'm afraid it's going to take time to break the power of the scholars, and the real problem is that we're going to need the lords to help us.'

Richard nods. 'And that's the problem. Preferably you'd use the scholars to unite with the people so that you can break the power of the lords. But if you want women's rights, the clerics will not support you, so now you need the great families to help you break the power of the clerics.'

'In short, that's the problem, yes,' Jalal confirms.

'I'm sorry, I still don't understand,' Anna Christina says. 'What made these families so important?'

'Some of them have ruled their respective provinces since the days of the Ottomans, and they have all fought with my father against the Turks during the great revolt—your First World War,' Jalal answers. 'When the war was won, my father recognised them all as governor of a Beledarian province and allowed them to keep their own armies.'

'That's something else I don't understand,' his wife says. 'Why do they have armies?'

'Because my father had been planning a revolution against the British Empire for years,' Jalal answers. 'He knew he would need a very large army for that, and this was the only way he could get the lords to pay for it.'

'So basically,' Richard says, 'all you need to do is create a national army, break the power of the clerics, and change the perspectives on women of at least half your population. Do you have any idea how you're going to do that?'

'I do. I'm going to allow the lords to command our new army. In exchange I will ask them to support the creation of a democracy, and then I will pray that, after we have broken the power of the clerics, the people will break the power of the lords.'

'You see, that is why I think I would make a dreadful king,' his friend says as he pours himself more whisky.

'As a matter of fact, what I'm worried most about is money. That army is going to cost us a fortune, but we also need to build roads, schools, and hospitals. How are we going to pay for all that?'

'You know why Hitler sent Rommel and his tanks here?'

'Oil,' Anna Christina answers before Jalal can say anything.

'Exactly! There are people who say Hitler lost the war because he didn't have enough of it, but I don't know. What I do know is that automobiles are going to change the future of transport, while transport is going to change the future of the world; a change that will be fuelled by oil!

'Friends, Europe needs oil, and you've got it. My countrymen may leave, but I have good contacts at Shell-Mex and the Anglo-Persian Oil Company, and I could try to broker a deal for you. If I'm successful, I'm sure that your oil will go a long way toward paying for that army of yours. There might even be something left for those schools and roads, and for the pockets of your lords.'

Jalal looks at his wife, who nods. 'I can see no harm in talking,' he replies before he goes on to explain who the lords are, what they believe, and how half of them are related to him.

Part III

NEW BEGINNINGS

CHAPTER ONE

ABDULLAH SON OF SAÍD
Mayasin

First Month of Drought 11, 1370 A.H. (17 February 1948 A.D.)

In the front of the classroom, Abdullah slowly closes his book and starts to put away his pen and papers. From the corner of his eye, he observes the rich kids as they run out of the classroom. Few of them will spend their afternoons on the homework that Mr Maghreb has assigned. The teacher can plead, shout, or beg, but they are indifferent. Their fathers pay vast sums of money so that they may be educated at the school where the king himself has enjoyed the largest part of his education, and this seems to absolve them of the obligation to study.

Abdullah detests their arrogance, yet he knows all too well that some of that money is going into the little purse that Mr al-Rubaie gives him every Gathering Day. A purse that contains more money than he generally made in a week on the streets and that allows both him and his brother to attend school and dream of a better future. And it is not just them. About a third of the kids at the school are from families like his, families that would have never been able to send their kids to school were it not for Mr al-Rubaie's generosity.

The first year was very difficult. Abdullah knew more about the English language than any of his fellow students, but neither could he read nor did he know anything about arithmetic or history. Even where it came to the Quran his knowledge was elementary at best. But Mr al-Rubaie himself tutored him after classes, and now, five years later, he can speak eloquently about Saladin and the revolt against the Turkish Sultan; he can even calculate the force with which his pen hits the ground if he drops it.

He stands up and starts moving toward the door. 'Thank you, Mr Maghreb.'

The teacher nods to him.

'Son of Saíd.' Behind the door, Mr al-Rubaie is waiting for him. 'Walk with me.'

'What is it, Mr al-Rubaie?'

Whenever he is in the presence of Mr al-Rubaie, he feels half a foot taller. This man is the greatest scholar of Islam in the world. He has personally taught the king, and he is friends with Lord Tali'a, yet he is inviting a boy like Abdullah to walk with him.

'Son of Saíd, I have come to tell you that your education is over.'

Your education is over. Abdullah's eyes grow wide, and it feels like all the oxygen is sucked out of his lungs. The hallway starts to swirl, and he stops walking. Mr al-Rubaie might as well have told him that his mother has died.

He looks at the scholar. Is it something he has done? His eyes narrow. Or is it something his brother has done? How many times has he told Samir that he should work hard, keep his mouth shut, and thank God every day that Mr al-Rubaie has given them this opportunity? Yet his brother will not listen. Once, Samir even got into a fight with the grandson of Lord Ismat, the prime minister! He feels his blood rising.

'Why, sir?' he asks a little too sharply.

The scholar smiles reassuringly. 'I have found you a job. In the palace.'

Abdullah frowns. Has he heard the old man correctly? Will he, a boy who grew up in Kobajjeb, soon be working for the king? Perhaps even serving him coffee? That seems highly unlikely.

'Do you mean that I am going to be a royal footman?'

'No. I mean you will serve the king, but you are not going to be a footman.'

He doesn't understand, and the scholar's smile broadens.

'The king is looking for a clerk, and you, Son of Saíd, are the ideal candidate.'

'What's a clerk, sir?'

'A clerk is someone who takes notes and citations and keeps records. A clerk in service of the king,' the scholar looks straight into his eyes, 'is the perfect start for a young man who has the intelligence to make his mark on the world, but lacks the network.'

He is going to take notes for the king. The king! He wants to say something; he *should* say something. But a lump in his throat prevents him from speaking, and he feels his eyes getting wet.

'Sir . . .'

The scholar interrupts him. 'You've earned it, Son of Saíd. Now prove that I have made a worthy choice.'

'I will not let you down, sir.'

Mr al-Rubaie's smile returns. 'I know you won't.'

'Name and business,' the man at the gate barks at him. He is wearing the ceremonial blue uniform of the Royal Guard, but there is nothing ceremonial about the man's rifle.

'Abdullah son of Saíd,' he answers. 'I have come to work here in the palace as a clerk for the king.'

'Taaraz!' the guard calls. 'Do we have a son of Saíd on the list?'

From the small house next to the gate another guard appears with a large book. 'What name?'

'Son of Saíd. Says he's come to work as a clerk.' Taaraz starts to browse through his book, and the guard at the gate snorts. 'Taaraz, how many times have I told you: write down a list of the people we should expect on a single sheet of paper in the morning so you don't have to go searching through that book of yours when people arrive!'

Taaraz looks up. 'You tell me how to do my job; tell me, can you read?'

The guard snorts again. 'If I could, I would be much better at your job than you are.'

'But you can't,' Taaraz taunts. 'So in the name of the Prophet, shut up and let me do mine!'

The guard makes a face at his colleague but doesn't say anything. Instead, he turns back to Abdullah. 'Can you read?'

Abdullah nods.

'Useful skill. Look at Taaraz. He can't fight and is stupid as shit, yet he makes a shilling more than me every week.'

'I heard that,' Taaraz says without looking up.

The guard raises his eyebrows and makes another face. 'Anyway, normally all staff go around the back, but I suppose someone will give you a tour later today. Have you ever been inside?'

Abdullah shakes his head.

'It's big; really big. And there's all kinds of art. And there is the queen . . .' The guard does not make any effort to hide his sinful veneration. 'I would happily give my life for one night with her.'

Abdullah can't believe what he is hearing, but he tries his best to keep his composure and replies, 'I have heard that she is exquisite.'

'Exquisite? Ha! You hear that, Taaraz? This son of Saíd has come to teach us a fancy word to describe our queen.'

'You are the only one here who needs to expand his vocabulary. As it is, I have always thought that "exquisite" was the perfect word to describe our queen.' Taaraz closes his book. 'Abdullah son of Saíd is the new clerk and he needs to be taken to the infidel upon arrival.'

'Which one? Lord al-Maseeh or Mr Petrakis?' the guard asks as he opens the gate, but before Taaraz can answer, the man turns back to Abdullah. 'Do you know who they are?'

He has read about the former in his history book and about the latter in the newspapers and answers, 'Lord al-Maseeh is the governor of the Baylasan province and the minister of war. Mr Petrakis is the king's secretary.'

Abdullah is pleased to see that the guard is impressed, but the man's face becomes irritated again when Taaraz says, 'So if he's a clerk, which infidel do you think we should send him to?'

'When you put it like that . . .' the guard starts, but he's cut short by a new voice, soft yet more authoritative than Abdullah has ever heard.

'I will take him.'

'Yes, sir!' both guards answer in unison, and now Abdullah sees that a man has appeared out of nowhere, and not just any man. It's Lord Tali'a himself, the commander of the Royal Guard!

He has seen Lord Tali'a before, in Mr al-Rubaie's Green Mosque during Gathering Day, but never up close, and even though the commander is much smaller than he had expected, he is also much scarier. He hears Taaraz coughing and realises that Lord Tali'a is holding out his hand. Quickly and clumsily, he takes it.

'Lord Tali'a,' the commander says.

He nods and answers softly, 'Abdullah son of Saíd.'

'Shall we?' Lord Tali'a gestures in the direction of the palace, and they start to walk.

Abdullah looks to his side. He knows he should not be intimidated by this man. He has God by his side, and he hasn't received this opportunity for nothing. However, Lord Tali'a is the second most powerful man in the kingdom.

But he is also disappointed. The commander of the Royal Guard is famous for his piety, yet if soldiers of the Royal Guard have such foul mouths, that reputation is clearly embellished.

'You disapprove of the remarks my guards made about the queen,' the commander says as though he has just read Abdullah's mind.

'Muslim men should not be talking like that about another man's woman, let alone about the queen.'

'Perhaps not, in a perfect world, but we do not live in a perfect world.'

'Yet those men work for you,' Abdullah counters. He cannot believe that he is arguing with the commander of the Royal Guard, but now that he has started, he does not know how to stop. 'If you tell them that it's not accepted, they will stop. If they don't, there are hundreds of other men who would give their lives to become members of the Royal Guard.'

'Son of Saíd, perhaps hundreds of men would indeed give their lives to become members of the Royal Guard, but would they also give their lives to protect the king?'

'It would be their duty, would it not?'

'Yes, it would, but while many men are heroes in their dreams, few are heroes in real life. I trust these men, and I will never fire them for a foul mouth. I might execute them if their lips became too loose, though. What goes on inside the palace must always stay inside the palace.' The commander stops and looks at him. 'Do you understand that?'

Abdullah stares at the commander. Is Lord Tali'a telling him this because troubling things are happening inside the palace, or is it standing procedure?

148

'I understand.'

'Good.'

The commander starts to walk again. Suddenly Abdullah remembers Ghulam's cousin—what is his name? Many times Ghulam used to come to him with stories from inside the palace told to him by his cousin from the Emir's Guard.

He wonders what has become of his old friend. After Mr al-Rubaie welcomed him to the Green Mosque, he only saw Ghulam a couple of times more. But it had not been the same and Abdullah didn't care too much when they completely lost contact.

Zahaar, that was the name. Clearly, Zahaar didn't care too much about the commander's rule, but maybe he'll know how Ghulam is faring.

'Is Zahaar still a member of the Royal Guard?'

'There was never a Zahaar who was a member of the Royal Guard,' the commander answers.

'But there must have been. He was the cousin of a friend of mine, and he was a guard, five years ago.'

They pass a couple of new guards as they enter the palace. The men salute, and Lord Tali'a nods at them. 'Son of Said, I have built the Royal Guard with my own hands, and there was never a man named Zahaar.'

Abdullah frowns. Was Ghulam's cousin executed because he shared information with Ghulam? Considering that the commander has just threatened him and the stories that are told in the city about Lord Tali'a, it is not impossible.

'Mr al-Rubaie and I go back a very long way,' Lord Tali'a remarks after they've walked about a minute in silence and have reached a door. 'He speaks highly of you. He says that your English is better than his and that you can understand the most complicated concepts in seconds. Is that true?'

'Mr al-Rubaie is too kind,' Abdullah answers modestly, yet the compliment from the scholar makes him glow.

Lord Tali'a opens the door, and from a sofa inside the room a man and a girl, half naked and about thirty years the man's junior, jump up. Abdullah averts his eyes. Is this the kind of thing the commander referred to?

'Jesus Christ! Can't you knock!?'

'Not Jesus Christ, just Ri'fat Tali'a,' Lord Tali'a dryly answers. 'And the question is not whether or not I can knock. The question is why you bring whores into the king's palace. It's very early for that, even for you.'

'What are you doing here, Tali'a?' the man asks, ignoring the sneer.

'I am here to bring you your new clerk. This is Abdullah son of Saíd. Abdullah, this is the king's secretary, Mr Petrakis.'

The girl has disappeared and the man is approaching Abdullah with his arm stretched out. For a second, he just looks at the infidel's hand, not knowing what to do. It is soiled, there is no question about that, but can he refuse the hand of his new boss? He sighs and accepts it, already disliking Mr Petrakis for forcing his vile hand on him.

'I will leave you to it, then,' Lord Tali'a says. 'Abdullah, I hope you will remember our conversation, and if there is ever anything you need to get off your chest, you know where to find me.'

'What did he tell you?' Mr Petrakis asks him the moment Lord Tali'a is out of earshot.

Abdullah frowns. For one, he has no idea where to find Lord Tali'a, but what's more, he does not think that the commander will appreciate it if he explains the threat.

'He told me that he did not fire men for talking disrespectfully.'

Mr Petrakis grunts. 'Those awful guards of his; I know all about it. Come and sit down. Let me get you some coffee. Have you had breakfast?'

Abdullah shakes his head, and Mr Petrakis rings a bell. Instantly, a footman appears. 'Bring us coffee and rolls.'

The moment the servant has disappeared, Mr Petrakis says, 'Listen up: Lord Tali'a may run the Royal Guard, but I run the king's life, his government, and the country. You work for me and the king, no one else. Is that clear?'

Abdullah nods. 'Yes, sir.'

'That's good. Now, your job is not very exciting, but if you prove that you're loyal to me, I will make sure that you're well-compensated and get ample opportunities for advancement.'

CHAPTER TWO

KHALID
Al Nawaara

Month of Pilgrimage 10, 1367 A.H. (13 October 1948 A.D.)

Khalid and Aadhil are lying under a tree twenty yards from the house. It's good to be home. Khalid doesn't mind living with his uncle and aunt in Taj al Wadi, and he is grateful that he can continue to go to school, but he does miss his family, especially his brother. Of course, if he were to come back more often, he would not get to see Aadhil too much either. His brother works for his father now and spends most of his time on the road.

'Shiya is going to school,' Aadhil says. 'Although it is not really school; there is woman from the capital who's teaching the girls all sorts of things in Mrs al-Tahtawi's house.'

That does sound a lot like a school. 'Why? What use is it for girls to learn things?'

'That is what I said too, and Father and Nourad and Saifan. But during those elections, there was a woman from Taj al Wadi here who was talking about how women should go and vote for her and that they should make sure their daughters receive an education. This made Mrs al-Tahtawi think. She still has gold left from the Banu Farud, and she used some of it to attract a female teacher from Egypt to teach her daughters, and now all around the village girls are going to her school.'

Khalid remembers the woman; everyone in Taj al Wadi had said that she wasn't right in the head. She had not been elected, of course, but she had been allowed to speak in the square and in coffee houses. Wherever she went, two men from Lord Tanvir had been with her to protect her and make sure that she was given a real chance—king's orders.

'But why Shiya?'

'It seems that she was listening to the radio when suddenly the queen came on and told everyone that in modern Beledar, women can become anything they want; Shiya decided that she wants to be a doctor.'

Khalid shakes his head. He has been away for two and a half months, and everyone seems to have gone crazy.

'That is not all,' Aadhil says as though he has read Khalid's mind. 'Mother has decided that we have to become a modern family.'

Khalid frowns. 'What does that mean?'

'Well . . .'

'Aadhil, there you are!' Saifan has appeared. 'Mother wants you to slaughter the ram!'

'Me?' Aadhil immediately sits straight up. He turns to Khalid. 'Do you hear that? I will tell you later, or you will see. Tonight.'

'Do you think you're up for it?' Saifan asks.

'Of course I am.'

The ram is a beautiful animal, and as Khalid looks at it, he can see the beast looking back. He is sorry that it has to die. Will it know what's coming, like Omar?

Probably not. The beast looks as though it trusts him completely.

'There is something else first,' Saifan says. 'Come on.'

They follow Saifan to the other side of the house, where they find their father.

'Son,' Mr Khan says to Aadhil, 'since this is your first Feast of the Sacrifice as a sixteen-year-old, I am proud to give you this dagger.'

Aadhil's eyes grow big with delight. 'Father, God is praised!'

He unsheathes it. The dagger is short, thick and plain, yet it has a beautiful curve, and it clearly is very well made. Aadhil carefully strokes the blade and smiles. Then he slashes it at his brother like he is going to attack him.

Quickly, Khalid takes a step back, and Aadhil grins.

'If God wants it, let's go kill the ram!'

He wants to run back to the other side of the house, but Saifan grabs his shoulder.

'Not so fast! First, you sharpen it.'

'But it is already sharp!'

'That is irrelevant. God wants you to do all you can to prevent animals from suffering. So whenever you slaughter an animal, you make sure that your knife is as sharp as possible.'

Aadhil scowls and looks to his father, but Mr Khan's iron stare confirms that Saifan is right. He walks to the grindstone and starts sharpening his new dagger.

As Aadhil is working, Khalid notices the blade's reflection in the sunlight. In moments like this he hates that his brother is older. Everywhere he goes, Aadhil will now carry his dagger, and nobody will dare to challenge him on anything, while Khalid will have to wait two years before he gets one. If he gets one.

There is one upside, though: at least he will not have to kill the beast.

'Don't show him your dagger,' Saifan says. 'You'll scare him.'

Aadhil nods and carefully holds the dagger behind his back as he caresses the animal's head with his free hand and moves behind the ram.

'You'll need to apply just enough pressure so you can cut the ram's throat, his windpipe, and the jugular veins in his neck, without getting stuck in his spinal cord. If you do get stuck, the beast will suffer, his meat will be forbidden, and we will be eating goat. Do you understand?'

'At least then the Christians won't be hungry,' Khalid jokes, and while Saifan smiles, Aadhil throws him an angry look.

He knows that his brother will never admit it, but he can see the anxiety in his face. Slaughtering an animal is a serious responsibility, especially during the Feast of the Sacrifice.

Aadhil brings his left hand under the ram's head and lifts its chin while he brings the knife in the right position. The ram still has no idea what's coming and stares satisfied at Khalid. He shivers and catches his brother's eyes. Aadhil grins like he has just won a prize.

'In the Name of God, the Most Gracious, the Most Merciful!'

There is a short shriek and a startled look in the beast's eyes; blood flows from the ram's neck, and his legs give way. The whole thing is over within seconds, and the next moment the three brothers are staring at a dead animal. Aadhil glows with pride.

Saifan applauds. 'That was very good work! When Nourad killed his first ram, we needed an extra two goats before he managed to do it right; Father was furious. Ha!'

They drain the ram and cut it up into pieces. One third will go to the poor in the village, who for four days a year eat better than the wealthy. Another third will go to their grandparents. The remaining third they bring to their mother, and a part of that is on the table that evening.

It becomes clear right away what Aadhil meant when he said that their mother had decided they were going to be a modern family.

Always, the men from the Khan family ate dinner by themselves, before the women, but tonight his mother, his brothers' wives, and even his little sisters are at the table.

And they're not just there—they speak too!

'Well, Aadhil,' Nourad's wife Yasmin says at dinner. 'You are sixteen years old now, a man. Are you going to find yourself a wife now and start a family someday soon?'

'Maybe when I am older.'

'Why? You have a good position with your father, and I am sure that girls are lining up for a man like you.'

'I am not going to work for Father much longer. When Khalid has finished school, we are going to Mayasin to join the king's army!'

They have spoken about this every time he's home from Taj al Wadi, and they have agreed that life is about honour and glory, not bargaining over pennies, and they never want to be dependent on other men to fight their wars. Yet Khalid has hoped to keep it a secret until he actually left school. He cannot believe his brother has just blabbed it like that.

But he isn't the only one who's flabbergasted. If a bomb had just dropped on their house, the silence would not be more deafening.

After a while, their mother says, 'Are you mad? Khalid is getting the best education a man can have, and you want to take him with you to the army!?'

'Forget that!' Nourad growls. 'You want to join the army, rather than continue to work for Father? We have just bought a truck; who is going to repair it if you leave?'

'It isn't difficult to repair a truck,' Aadhil counters. 'Even you could learn it. And it is as Yasmin says: I am a grown man, and I can make my choices!'

'But surely not the king's army?' Saifan's voice is soft, although the incredulous tone is difficult to miss. 'Why not join Lord Tanvir's militia? That is nearby, and what's more, they are our people.'

'The king's army are our people too, and the king does not have dozens of children, grandchildren, and nephews to promote before boys from local villages.'

Aadhil is completely relaxed, and even though Khalid is afraid that this is going to turn out all wrong, he once again admires his brother's courage.

'But what will you be fighting for?' Saifan asks.

'Well, for our king and our country, of course. The king is a descendant of Muhammad and it is our duty to fight for him. We will be winning the next war against the Jews, and one day will we conquer all of Arabia, and then we will make you all rich!'

Out of nowhere, their father slams his hand on the table.

'You cannot go! The king is a foreigner, and he lost the war against the Jews on purpose! Besides, what does he know of the desert? Have you ever seen him here? Can he even ride a camel?'

Khalid stares at his father, but Mr Khan isn't finished. 'Nourad is right. We have just bought a truck, and if all goes well, in two years we're going to buy another one. You have proved that you can repair it, so you cannot go!'

'And neither can Khalid!' their mother adds. 'After he is finished with school, he will go to the university in Mayasin. He is not going to waste his life in the army!'

'You and your schools!' Their father now turns on their mother. 'This is all your fault! Saifan and Nourad never went to school, and they turned out great, but look at those boys'—he gestures to Khalid and Aadhil—'they're getting all kinds of crazy ideas in their heads!

'And now you are letting Shiya go to school as well! It is offensive to the natural order of things, and I promise you, God will punish us for it! Perhaps he has already started, and that is why those boys are suddenly getting crazy ideas!'

Khalid's father has turned dark red, and for a moment the table is completely silent, but then Shiya, who either doesn't understand the gravitas of the situation or simply wants to break the tension, says softly, 'I like going to school.'

'You see!' Mr Khan explodes, pointing at his wife. 'You have turned my daughter into an infidel and my sons into men who betray their own people!'

'Don't you dare talk to me that way!' Khalid's mother counters. 'Aadhil is completely correct about Lord Tanvir and his militia. One hundred and twenty percent corruption and nepotism; it is written. And so what if they go—you have two more sons! Let them learn to repair your stupid truck; you never wanted that thing in the first place!'

Mr Khan slams his fist on the table again, even harder than before, and Yasmin's plate falls on the ground. Then he takes his own plate throws it at Aadhil, missing him by inches.

'Aadhil is not going into any army, nor is Khalid! In fact, Khalid isn't even going back to school. Next week, he will come with us on an expedition, and if God wants it, he will learn what it is to be a merchant. Furthermore, from this day on, Shiya is forbidden to leave this house! Let her clean; let her cook; school is not for women!'

He appears to be finished, but then he reconsiders. 'And finally, women are no longer allowed at my table! In the name of God, this farce has lasted long enough!'

He snorts and walks away, followed by their mother. At the table, no one speaks, but Shiya and Aisha, Khalid's youngest sister, are softly sobbing. In the distance they can hear the screaming continuing.

'I never want to go to school,' Aisha says, and the tension breaks.

'Anyone interested in more stew?' Saifan has picked up the bowl and is looking around the table. 'Come on, it is the Feast of Sacrifice, and we should not be fighting, even if they are.'

'I'll have some,' Yasmin replies.

Khalid puts his plate forward too, distractedly looking at Shiya, who has started to sob louder.

'I like school!' she cries. 'And I don't want to stay at home!'

Yasmin puts a hand on her shoulder while Nourad growls, 'Don't worry, you will still be going to that stupid school of yours.'

Everyone looks at him.

'What? We all know who is the real boss in this house. There is no way that Father is going to let Aadhil join the army, but three days from now Khalid and Shiya are going to be back in school; it's written.'

From his tone it's clear that Nourad disagrees with this state of affairs, but he *is* correct, and three days later, Saifan and Aadhil take Khalid back to his uncle and aunt in Taj al Wadi, where he can continue his education.

CHAPTER THREE

ABDULLAH SON OF SAÍD
Mayasin

Month of Separation 4, 1370 A.H. (10-11 May 1951 A.D.)

Abdullah has been staring at the papers on his desk for at least an hour, but so far he has not read a single word. He cannot get the argument he had with his brother last night out of his head. At first he was so proud when Samir was admitted to the University of Mayasin, yet lately . . .

He shakes his head. He does not really dare to admit it, even to himself, but lately he has been thinking it was a major mistake. That it would have been much better if Samir had simply found himself a job, like Abdullah, and started to take some responsibility for his life. And yesterday it all came out, and Abdullah told his brother that he was going to stop paying for his extravagances. In response, Samir yelled that Abdullah was small-minded and understood nothing.

Has he taken the correct decision, or was his brother right? He sighs. He loves Samir, and every nerve in his body tells him that the only way to bring him back to God is to force him to start taking responsibility, yet somehow he cannot shake the feeling that . . .

'Abdullah Saíd!'

He looks up. Mr Petrakis is standing next to him. He has worked in the palace for more than three years now, but he can count on one hand the number of times the king's secretary has spoken to him directly.

'What is it, sir?'

'Half an hour from now, the American ambassador will arrive at the palace for a meeting with the king. I need you to take minutes.'

'Me, sir? Where is Mr Hashem?'

'All I know about Mr Hashem's whereabouts is that he is not where he should be.'

'And what about Mr Zubi and Mr Tanvir?' He gestures at two of his senior colleagues, who normally ignore Abdullah's existence but are now staring at Mr Petrakis and himself as though they have just discussed the murder of the king.

'It is my understanding that Mr Zubi and Mr Tanvir do not speak English, which makes them somewhat useless in a room with the American ambassador. Now, I really don't have time for questions; get up and follow me.'

Zubi and Tanvir avert their gazes and start whispering to each other, no doubt plotting some form of retaliation for the insult, but Abdullah does not really care and jumps up. He is going to meet the king!

Mr Petrakis is making great haste and leads him through hallways he's never set foot in. The first day he arrived at the palace, he thought he would be at the epicentre of power from that moment on. Instead, from the second day onwards, he's entered the palace through a back door to spend his days in a back office where he has worked on translating unintelligible, badly written orders from ministers and writing letters that are dictated to him by assistants of the ministers.

After the Zionists cheated their way into Palestine and the war started, he spent most of his time translating foreign newspapers. His colleagues looked at him with clear envy, which was just one of the reasons why it was very exciting work, but when the war was lost the outside world appeared to become much less important. Now, occasionally, a member of the Royal Guard will barge into the office and demand that he drops all of his work to translate foreign newspapers or documents, but no one in his office seems to care, and a lot of the things he translates he does not understand. He has not met Lord Tali'a again since his first day.

Still, Abdullah thanks God every day for his job. He is so well paid that he has been able to move his family to a small private house in Juban, and few boys from Kobajjeb can say that they work in the palace!

'We are here,' the king's secretary says as he stops in front of a door, where two Royal Guards are standing watch, accompanied by a footman. Turning to the latter, he asks, 'Is he in?'

'No, sir.'

The infidel opens the door. The king's office is larger than Abdullah's family's house, but there is very little furniture. In front of the window there is a giant desk facing two comfortable chairs. There are two large sofas, and one of the walls is lined with cupboards that are stacked to the ceiling with books. For a second Abdullah wonders how the king gets his books from the top shelves, but a cough from Mr Petrakis brings him back to the moment.

'This is you,' the infidel says, pointing to a desk that is so small, Abdullah had not yet noticed it. He sits down. There is a small stack of papers waiting for him alongside three pens and two bottles of ink.

'Against my advice, the king wants records from all of his official meetings. So you take minutes, you copy them out—

either on a typewriter or in your very best handwriting—and then you bring them to me. No one else gets to see your notes. Do you understand?'

Abdullah looks at Mr Petrakis and replies, 'Yes, sir.'

'Good. Furthermore, I want you to swear by the Quran that you will never tell anyone about what went on in the meeting, or in any other meeting that you attend that involves the king. Do you swear it?'

'I swear by the Quran that I will never tell anyone about what went on in this meeting, or in any other meeting that involves the king.'

'Good. Now, it is important to remember that you should behave as though you are invisible. You will take minutes, but you will not make a sound. You will not move, you will not cough, and you will not breathe loudly. When the king arrives . . .' Mr Petrakis does not get to finish this sentence, because the doors open, and in walks the king. Instead, the infidel hisses, 'Stand up.'

Abdullah has seen pictures and statues of the king, but they do not do justice to the tall man in the dark blue suit who has just entered the room. He is reminded of the men in suits whose shoes he used to shine in front of Pervaíz's coffee house, but the king appears stronger and much more much confident.

'Where's Hakim?' is the first thing the king asks when he has turned his gaze in their direction.

'We do not know, Majesty,' Mr Petrakis answers. 'This is Abdullah Saíd.'

The king looks at Abdullah, who wonders if he ought to bow or kneel, but he is too late; the king is already speaking to him. 'Is Saíd your father's name?'

'Yes, Your Majesty,' he mumbles.

'Hmmm. And what were your grandfathers' names?'

He looks down and softly answers, 'I don't know, Your Majesty.'

'Is he one of the boys Tali'a has selected?' the king asks Mr Petrakis.

'He is, Majesty. He came to us a couple of years ago. Before that he was one of Mr al-Rubaie's projects.'

'I suppose we should be grateful to Mr al-Rubaie, then. If it weren't for him, the only people who could write in this palace would be Ismats, Raslans, and Kalaldehs.'

There is a knock on the door, and the footman steps in. 'The American ambassador, Mr Williams.'

The king turns around, and Abdullah, remembering that he should be invisible, sits down behind his little desk and stares at the door through which Mr Williams comes in, a half-smoked cigar in the corner of his mouth.

Mr Petrakis leaves, and after the American ambassador has asked for a whisky, the king turns to a side table and personally pours two glasses. Abdullah tries not to stare, but he can hardly believe that the king, a descendant of Muhammad, drinks alcohol. Of course, it would be impolite for the king to let the man drink alone, but why is there a whisky tray in his office?

'Mr Ambassador, I called you here today because we have a problem: your Texas Arabic Oil Company in Bab al Din. People are being expelled from their lands without any compensation, and this cannot go on.'

'I am very sorry to hear this, sir, but you should know that TAOC has made an agreement with Governor Lord Raslan. He has assured them of his complete cooperation, and he does not have any objection to their way of doing business.'

'I know he does not have any objections, Mr Ambassador. It is his militia that is driving the people away from their homes. My problem is that the people have objections, and therefore I have objections.'

'Sir, that is a problem indeed. I will talk to the board of directors and see what can be done. However, I cannot make any promises.'

'Mr Ambassador, I have allowed a small concession for your Texas oil company, because at the moment the British profit too much from our oil. Nonetheless, it took Shell-Mex and the Anglo-Persian Oil Company years before I gave them any large concessions. When I look at the size of the American operation, it is completely out of line. What's more, I never sanctioned any military actions against the people in my country. I could send in the army and nationalise all the assets of your Texas company, but I would not like to harm the good relationship between our countries.'

Governor Lord Raslan is the father of the secretary of state and the most important nobleman in the country. Is it true what Abdullah is hearing, that his militia is attacking his own people? He wishes he had more time to think about it, but he has never before taken minutes in English, and he needs all of his attention to keep up with what's being said.

'Of course, sir. I will contact them at once and tell them they will have to scale back their operations. Now, the last time we spoke, you promised me you would give our military base some thought. Have you?'

'I am afraid an American base on Beledarian soil is impossible, Mr Ambassador. After having the English here for thirty years, I cannot have another foreign army in my land, not even as guests; the people will not accept it.'

K. 30 years English. New foreign army unacceptable, Abdullah writes. Of course it is unacceptable.

'I understand, but it appears that there are a number of your lords who do not share those objections. I have spoken to representatives of Lord al-Maseeh and Lord Kalaldeh, and both have assured me that they do not hold any objections to a base on their lands, if they are duly compensated, of course.'

'The lords and the people are not quite the same thing,' the king says.

'And yet both Lord al-Maseeh and Lord Kalaldeh have sons in your government, and the people elected them as governors only recently.'

Ah yes, the elections for governor. There have been many letters of complaint from people who say that they were unfair, yet Mr Petrakis has ordered all these letters to be burned.

'Mr Ambassador, you see it the wrong way around. *I* represent the people; the family members of the lords represent their own interests. And you know very well that if I allow your bases, the newspapers will not be writing about al-Maseeh or Zubi; they will write about me. The lords will get your money, but as you put it in your country, I will get the shit.'

'I've got to say, you have not made a very good deal, sir,' the ambassador mockingly says.

'It was the only deal there was,' King Jalal snarls. 'Now, Mr Ambassador, if you will excuse me. I am a very busy man.'

Is this it? On the one side, Abdullah will be happy once this awful man leaves, but he's also disappointed that his moment with the king is over so soon. He looks up and sees that the ambassador has no inclination to get up. Instead, he smiles a crooked smile, relights his cigar, and says, 'Sir, I implore you to remember that the United States of America has always been there for you. True or not?'

The king sighs. 'Mr Ambassador, that is certainly true, as I have always been there for you.'

'Exactly, because as you said, we are allies. When you wanted to be independent, we backed you. When you needed money, we lent it to you. We gave you jeeps, tanks, airplanes, and a huge bag of money, for absolutely nothing. Sir, almost all the weapons your soldiers use were manufactured in the United States. Now, we are asking this tiny thing in return . . .'

'Mr Ambassador,' the king tries to interrupt Mr Williams, but the American doesn't stop talking.

'Sir, we read the newspapers here, and while we respect the way you handle your communists, they are our problem too. All we want to do is help, and if we build even just a very small base, the Russians will understand that there is no beef for them here. What's more, we are offering handsome compensation for a base like that, and you can rest assured you will not be having any more problems with the Texas Arabic Oil Company.'

Did the ambassador just admit that this Texas Arabic Oil Company is causing problems because the Americans want to build a base in Beledar? Abdullah looks back at his notes, but the last words he has written down are, *Only deal. Busy man. Goodbye.*

Fortunately, the king still has not answered, and he takes his pen and starts to write as rapidly as he can. From the corner of his eye he can see the king stand up, and then King Jalal starts to talk again.

'Mr Ambassador, after our revolution, in which my father fought the Turks together with the English, we never got independence. We got promises, from your President Wilson, amongst others, and a temporary mandate for the British to rule us, which lasted for almost thirty years. Yet did we complain? No.

'What did we do? When the British asked us to support you in the War of the West, we supported you. I was there at the front, fighting side by side with Englishmen against German, Iraqi, Vichy French, and Syrian soldiers in a war that was not ours.

'Thirty years later, you made good on your promise, and I am grateful, but my father did not live to wake up in the independent Beledar that he had won for us.

'As for the weapons you have been selling us these last years, both you and I know that your country produces so many weapons that you would have to fight at least three Korean wars at the same time to use them all. If you don't sell them, soon you will have to shut down the factories, but in doing so you will endanger the livelihoods of hard-working American families.

'We don't need to buy your weapons. The French and the English will sell us weapons too, but since your weapons are good and your loans fair, I never had any reason to shop anywhere else.'

Abdullah wishes he could ask the king to pause for a second so that he can catch up, but he must remain invisible.

'As for those "free" jeeps, tanks, and airplanes, and that bag of money, we both know they were a bribe I took in exchange for letting it pass that President Truman broke his predecessor's promise that there would never be a Zionist state.

'Mr Ambassador, I remember as if it were yesterday when your predecessor was here to offer me my, how would you describe it in your culture? *My thirty pieces of silver*. My country wanted war. My people wanted war, but he begged me not to send my tanks, and I took the silver.

'I, and many of my neighbours, as an act of friendship to your country, have allowed Israel to exist, and look at what it has caused: Shukri al-Quwatli, president of Syria, overthrown by his army and exiled because he did not send enough soldiers to Israel. Mahmoud Nuqrashi Pasha, prime minister of Egypt, executed for accepting the ceasefire. King Abdullah of Jordan, one of the wisest leaders ever to walk this earth, murdered because he thought the time for peace had come.

'You talk about a "free" bag of money and "free" jeeps, but for me these were never free at all. Every day my people wake up in anger, because eighty miles from here there is a European proxy state where Arabs are mistreated and suppressed. I do not blame the Jews, I really don't, but I do blame you, and I blame myself.

'Thus, Mr Ambassador, I owe neither you nor your country anything at all. Not a tiny military base, nor a blind eye toward your oil company. I expect it to be scaled down completely before the end of this week, or I will nationalise all of its assets, and I will start buying my weapons from the Frogs. Do I make myself clear?'

'Very clear, Majesty,' the American ambassador says, and thirty seconds later he is out of the office, his tail between his legs, and in comes a Royal Guardsman whom Abdullah recognises as Taaraz.

'Mr Saíd, come with me.'

Abdullah looks at his notes. They are not yet finished, but he does not object. He follows the guard, thinking about the last words he wrote down. *Bribe. Thirty pieces of silver. Blame myself.*

He does not understand it. Beledar had fought the Zionists. They had lost, yes, but the king had sent their army. What kind of bribe had King Jalal been talking about? And what is the connection between the king and the murdered leaders he mentioned? Is the king thinking about making peace with Israel? That would be outrageous!

'This is where you copy out your notes,' Taaraz says as he opens the door to a nondescript little room with only a desk and chair inside.

Abdullah nods and sits down behind the desk. Taaraz does not leave. Should he copy out his notes in English or in Arabic? For a second he considers asking Taaraz, but then he realises that no one else is supposed to know what was said, and since he knows Taaraz can read Arabic, he decides to go for English.

He is almost finished when Lord Tali'a walks in and takes his papers out from under him. He does not object. He has sworn that he will not tell anyone about what was going on in the room during the meeting; he is not going to protest when the commander of the Royal Guard confiscates his notes. He sits back and looks at the commander while he reads.

When Lord Tali'a has reached the last paper, the commander looks at him. 'Is this your true account of what happened during the meeting?'

'Yes, sir.'

The commander gives him back the papers but keeps the last two. 'I understand that you are a very meticulous clerk, yet I am sure that the American ambassador left after the king told him he was a very busy man. Wouldn't you say that that is in fact a more accurate account of what happened?'

'But sir, Mr Petrakis . . .'

'Mr Saíd, you work for the king, not for Mr Petrakis. For King Jalal the meeting was over the moment he told the ambassador that it was time to leave. Do you understand?'

Abdullah nods. 'Yes sir.'

'What ails thee, Son of Saíd?' the scholar asks when Abdullah lingers in the mosque after the prayers of Gathering Day are over.

'It is my brother, Mr al-Rubaie.'

'Samir? I have not seen him in a long time. Is he sick? Should I contact my doctor?' the scholar asks.

'I am afraid, Mr al-Rubaie,' Abdullah replies, 'that the doctor cannot help him, for he does not suffer from any sickness of the body. He suffers from a sickness of the soul.'

The scholar shakes his head. 'That is grave indeed. How does this sickness of the soul manifest itself?'

'As you know, after leaving your school Samir went on to university. I have funded him, but I now fear it has been a mistake. Recently, I have learned that my brother spends money on alcohol and hashish. He also spends much of his time with women, and many nights he does not come home to his mother.'

Mr al-Rubaie stares at him reflectively. 'Are you sure that this is not merely a symptom of youth, rather than a sickness of the soul?'

Abdullah frowns and says, 'Please, Mr al-Rubaie, explain to me what you mean by this?'

'When you first came here, something had happened that made you crave God's love and forgiveness. I have never asked you what it was, because for me it is not of any importance. All that matters is that you never lost your way again.

'Not all men encounter such an event during their lives, though, and many, once they reach a certain age, are driven away from the path of God for some time. But when the heart is good, God willing, they inevitably return.' The scholar pauses a moment before asking, 'Tell me, Son of Saíd, is your brother's heart good?'

Abdullah bows his head and thinks back to the fight he had with Samir. 'A month ago, I would have full-heartedly said yes. Now, I am not so sure.'

'Young man, if you would have full-heartedly said "yes" merely a month ago, you should not have doubts today. To doubt your brother is to doubt God. If God wills it, Samir will find his way again. It may take a month or it may take ten years, but I have faith, and so should you.'

Abdullah sighs; he cannot stand feeling powerless. He asks, 'So I should continue to fund him?'

The scholar shrugs. 'You must do what you feel is right, but you must also give him room to find his own way to God.'

The words of the scholar sound definitive, but he is not yet ready to leave. Instead, Abdullah stares into the void and thinks back to the conversation between the king and the ambassador. Should he ask Mr al-Rubaie's opinion?

'Is there something else, Son of Saíd?' says the scholar, who notices his reluctance to leave.

Abdullah is sure that the scholar will be able to make sense out of it all, yet he has sworn by the Quran that he will never speak to anyone about what happened in that room. Besides, Mr al-Rubaie is very friendly with Lord Tali'a. What if he were to tell the commander that the young clerk cannot be trusted to keep his mouth shut?

He shakes his head. 'No, sir. Thank you, sir.'

'Thank not me, Son of Saíd. Thank God, for it is He who gives and He who takes.'

CHAPTER FOUR

KHALID
Taj al Wadi to Camp Mayasin

Month of Separation 9-13, 1370 A.H. (15-19 May 1951)

He is making his way from the school to his uncle's house, thinking about what he's going to do when he leaves school. Perhaps he'll get a law degree. A couple of months ago a man from the university came to tell them about the importance of the law. The law is what keeps the peace in any civilised country, and according to the man, the king needs dozens of lawyers in the coming years to help him write new laws for their young country.

Or he might go into medicine and be a doctor. At the medical school, there are doctors from Egypt, England, and even America who are teaching the latest medical discoveries to Beledarian students. If he becomes a doctor, he will be able to save lives; one day he might even make up for Omar.

He shakes his head. He doesn't want to think about what he has done and tries to put it out of his head. Perhaps law is the better choice; if he becomes a doctor, Omar will keep on haunting him. But still, saving lives would be a perfect way to spend his life.

Fortunately, he doesn't have to make up his mind for another year. He can . . .

'Khalid.'

He looks up. He's been so preoccupied with his own thoughts that he hasn't seen his brother standing in front of his uncle's house.

'Aadhil! What are you doing here?'

'I've run away from home, and I'm joining the army. I have come to get you too.'

The army. Sometimes Khalid walked by the army office in Taj al Wadi and paused for a second, but lately he hasn't given it any serious thought. Since the terrible scene during the Feast of the Sacrifice, he has even stopped discussing it with his brother. But clearly Aadhil has not forgotten, and he is now here to bring Khalid with him.

'You ran away?' he asks. 'What about Mother and Father?'

Aadhil shrugs. 'They live in the previous century. Besides, mother has Aisha and Shiya, and father has Nourad and Saifan. They'll manage without us.'

'But I can't leave school. I have just one more year, and then I'll have a degree and . . .'

'That's why we have to go now!' Aadhil interrupts him. 'Can't you see? The closer you'll get, the more suspicious they'll become! Mother has all kinds of plans for you, and she keeps on telling Father to ask everyone here to keep an eye on you. Trust me, when you've finished your school, it will be too late.'

The last time he trusted his brother it didn't end well. On the other hand, there's a good chance that Aadhil is right this time; he knows his mother well enough. But his mother was also right: few boys in Beledar are fortunate enough to go to school as long as he has, and if he also were to get a university degree, all doors will open to him. *God, please tell me what to do.*

He looks at his brother, who appears to be waiting for him to rush into his uncle's house, retrieve his stuff, and follow him. Will Aadhil understand if he decides not to go?

Probably not.

He sighs. 'I need to get my things.'

Aadhil shakes his head. 'No, you don't. The army will take care of us.'

Khalid and Aadhil hide in the office for three days and three nights. The days are not too bad; Khalid had just borrowed a big English book from the library, and when there is light, he loses himself in the adventures of a man named D'Artagnan and a group of French knights. But at night, every little sound wakes him, and when he falls back to sleep he dreams of his father and brothers coming to get him.

On the fourth morning, though, they embark on a lorry for Mayasin alongside fourteen other recruits. With every mile the lorry puts between them and Taj al Wadi, Khalid begins to feel more at ease, and gradually his unrest makes way for excitement. Now that their father can no longer get to them, the adventure can truly begin.

There is some disappointment when they learn that the training camp is not actually in the capital—the soldiers at Taj al Wadi merely called the camp Mayasin because it is the nearest city. But all that is forgotten the moment they set foot in the camp.

At the far side of the camp there are stone buildings, barracks and the mess for the soldiers and officers, while the tents for the recruits are situated right next to the entrance. Together with the other kids from Taj al Wadi, they are assigned a tent. With about forty recruits already in it, it is completely crowded. There's hardly room to move, but they're sleeping about a foot away from each other, and they're on their way to living their dream.

Despite his tiredness, Khalid does not dream much that first night. His stomach hurts (no one had fed them when they arrived at the camp) and every time he closes his eyes he hears his mother's voice. What did his parents do when they discovered that their sons were gone?

The next morning before the sun is up there are men in the tent, yelling things like, 'Lazy bastards! Open your eyes! God hates idleness! In the name of God, get outside now!'

Khalid thinks he is still dreaming, but when he receives a kick in his ribs he realises that it is probably best to '*get his ass outside as soon as possible, unless he wants to get acquainted with the wrath of God,*' as one of the men delicately puts it.

Rubbing the sleep from his eyes, he follows his nose toward the fresh air and lines up alongside the other recruits outside the tent. He looks at his brother, but Aadhil does not look back. Instead, he stares straight ahead, and Khalid decides to follow his example.

In front of them, illuminated by the last rays of moonlight, is a man. Judging by the three stripes on his shoulder, he is a sergeant, and he is patiently waiting until the recruits are assembled. Khalid looks back at the tent and sees that the slow kids have been woken slightly more harshly.

'Empty!' He hears a man call from the tent, and once the latecomers are lined up in front of the rest, the sergeant starts to shout.

'My name is Mr Aazim, son of Ghazwanand, and I am your drill sergeant, which means that I will be your commanding officer, your general, your god, your king, your reverend, your father, and your prophet for the next three months! You may address me as Mr Aazim or Mr Ghazwanand, sergeant and sir! You will not speak unless you are spoken to, and you will always speak politely! Do I make myself clear?'

From the group, there comes a weak, 'Yes, sir.'

While all the recruits are physically there, most of their minds are still asleep; those who are awake are ill at ease, and nobody, including Khalid, considers this a good moment to stand out.

The lack of enthusiasm in the reply does not please Sergeant Aazim, though; he responds by roaring even louder than before. 'Perhaps I am getting deaf, but I have heard newborn babies cry louder than that! Could you, in the name of God, repeat that?'

'Yes, sir!' Khalid tries to say it as loud as he can, but since the recruits do not manage to answer in unison, the response is mostly chaotic, and Sergeant Aazim regards them with dismay. He paces up and down alongside the boys, staring each of them in the eyes. The sergeant is over six feet tall, clean-shaven, and he has more muscles than Khalid has ever seen on a man. As he walks back and forth in front of the recruits, Khalid tries to breathe as little as possible.

Around him, the young men clearly share his fears, and all eyes meticulously follow the sergeant's movements. *Merciful God, You have always supported and helped me. Now I ask You, don't let him stop in front of me.*

His prayer is answered. Aazim stands still before a boy in front and to the left of him. God is praised. 'For some reason I did not hear you.' The sergeant speaks softly now, yet no one has a problem understanding him.

'I am sorry,' the boy replies.

Clap! The giant hand of the sergeant comes down on the recruit's ear, and the boy, who is so small that Khalid doubts he is actually seventeen, has great difficulty staying on his feet. When the kid regains his composure, Khalid can see that a giant scar splits his face in two.

'You are sorry, what?' The sergeant's face is less than a foot away from the boy's, and Khalid can see saliva following his words.

'I am sorry, Sergeant, sir!' the kid shouts. Until the sergeant stopped in front of him, Khalid had taken no notice of the boy, but he respects the speed with which the kid has straightened himself and the fact that the boy does not look down. On the contrary, the scar-faced kid stares indignantly back at the sergeant.

For at least half a minute, the boy and the sergeant keep on staring at each other, while the rest of the recruits hold their breath, but then Sergeant Aazim turns around, takes a few steps back and faces the whole group again. 'You may find your tent a bit crowded at the moment,' he says. Although he is not shouting anymore, his voice is still sharp, 'but since you are the most pathetic group of recruits I have ever seen, I promise you that at the end of the day there will be a lot more space. At the end of this week, if God wants it, you will feel like you are living in a castle.'

He follows this remark with a malicious laugh. 'The first month of your training we will get you into shape. You all look like you have spent your entire life sitting on your asses, sucking your mommy's titties. Yet if God wants it, that will be changing shortly. We start now!' He starts to turn, but then he reconsiders. 'Does anyone have any questions?'

If they are stupid or simply tired of life, Khalid doesn't know, but a couple of kids raise their hands, and Sergeant Aazim points at a boy that is so fat, Khalid wonders what he was thinking when signed up.

'Shouldn't we have some breakfast?'

The fat boy is standing in the second file, and as the sergeant makes his way to him, the two boys in front of him immediately step aside. The moment Sergeant Aazim is in range, he slaps the fat boy in the face. He is neither as strong nor as resilient as the small kid, and immediately the fat boy cowers.

'Should we not have some breakfast first, what?' the sergeant shouts.

The boy gets back to his feet and says loudly, 'Should we not have some breakfast first, sir?'

Clap!

Another slap is his reward, and this time he literally falls to the ground.

'Are you stupid!?' the sergeant shouts as he kicks the boy in his stomach. 'Do you think that when you are running from the enemy, they will wait so that you can have some breakfast first?'

He kicks him again. 'Food is a luxury. A good soldier can go without food for a month. Looking at you, I'd say you should be able to go without food for a year!'

Another kick, and then the sergeant turns to the recruits. 'Look at him. It's boys like him that caused our defeat against the Jews! The Jew will not wait until you have eaten! He will not wait until you have prayed! The Jew does not care, and if you are weak, he will kill you!'

Sergeant Aazim is so angry that for a second Khalid fears he will give the fat boy yet another kick, which might kill him, but instead the sergeant turns away, and when he is back at his original position, he looks at his recruits and says, 'When you see food, you eat! When you do not see food, you do not eat! Always make sure you have your own water, and always carry food on a mission in case you get lost. The army takes care of you, if God wants it, but never, ever, ask for food! It is ungrateful! Any more questions?'

It seems that all the questions had been about food, and no one raises his hand this time. The sergeant waits for a second, laughs, and gives the order to start the first run.

Before they are ten minutes away, Khalid has started to feel sympathy for the fat boy; running on an empty stomach is much tougher than he had expected. He also realises that if they keep going at this pace, he will not last very long. Already he's breathing heavily, his legs have begun to feel weak, and his feet are seriously hurting. He looks down; his scandals are unfit for running. On the other hand, next to him there is a kid without shoes. If that kid can keep going, so can he.

But he wouldn't mind a little more air. And there's a pain in his right side, like someone's cut him. Well, at least it distracts him from the pain in his feet.

Khalid passes two boys who have stopped running. Should he stop too? Just a little break might make the pain go away. His brother is running in front of him, though, and Aadhil will be terribly embarrassed if his little brother is kicked out on the first day.

Of course, once his legs are no longer able to carry him—and it feels like that moment may arrive any minute now—there won't be much he can do about it. He will be sent back to Al Nawaara a failure.

'Listen here, boy . . .' A man in uniform has appeared next to Khalid. 'I am going to be honest with you. There is simply no way that you are going to make it. You already look like you are going to die, and this is just your first day. You would do yourself a great favour by going home now; it is written. In fact, you would be doing the army a great service. Even if you do not die, what kind of soldier do you think you will make?'

Maybe the man is right, but if Khalid gives up, it will be because his legs give up, not because this soldier is telling him that he is too weak. He keeps on running, and everywhere around him he now sees soldiers running alongside the recruits.

'I am sure the Prophet, may God bless him and protect his soul, is deeply ashamed of the fact that you are a Muslim,' the soldier continues. 'Although, are you sure that you are a Muslim? You look more like a little Jewish boy to me.'

Khalid still does not say anything, and the soldier seems to accept this as a sign that he has hit a sensitive point.

'Guys, I have a little Jew boy here!' the soldier shouts before he spits on Khalid.

He cannot remember anyone ever spitting on him before, and he wants to stop and attack the soldier, but if he does it might end his career in the army before it has even begun. Nevertheless, an insult like this must not go unpunished, and he must think of another way to repay the insult.

'Your father must have been drunk when he mounted the sow that bore you! Why won't you look at me? Are you scared of me? Are you dumb, boy? Or don't you have enough energy to speak? If you don't have the energy to speak, how are you going to fight?'

In fact, Khalid does have the energy to speak. His rage has driven away the pain in his feet, and it has given him a new strength that he does not want to waste on the man next to him. He walked to Arabia as a boy; there is no way that he is going to give up during some little run!

The sun is showing itself, and Khalid can smell the dew, a scent that reminds him of home. Will he ever see it again? He does not know, but Aadhil is still in front of him, and as though his brother can hear what he is thinking, Aadhil looks back over his shoulder and winks at Khalid.

And then, abruptly, they stop.

Khalid promptly bends over and starts to cough; it feels like he's going to cough up the inside of his lungs, while at the same time he's sure that his head his going to explode. Around him, the Earth is spinning.

Someone slaps his cheek; it's the soldier who was running next him. 'Don't worry, boy, God willing, you'll make it. First run is the hardest.'

'Line up!' Obviously the sergeant feels like they have had more than enough time to catch their breath, and, grudgingly, the recruits follow the order. Khalid looks around, and only now does he notice that they are back at the camp. There are at least ten fewer boys than when they had set off to run.

'You are a bunch of wimps!' the sergeant begins. 'Do any of you know how far you ran?'

Nobody says anything.

'You ran five miles, and it took you over forty minutes! Do you know who runs five miles in forty-five minutes?' Still not a sound from the recruits. 'Neither do I! Pigs are faster! Jews are faster! In fact, I have heard of women running five miles in less than thirty! You boys are slower, not just slower than women—you are snails compared to them!'

Khalid stares at the sergeant. Normally he would probably be angered by the comparison with women, but at the moment he still does not have enough energy to care.

'I have to admit, though, that I am partly to blame, for I could have made you run faster. After all, there are still too many of you sorry lot left. But do not worry, God willing, I will correct this mistake during the coming weeks!' The sergeant pauses for a second to let them contemplate that, but then he says, 'For now, you may thank God and the king that we have provided food for you!'

The 'food' is porridge, something that Khalid and many of the boys have never eaten before. It's not too bad, especially since Khalid has not eaten in over twenty-four hours, and he is so hungry he could eat anything.

Breakfast is followed by more training—in fact, they only pause for prayers. They do push-ups, sit-ups, pull-ups, more running, and, at the end of the day, their first boxing exercise.

It seems simple: three left-hand punches whilst moving forward, followed by a right-hand punch, and then three left-hand punches whilst moving backward, before finishing off their combination with a right-handed punch and returning to the starting position to start over. But the devil is in the footwork.

'Boxing is easy, like dancing,' Sergeant Aazim shouts. 'As long as you move gracefully and do not step on the lady's toes, you should be fine.'

Khalid cannot remember ever having seen anyone dancing in Al Nawaara, which sounds like it is a sinful exercise, and while he is pondering if that might be different in the capital, he stops paying attention to his feet and receives a whack from the sergeant's stick as a reminder that he just put the wrong leg forward.

He screams, and for a moment he feels embarrassed about it, but then the boy next to him screams too. And another, and another, and it goes on until a captain appears.

'Sergeant.'

'Captain Hussein!' Sergeant Aazim salutes him formally before turning to his recruits. 'There is a senior officer in the vicinity! Why are you not saluting him?'

The recruits turn to the captain to make up for their apparent mistake, but their timing is uncoordinated, and it is appallingly chaotic.

'First day,' Sergeant Aazim says apologetically.

Captain Hussein grins forgivingly. 'The commander asked me to check whether you had exchanged the recruits for pigs at some point during the day, for in his tent it sounds like there are a bunch of pigs being slaughtered out here.'

'Sir, I am sorry, but these are the worst recruits ever. They have no stamina, no muscles; I think I would rather have pigs.'

'Well, if God wants it, perhaps you could do something that doesn't make them squeal; the commander is getting annoyed.'

'Certainly, sir!' The sergeant salutes again, and after giving a casual salute in return, the recruits' saviour walks away.

'Sons of whores! You have embarrassed me before two senior officers! If you ever do that again, in the name of God, I will whip each and every one of you until you really have reason to squeal like pigs. Do I make myself clear?'

'Sir, yes sir!'

It's loud and almost in unison, and the sergeant looks so surprised that Khalid has to control himself. If he starts to laugh now, the sergeant will certainly punish him for it, while the only things he wants are some food and his bed.

CHAPTER FIVE

ABDULLAH SON OF SAÍD
Mayasin

Month of Separation 22, 1370 A.H. (18 May 1951 A.D.)

When Abdullah arrives at the small gate on the First Day, he finds Taaraz there.

'Peace be upon you, Abdullah Saíd,' the guard says.

'And upon you, peace,' he answers. He narrows his eyes. It is very unusual for Royal Guardsmen to greet the men who enter the palace. 'Are you waiting here for me?'

'I have orders to escort you to your new office.'

'What new office?'

'Just wait and see and have faith in God.'

Abdullah frowns. He does not know anything about a new office, and there is something in Taaraz's voice he does not like. And by 'God,' does the guard mean God or Lord Tali'a? It is difficult to tell with the men from the Royal Guard. Nonetheless, there is not much he can do but follow him.

Is he in trouble? There was the conversation between the king and the American ambassador two weeks ago, but he has not told a soul about that.

Nevertheless, he is well aware that clerk has become a dangerous profession. Mr Maghreb never returned—not even his family know where he is—and last week a second clerk disappeared. In his little back office, he has heard men whisper about Lord Tali'a and the Royal Guard, but no one dares to voice accusations like that too loudly.

His new office isn't in the back of the palace. In fact, Taaraz is taking him to the little nondescript room where he copied out the minutes for the king's meeting two weeks ago.

'How do you like it?' the guard asks.

'It is perfect,' he answers. It's true. It may be small, but it is a private office almost at the heart of the palace. 'God is praised, but to what do I owe this?'

'Son of Saíd, you are now one of three private clerks for the king.' As if out of thin air, Lord Tali'a has appeared. 'Your prime responsibility will be to take minutes for all cabinet meetings and all other meetings the king holds with his ministers, but you will also assist the king in any other endeavours where he wants assistance. Do you understand?'

'I do, sir. But isn't Mr Petrakis in charge of all secretarial staff?'

'If Mr Petrakis were to keep a better eye on his staff, there would be no need to assign new men. But you do report to Mr Petrakis, yes. Now, tomorrow you will buy yourself a suit, but this week's cabinet meeting is starting in less than two hours, and you'd better prepare.'

Abdullah is sitting in the corner of the great conference room, and opposite him are the king's other two private clerks, who introduced themselves, just before the meeting started, as Haidar and Rashid. Apparently it takes three clerks to take notes for a cabinet meeting, and when the meeting is over they should write the report together, after which Mr Petrakis will read it and order changes to specific details.

Abdullah does not understand this, but today he is glad that he is not alone. While he knows all the ministers' names, he does not know all of their faces yet, nor their voices.

'Majesty, once again I would like to emphasise that it is the position of all of us that those provinces that do not have ministers in this government should not get highways. However, since you are insisting that your highways run straight, we have come up with a new plan,' says the prime minister, Lord Ismat.

The king sighs audibly. 'You want to build three highways.'

'All credit is due to the minister of transport for this brilliant plan,' the prime minister says in a tone that clearly betrays he has come up with the plan himself. 'You will have one highway to Baghdad, one to Riyadh, and one to connect the two!'

'And how much more will this extra highway cost?'

'Majesty, Lord al-Rikabi has inquired with the Germans, and they say that their government will gladly lend us the money if their companies are allowed to build it. Then Lord Raslan did some more inquiring, and he has received similar offers from the French, the Americans, and the British, although we all agree that the British should not be granted the privilege.'

'And how are we going to pay them back?' the king asks.

The prime minister coughs. 'Mr Dagher can tell you all about that part.'

Mr Dagher is the chancellor of the exchequer. The executive orders that used to cross Abdullah's desk in the back office were often chaotic, but when Mr Dagher's name was on them they were always very clear and organised.

'Majesty, since my ministry won't be ready on the First Day of the First Month to implement the new tax system . . .'

'How do you mean your ministry won't be ready?' the king asks sharply. 'You started to prepare for this tax plan years ago. How can you still not be ready?'

'Majesty, when my great-grandfather started my family's book-keeping firm, a hundred years ago, the records of all the companies in Mayasin were so meticulously kept that he struggled to survive. However, when the sultan started to increase his taxes about 1300 years after the Prophet's migration to Medina, companies began to hide their income, until they they just stopped keeping records altogether. Before the revolt started, bookkeeping had become a forgotten skill.

'Majesty, I cannot deny that my family has profited considerably from this, but when I arrived at the treasury, there were forty-three people working there, of whom only seventeen could read. There are approximately twenty thousand people and businesses that will have to pay the tax, and unless we go about it with the utmost care we will create chaos, and we will suffer from that for many years to come.'

'Is that why you brought up the aversion against the income tax three weeks ago?'

Briefly, Abdullah glances up from his paper. The king is speaking to the prime minister, who smiles and says, 'I thought if God wants it, we might announce that your government has postponed the tax for another, say . . . six months. It would be a much better announcement than that we are incapable of enforcing it at this moment.'

'Majesty.' This voice Abdullah does not know. He looks up, but he does not know the face of the man either. 'According to my father, it will also be much better if the income tax is postponed for another year. The police in Mayasin are very worried about what will happen to their income if businesses have to start paying a separate tax to the state. If he cannot guarantee that there will still be enough money for them left after your tax, there might be trouble.'

Abdullah narrows his eyes. This can only be the son of Lord al-Rikabi, the mayor of Mayasin. He writes down: *Father Al-R.*

agrees postponement tax. Police worried about own thieving. Then he crosses out the word 'thieving' and replaces it with 'tax collecting,' albeit with pain in his heart.

'All right,' the king says. 'Lord Ismat, if God wills it, you may announce that we are going to postpone the income tax. Give the people a little more time to prepare.'

Abdullah wants to snort, but he controls himself. He is invisible. The prime minister says, 'Thank you, Your Majesty. Mr Dagher?'

'Yes, Majesty,' the chancellor says. 'To pay for the extra highway, we could shelve building the hospitals in Oyoun al Jabal and Al Jaboulía.'

'Why don't we shelve the hospital in Bab al Din?' the king asks lightly, but the question is followed by one of the men jumping up and slamming his hand on the table.

'Then where do my people go when they get sick?' This must be Lord Raslan, the secretary of state and the son of the governor of Bab al Din.

'Where do they go now?' the king asks.

'Majesty, I am a minister. It is unthinkable that my people don't get a hospital, while the people in Oyoun al Jabal do, when they don't have any ministers!'

'Perhaps, but in Oyoun al Jabal there are more people than in Bab al Rabi and Bab al Din together.'

'Unthinkable!' Lord Raslan repeats.

'And I suppose those schools you want to postpone are in Al Jaboulía and Oyoun al Jabal as well?'

'Majesty,' begins Lord Ismat, 'Al Jaboulía and Oyoun al Jabal should be thanking God that they get this beautiful highway. In fact, this one will even be better than the one you designed, for it will be connected to every important city in the country.'

'Almost every important city,' Lord al-Rikabi says. 'Mashta Gazal won't be connected.'

'Mahsta Gazal doesn't provide any ministers for His Majesty's Government, and all the people there have to trade is salt. I say they can keep it!' Lord Raslan comments.

Except for King Jalal, everyone at the table laughs.

'What if we were to postpone all girls' schools in Bab al Rabi, Baylasan, and Bab al Din and use that money to pay for the highway?' the king asks.

Abdullah nods approvingly to himself but wonders why they had wanted to build schools for girls in the first place. Girls do not need school; they need to raise children and cook.

'Majesty!' Lord Ismat exclaims. 'That is the best plan I have heard in months.'

The prime minister applauds loudly, and the rest of the table follows his example.

'Lord Raslan,' the king says when the table is silent again, 'you may inform the French that they may come to build our highways. I have just postponed the building of at least twenty schools for girls. I will need something to appease my wife.'

More laughter and applause. 'Of course, Your Majesty!'

Abdullah looks at the agenda. The meeting is already well over an hour underway, and they have just crossed off the first point. Seven more to go.

'What do you think?' Haidar asks him when the meeting is over. It is the end of the afternoon, they have only paused briefly for prayers and Abdullah's head is spinning.

'I do not know if my notes are good enough to write a full report,' he answers. 'And I am hungry.'

Haidar smiles. 'They will bring food to your office while you are working on the report. Generally, we all take two hours to work in private on our reports, and then we put everything together. Do you think you can do that?'

'We put everything together tonight?'

'I suppose they did not tell you that your life was pretty much over once you made it to private clerk. But don't worry, you will be compensated in your salary.'

They had not told him, indeed, Abdullah thinks as he walks the short distance from the conference room to his new office. On the other hand, he does not have much of a life to go home to anyway. He . . .

His mind stops working. Around the corner of the hallway comes the most beautiful woman he has ever seen. She is very white, but she has auburn hair, and from fifty feet away he can see her hazel eyes shining. This must be the queen, and she is coming toward him.

He takes a couple steps to the side and presses himself against the wall so that she has ample room to pass him. His heart starts beating faster. What should he do if she starts to talk to him?

He told the guards that he had heard she was exquisite, but now that he has seen her in real life, he realises that the description was completely wrong. This woman is a goddess.

No, that is blasphemous. And what's more, she is not wearing a headscarf. And not only that, she is wearing a dress that clearly shows her left leg every time she puts it forward. And it shows her neck, her shoulders, and her arms, yet Abdullah cannot avert his eyes.

He feels his heart pounding. He feels his penis . . . He looks down; thank God it does not show. He has not felt like this since he was in Siraj's House of Dreams, a lifetime ago. *Please God, forgive me.*

Of course, it is mostly the queen's fault. How can this woman walk around like this? How can the servants work in this palace—how can anyone work in this palace when there are women walking around like this?

The queen does not give him a single look, but his eyes follow her even after she has passed him.

'Hello.' He hears a high female voice, followed by giggles.

In front of him is a girl, while the giggles come from a group of girls following the queen and looking over their shoulders at him.

'Hello,' he answers sheepishly. Thank God the group of girls is now out of earshot.

'And who may you be?' the girl asks.

'My name is . . .' He cannot think of it. He has thought about girls, quite regularly, actually, yet he has never really spoken to one, and now he cannot think of his name. 'I am the king's new private secretary.'

The girl giggles again. This girl is decently dressed and shows only the skin of her face, although her headscarf is tied rather casually, and most of her hair is showing. 'I am one of the queen's ladies, and my name is Kalima Raslan. What is your name?'

'Kalima is a beautiful name,' he says, and as he says it, his own name comes back to him. 'I am Abdullah son of Saíd. Are you the daughter of Lord Raslan, the secretary of state?'

'He is my uncle, and it's Lady Raslan to you,' and with that she pivots and continues in the direction the queen has gone.

'Wait, Lady Raslan,' Abdullah calls. 'Will I see you again?'

She pauses and looks over her shoulder. 'If you are the king's new private clerk, that is very likely.'

Chapter Six

Khalid Khan
Camp Mayasin

Month of Burning 6, 1370 A.H. (10 June 1951 A.D.)

Apart from the fact that the sergeant has moved boxing practice a mile outside of camp, the first weeks are exact replicas of the first day; except for the afternoons of Gathering Day, they are always training, and even though the recruits rise earlier and go to bed later as soon as the holy Month of Burning begins, there is no change to the schedule.

'Jews do not have holy month, so unless you want to be killed on your praying mat, you train.'

It amazes Khalid how quickly his body adjusts to the physical exercise. The first couple of days there were moments when he had considered going home and begging his father for forgiveness. Then, quite suddenly, he felt like he could keep up with the rest of the group. He is not the strongest, the fittest, or the fastest recruit, but he is not the worst either.

They train so hard that they are always hungry, and the only thing they get to eat is porridge, three times a day. Sometimes—these moments seem to be chosen completely at random—there are olives, raisins, or dates added to it, but there is one constant:

it is never enough to satisfy their hunger completely, and they are always looking forward to their next meal. The first day of the Month of Burning, some of the boys had refused the food, since meals were still served during daytime, but Sergeant Aazim said, 'You don't eat, you cannot train. You cannot train, you'll be too weak to fight the Jews. You can eat, or you can go home!'

No one went home.

The first significant change comes after three weeks. So far they've only boxed without an opponent, but today the sergeant has decided they have moved enough air around, and it is time for the recruits to start fighting each other. Khalid finds himself facing a short and skinny boy whom he recognises by his scar as the kid who had stood up to Sergeant Aazim on the first day.

He wonders if the sergeant will still be using his stick to correct their footwork. By now most of the boys can take a couple of hits from it without screaming, and, as he's considering this, he pays no attention to his opponent, who jumps on him the moment the sergeant says, 'In the name of God, go!'

Next thing he knows, he's on the ground with the boy on top of him, and he needs all his energy to protect his face from the blows that are being launched at him.

'Aargh!' he screams. He tries to kick the boy with his knees, but it does not help; he cannot put enough strength behind his legs.

Now the boy is pounding on his chest too. This guy is crazy; if Khalid had dishonoured his sister, the kid would probably not be any more aggressive. For a moment, Khalid wonders what to do. If he calls for the boy to stop or for help from his brother, nobody will ever take him seriously. No, he has to break free, and, in order to do so, he'll have to take some mean punches to his face. Not a cheerful perspective, but he doesn't have any choice. One, two, three . . .

He removes his hands from his face and grabs the boy's shoulders. He feels a punch land on his ear; one on his eye. Now he can reach the boy's face too, and he tries to punch it, but the kid easily diverts his blow.

Another punch lands on his face, but then he manages to put all his weight behind his body and push himself up.

The boy falls off him but is directly back on his feet. Khalid gets up too, albeit a little bit slower. Fortunately, the kid gives him time. The boy's feet are bouncing on the ground, his fists in front of his face and a sinister smile on his lips. 'You want some more?'

'If God wants it, come and get me.' Khalid puts his arms up too.

As they have been practicing, Khalid deals out three straight punches with his left hand, aimed at the boy's nose, and then a full power blow with his right. The boy blocks all four punches and directly comes back with a counterstrike aimed at Khalid's kidney. His block is too slow, and he feels his stomach burning, yet the boy does not stop.

Punch after punch after punch comes his way. Khalid tries to block them, but the boy is so fast. He hits hard, much harder than the kids back in Al Nawaara, harder than Khalid's brother and perhaps even harder than his mother. Meanwhile, Khalid cannot get a single one of his own punches past the lad's defence. Why is he so ferocious?

Another hit; this time he feels his ribs burning. He considers his options. If he isn't going to get a punch in standing, he will throw the boy to the ground and batter him like the boy did to him when their fight started.

God help me, he prays silently before jumping at the boy, who has not expected this, and the next moment he is on top of him. This time it is the kid's turn to protect his face from his blows, but since Khalid's arms are longer, it will be even more difficult for the kid to get out. With all of his strength he pounds at the boy's face and at his body, and to his delight he can hear his opponent grunt.

Then he feels the kid's knee in his balls, contact that is followed by the excruciating pain only a man can feel. That is completely unwarranted! Despite the pain, he is incapable of screaming; the blow sucked all the air out of him. He rolls off the boy, and while he can't even think due to the pain, the boy is already on top of him. He puts his arms up again, but he no longer has the strength to really protect his face.

This is it. The boy will kill him, and Khalid doesn't even know what he has done to deserve it.

'Enough!' It sounds really far away. 'Enough!'

He feels how the boy is pulled off him, and when he looks up, he recognises Sergeant Aazim as his saviour.

Next thing he knows, the sergeant slams the kid in the face with his giant fist. His attacker directly falls down next to him, and then the sergeant kicks Khalid in the ribs. After all the punches he already received, he does not feel the pain, but for the second time in two minutes he is gasping for air.

The sergeant looks around the group. 'When you are on the battlefield, you fight until you are dead. Here, when I say enough, it is enough! When I have to say it more than once, you will be fighting me. Do you understand!?'

'Sir, yes sir!' all the recruits shout, except for Khalid and the kid, who are both lying exhausted on the ground. Khalid prays that he doesn't get another kick to pay for his silence, but the sergeant does not take any more notice of him. Without another word, he turns around and leaves the group. Khalid rolls on his back, closes his eyes, and silently prays.

Gracious God. Thank You for not letting me die here today. Merciful God, with Your help I will never again be careless and let myself fall into the hands of a madman. I bear witness that there is no God but God, and Muhammad is his Prophet.

'Khalid, Khalid,' the voice of his brother says. 'Are you okay?'

'I am alive,' he grunts.

'God is praised, but why did let yourself get beat up like that?' Aadhil reproaches him.

Before he can answer, there is another voice. 'He was stupid; he underestimated me.'

Khalid opens his eyes. Next to him, on his knees, is his brother, and gazing down at him is the kid, who looks even uglier than he did before the fight; his right eye is swollen and his lip is bleeding. He reaches out a hand, and for a second Khalid is doubtful. Should he accept a hand from the guy who has almost beaten him to death? The kid notices his hesitation, and the sinister smile appears again.

He sighs. Not accepting the hand will only show that he was scared. He lifts his arm, which takes more effort than he had anticipated, and the boy pulls him up. Every bone in his body aches.

'Ghulam al-Farooq,' the boy says.

'Khalid Khan,' he grunts, and gesturing with his head to his brother, he adds, 'My brother, Aadhil Khan.'

Ghulam reaches out his hand to Aadhil, but his brother is in no mood to accept it. Instead, he gives him a push, and the kid almost loses his balance. Directly the fists are up again, ready for the next fight.

'Why did you almost kill my brother?' Aadhil demands.

'I did not almost kill him,' Ghulam answers coolly, his fists still up. 'Look, he can stand. If he was almost dead, he would fall to the ground.'

Khalid does feel like falling back to ground, but he does not want to show how badly he's hurting.

'You're crazy!' his brother says angrily, and he spits on the ground. 'I am sure that your mother was a whore and your father a Jew!'

'Aadhil,' Khalid lays his hand on his brother's arm, holding him back, 'it's okay. I am alive.'

His brother shakes his head and spits on the ground again, while Ghulam keeps his hands in the air.

'Your little brother is soft because you protect him,' Ghulam says. 'If I really had been a Jew, he would have been dead; he needs to toughen up.'

Aadhil snorts and looks at Khalid. 'Maybe it is true; you are soft.'

'Of course it's true. Look at him, he is more than a foot taller than me. If he is not soft, how else could I have beaten him?'

'You beat me by cheating.' While Khalid is pleased that his brother and the kid have found some common ground, he does not appreciate that their bridge is being built over his flaws. 'We were supposed to be boxing. You just jumped on me; that is not boxing!'

'We are soldiers, not boxers.' Now it is Ghulam's turn to spit on the ground. 'When you meet the Jew, do you think that he will stick to boxing rules? When the sergeant decides it's time to test you and calls you forward so that you can box him, do you think that he will stick to boxing rules? No. He will kill you.

'This is where we train, and in order to survive we need to fight each other with everything we've got. We need to learn new and nasty tricks, and we need to learn to defend ourselves from those tricks. That is the only way we can get stronger and make ourselves better. If you don't feel like you're dying at the end of the training, you have not trained hard enough.'

'God is great!' Aadhil exclaims. 'The boy's got a point!' He walks toward Ghulam and extends his hand.

After a brief moment of hesitation, Ghulam lowers his fists and accepts the handshake. His brother looks at Khalid. 'God wants me to change my mind. I like this guy.'

Except for the kid who was practicing with Aadhil, a boy named Namdar, the rest of the recruits are already out of sight when they start to make their way back to camp; Ghulam and Khalid are both limping. Aadhil is the only one talking, but his predictions about what they may find in their porridge that evening are interrupted by three jeeps that stop next to them.

They wait to look. Soldiers leave the jeeps first, and then a man in dark blue suit, which is incredibly clean for a man who has been driving through the desert, gets out and slowly makes his way to them.

The man is in his early forties and easily the best-groomed man Khalid has ever seen. He wonders what a man like this is doing here, and clearly his brother is wondering the same.

'Are you lost?' Aadhil calls, and Khalid smiles, but then he feels a hand on his ankle.

He looks down, and on the ground he sees Ghulam, his head pressed deeper in the sand than Khalid has ever pressed it while praying, no matter what sin he had committed. Next to him is the boy named Namdar, who is following his example.

'That is the king, idiot,' Ghulam hisses.

Aadhil starts to laugh, and Khalid can't help but follow. 'Sure he is, and I am an Egyptian pharaoh!'

The soldiers are still standing next to the jeeps, but the man is almost upon them. 'May peace be upon you.'

'And may peace be upon you too,' Aadhil answers. 'My friend there says you are the king.'

'Your friend is right,' the man answers. 'I am King Jalal Amin of Beledar, son of Emir Hussein Amin, who drove out the Turks

199

during the Great Revolution, and descendant of the Prophet Muhammad.'

Startled, Khalid looks at his brother for a fraction of a second before both boys throw themselves to the ground; all of Khalid's limbs punish him for this rash action.

'I told you!' Ghulam hisses, almost inaudible.

They hear the king chuckle. 'Please, young friends, stand up. I am your king, not your god, and I want my soldiers to look me in the eyes.'

Khalid turns his head to his brother, who shrugs and very slowly gets up. He wants to follow his example, but a sharp pain in his back stops him; he can only just keep himself from shouting out.

Then he sees a hand in front of his face. He looks up; it is the hand of the king! Should he take it? Not taking it would mean insulting the king, but he is simply a boy from Al Nawaara, and his hands are extremely dirty; taking it would mean insulting the king as well!

He lifts his hand from the ground, about halfway to the hand of the king, and from there the choice is made for him. King Jalal grabs his hand and pulls him up.

'Rough day?' The king's dark eyes meet his own.

The king is asking him. Not his brother, not Ghulam—him! He feels his comrades staring at him, silently shouting that he should answer. He takes a deep breath.

'If you don't feel like dying at the end of training, then you have not trained well, sir.' Ghulam's words are the only words he can think of, and it is deeply gratifying to see the king's eyes light up.

'That's the spirit! Keep up the good work, and one day I am sure that I will welcome you all as officers in my palace.'

'Thank you, sir.'

The four boys salute their king, who nods at them and turns back to the jeeps.

When the jeeps are long gone, they are still standing there, staring at where the jeeps had been. Eventually it is Ghulam who opens his mouth.

'Sir.' He pauses a second. 'Majesty is what you should have said!'

Khalid looks at him. 'What do you mean?'

'The right title for the king is not "Sir" but "Majesty." Imagine how dumb he must have thought us!'

Aadhil shrugs. 'I don't know. I suppose we should praise God that you had given Khalid a good line just minutes before. Otherwise he would have thought us really dumb. Ha!'

Khalid looks at his brother and their new friend. He wants to say something, but he still cannot speak. The king has just pulled him up from the ground, and he knows that he would die for the man without hesitating.

Chapter Seven

Abdullah son of Saíd
Mayasin

Month of Burning 6, 1370 A.H. (10 June 1951 A.D.)

Abdullah is sitting behind his desk, working on a letter from the king to Lord Tanvir. There have been disturbing reports about slavery in Oyoun al Jabal—just the fact that it still exists is extremely disturbing in the eyes of Abdullah—and the king wants the governor of Oyoun al Jabal to crack down on it. The letter has to be perfectly worded; it cannot lay any blame on Lord Tanvir, while it also has to make clear that if the governor does not put an end to this business immediately, the king will send General Lord Raslan and his regiment to Oyoun al Jabal to intervene.

But he cannot concentrate. Outside his office there appears to be a heated debate going on, and there are actually men screaming. He sighs, stands up, and throws open his door. There is Jafar, the young man who was recently promoted to under butler, two footmen, Taaraz, and two other guards Abdullah does not know.

'In the name of God, could you take your discussion elsewhere?'

'There is no discussion,' Jafar says. 'I am the under butler, and these men have to listen to me!'

'What he is saying is stupid,' Taaraz counters. 'He is forgetting that he works for the king *and* the queen.'

'The butler is my boss, and I follow his rules! We are not going to have a repeat of the situation with Lord Richard. It is my . . .'

'It's your nothing . . .' Taaraz interrupts him. 'I am . . .'

'Shut up!' Abdullah calls, and he does not know if it's his new position or his new suit, but the men listen to him. 'What is the problem?'

'There is a man who wants to see the queen,' Jafar says, 'from France, her home country. And the queen wants to receive him in private!'

Abdullah frowns, but he does not really see the problem. 'You mean in private with her ladies in waiting?'

'I mean *in private*. No ladies. No servants. Just the queen and this Mr Lestrade.'

'That is impossible,' Abdullah says. 'We cannot allow the queen to receive a man in private. What will the king say?'

'The king does not care,' Taaraz barks. 'The king trusts the queen completely. Jafar just referred to Lord Richard; I remember him. He was an Englishman, and when the king was still emir, he visited us. We brought him to the queen because the king was in a meeting, and King Jalal thanked us for it!'

'The king may have thanked you, but my boss scolded me!' Jafar counters. 'The butler decides on etiquette, and in Mr Pasha's absence, that means me.'

Abdullah looks at Jafar. That is strange; the butler is always in the palace. 'Where is Mr Pasha?'

Jafar sighs. 'Replacing the king's valet on some trip; Mr Badran is ill.'

'And what about Lord Tali'a and Mr Petrakis?'

'They have all gone with the king, and now Jafar here believes that he is the man to hold the fort, but he forgets that we work for both the king and the queen,' Taaraz says. 'Abdullah Saíd, you are a man of sense. Tell him!'

'I agree with Jafar,' Abdullah says. 'We work for the king, not for the queen, and it is our duty to protect her and her honour. The queen is a woman and does not understand how men think, which makes her ill fit to make these kinds of decisions. This man Lestrade, she cannot trust him.'

Taaraz snorts and says, 'I was wrong, Abdullah Saíd. You are not a man of sense!' before storming off, followed by the other two guards.

'Don't mind him,' Jafar says. 'I am sure that he will have forgotten all about this by tomorrow.'

Abdullah nods and returns to his office. He is not so sure, and he still can't concentrate on the letter. What in the name of the Prophet can the queen be thinking that she wants to receive a man alone, and how is it possible that this man comes to the palace on the exact day that every man of importance is away?

Hours have passed, but he still hasn't finished his letter. It's useless, and maybe he should take a walk through the palace garden. The jacarandas are blooming, and now that he's a private clerk, he has access. He stands up and leaves his office, but he doesn't get far. In the next hallway there's a girl leaning against the wall, crying.

'Lady Raslan?' he asks.

She looks up but does not reply.

'What is it?'

She shakes her head, and suddenly he wonders if they are tears from sorrow or from anger. 'She made us sin.'

'What do you mean, she made you sin?' Abdullah asks.

'She forced us to drink alcohol so that she could speak with a man in private. Either we drank champagne or she would send us home! Can you imagine me being sent back to Bab al Din? If my father didn't kill me, I would die there!'

Abdullah does not exactly understand what Lady Raslan means by that, yet he is enraged that the queen has made Lady Raslan drink alcohol. He has committed the sin himself out of his free will, but he was very young. To force someone, a girl, is monstrous! To do it during the Month of Burning . . . He does not know a word for that.

If it were allowed, he would hold her and tell her that everything is going to be okay, but he does not dare touch her and instead offers her his pocket square so that she can use it to dry her tears.

'Can I get you something, Lady Raslan? A glass of water, perhaps, or some tea?'

The girl blows her nose and looks into his eyes. 'It's not that I don't want to leave the palace, you know. If I could, I would leave tomorrow. But I want to go in a respectable way, and I definitely don't want to leave Mayasin.'

Abdullah looks down; the girl's eyes are too much for him. Why is she telling him this? It's not like there's anything he can do about it. To change the subject, he asks, 'Do you know what the queen and Mr Lestrade spoke about?'

She tilts her head a little and he realises that she had not told him the man's name. But she does not question him about it, and he is glad that he doesn't have to admit that he is, partly, responsible for what happened.

'They were speaking in French, and the queen said she did not know anything about politics, which I know is not true. I swear by the Quran that she reads most of the cabinet reports. Anyway, they started to talk about a woman named Coco, and the queen said that this woman was only exiled for her anti-Semitism because she was famous, and that twenty years ago everyone in

Paris hated Jews. And then he said that a man named Salvador had become *persona non grata* as well and that an Italian priest had performed a successful exorcism on him, and that he was now crazier than ever.'

He raises his eyebrows. Either she is still drunk or the queen and Mr Lestrade have been talking in some kind of code. 'And that was it?'

She shakes her head. 'They also spoke about her brother. That he is a communist and that he will go down in the history books as a war hero, but that this was because French historians loved fiction. And there was more, much more, but the queen kept refilling our glasses, and I could not concentrate, and then they went into the garden, and I could no longer hear them.'

Lady Raslan starts to sniff again, and Abdullah can see the tears flowing down her face. He feels terribly guilty. If he had sided with Taaraz, Lady Raslan would never have been in the room, and she would not have been forced to sin.

'Is there anything I can do?'

She shakes her head, but then she appears to think of something. 'You could get me out of here.'

'And how would I do that?'

'You know how.'

Is she implying what he thinks she is implying? Does she want him to marry her? That is absurd; her family would never allow it!

'I am just a boy from the worst neighbourhood of Mayasin,' he says.

'No,' she answers suddenly, much more firmly, 'you are a private clerk of the king. Will you think about it?'

He nods, and in that second he has thought about it. It is impossible, but who knows, maybe in a couple of years. 'I suppose I will see you later then, Lady Raslan.'

It is her turn to nod, and he turns around and starts to walk back to his office. Suddenly a hand grabs his arm. It is a small hand, her hand, and it sends a shock through his body. Electrified, he pivots.

'And Abdullah, in the name of God, never tell anyone that I speak French.'

He shakes his head.

'Swear it!' she demands.

'By the Quran, I swear it.'

She nods and leaves him behind, befuddled.

'Son of Saíd, tell me, has your brother returned to God?' the scholar asks. It is Gathering Day, and while Abdullah is much too late for the most important prayer, he has decided to visit the Green Mosque anyway.

'I do not know. All I know is that he has found a job in a hotel to support himself and that his grades are good.'

The scholar smiles. 'Then he is on his way. We will continue to pray for him, and if God wants it, he will soon take the last steps too.'

'God is Merciful, Reverend.'

'God is Merciful,' the scholar confirms, and he looks at Abdullah, who is clearly still troubled. 'Tell me, why have you come?'

Abdullah sighs. He has thought a long time about whether he should confide in the scholar, but now that he is here, he does not know if he can speak. Mr al-Rubaie waits for him to say something and when it is clear that he won't, the scholar says, 'I am afraid I cannot help you if I do not know what your problem is.'

Abdullah sighs, but still he cannot say it. The scholar is not in haste, though, and patiently waits, while all he can do is stare at the floor until finally, Mr al-Rubaie says, 'Is it a woman?'

He nods, and the scholar continues. 'Of course it is a woman. Dangerous creatures, women. Ever since the Lady Helen—do you know the Lady Helen?' Abdullah shakes his head. 'Three thousand years ago, she was the most beautiful woman in the world. When she was taken from her husband, all the lords of Greece united to get her back. Many wars have been fought over women since Lady Helen and even more to impress them.

'But this is irrelevant. Is she married? That would be a problem indeed. Nevertheless, you are not the first man to face this problem, and God will give you strength if you ask for it.'

'Reverend, I fear that the queen is playing a trick on the people of Beledar,' he blurts out before he bows his head again. He has said it, and he cannot say more, even though he feels the friendly eyes of the scholar on him.

'We are all sinners, Abdullah, but that does not condemn us,' Mr al-Rubaie says. 'I believe that it is best if we let God judge the queen, while we look after our own lives.'

Not in this case. Mr al-Rubaie does not know what Abdullah knows. 'I know, but I . . .' He sighs and looks straight into the eyes of the scholar. 'The queen walks through the palace like a whore, and she forces her maids to drink alcohol during the holiest of months so that she can plot with men from her country.'

'Son of Saíd.' Suddenly the scholar's voice is very strict, and Abdullah realises he has just compared the queen of Beledar to a whore! 'I am going to pretend that I have not heard what you have just said, and you will never repeat it to anyone.'

He nods and says, 'Yes, Reverend, I'm sorry.'

'Do not ask me forgiveness. Ask God. Now, for the matter at hand, you are a grown man, you have a good position and you do not have a wife. Tell me, what are you doing about that?'

The scholar is right, of course. He should never have spoken like this about the queen. Instead, he should be here to discuss his own life. Just so that he does not seem completely worthless when it comes to taking care of himself, he answers, 'In fact, there is a girl . . .'

'God is praised!' The scholar sounds truly joyful, as though he has already forgotten Abdullah's outrageous words. 'Tell me about her!'

'She is beautiful,' Abdullah answers. 'But I fear that she is not for me.'

'Why not?'

'She is the granddaughter of Lord Raslan, the governor of Bab al Din, and the niece of Lord Raslan, the secretary of state.'

'In the eyes of God, all men are equal, no matter their title or position,' the scholar counters, once again strict.

'Of course they are,' Abdullah answers a little too quickly, since he knows the scholar is right, and he has not thought of anything to follow these words. 'But still, her family will never allow it.'

'The Raslans are good Muslims,' the scholar says. 'They know that all men are equal. Let's make a deal: I will write to her father that you are a good man with good prospects, and when he answers me that he will gladly accept you as his son-in-law, you will take your family to dinner at her uncle's house.'

'My family to dinner at the house of the secretary of state?'

'Of course! They will need to know where you come from, and since you have God at your side, what can go wrong?'

He can think of a million things. First of all, what will they say when they see his mother? He sighs. It was Lady Raslan herself who had suggested it, and with Mr al-Rubaie's introduction and God at his side, he might just have a chance.

'You know what?' says the scholar, seeing him doubt, 'I will even accompany you!'

'You would do that for me?'

'Son of Saíd, every man needs a good woman, and if you have found one, it's my duty to make sure that you get her.'

CHAPTER EIGHT

CORPORAL KHALID KHAN
Camp Nardin

Month of Respect 13, 1371 A.H. (7 April 1952 A.D.)

'You're too young to be a corporal. It is written,' growls Colonel Issa, a small man with a big moustache, while smoke comes out of his mouth. Khalid does not answer. The commander puts the cigar back in his mouth and gives him a long stare. Eventually he shakes his head, and without removing the cigar, he adds, 'The men will not like you.'

Khalid stands as straight as he can, yet he still does not answer. He has earned his position and takes great pride in the fact that he was promoted before his brother and Ghulam. Whether or not the men will like him, he is not going to give it up voluntarily.

'You're going to lead men who have been in the army for years, some of them twice your age,' the colonel continues as though he has read Khalid's mind. He takes his cigar from his mouth, throws the ash on the ground—even though there is an ashtray on the table—and puts it back. 'But if Command says you're to be a corporal, if God wills it, you are going to be a corporal. By the Prophet, if someone up there decided that you were going to be a lieutenant, I'd give you your own platoon. If the king made you a general, I would salute you. That's how our modern army operates.

'A couple years ago, there was a battalion that tried to implement the natural order of things, God's order. The kids that got demoted didn't complain; they knew that was how it was supposed to be. Nonetheless, Lord Tali'a hanged its commander.'

'Why, sir?' Khalid asks.

'Why?' The colonel spits on the ground. 'Because Lord Tali'a is no fool, and we already have enough stupid men in senior positions. It has been 1,370 years since the Prophet emigrated to Medina, and with modern weaponry one dumb decision can cost us a platoon, a company, or even a whole battalion. We do what we can to limit the amount of dumb people making decisions. Sometimes we are more successful than other times.

'But in peacetime, the most senior men in the most senior positions will do just fine . . . Causes the least amount trouble, so to speak.'

'Perhaps you could assign me only new soldiers, sir, if God wills it. There were some other kids on the truck who were pretty young, too,' Khalid ventures.

The commander shakes his head. 'That is not possible either. You're new and they're new. We need to split you new kids so that you can integrate and adjust. If God wants it, you will get one kid from your draft in your section."

Khalid nods. 'Sir, I don't know if I get any say, but if I do, can he be Namdar Jumblatt? We worked together really well during training.'

After they met the king, there had been a special bond between the four boys, and they had agreed that they'd always support each other. *One for all and all for one*, like in the book Khalid had brought with him. But Aadhil and Ghulam were sent to different regiments, and only Namdar has come to Nardin with Khalid. He hardly knew the rest of the kids on the bus.

'I really don't care,' barks the commander before pausing for a moment. 'Sure, take Namblatt. Now, Alif company is short of a corporal. You are to report to Captain Madani.'

Khalid doesn't bother to correct the commander on his friend's name. He salutes and says, 'God is praised, sir!' before leaving the commander's tent as quickly as he can.

Captain Madani doesn't look like he's ever undergone the same kind of rigorous training as Khalid went through. He's incredibly fat, and he has a huge beard from which Khalid can tell what he has eaten for dinner the previous evening, while the caterpillars under his eyes make him look as though he has not slept for days.

'At ease, Corporal,' he utters lazily.

'Captain, Colonel Issa sent me to report to you.'

'I'm sure he has. A little bird told me that a new corporal would be joining my company one of these days. Nonetheless, you look more like a toddler than a corporal. How old are you?'

'Almost nineteen, sir.' In fact, Khalid is barely eighteen, but 'almost' is a relative concept.

'Almost nineteen, eh? You know, I was nineteen when I married; daughter of a great lord. Figured I would not have to work too much after that, and I could out live the rest of my life in peace.

'And I did; many years I had complete peace—apart from the wife and children, of course. Then one day my father-in-law comes home from Mayasin and tells me that he has found me an honourable position. Two months later, I am an officer in the king's newly formed army, imagine that.'

'It's very honourable, sir.'

'More like very tiring,' he grunts. 'Very honourable, ha! At home I have five children, and when I was there, most of the time I thought that was five too many. Here I have seventy-three, and it seems that the older they get, the less mature they become. So perhaps it is a good thing you are a young man, right?'

'Perhaps it is, sir.'

'We'll see. Now, if God wants it, go and report to Lieutenant Fakeih from second platoon.'

Lieutenant Fakeih is a man in his mid-thirties, and when Khalid walks into his small tent to report, the lieutenant looks even more incredulous than the colonel.

'You are my new corporal?' he exclaims. 'But you are just a boy! By the Prophet—may God bless him and protect his soul—is this a joke?'

Khalid does not want to appear weak in the eyes of his new commanding officer and says, as loudly as he can, 'Colonel's orders, sir.'

'Well, in that case . . .' the lieutenant replies sarcastically and sighs. 'Let it be noted that I am accepting you under protest.'

Khalid looks around; there is nobody to note anything, and he wonders if he should make that note, but before he can ask, Lieutenant Fakeih continues, 'You'll take the section of Sergeant al-Jasser. Go find him, if God wills it. It might be difficult, because he's always running around doing'—the lieutenant makes a weird gesture with his hand—'*things*.'

The sergeant indeed proves tricky to find. Several times Khalid is pointed in the wrong direction, but when he has almost given up hope, he literally bumps into him right in front of his platoon's tent.

'By the Prophet, man, watch where you're going; you've made me lose my smoke!'

'I am sorry, sir,' he says softly. 'I am looking for Sergeant al-Jasser . . .'

'Well, you've found him.' The man cuts him off before lighting a new cigarette. 'You the new corporal?'

'Yes, sir,' Khalid answers, looking up. The sergeant is gaunt and tall. Very tall.

'Finally.' The sergeant grabs Khalid's hand and squeezes it as though he is testing how much pressure the young man's bones can withstand before they break. 'Finally, our platoon is complete! For the past two months I have had three jobs, did you know that? The lieutenant, you've met him, right?'

'Yes, sir.'

'In the name of God, don't call me *"Sir."* Non-coms address each other on a first-name basis, and my name is Shamil.' The sergeant starts to walk again, and Khalid follows while trying to pay close attention to the man's words. Never before has he met a man who speaks as rapidly as Sergeant Shamil. 'The only non-coms you address as "Sir" are the sergeant major and the master sergeants. Don't forget; they're not the friendliest chaps 'round here, but don't hold that against them. A friendly SM or MS isn't very useful. Do you understand?'

'Yes, *Shamil*.' This feels outlandish.

'All right, first things first. You've met the lieutenant, right?' Khalid nods a little hesitantly. Has the sergeant already forgotten that he asked that half a minute ago? 'So you know that he's an idiot. Of course, it is natural for a platoon sergeant to take on a lot of work from a lieutenant, just like it's natural for a master sergeant to take on work from the captain, but in our case it's a disgrace. I mean, Captain Madani's a bit off, but Lieutenant Fakeih's an idiot; the man can't even read. He pretends to read, but he's actually looking at dirty drawings. I've tested him; can't read for shit. Can you read?'

'I can.' Khalid looks around. Surely, if someone overhears Sergeant al-Jasser, he will be severely punished for these remarks; maybe they will even hang him. But there is nobody around to hear.

The anxious look in his eyes does not go unnoticed by the sergeant. 'I know, better not say that shit, but it's true. He can't write, he can't read, not even a map. We all know it. You know he's been in the army from the start?'

The sergeant takes a new cigarette from the inside of his pocket and uses his old one to light it. 'His uncle's Lord Raslan, know him? Governor of Bab al Din. That's why he's a lieutenant. Six years and a governor for an uncle; should have been a major by now. Bad luck they didn't send him to Palestine. Now he'll get us killed in the next war.'

Picturing the man Khalid had met half an hour ago in an actual war causes enough distraction for him to lose track of the story the sergeant is telling him, and when he realises that he's not listening anymore, he tries to bring back his focus.

'. . . both the job of platoon sergeant and the job of section commander. D'you think I get extra money? No. Let Shamil do all the work, but don't give him extra money. Shamil, write the report! Shamil, command Muhammad's old section! Shamil, update the logbooks . . .'

Khalid just nods, and fortunately no answer is expected as the sergeant continues. 'All right, let's talk about your duties. D'you know what we do at this station?'

'We guard the border with Iraq?' It sounds more like a question than Khalid had intended.

'Yes. No. Yes, but not really. There is one battalion here and no artillery; if the Iraqis attack us here, better run. D'you know where you run to when they come?'

'Nardin?' It's the nearest city.

Sergeant Shamil laughs out loud. 'That's not even a bad idea. Run to the Forbidden Chambers in Nardin for one last quickie with your favourite chickie. However, first you run to the M38s, and you take one. Once you have made sure that I'm on one as well, we ride north to Nareng, where the real base is situated.'

For a second he is quiet, and Khalid uses the opportunity to ask, 'M38s?'

'Yes, M38! Due to lack of tanks, the pride of our battalion. Jeeps!' the sergeant clarifies in a tone that says Khalid should have known this already. 'Now, If all M38s are gone, you can go to Nardin. I'll even come with you. Whatever you do, though, do not stay here and fight. There are no bunkers, nor is there any other kind of protection. In short: you will die. D'you understand?'

Khalid nods.

'All right, because we don't guard the border anyway, we're more like a customs station. D'you know what that means?'

'We check whether there are illegal products being smuggled into Beledar?'

'Exactly! And d'you know what illegal products are?' the sergeant asks.

'Weapons.' In camp he had read in a newspaper that the government instituted a new law that said only soldiers and policemen were allowed to own weapons.

'That's correct. What else?'

What else? He thinks long and hard, but he cannot think of anything. 'I do not know, sir.'

'Don't call me sir.' Khalid wants to apologise, but the sergeant does not give him the opportunity. 'All right. The point is, stuff's illegal as long as nobody's paid any taxes. It'll be your duty to levy those taxes. Everything that goes out of Beledar's taxed, and everything that comes into Beledar's taxed as well. The same with people. People who leave Beledar have to purchase an exit visa, and people who come into Beledar an entrance visa. The more money they've got, the more they'll have to pay. D'you understand?'

'Not exactly.'

'All right. You get paid nine shillings a week, correct?' Khalid nods. 'Now that's three shillings more than a normal soldier, but still, it's hardly enough to take care of a family. In times of war, we can look forward to the spoils of victory. You know: loot, women, that kind of thing—or so we've been promised. In times of peace we have to supplement our income ourselves, and we do that here.

'It's your job to determine how much every man that passes our station is worth, and a good corporal makes sure that he makes a lot of money, for his superiors but also for his men. There are a couple of real bastards in your section, and if you don't make them rich, they'll only get worse. On the other hand, if you do make them rich, they'll eat from your hand. Understand now?'

Khalid nods, but he does not like it. If he had wanted to hustle for pennies, he might as well have stayed at home.

'All right! Let's go over the rules. Make sure you write them down, or at least that you don't forget them.' Khalid has a note-book, but the sergeant doesn't wait for him to get it out. 'The first rule is: everybody pays! It doesn't matter how poor, young, old, pretty, dangerous, or important someone is, everybody pays! If the king's standing in front of that boom bar, you're allowed to make an exception, but everybody else pays.'

'What if someone comes here who does not have any money?'

'Then that man is a fool. Everybody knows that one must pay to cross the border.' The sergeant pauses for a second. 'But you're right, some men really don't have any money. If these idiots want to cross, they'll have to work at the camp to pay for their crossing. There are always some privates who have nasty jobs or *some need* that could be fulfilled in exchange for a little money.'

Khalid nods again; this is not making it any better.

'All right,' Shamil continues. 'Rule number two: foreigners pay double. Foreigners don't pay any taxes, but when they visit our country they do use our facilities. It's only right that they should contribute. D'you not agree?'

'I do.' It seems to be the only acceptable answer.

'Good.' They have entered a small tent, and the sergeant sits down behind a desk and gestures to Khalid to take a chair in front of the desk. 'Then there's rule number three: all travellers are stingy, and they'll do everything they can to pay as little as possible to cross the border. Rich men'll dress themselves up as poor men, and merchants carrying gold and jewels will hide them in cheap foods or blankets. It's your job to distinguish the rich from the poor and to determine how much a man can pay.'

Khalid nods again, even though he has no idea how he's going to determine that. The sergeant doesn't even look at him, though, and continues. 'There are certain tariffs. The starting tariff is a shilling for the poorest people from Nardin, while the maximum for a rich man from Nardin is a pound. You will soon get to know the people there; learn who's rich and who's not. It shouldn't be difficult for you to distinguish between them.

'For the rest of the travellers from Beledar, you should charge anything between two shillings and two pounds, depending on how much money you think they have. But with merchants, it's slightly different. You don't just charge them to enter or to leave our country. They'll need permits as well.'

He takes a stack of different coloured pads from a drawer in the desk. 'Look, these yellow ones are permits to use our roads; red are export permits, which means that you're allowed to take stuff that was produced in Beledar over the border to sell. These green ones, are import permits.' The sergeant keeps putting different sheets on the table, one by one. 'Gasoline permit; general trading permit; gemstone trading permit; silk trading permit; alcohol permit; permit to employ people here, for when someone brings a chauffeur or servants; and a blank permit for occasions when you think special permits are required.

'A small merchant, he will need a general trading permit. Generally, it will cost one pound; maybe he'll also need an import permit, but beware: if you overcharge him, he cannot make a profit, and he will not come here next time. You don't want to do that, because no merchant means no taxes. A large trader, on the other hand, with jewellery, more than two camels, or even a truck, he will need many permits, and because he has much stuff to trade, they will also need to be more expensive.'

The sergeant pauses for a moment to light his next smoke, and Khalid realises that his father would be a large trader. Perhaps one day his father will even pass through here. If he is the man levying taxes on his father that day, his old man will definitely not be proud.

'I should warn you,' the sergeant continues. 'There can be no complaints that you're overcharging. Should a traveller or merchant complain about you to the colonel and Commander Issa decides that he has good grounds for it, you have a problem. You and your squad will get only night shifts for at least two months, and they will not thank you for it. Merchants do not travel through here at night; savvy?'

Khalid nods. 'Everybody pays the right amount.'

'Exactly, everybody pays, but some pay more than others, which brings me to rule number four. You can import and export everything as long as you are willing to pay the price. We are not policemen and we are not judges; we are soldiers. Fighting is our business; this is how we feed our families. After all, why would we risk our lives if our families are starving back home?' It is a rhetorical question, and without taking a breath the sergeant continues. 'Somebody wants to come into this country or leave it without any papers? You say no problem, as long as you pay enough. You find boxes of liquor? These people will need an expensive permit for that, or they can leave it at the border station.'

Khalid shakes his head. His job description does not sound like something the Holy Quran would approve of, but these men have been here for years; they must know better. 'So what is the fifth rule?'

Shamil looks straight at him and says gravely, 'A soldier always shares,' before taking a drag from his cigarette.

'Half of all the taxes your squad collects is for us. Of that half, a quarter is for yourself, a quarter is for me and the lieutenant— God knows why we give him money, but that's the rule—the rest is for your men. The other half we give to the sergeant major, who makes sure it ends up in the places it is supposed to end up.

'If you should somehow forget about the first rule, you can always pay people yourself at the end of the day. If you forget the fifth or decide that you think fifty-five percent for us and forty-five for the sergeant major is fairer, or if someone in your squad decides that he can slip an extra shilling into his pocket when nobody is watching, nasty accidents happen. The previous corporal that led your squad was not a very good mathematician.'

Khalid gets the message, but the sergeant feels the need to elaborate anyway.

'You are a young man, so I suppose you were given this position on merit. I have high hopes for you, and I'd hate it if your career in the army came to the same abrupt ending as your predecessor's did, not least because it would mean that I would have to take on an extra job again. Do I make myself clear?'

'Yes, sir. Very clear.'

Shamil gives him an angry look.

'I mean yes, Shamil.'

Chapter Nine

Abdullah son of Saíd
Mayasin

Month of Respect 18, 1371 A.H. (9 April 1952 A.D.)

'Mr Saíd.' Abdullah looks up and sees Mr Petrakis in the doorway. 'The American and the British ambassador are visiting the king tonight. Please inform Haidar and Rashid that they will be working late. You may decide for yourself who to send to the Yank and who to the Brit.'

'Mr Petrakis, Haidar and Rashid have both been working very late all week. What if I were to take on one of the meetings, while we let one of them have an early night?'

'Certainly not, Mr Saíd. You are senior clerk, and that means you delegate work like this. You already work late every First Day, and if you start doing the work of your juniors, soon people will start saying, "Why are the clerks always working late while the king's secretary is playing cards?" We would not want that now, would we?'

'No, sir.'

The king's secretary shakes his head. 'Go home to your new house. Let your wife cook for you, and if she bores you, go into the city and have some fun!'

Abdullah sighs. Haidar and Rashid are more than ten years his senior, they have held the position of private clerk for much longer and they both attended university, yet two days before his marriage, he was promoted to senior clerk. No new clerk was appointed to replace him, and a lot of his work simply fell to Haidar and Rashid, yet they never complained.

At first he thought it was Lord Raslan, the uncle of his Kalima, who had arranged his promotion, but as the months went by, a pattern emerged. Aside from passing on orders from Mr Petrakis to Haidar and Rashid, he has not received any real new responsibilities. However, he is no longer privy to any meeting with foreign ambassadors and businessmen, and letters to the governors with no family members in the cabinet no longer originate from his pen either. He is sorry about that. These were complicated letters, and signing the king's name made him feel terribly important.

Standing in front of his house in Dhamar, he has already forgotten all about his worries. Every day when he gets home he spends at least ten minutes standing outside, staring at the mansion and thanking God that he, Abdullah son of Saíd, a boy from Kobajjeb, owns a house in Dhamar!

Of course, Abdullah knows that this is mostly thanks to his new father-in-law, who presented him with a very gracious dowry on the day that he married Kalima. Yet it is he who has given the money a great cause.

The house has five bedrooms, and while two of them are occupied by his little sisters and his mother at the moment, when his sisters get married they will provide ample room for a very large family. With the money that has come with his new job he is even able to afford a servant woman who cleans and cooks. The latter is especially fortunate; he quickly discovered that Kalima never learned to cook, yet she refused to give control over the kitchen to his mother.

His wife has other qualities, though. For one, she is already pregnant, and she has promised Abdullah that his first child is going to be a boy.

'Abdullah.' He recognises his brother Samir's voice, but the young man who calls him bears little resemblance to the boy with whom he argued a year ago about behaving like a good Muslim. This man wears a spotless tunic instead of worn jeans, and he has a small beard that makes him look five years older.

'I have come to apologise,' Samir says. 'I understand now that I did not have my priorities right and that my duty lies to God.'

Abdullah smiles. Mr al-Rubaie was right: his brother has returned to God! 'Fortunately, God is merciful.'

They hug and kiss each other. 'Of course, I also could not let you live alone in this big house with all these women!'

Abdullah raises his eyebrows. 'You know, I will not be living alone with these women for too long. I have a son coming soon!'

'God is praised!' his brother exclaims, and they hug again.

'Come inside, and I will show you the house. Now that you are here, I will tell Kalima that from this moment on we will be taking our meals together, and that the women can eat after us.'

When he enters the bedroom later that night, Kalima is not yet asleep. That is unfortunate. She always wants to talk, whereas Abdullah just prefers to undress as quickly as he can, lie down, and close his eyes, especially after a night like tonight.

After their marriage, Kalima asked him if he wanted to take his meals alone. Afraid that would be terribly dull, he told her no, but it was a decision he spent the next year regretting. Listening to his wife, his mother, and his sister babble on about the most meaningless things has been excruciating. Now that his brother is here, there is no longer a reason to eat with the women, and tonight he has made the most of it, only speaking to Samir while avoiding the rest of them altogether.

'How was your day?' Kalima asks.

'It was fine,' he answers. 'Not much happened.'

'How is the queen?'

'I haven't seen the queen today.'

'And the king, did anything interesting happen in the meetings?'

He sighs. The same questions every day. 'You know I cannot tell you about that; it is forbidden.'

'Fine,' she answers, but instead of the normal 'who am I going to tell' routine, tonight she asks, 'How is your brother?'

'As a matter of fact, he's doing very well. I am pleased to say that he has returned to God and that we can be very proud of him.'

'I am very happy for you. Is he still working in that hotel?'

'No. In fact, in his free time he's now working for an organisation called the Muslim Brotherhood.'

'What is that?'

'It's a religious organisation that provides healthcare and education to people who cannot afford it. At the moment they mostly operate in Gorgan, that new quarter in the east of the city, to where all those people from the country and the people who can no longer afford Kobajjeb are moving.'

'Why is the king not providing healthcare and education there?'

Abdullah shrugs. 'I believe the king is spending most of the money on the army these days. And he is building girls' schools in the country . . .'

'That's the queen's doing,' Kalima interrupts. 'She was always talking about jobs for women and schools for women.'

'Maybe,' Abdullah answers, irritated by the interruption, as he turns off the light. 'Goodnight.'

Intermission:

King Jalal
Mayasin

Month of Pilgrimage 20, 1372 A.H. (9 September 1952 A.D.)

Normally, Jalal sits on the windowsill of his office when he drinks, but tonight he has a terrible longing to talk to someone. He could pay a visit to his wife's bedroom, but considering that he is already quite drunk, that can only end in one of two ways: in half an hour they'll either be having sex or she will be scolding him that he isn't improving the position of women in the country rapidly enough. And the latter is really unfair—he's doing all he can and she knows it.

But perhaps he's also being unfair to her. She won't scold him; she never does. But they may end up discussing the position of women, and he is definitely not in the mood for that tonight.

Perhaps he should pay a visit to Lord Tali'a. He looks at his watch. Only thirty minutes past midnight, not a very disrespectful time for a king to pay a visit to his most important servant. He takes his glass and starts to make for the door, but then he reconsiders. Better take a bottle too.

Outside his door, a footman and two guards are standing. 'Men, I just want to take this opportunity to tell you that you're all doing an excellent job!'

INTERMISSION

'Thank you, Majesty!' the men answer. Look how proud they are! He should get out of his office more often when he is drinking.

He starts to walk, not in any particular direction, and in the next hallway he runs into his new senior clerk. Once this lad had high potential, like Rashid and Haidar, sent by Mr al-Rubaie, fluent in English and highly intelligent. But his marriage is a serious cause for concern.

'Good evening, Mr Saíd,' he says.

'Good evening, Majesty,' the young man answers. Is there a look of disapproval in the clerk's eyes? He takes a sip from his whisky; there it is.

'How's Lady Raslan treating you?'

'Very well, Majesty, thank you.'

'Raslan.' He nods and repeats it, placing extra emphasis on both syllables, 'Ras-lan.'

The clerk gives him an uncomprehending look, and he decides that the lad will not make for interesting conversation. 'Well, keep up the good work.'

He continues his expedition until, after a couple of minutes, he realises that he has no idea where the commander's office is. He looks around and sees two guards at the end of the hallway.

'You men!' he shouts, and they start to approach him. 'Take me to your commander.'

'Of course, Majesty,' one of the men answers, and they start to lead him through hallways he cannot remember visiting before.

As a child, he had roamed through the palace once or twice, but it had been very dull on his own. If he'd had any brothers, perhaps he would have gone exploring more often, but despite his many wives, his father had not fathered any children aside from Jalal. None that lived, anyway. He vividly remembers his

229

father cursing at God when the Most Merciful had taken another of his sons.

'Here we are,' a guard says when they arrive at an open door in one of the most distant corners of the palace, although Jalal isn't sure if they are still in the palace at all.

He looks through the opening, and the first thing that catches his eye is a map on the wall opposite to him—a wall that is much too close to the door.

'Majesty, what can I do for you?' Lord Tali'a is sitting behind a tiny table, although perhaps not tiny compared with the rest of the room, and apart from a small chair and some candles, there is nothing else in there. No books, except for the one in the commander's hand, no papers, no cabinet—nothing.

'Is this really your office? No wonder it took me ten years to find this place!' Jalal says. 'I came to bring you a drink.'

'No, thank you, Majesty.'

'Oh, come on Commander, I order you to have a drink with me!'

Lord Tali'a gives him a look that would certainly have scared him if he were not the king, but then the commander says, 'In that case, I would be delighted.'

'Excellent!' He steps forward, but then he realises he only has his own glass. He looks back at the door; the guards that led him to the office have disappeared.

It doesn't matter. He can drink from the bottle. He refills his glass, gives it to the commander, sits down, and raises the bottle.

'Lord Tali'a, why didn't you let my uncles betray me? You are, by all accounts, a good Muslim, so why did you save me? I mean, I know myself, and I am sure that they were better Muslims than me.'

The commander looks at his glass and takes a little sip before answering. 'Majesty, when you were in England, your father used to pass on your letters, and I was impressed with the observations you made. In fact, I still remember what you wrote.

' "*The English, they see their people as capital and by investing in them—educating them and improving their health—they increase their productivity, which in turn increases the wealth and power of the nation as a whole.*"

'And you had plans to end the corruption of the lords, the unfair treatment of women, and to make this country the greatest in the region.

'Majesty, despite what people say, to be a good Muslim is not about praying five times a day or making pilgrimages to Mecca; it is about doing what is right. You wanted to improve our country; your uncles wanted to be king.'

'Well, in that case I suppose I must be a bitter disappointment. It takes a crippled old man less time to cross the desert than it takes me to build enough schools for the people. The lords are mightier than ever, and I am actually sustaining their corruption in order to achieve my wife's ideals.'

'But they are good ideals, Majesty! And I never thought that you would achieve your goals overnight; you must remember that it took Gabriel twenty-three years to reveal the Quran to Muhammad. What matters is that whenever there is no good choice, you keep on making the right one.'

The commander's glass is almost empty, and Jalal decides the man needs a refill. 'What about the map? Why do you have that map on the wall?'

'It helps me set my priorities.' Lord Tali'a stands up, and Jalal follows his example. The commander points at Syria. 'As you know, a couple of years ago President al-Atassi tried to unite his country with Iraq, a move which would have started the struggle for a great Arab empire. Nonetheless, Iraqi ambitions have not disappeared without Syria, and less than a year from now, Faisal's grandson, Faisal II, will be king. Since he cannot have Syria, he will come after Beledar.'

'We're going to have a war?' That was not exactly what Jalal had expected to hear when he decided to go out and find Lord Tali'a's office an hour ago.

'Only God knows these things for sure, but I believe it to be highly likely.'

Jalal puts the whisky bottle to his lips and takes a large swig. 'Wars are expensive.'

'Yes, they are, but they are also opportunities.'

'How do you mean?'

'They are opportunities for men who are not related to the lords to make a name for themselves. They are opportunities for us to start putting men who are loyal to us in key positions in the army.'

'You mean men like Issa and al-Dahabi?' The commander nods. 'We are going to need a lot more than one war to cleanse the army of the lords' family members.'

'We definitely will.' Lord Tali'a looks at him and kills his drink; somehow Jalal has never felt this close to the man. 'But it's a start.'

Part IV

WAR

CHAPTER ONE

CORPORAL KHALID KHAN
Camp Nardin

Month of Respect 20, 1372 A.H. (4 April 1953 A.D.)

Victory. Khalid can still feel the adrenaline shooting through his veins. It was very close, but in the end his plan came together perfectly. Behind him, his men are celebrating enthusiastically, and Khalid is reminded that they are quite decent fellows—as long as they win.

To keep the soldiers focused on their training, every week games are organised at the camp. Prizes are things like extra meat and furlough days for the winners, while losers get latrine duty. Khalid's squad is on a winning streak that has lasted for over three months now—he can't even remember the last time his squad had latrine duty. To say that his squad loves him would be an exaggeration, but at least they have started to respect him.

To win the love of your squad, Khalid has learned, you have to make them rich. Unfortunately, to make your squad rich you have to get the right shifts at the border station, and Khalid isn't getting them. And even if he got them, he would still be no good at it.

At first he had really tried his best to bully all travellers into letting go of as much money as seemed reasonable—Sergeant

Shamil was not wrong when he had said that soldiers make much too little to raise children and support a family, and Khalid felt responsible—but it did not take long to learn how the soldiers actually spent their money: on whores at the Forbidden Chambers in Nardin and on arak. From that moment on, he has been rather lax when it comes to extorting money.

Sometimes he even puts up a shilling of his own money to pay for the passage of a traveller. He does not need much money anyway. The army pays for his food and his clothes, while his mother has raised him too well to spend money on whores and arak; occasionally he goes into Nardin to buy a book, but that's it.

'Corporal!' He looks up. In front of him is Sergeant Shamil, the traditional cigarette in the corner of his mouth, but his tone is serious and the usual smile is not present. '*He* wants to see you in the tent.'

He is Lieutenant Fakeih. 'Do you know what's waiting for me?'

Shamil takes the cigarette from his mouth and shakes his head. 'Not a pretty girl.'

Khalid nods and walks into the tent, where he finds Lieutenant Fakeih behind a desk, staring at a logbook in his hands. Khalid salutes and stands at attention; the lieutenant ignores him.

He wonders what he has done that has led him here. He also wonders what Fakeih is trying to achieve by letting him stand here at attention and why the lieutenant never turns a page.

Is it something his soldiers have done? They are certainly no paragons of virtue. Given too much freedom they loot, neglect their hygiene, go joyriding in the M38s, and do all the other things soldiers do when bored. Nevertheless, Khalid does not believe that his men behave much worse than the other soldiers in the camp.

On average they are fairly clean; they have broken only one M38 jeep in the last month—which they repaired themselves—and he hasn't received any complaints about thievery since the problem with Ayden and the boots of the soldier in Ba Company.

As for visits to the Forbidden Chambers, this is not something he can stop. Nardin is not a big city, and the Forbidden Chambers are mostly there because a battalion is stationed right next to the town. If the commander really wants it stopped, he can easily have it shut down, but by now Khalid is sure that the commander cares less about the hookers than Khalid does.

His back starts to ache and he suppresses a yawn, which is fairly difficult without moving, yet it takes at least half an hour more for Fakeih to put down the logbook and walk up to him. 'Well, you know what you are here for . . .'

Khalid doesn't even know if this is a question or a statement, and only when it becomes obvious that the lieutenant is waiting for a reply does he decide that he better give the man one. 'Sir?'

'I said, you know what you are here for.' Fakeih takes a step closer.

'I heard you, sir.' Khalid does not intend to be disrespectful; the words come out completely wrong.

'If you heard me, then what are you "sirring" me for?' Fakeih scowls.

'Sir, in the name of God, I do not know what I am here for.'

The lieutenant takes another step closer. Khalid doesn't like it when any person stands too close to him, but not many are worse than the lieutenant. Apparently, Fakeih has no idea what a teeth-cleaning twig is, and Khalid can smell the man's foul breath.

'Again!' the lieutenant observes despairingly before he swings his arms in the sky. 'You have won again! Why do you not understand?'

'Understand what, sir?'

But the lieutenant does not answer. Instead, he starts pacing up and down in front of Khalid. Twice he stops and looks at

Khalid, but then he shakes his head in disappointment and continues his parade.

The third time, he asks venomously, 'Are you pulling my leg?'

'No, sir,' Khalid replies.

'Are you thinking stupid Fakeih, simple lieutenant. Why, he ought to have been a captain, major even, if God wanted it. Yet here he is, giving directions to a platoon of apes, and he has no idea what is really going on. Is that what you're thinking?'

'No, sir.' Khalid is not lying; he does think Fakeih is stupid, but he definitely does not think the lieutenant ought to be a captain, let alone a major.

The lieutenant spits on the ground, missing Khalid's boot by not much more than an inch.

'I'll let you know, the only reason your lieutenant is not a major is because of politics. It is because of my uncle. The king dislikes him, and therefore I will not be promoted. In fact, in order to punish my uncle, the king has sent me to a battalion led by a Shi'i, did you know that? Your commander is a Shi'i!'

Khalid frowns; even if the commander were to be an infidel, he cannot see why this is relevant. He has never seen Colonel Issa favour the Shi'a, and while Fakeih might call himself a Sunni, the lieutenant won't see Paradise, no matter what religion he chooses.

As for the other thing, it is highly unlikely that the king gives a man like Fakeih any thought at all, let alone takes the time to hinder his military career. Besides, Lord Raslan's son is the most important general in the military, which makes this accusation completely bizarre. But since Khalid cannot say any of these things, he decides to say nothing and stare silently back at the lieutenant.

Fakeih cannot handle this for long and sighs. 'Since you appear determined to remain uncooperative, I will spell it out for you.

You are here because you are an embarrassment to your platoon. Every training, you are out to shame your fellow corporals, the ones in your platoon, and the ones in your company. You take an assignment and you tell your men, "Shame your fellow men!" Is it not so?'

'Sir?'

Clap. The lieutenant slaps him, not nearly as hard as his mother used to do, and he does not flinch. This annoys Fakeih even more, and he slaps him again, this time with his other hand, which is clearly the weaker one.

'Stop playing stupid!' the lieutenant shouts. 'I wish that on the night you were conceived, your father visited a mosque instead of your mother, you cowardly jackal! Does your father visit mosques, or are you secretly an infidel?'

'I pray five times a day, and my father has made two pilgrimages to Mecca in his life—so far,' Khalid answers calmly; he leaves out that he is a Shi'i like the commander, seeing as the lieutenant clearly does not like the Shi'a.

Fakeih snorts, pivots, takes a step back, and pivots to face him again. This is an improvement; Khalid can no longer smell the man's breath. 'In the name of God, it has to stop. You cannot defeat your senior officers, let alone shame them. It is written. Do you understand?'

'Sir, when the squads are playing against each other, I am playing against other corporals. These are not my senior officers.'

The lieutenant steps forward again, and this time Fakeih puts all of his strength behind his right hand.

Clap!

This time Khalid flinches—albeit just—and Fakeih looks pleased. 'They are older, and therefore they are your seniors. You must respect your seniors; it is written. Have your parents taught you nothing?'

Khalid takes a deep breath. He has not missed the bitter looks from his colleagues, but since Commander Issa actively encouraged competition, he has never cared about them.

Yet here he is, being punished by his superior officer for doing his work. Punished for pushing his men harder than the other corporals, despite the fact that they did not like him; punished for using his brain when given an assignment.

There are a dozen things he wants to say, mostly not nice things, but he takes another deep breath and uses all his energy to keep his voice even when he asks, 'Are you commanding that my squad can no longer win any of the assignments, sir?'

The lieutenant stares at him, and Khalid decides there is no intelligent life behind those eyes. 'You see, you do understand. You are a boy, and boys do not defeat men. You bring shame upon your parents, and, more importantly, upon me. If I ever hear of you shaming one of your seniors again, God willing, I will cut off one of your ears. Not only will you no longer win, you will start to lose. Do you understand?'

Start to lose . . . The one thing he has going for himself is being taken from him. He feels a strong inclination to slap the lieutenant and ask him if his uncle minds that he is a coward who can't read, but once again he controls himself.

'Yes, sir!' he manages to spit out.

'Good.' A satisfied smile appears on the lieutenant's face.

'Anything else, sir?'

'Nothing else, Corporal.'

CHAPTER TWO

ABDULLAH SAÍD
Mayasin

Month of Respect 29, 1372 A.H. (13 April 1953 A.D.)

When Abdullah saw the agenda for the cabinet meeting this morning, he thought it might just be the shortest meeting in history, but that was before the newspapers arrived.

The *Communist Gazette* opened with the news that Lord Raslan and Lord Ismat have used the construction of the highways in their provinces to enrich themselves. It claims to have documentation that proves their family members bought land weeks before the order to build the highways officially passed, land that they sold to the government just a couple months later for three times its price. It also claims that not all the people were willing to sell their land in the first place and that force was used to coerce people into selling.

Meanwhile, all the other newspapers have opened with the news that the king wants to abolish the courts of divine law. It is true, Abdullah knows it, but he does not understand how all the newspapers can have the news on the same day.

Lord Tali'a must be furious, but so far the commander is the only person in the meeting who has not opened his mouth. As to the rest . . . There is basically a small war going on.

'Majesty, we must act!' the prime minister, Lord Ismat, calls for the third time. 'These journalists, they think they can print lies. They think that they can steal confidential information. It is outrageous!'

Some of the ministers slam their hands on the table in agreement, but Lord Kalaldeh stands up, points his finger at the prime minister and shouts, 'You know what's outrageous? That your lot is stealing from the people of Beledar! We have no money for schools, no money for hospitals, because Lord Raslan and Lord Ismat want to buy cars for their children!'

Other members slam their hands on the table in support of Lord Kalaldeh, but then Lord al-Rikabi gets up. 'I believe the main issue here is that we should reconsider our decision to abolish divine law. They are calling it "an attack on Islam." How can the Islamic government of an Islamic country attack Islam?

'With divine law, everyone knows what he is in for, and everyone knows that it is just! Who gives us the right to decide what is just and what is not just? Certainly not God; He has given it to the scholars!

'When we agreed to abolish the courts of divine law, no one told us that we would legalise sodomy, fornication, and adultery in the process. But it is right here, written on the front page of every newspaper! Majesty . . .'

'We are not going to legalise sodomy, fornication, and adultery,' Mr Petrakis interrupts before the king can answer. 'These are very grave crimes, and the royal courts will condemn people who are guilty of these crimes, just like the courts of divine law used to do.'

Everyone is silent and looking at the king, Abdullah included. He too has not known what to think about the decision to abolish the courts that were presided over by the scholars, Mr al-Rubaie amongst them, yet he has not dared to discuss it with anyone.

'First of all,' the king calmly begins, 'I would like to point out that we are not going to abolish divine law. We are but men, and we could not abolish the laws of God if we wanted to. What we are going to do is let God be the judge on His divine laws, while we'll be the judge on our own laws—human laws.

'At this very moment there are some very dedicated lawyers writing these human laws, and they will cover areas like stealing and killing, but will they cover sodomy, fornication, and adultery? I think not.'

'But Majesty,' it is Lord al-Maseeh who speaks, 'every God-fearing man, whether he is Christian or Muslim—even the Jew—knows that these sins are so great that it is the duty of any government to protect its people from them! Besides, those laws you are speaking about should be written by the government and presented to Parliament!'

'Lord al-Maseeh, I commanded the previous government to start writing new laws five years ago. Although officially this is a new government, I do not see any new faces, and therefore I don't have much faith that this government will make much progress. It's my turn now, and as for *duty*, we all know that no law can stop fornication. There's a whorehouse in every major city in Beledar, yet I have never heard of the divine court condemning a man for visiting it. What I have heard of are girls being stoned to death right here in the streets of Mayasin for fornicating with a boy without being married to him.

'As for adultery, our secretary of justice here has done some research on that, and it appears that nine out of ten convictions by the courts are of women, but look me in the eyes and tell me truly that you believe women commit adultery more often than men. Because if that is so, where are the whorehouses filled with men? I have never heard of their existence!'

'Majesty, that research was not meant for . . .' the secretary of justice starts, but the king interrupts him with a roar.

'Not meant to make this argument? We all know it is true, and five months from now it will be over! My laws will protect the people, and by people I mean both men and women.'

All the ministers start shouting at the same time, while Abdullah realises that Kalima was right. This is the queen talking. She is the one who walks around indecently and wants all those other things for women. Sometimes she even gives radio addresses to the women of Beledar; his mother mentioned them once. And she has bewitched the king.

It is very dark and well after midnight when he gets home, and all he wants to do is eat some dates and go to bed, but there is a man standing in front of his house, waiting for him.

'Mr Abdullah Saíd, my name is Nouri al-Abadi.'

Abdullah looks at him. Even in the dark it is clear that Nouri al-Abadi only has one eye, and it makes him look very freakish. He sighs. 'What do you want, Mr al-Abadi?'

It comes out a little less polite than he had intended.

'I work for governor Lord Raslan, and I have something I need to discuss with you, but not out here. Inside.'

Abdullah looks at the door. If he lets this man in, when will he leave? On the other hand, if this man really does work for his wife's grandfather, it will be a great insult if he does not oblige.

'Would you like some dates, Mr al-Abadi?' he asks when they are standing in the kitchen together.

'No, thank you.'

Abdullah nods. He is too tired to be polite and doesn't invite the man farther into the house. 'What do you want to discuss?'

'This business in the newspapers today.' Mr al-Abadi shakes his head. 'Most unfortunate.'

'Which business are you referring to?'

244

'Everything, actually.'

Abdullah cannot disagree.

'Lord Raslan believes that it could have all been prevented, you know? If the king would be just a little more generous with information; if all this secrecy that surrounds everything that goes on in that palace were toned down a just little bit, it would make everyone's life much easier.'

'I suppose he should go and talk to Lord Tali'a then.'

Mr al-Abadi smiles at the suggestion. 'Unfortunately, everyone knows that Lord Tali'a does not believe in transparency, and I can tell from my own experience that he is an extremely unreasonable man to argue with.

'On the other hand, we can hardly blame Lord Tali'a for his obsession with secrecy. Just consider what happened today. Most unfortunate. No, I'm afraid that you misunderstand. Lord Raslan doesn't want everything that's going on in the palace to be thrown into the open. Those journalists definitely have no need to know. What Lord Raslan wants is some more information for himself. It would be so much easier to help the king if he had a little more information.

'And soon, when the time is right, he wants to ask the king for it, but first he wants to show that he is worthy of being informed. He wants to show that he will do the right things with whatever the king is willing to give him. And I told him that he could prove it, if we just ask his new grandson to start giving us a little access; very temporary, of course.'

Abdullah sighs. 'I am sorry, but I cannot help you.'

'You see, I believe you can. Lord Raslan is not a man who is used to hearing "no" when he asks for something, and definitely not when this "no" comes from the new grandson to whom he has donated a considerable amount of money for his new house!'

Abdullah's heart starts pounding. He is being threatened again, and this time by his wife's grandfather! Or is this man one of Lord Tali'a's agents?

Someone leaked information about the abolition of the courts to the newspapers; is this the commander's way of determining who can be trusted? It seems more logical than his wife's grandfather sending a man he has never met to spy for him.

As calmly as he can, he says, 'Mr al-Abadi, please get out of my house right now. I believe you're a fraud. My wife's grandfather would never ask me to do such a thing.'

The man grins. 'Then you do not know your wife's grandfather, Mr Saíd. If you wish it, I'll leave, but I will be back.'

Much too loudly, he closes the door to the bedroom, and when he turns on the light, the baby starts to scream. *God, why are you doing this to me!?* He is very proud of little Muhammad, but he wishes the boy would just keep quiet—at least until the sun comes up.

'Are you all right?' Kalima asks.

He sighs deeply. 'I will sleep in the spare room.' He moves to turn off the light, but then he reconsiders. 'Is it true?'

'Of course not!'

'How do you know what I am talking about?'

'My brother came by in the afternoon to bring a present for Muhammad. He told me that the *Communist Gazette* was writing all kinds of lies about our family!'

'They say they have proof.'

'They are liars; they don't even have God. How can you possibly believe people who don't believe in God?'

He nods. She is right. How could he have believed those infidels, even for a second?

It was that Abadi. He had made Abdullah doubt his wife's family's integrity. He grunts and goes to turn off the light again, but Kalima stops him.

'Who was the man?'

'What man?'

'I clearly heard a man's voice.'

'I think you were dreaming. It is very late.' It is the worst explanation ever, but he is too tired to come up with a better one.

'And what about the other thing in the newspapers? The courts?'

Abdullah sighs. 'That is true.'

'How can the king do that? How can he abolish God's laws?'

'He is not abolishing God's laws; he is simply putting God back in charge of declaring judgments. Good night.'

He closes the door, and not until he has reached the spare room does he realise that he left the light on. That is not very nice of him, he thinks as he sits down on the bed without taking his clothes off. He closes his eyes and lies back. He can still hear his son and wants to get up again to tell Kalima to do something about it, but when he opens his eyes he is ten years younger and Rizq is hunting him through the streets of Mayasin.

CHAPTER THREE

CORPORAL KHALID KHAN
Camp Nardin

Month of Separation 21, 1372 A.H. (5 May 1953 A.D.)

Khalid is sitting in the shade of the border station, his eyes closed, dreaming about his parents' house back in Al Nawaara. It has been two years since he last saw his family, and lately he has been wondering more and more often how everyone is doing. Does Aisha still wind everyone around her finger? Does Shiya still go to school? Is his father still angry?

His thoughts drift off to Aadhil. It was a bad decision to follow his brother, he knows that now, yet he does not regret it, and he wonders how Aadhil is faring. It has been quite some time since he last received a letter from his brother. After the camp in Mayasin, Aadhil was assigned to the Second Armoured Division. With his fearlessness, he'll probably have his own tank by now. If they have not given it to him, surely he will have taken one. The thought makes Khalid smile.

Or is he dead? Killed in a row with a fellow soldier or for disobeying a senior officer? This thought makes him sad, and his mind wanders to Ghulam.

Ghulam became a member of the newly formed Green Berets, the Special Forces. It is said that there is no place where soldiers receive promotions as quickly as in the Green Berets. Khalid hasn't heard from his friend since they said goodbye at Camp Mayasin, but he is sure that Ghulam, if he is still alive, is a sergeant by now at the very least. He feels slightly jealous that his friend has been placed in a regiment where there are no outdated ideas about seniority through age, and no border duty.

The shift is almost over, and it has been a very slow day, like the week before and the week before that, and in a way he is grateful for that. Every time some merchant hands him his shillings and pounds in exchange for the bullshit permits, he feels like he is extorting his own father; he'd rather lose the respect of his squad than squeeze those men for every penny they have to spare.

And he is losing the respect of his squad—fast. Two latrine duties in two weeks, and both times a portion of their respect for him was flushed down the toilet. To make matters even worse, the day after the lieutenant ordered him to start losing in the games, orders arrived that every man needed to spend at least two hours a day digging trenches and building the bunkers that had so far been conspicuous in their absence; every time Khalid puts his squad to work, he feels like they are on the verge of a mutiny.

Now would be a good time to be attacked or to revisit the war against the Jews . . .

'Khalid, Khalid.' Namdar's voice in his head. Good old Namdar. He has to admit that his brother in arms has not completely abandoned him to find favour with his new comrades, but sometimes he can see the regret in his friend's eyes. Regret that he can't go full out when the others are making jokes behind his corporal's back; regret about the promise between the four boys. *Brothers in arms, in the name of the king. One for all, and all for one.*

Namdar does not seem to care about getting promotions. As a Druze growing up in Taj al Wadi, he had always been an outsider, and now he mostly cares about being accepted. If it wasn't for his friendship with Khalid, he'd be the most popular guy in the squad.

'Khalid!' Someone is shaking his shoulder. Perhaps the voice isn't in his head. 'Khalid!'

He opens his eyes to find Namdar in front of him, pointing to a car that's waiting on the Iraqi side of the border. 'Look!'

He takes his binoculars and directs them at the Iraqi border station. There is a car, unlike any car Khalid has seen before. Had he ever seen a carriage, he would describe it as a carriage without horses, burgundy, with three prominent headlights and sand-coloured tires.

'What is that?' Khalid asks.

'A car,' Namdar answers.

He sighs. 'I can see that, but what kind of car?'

Namdar shrugs. 'An expensive car.'

He sighs again. At the Iraqi side of the border, a man with a top hat and white gloves has gotten back behind the wheel, and, slowly, the luxurious vehicle starts to move toward them. Khalid gets up. All of his men are on their feet too, anxiously anticipating what is about to happen.

'In the name of God, that car is going to need a lot of permits,' Ayden says. 'Corporal, you had better let me handle this.'

Khalid looks over his shoulder. This is not the first time Ayden tries to step in, but if Khalid gives in to the private and Ayden walks away with a big sack of cash, he will lose all control of his squad.

'Thank you, Private, but that will not be necessary.'

'But Corporal . . .'

'I said thank you,' Khalid interrupts, trying to avoid a discussion that will only further undermine his authority.

Ayden has no plans of stepping aside, though. He stands in front of Khalid, his eyes flashing. Is he going to attack his corporal? Khalid wants to look around to see where the rest of his men are standing, but he does not want to lose eye contact with Ayden. Namdar is at his side, he thinks; he would not vouch for the rest.

'It's a Rolls-Royce,' Rasmi says, breaking the tension just before the car stops at the boom bar. 'The owner is very rich.'

Khalid does not know what a Rolls-Royce is, but as he walks over, he can see the greed in the eyes of his men in the reflection of the blinded windows of the car. He must not mess this up.

He taps on the window next to the chauffeur, which slowly opens.

'Peace be upon you,' he says.

'And upon you be peace,' the driver answers. Not a Beledarian accent, nor an Iraqi one. He wonders where the man is from.

'God willing, may I inquire as to the purpose of your journey to the beautiful Kingdom of Beledar?'

'You may not,' the man answers curtly.

For a second, Khalid is taken aback by this answer. This is new. Where would this man have learned this ill-guided rudeness? Does he have some knowledge that Khalid is unaware of? Or perhaps some connections . . .

'All right . . .' He mimics Sergeant Shamil's tone and voice, trying to sound as casual as possible while regaining his composure. 'Your papers, if God wants it, and your passengers' papers as well.'

The man hands him three sets of papers, and when Khalid turns around to study them, he almost bumps into Ayden, who clearly does not want to miss even a whisper of the conversation and is standing irritatingly close by.

The driver is from Oman; his passengers are French, a man and a woman. A couple? They do not share any name, as is common in Europe. Why would a French man and woman with an expensive Iraqi car and a driver from Oman want to cross the Beledarian border at Nardin, of all places? There is nothing here for miles and miles, except for a dirt road. He turns back to the car.

'Where are your visas?' he asks.

'They are in there.'

Khalid looks again. Nothing in his hands resembles a Beledarian visa.

'If God wants it, look at the green piece of paper!' the chauffeur says.

Khalid does. There is no stamp from a Beledarian embassy or from the army, the king or any of the ministries. Instead there is a message, handwritten and difficult to decipher:

This oficial dokument from the Beledarian Ministry of Travel, is valit as a Free Travel Visa for . . .

This is a joke. No Beledarian agency would produce a document like this, and if there is such a thing as a Ministry of Travel, Khalid has never heard of it. Someone has been making a lot of money off these people, probably the Iraqis. He gives the green piece of paper back to the man, who, according to his passport, is named Masoud al-Rashdie, but keeps the passports.

'Quite a lot of spelling mistakes for an official document, wouldn't you agree?'

The chauffeur looks at the sheet for no more than two seconds—not long enough to actually read anything—and replies, 'I didn't know it was the duty of a corporal to check official documents for spelling errors.'

Khalid smiles. 'If you could read, you would have probably noticed them yourself.'

His insult does not work. Al-Rashdie returns his smile and says, 'If God wants it, perhaps you could give me the passports back. We should really be going.'

Khalid sighs and shakes his head, acting disappointed. 'I'm sorry. There is nothing I would like to do more, for I can see that you are clearly chauffeuring important people, but I can't. You need the right paperwork to enter our country, to use the roads, and all those kinds of things. Besides, forgery of an official document is a grave crime here in Beledar. Perhaps you would like to step outside?'

The chauffeur shakes his head. 'I have the right paperwork. This document,' he waves the green sheet of paper around again, 'is the real thing, no forgery. Your commander, I believe his name is Colonel Issa, knows about it. Go and call him!'

Both he and the chauffeur know that he will never call the colonel over an issue such as this. Thus, if al-Rashdie is telling the truth, and he does not let this man pass, he will probably not be a corporal tomorrow morning; the ball is in his court.

He turns around again, and in the eyes of Ayden he sees doubts. 'Give me a cigarette,' he hisses to the soldier.

Ayden does not respond. Instead the private stands paralysed, looking stupid.

'A cigarette!' he repeats. This time Ayden understands. He hands him a cigarette and lights it. Khalid has never seen any use in smoking, but since he feels like this may be a turning point in his life, he reckons it's as good a time as any to start. He inhales deeply and closes his eyes, suppressing the urge to cough.

If they demote him, life will be a lot easier. If he is going to be kicked out of the army, at least all the fuss will be over; he can go home and beg his father for forgiveness. If his family does not welcome him back, he can always go to the capital and see if he can find a job there.

He inhales again and turns back to the car. In his head he can hear Sergeant Shamil's voice. *Everybody pays.*

'Mr al-Rashdie . . .' the chauffeur nods, 'my commander is a very busy man, but if you have your own radio, feel free to contact him. If your document is the real deal, I am sure that he will make time for you. Otherwise, you will just have to pay us for the visas and permits you are going to need in the coming weeks, which will amount to,' he makes a quick calculation in his head, 'two hundred and thirty pounds.'

He hears Ayden gasp behind him, and the chauffeur exclaims, 'Two hundred and thirty pounds! In the name of God, that is ridiculous!'

The chauffeur is right—it is ridiculous. Two hundred and thirty pounds is more money than he has ever seen, more than he can imagine, actually. But for the first time he is looking at a man who deserves to be squeezed for every penny he has, and since he is going all-in anyway, he'd better go all the way and pray that God will protect him.

'Maybe it sounds ridiculous,' he replies calmly, 'but when you think about it, it's really not. Your own visa is five pounds, as you are from Oman but employed by Europeans. You will also need a working permit, since there are countless Beledarians who would love to drive your masters around. I could send Ayden here to Nardin to collect one right now.'

'This car belongs to my boss, the sultan of Oman,' the chauffeur counters. 'It is my duty to keep it safe!'

Khalid shrugs. 'That is not my problem. You are a foreigner working in Beledar, and therefore you will need a permit, which costs fifteen pounds. Then there are your masters themselves; they are French. Since our government does not have a visa treaty with France, their visas cost twenty pounds each.'

He has no idea if this is true, but it sounds great, and Khalid gives himself an imaginary tap on the shoulder before continuing. 'Next thing is the car, which is, I have to say, very beautiful. In that car you will have much pleasure from the roads that we have built, once you have reached them; much more than the

Beledarians get from the roads themselves. So it is only fair that you should contribute to the costs of the road. The standard contribution for a car like this is another ten pounds.

'And finally, there is a sixty pound fine for the fraudulent papers and an extra hundred to keep your business secret, which is what you want, is it not?'

The chauffeur grunts and starts to explain what Khalid has said to his passengers. The nearest border station is no more than two hours away, but Khalid can think of a number of reasons why the man from Oman would not like to turn around. Apart from the fact that he will have to pass the Iraqi border station again and face the humiliation of the Iraqis laughing at him after their little swindle, they will also make him pay again.

A passenger door opens, and out of the car steps a tall man in a dark suit. 'Do you know who I am?'

For a second Khalid needs to adjust; it's been a long time since he last spoke English, but the teachers at Taj al Wadi have taught him well. He opens one of the little books with the word 'passeport' in Latin letters and smiles at the Frenchman.

'It says here that you are Patrick Dombasle. Do I pronounce that right?'

'Ah! You speak English! That means you are not a complete moron! Do you think I like coming here?' He speaks rapidly, but since he articulates carefully, his words aren't difficult to follow. In fact, Khalid realises that for some reason this man's English sounds very beautiful, almost as if the man is singing angrily.

'I should think you do,' he counters. 'After all, Beledar is a wonderful country, and with a car like that and a young lady next to you, it must be very comfortable to travel.'

'Do you think you are funny?' The anger is dripping from the man's face; Khalid doesn't reply. Instead he tries to take another casual drag from Ayden's cigarette, but it has gone out. He realises that he is in very real danger of looking stupid and throws it in front of Mr Dombasle's feet to compensate. The Frenchman looks at it and says, 'You have no right to harass us like this. We are diplomats.'

'Maybe,' Khalid replies, 'but if you are, then where are your diplomatic passports?'

The man snorts. 'I work for a very important and big company; I am here to help your country! I am here to help you, and you treat me like this!' He takes a step closer. 'I demand to speak to your commander!'

'Certainly, sir, the camp is just two miles that way.' Khalid points at the road. 'I am sure that Colonel Issa will be honoured to receive you. However, in order for you to go down this road with your car, you will have to purchase the permits and visas first.'

'*Mon dieu!*' the man exclaims, and he stamps around helplessly. While Khalid's men cannot follow the conversation, he can hear some suppressed giggles. Then the Frenchman's eyes light up. 'But I have just told you that my purpose is business and that I am here to help your country. Surely I will no longer have to pay your hundred pounds for secrecy.'

'Indeed you will not,' a sigh of relief comes from Mr Dombasle, 'but you will have to allow my men to search your bags. Do not worry, though, my men are very . . .' he looks for the right word, and finding it brings a small, sadistic smile to his lips, '*discreet* when it comes to searching luggage. Especially with the private underwear of a European lady.'

Mr Dombasle looks appalled but does not say anything. He sticks his head back in the car, and Khalid hears him talking to the woman. '*Enfoiré*,' is one of the words he catches.

He remembers how in Taj al Wadi there was a boy from Syria in his class. The boy always claimed he spoke French, but everyone knew that he only knew the bad words. *Enfoiré* was one of his favourites.

'I only have dollars,' the Frenchman says when he comes back out.

'Fine,' Khalid answers. 'It will be a hundred and fifty dollars American.'

'What! Two hundred and thirty Beledarian pounds is no more than a hundred and twenty dollars.'

'The other thirty is for calling me "*enfoiré*," 'Khalid says. He knows that he is pushing it, but finally he can pay someone back for the injustice he suffered from his lieutenant a month earlier.

Mr Dombasle stares at him, and he stares back. He is determined not to look away, and for almost two minutes, the men just stare at each other. Everyone around them is quiet, but then Mr Dombasle snorts and turns to the chauffeur.

'Masoud, get back in the car.'

Khalid sees the Frenchman take the money, and for a second he thinks Mr Dombasle is simply going to throw it on the ground. He decides that if the Frenchman does this, he will make him pick it up, and, seeing how many dollars there are in the wallet, he will make him pay another fifty.

But the Frenchman is not that stupid. He takes a step toward Khalid and silently hands it over to him before turning around and stepping back into the car.

'Can we go now?' the driver asks through the window.

'Almost,' Khalid answers, and he turns back to Ayden, who this time automatically offers him another cigarette. He takes it, accepts Ayden's matches, and turns back to the chauffeur. 'I would not want you to leave without your visas and permits.'

He walks away from the car and gestures to his brother-in-arms. 'Namdar, go and draw up some permits for me. Take your time, though; they are sitting in a very comfortable car, and it is only a little hot.'

He recognises the smirk on the face of his friend, and he knows that the expression is mirrored on his own. Adrenaline is blowing through his veins, mixed with a strong feeling of exuberance. He has not felt this alive in a long time.

CHAPTER FOUR

ABDULLAH SAÍD
Mayasin

Month of Separation 21, 1372 A.H. (5 May 1953 A.D.)

Abdullah is putting away his seventh cup of coffee since he woke up, but it's not helping him. Yesterday, Haidar did not show up for work, and Abdullah had to work out the entire cabinet meeting with Rashid. As usual, it lasted much too long. When he arrived home, Muhammad was screaming, and there was not a single place in the house where he could sleep in peace. His head hurts, and so does his back, and Haidar is still not in. Where can he be?

He returns his attention to the letter Mr Petrakis threw on his desk yesterday. Apparently some merchant in Oyoun al Jabal wants the king to intervene in a dispute with Lord Tanvir about a truck. At first he didn't think anything in particular about the situation—disputes like this happen all the time, and lately an increasing number of people find their way to the king, which, according to Mr Petrakis, is one of the reasons why the king is making new laws—but now that he's looking at the letter again, it strikes him how beautiful the handwriting is and how well its words were chosen. Where would this Mr Khan have learned to write like this?

Abdullah sighs. He doesn't have time for questions, but he cannot focus on his reply, or on any of the other things he has to do. He stands up and walks to Rashid's office. 'Have you heard from Haidar?'

His colleague shakes his head. 'I knocked on his door this morning, but no one answered. I don't understand. I've been here for six years, and I swear by the prophet that in all those years, Haidar has never missed a single day. Never.'

'Gentlemen.' Abdullah turns around to the voice of Mr Petrakis. 'Has the great Haidar returned yet?'

Abdullah and Rashid shake their heads, and the infidel's eyes narrow. 'That's unfortunate. The king has an extremely busy day. Rashid, you take the king's meetings with ambassadors. Mr Saíd, you handle all domestic matters. I will go and find Tali'a; no doubt he will know what's going on.'

'What did that mean?' Abdullah asks Rashid when Mr Petrakis is out of earshot, thinking about Mr al-Abadi, the man who visited him late at night two weeks ago. Is there a connection?

But Rashid clearly does not think much of the remark and shrugs indifferently. 'You know, Lord Tali'a knows everything that's going on this city. If he doesn't know where Haidar is now, he'll certainly know it by the end of the day.'

Abdullah nods and makes his way back to his office. Chances are that Lord Tali'a knows exactly where Haidar is.

There is a knock on his open door, and he looks up from his desk. 'Taaraz, what is it? I don't have much time; I have to be back in the conference room in . . .' He takes a look at his watch. 'Three minutes.'

'Lord Tali'a wants to know if you've noticed anything strange about Haidar lately. Anything.'

'No, why?' Abdullah asks as he picks up some papers and stands up.

'Are you very sure?'

He sighs and scowls at Taaraz. He really does not have time for this. 'If I had, I would have told you. In fact, I would have told you yesterday evening. At the moment, we should be doing our work with five clerks. Instead, there is just Rashid and me.'

'And it will probably just be you and Rashid for some time,' Taaraz answers.

'What do you mean?'

'We've found Haidar and his family in their house. Someone has cut them up into very little pieces.'

Abdullah sits back down. 'Dead?'

'Unless you know a way to glue them back together.'

The guard's tone is deadly serious. Abdullah has feared something like this, but he expected the Royal Guard to be responsible. Yet as he stares at Taaraz's face, he is positive that this guard definitely didn't have anything to do with it.

'We surely belong to God, and to Him shall we return,' Taaraz mutters in a more friendly tone.

Abdullah nods and picks up his papers again. The king won't wait for a dead clerk.

'Son of Said.' Lord Tali'a is standing in the doorway. The last time the commander of the Royal Guard visited Abdullah's office was at least a year ago. 'Tonight, the queen's brother is having dinner with the king and the queen. The king regards this to be a business meeting, and he wants minutes kept.'

'What about Rashid?' Abdullah asks. Surely this is more his cup of tea; even with Haidar gone, Abdullah has not been privy to any private or secret meetings, and at the moment he just wants to get home as soon as possible.

The commander shakes his head. 'I have sent Rashid home. If God wants it, I will send you a new clerk tomorrow to replace Haidar, and if Rashid is still not fit to work, I will send two.'

That is the first good news he's had all day. 'Dinner, so we go to the dining room?'

'Not really. The queen's brother does not need to know that you're listening. Come with me, if God wants it.'

He follows the commander in the direction of the dining room, but suddenly Lord Tali'a stops in front of the wall. 'Turn around, please.'

Abdullah obeys, and when he is allowed to look again, the wall is gone and there is a hallway. 'The old Emir never trusted anyone and always wanted to know exactly what everyone was saying. His father had started to build this palace, but he finished it in such a way that few places remain where the walls do not have ears.'

Apparently keen to take away some of Abdullah's stress, the commander keeps on talking as they walk through the secret hallway. 'The queen's brother, François Marceau, was driven here in a Rolls-Royce from the sultan of Oman—you know what a Rolls-Royce is?'

He shakes his head.

'It's a very expensive car. Some company gave this car to the sultan to impress him, but they didn't know that the sultan only drives in white Cadillacs. He has lent the Rolls to Monsieur Marceau, and the queen's brother believed that using the car he could cross the border incognito, but that hasn't turned out quite as he hoped.'

'And what is the queen's brother doing here?'

'He's here to sell things for companies that are willing to pay him a large commission, which is why the king regards this as a business meeting. He's a very bad-mannered person, the queen's brother; I don't think you'll like him much.'

Lord Tali'a stops walking. 'You can sit here, and you'll hear everything that is being said at the dinner table. I will send Taaraz to collect you when they are done.'

'Yes, sir,' Abdullah says, and before he knows it Lord Tali'a has disappeared again. He is confused. Why this charm offensive from the commander of the Royal Guard? Has the man suddenly decided that Abdullah is trustworthy after all? Or is he in greater danger than ever? Is Lord Tali'a trying to make him feel overly comfortable because Haidar's fate is awaiting him too?

He does not get much time to ponder this, for he hears the voices of the king and the queen coming, and less than a minute later, a footman announces the queen's brother and a lady with a French name.

After asking for champagne and complaining about corrupt soldiers at the border station, Monsieur Marceau says, 'You have a very nice palace!'

'Thank you. My father and my grandfather built it.'

'It would be a shame if it were to become a townhouse for King Faisal.' Abdullah frowns. It is a very strange thing to say, and besides, why would the palace become a townhouse for the king of Iraq?

Apparently the king feels the same. 'And why would that be?'

'The young king of Iraq is almost of age, and everyone knows that he is planning to unite the Arab world, a dream your father once held too, I believe. We have information that he wants to begin his quest in Beledar, since you have strayed from what the mob believes to be the true faith.'

'Monsieur Marceau, every king on the Arabian Peninsula wants to dominate the Arab world. Should Faisal decide to start here, we will have a warm welcome waiting for him.'

'I believe you, but you should know that he has a superior army with superior weapons. Fortunately, I know just the right people to help you. I can get your army the best weapons available in the world today.' Abdullah has to admit the man sounds generous.

'That is a most kind offer,' the king answers, 'but at the moment we need schools and hospitals rather than more weapons. Besides, my generals are very satisfied with the weapons they have.'

'Majesty, with all due respect, your ministers disagree. I have spoken with them, and they all support me; even your minister of education.'

'And how much are you paying my ministers to agree with you?'

'What are you insinuating?' The queen's brother is not quite shouting at the king's table, but it is close.

'Monsieur Marceau, I do not mind talking business at the dinner table, even in the presence of ladies. I am willing to overlook the fact that you are only here to sell me things, because you will be receiving a commission. I do not even really care that you are bribing my ministers. They will agree with you on anything as long as you pay them enough. But I do mind your tone, Monsieur Marceau.

'Besides, it is not really news that my second cousin is planning an invasion of Beledar. The Iraqis have been preparing their army for over a year. What amuses me is that the weapons you are trying to sell me are the same weapons you have tried to sell to Faisal's government in Iraq.'

'Is this how you treat your guests!?' Now the queen's brother is actually shouting, and this time at the queen. 'Have your husband insult them! Accuse them! Remember, I am your family! I will . . .'

'That is quite enough, Monsieur Marceau,' King Jalal intervenes sharply. 'Another word to the queen of Beledar and I will have you thrown in a very small room without windows.'

The queen's brother snorts, and Abdullah can hear him stand up. 'If you lose this war, you will regret treating me like this. And even if you don't, you will regret it! You will pay for this! Trust me, I have more power than you think!'

At least the meeting was short; that's the second good thing that has happened today. But whether it balances the shock that war is coming ... And not just some war, war with another Muslim country!

Or were the men bluffing?

Abdullah sighs. Here he is at the very centre of power, and he has no idea what is going on around him. If it weren't for Lord Tali'a, he would ask his wife's uncle.

CHAPTER FIVE

CORPORAL KHALID KHAN
Camp Nardin

Month of Separation 22, 1372 A.H. (6 May 1953 A.D.)

Back at the camp, doubt sets in. Did he overdo it? While nobody has heard or seen a Rolls-Royce rolling in, the Frenchman might be complaining somewhere else—in the capital, for example. It could be days before news reaches the camp that Corporal Khalid Khan will be be court-martialled.

Nonetheless, for the first time since he has arrived at Nardin, his men are actually singing his praises throughout the camp. *Dollarboy*, they call him. Suddenly he is famous, and during dinner, men whom he has never met before come to congratulate him.

'Quite a lot of spelling mistakes for an official document. That is most odd, considering on most of the documents from our *Secret* Ministry of Travel there isn't a single typo to be found,' one of them says as he is shaking Khalid's hand, while another remarks, 'Did you know that the documents from our Travel Ministry are so very secret that if this was a real document, it would be invisible?'

After dinner, he sits with his men around a small fire, and

Rasmi conjures up a bottle filled with a liquid that looks like water. 'Give me your cups. We are going to celebrate that our corporal has made us all rich!'

As Khalid passes his cup, he asks, 'What is that?'

'Our corporal knows English and French, he knows the rules of war and the book of strategy better than the commander, but he does not know arak!'

A day ago Ayden might have spoken the exact same words, and this would have sounded spiteful. This evening, though, the words are intended in genuine good spirit.

From Khalid's cup comes a strong smell of anise, mixed with the liquid the soldiers use to clean their wounds. Alcohol. He hesitates. Alcohol is Forbidden, yet if he snubs his men now, they may not give him a second chance. He takes a deep breath. God is merciful. The most merciful. He will understand.

'Add some of your water,' Namdar says next to him.

How does he know? Has Namdar drunk this before? Of course. This isn't the first time these men are drinking together; this is simply the first time that he has been invited to join. He follows his friend's advice, and in the light of the fire he can see how the content of his cup magically turns white.

'To the corporal!' Rasmi calls and raises his glass.

'The corporal!' The rest of the men repeat the toast, and they all raise their cups and drain them. Khalid is last to lift his cup, and when he puts it to his mouth, he says a quick prayer.

The liquor is sweet, but when his cup is empty he gags and feels how the arak is directly looking for a way out of his gullet. He closes his mouth; some of the liquid finds its way back onto his tongue, but he swallows it again. Nausea rises inside of him, and he closes his eyes.

'Take a deep breath,' Namdar says, and after following his friend's advice he feels a little better. He takes another, and the nausea starts flowing away. Another breath, and he opens his eyes again. Around him, the men are laughing.

'One more!' Rasmi calls. The private receives a loud cheer from the rest of the men, and reluctantly Khalid puts his cup forward for a second round.

'To Dollarboy!' they announce.

This one goes down easier than the first.

'What exactly was it you said to him?' Namdar asks.

This isn't the first time he has been asked that question, and so far Khalid has stayed fairly factual and reserved in his responses. 'I told him that it did not matter which way he went. However, if he did not pay us, we were going to have to search through all of his baggage, and I said that I could not blame my men if they were to show a healthy interest in the underwear of a French woman.'

The men laugh, but when he looks at their faces, dead silent and waiting for a great story, he decides that a little embellishment cannot hurt. 'I also told him that we did not have much of a liking for the French and that many folks in Beledar knew people who had died fighting the French traitors in Syria during the War of the West, and that therefore he had to pay punitive damages. Being French, I supposed he understood the irony.'

Although his men do not get this irony, it does not stop them from laughing harder.

'Finally, I said that American dollars were much better in our hands than they were in the hands of a Frenchman.'

'Dollarboy!' Ayden calls, and Rasmi starts to refill the cups once more.

'Corporal Khan!'

Khalid hopes it's a dream, but he knows better. He opens his eyes. The world is spinning, and his head feels as though someone has hit him with a war hammer. He is in his own bed, but how did he get there? The last thing he remembers is that his drink magically turned white when he added water. He has drunk alcohol! Is this feeling in his head God's punishment?

'Corporal Khan!'

It is the sergeant major!

He gets up and violently hits his head on the bed above him. Normally this would have hurt terribly, but at the moment it seems impossible for the pain in his head to get worse. He stands up and salutes.

'At ease, Corporal,' the sergeant major says.

He has slept in his uniform. It is rumpled, and he looks far from presentable, but he does not have a spare.

'You are to report to the commander immediately,' the sergeant major continues.

'Yes, sir.' It is a weak sound that comes out of his mouth. He has to go and see the commander, in his ragged outfit, feeling awful! This is definitely God's punishment.

Is he in trouble? He looks at the sergeant major again, but the man's grim face does not betray anything.

As he follows the sergeant out of the room, he can see the faces of his men. Ayden makes a drinking gesture with his hand and shows him his ugly missing-teeth smirk.

When they step outside, his eyes are blinded by the sunlight, and the pain in his head does something Khalid had deemed impossible a mere minute ago: it grows worse. He tries to regain his wits, and with all his strength he succeeds in bringing back some images from the previous evening. He sees himself drinking, and he vaguely recalls embellishing his discussion with the Frenchman; the rest of his mind stays blank.

Why has he been summoned to the colonel? Did the men trick him? Maybe one of them does speak English and has told the rest that Khalid was exaggerating. Maybe they have finally found a way to get rid of him, and this is his walk of shame.

Or maybe the colonel has received word from Mayasin, where Mr Dombasle, who really is a diplomat, has told the minister all about the shameless corporal at Nardin, and now Khalid is going to have to answer for his actions. But if the Frenchman is a diplomat, wouldn't his passport have borne a diplomatic seal? Or had it? Did he make a mistake?

He needs to set up a line of defence, and he has very little time to do it, yet his brain is malfunctioning. If only that infernal pain would go away; it is impossible to think rationally like this, and before he knows it, they have arrived at the tent of the colonel. The canvas is open, and the sergeant major steps aside, allowing Khalid to enter first; now it's too late.

The commander is sitting behind his desk; Major al-Attas is sitting in a chair next to the desk, and Captain Madani is standing in the room. Khalid salutes and stands at attention.

'At ease, Corporal,' Colonel Issa says.

Khalid relaxes his stance, but he does not feel at all at ease. There is too much light in the office, and simply keeping his eyes open and focused on the colonel costs him all of his energy.

'You do not look too well,' Captain Madani remarks drily.

'The corporal bumped his head against the bed of his upstairs neighbour rather violently,' answers the sergeant major, who has silently followed him inside. 'He might have a small concussion.'

Why is the sergeant major defending him? The man must have noticed what kind of state he woke up in . . .

It's not important. At least one of the scarier men in the camp seems to be on his side.

'Did his encounter with the bed also ruin his clothes?' Major al-Attas asks.

What can he say to this? Although prohibited by God, drinking is not illegal in the king's army as long as one does not have duty the next day. But before he has found the right words to bring this point up, the colonel bluntly ends this discussion with the words, 'Thank you, Major.'

'Now, Corporal.' Colonel Issa turns to him, and Khalid holds his breath. This is the moment where the commander is going to tell him that he will be taking away his stripes, or maybe he really is going to court-martial him.

'From the moment you arrived here, it was clear that you were going to present a problem for all of us. While we obviously applaud young, intelligent, and ambitious men—and the army most certainly needs them—it is never a good thing when they rise too quickly and embarrass the more senior men around them.'

'It is written,' the major and the captain confirm in unison.

'Since your arrival here,' the commander gravely continues, 'you have shamed your seniors in training, thereby making the men lose respect for their officers. Am I wrong?'

'No, sir.' Arguing is of no use; it would be his word against that of Lieutenant Fakeih, and he cannot possibly win that battle.

'And now it appears that you have charged a Frenchman, who claimed to have papers allowing him to travel through our country without any harassment, an absurdly large amount of money for his visa and permits. Is this true?'

It is as he feared. Mr Dombasle is a diplomat, and he complained to somebody important. 'It is, sir.'

'Well, explain yourself!' the colonel commands.

'Sir . . .' He hesitates. If only his brother was here; Aadhil would know exactly what to say. But he is not, and thus Khalid takes a deep breath and continues. 'The Frenchman presented handwritten papers from the Beledarian Ministry of Travel. Since I have never heard of a Ministry of Travel, and there were many errors on the documents, I decided that they were fraudulent, and I gave the man a fine for that. Aside from the fine, I believe I charged the man fair amounts for the regular taxes that a man in his position ought to pay when entering our country.'

'Hmmm.' The commander gives him an inquisitive stare before continuing, 'I have also heard that you have, once again, shamed your superiors, this time by showing an impressive proficiency in the English language. Is that true?'

'I would not call my English language skills impressive, sir,' Khalid replies. He knows that all eyes in the room are upon him, but he concentrates on Colonel Issa. 'I have been taught English at school, and sometimes I still read English books.'

The commander nods. 'Is it true that your men call you Dollarboy?'

'Some of them appear to think it is funny.'

'Funny? Well, I will tell you something funny. Last night, very late, a courier came to the camp with a message from Lord Tali'a.'

For a second Khalid's mind drifts back to a night by the campfire in the desert, more than ten years ago. It is hard to believe he has taken this big risk, and it has instantly been sent to the desk of the man who has been his hero for so long.

'The man you harassed at our border was none other than the queen's brother. What do you say about that?'

Suddenly, Khalid forgets all about his headache. The queen's brother! He isn't just going to be demoted—he will be court-martialled, probably condemned to death and it will be completely justified! *Please God, have mercy,* he silently prays, but his prayer is interrupted by the colonel.

'Well?'

'I did not know, sir. He never said anything about being the queen's brother. He said he was a diplomat, but he did not have a diplomatic passport. Combined with the fraudulent papers . . .'

Khalid wants to say that he had assumed he was a fraud, but the colonel interrupts him again.

'Lord Tali'a also wrote that there were few times in his life when he had seen a man more furious than Mr Marceau.'

Khalid looks down.

'However, it appears that the queen doesn't particularly like her brother, and while Mr Marceau has demanded we hang you, she has decided that, if God wants it, you are to be given a medal and a promotion instead. Do you understand what I am saying?'

It does not sound so bad, but maybe he has misunderstood. 'Sir?'

'I am saying that you are a very lucky man, Dollarboy.' Colonel Issa is speaking calmly. 'And to add to your luck, this morning I was presented with a different problem. Major?'

The commander sits back with a contented smile, and Major al-Attas starts to speak.

'Corporal Khan, it has come to our attention that there is a serious problem in your platoon. It seems that your Sergeant Shamil al-Jasser hasn't always been giving Lieutenant Fakeih the respect that he is due. Do you know anything about that?'

How can he answer this honestly without incriminating Shamil, for whom he feels a strange affinity? He opens his mouth, but Captain Madani cuts him off before any sound comes out.

'You do not have to answer that. We all know how Sergeant al-Jasser feels about the lieutenant. Unfortunately, though, as of this morning, Lieutenant Fakeih knows it too, and he is demanding the sergeant's head.'

Khalid's eyes grow wide. Are they going to hang Shamil? The four men around him notice his distress and begin to laugh.

'Do not worry,' Colonel Issa says. 'As long as God protects me, I am not in the habit of sacrificing perfectly capable sergeants to please the whims of self-indulgent lieutenants. Sergeant al-Jasser is very capable. Lieutenant Fakeih an idiot.'

That is a relief.

'The commander has decided that Sergeant al-Jasser will receive a whipping, and then he will be sent to Mayasin with a recommendation for a promotion to lieutenant, if God wants it.' Major al-Attas is talking again. 'You will replace him. Do you accept?'

Does he accept? It is a great honour, of course, but it will also be very difficult. 'Sir,' he is speaking softly, 'what about Lieutenant Fakeih? What will he say?'

The colonel gives him a stern look. 'Let us worry about what the lieutenant will say, Corporal. If he does not like it, he is free to resign his post. Despite the odds, you have gained the admiration of all the men in your platoon, and not just in your platoon; in your company and this battalion as well. More importantly, though, you have gained the admiration of our queen, and for that you should praise God.

'If you were a sergeant, we would have fewer problems with corporals being embarrassed that a boy's section defeats their own during training. If your platoon performs like your section did, all the credit will go the lieutenant. So do you think that you can work with Lieutenant Fakeih?'

He will never get another a chance like this. 'Yes, sir!'

'Perfect. Captain?'

'Sergeant Khalid Khan, allow me to present you the Iron Crescent.' Captain Madani pins the medal on his chest, and Khalid glows with pride.

'Now,' the colonel says, 'you'd better be off before I change my mind.'

'Thank you, sir! God is praised!'

He salutes, and just as he is about to turn around, the commander says, 'Sergeant, one more thing. You can select one of the men from your section to take over as corporal. Consider it a bonus for the dollars you've brought us.'

'Thank you, sir!' He salutes again. Sergeant! It sounds fantastic, and as he steps out of the office, his headache has substantially lessened. What's more, the light that seemed his enemy just ten minutes ago now brightens his day.

But then he remembers the promise he has made. *One for all, and all for one.* Since it will be his choice, the only person he can select as his corporal is Namdar; his men will not like that. He sighs, but then he realises something else, and his smile returns.

His men? They are Namdar's men now; Namdar's problem. *Praise be unto God!*

With that last thought comes also the awareness that he has missed at least two prayers since the previous day, even though he has been given much to be thankful for, and he quickly goes to clean himself so that he can make up for it.

CHAPTER SIX

ABDULLAH SAÍD
Mayasin

Month of Burning 8, 1372 A.H. (21 May 1953 A.D.)

As has become customary, it is well past midnight when Abdullah arrives home, and he tries to remember the time when he thought Mr Petrakis and Lord Tali'a were shutting him out of everything interesting that was happening. He cannot believe he was jealous of Haidar and Rashid in those days.

It has become clear that the queen's brother was right. Was is imminent; the question is when it will start. The only thing everyone seems sure about is that the Iraqis will hold off their attack until the Month of Burning is over, which means it's going to be a very short war; once summer starts, it will be too hot to fight.

Until two weeks ago, Abdullah thought that wars are fought with tanks and guns, and he still finds it hard to believe how much paperwork is involved in the preparation. What makes it even more complicated is that Lord Tali'a is demanding complete secrecy from everyone involved. Not only does this mean that he only has Rashid to help him while the two new clerks have to take on all the other work, but it is also very difficult to write letters to governors and large merchants to inform them that they have to prepare for war without telling them that they have to prepare for war.

Someone has left the light on in the sitting room. He walks in to turn it off, but he finds his brother there. 'Samir, are you still awake?'

'I was waiting for you, brother.'

'I am afraid you will have to wait a little longer. Mr Petrakis has ordered me to be back at the palace tomorrow an hour after sunrise.'

'I have dates . . .'

He looks at his brother and the plate of dates he is holding up. If Samir has stayed up this late to talk to him, it will probably be important. Perhaps his brother is even getting married! He walks into the living room, takes the plate, and sits down.

'You have five minutes,' he says before biting into of one of the dates.

'Brother,' Samir says, 'a long time ago you told me that it was time to return to God. I was too stubborn to listen to you back then, but I know that you are a good Muslim, and I hope you will listen to me when I tell you that it is time to return to God.'

'I don't understand you,' Abdullah says and picks up another date.

'Abdullah, you do not have to pretend any longer! I know what is going on in the palace. Everyone in the Brotherhood knows what is going on in the palace. The king is not a real descendant of Muhammad—may God bless him and protect his soul. He is corrupt. He doesn't care about the people. On the contrary, he is trying to lead them away from God so that he can sponsor the luxurious lifestyles of his friends.

'The queen plots with foreign agents. She forces her ladies-in-waiting to drink alcohol during the Month of Burning, and then she organises great orgies at the palace; that is also why the king has abolished the courts of divine law. Tell me, what descendant of the Prophet would do such a thing?'

It is a rhetorical question, and Samir does not wait for an answer. 'There are orgies with all the servants, and the king takes whoever he pleases: girl, boy . . . But his lust is so insatiable that he even keeps a secret harem of Jewish girls on the side.'

Despite his tiredness, Abdullah cannot help but laugh out loud. A little too loud, even, and he promptly corrects himself; he doesn't want to wake Muhammad. 'Where do you get this nonsense?'

'Nonsense? Tell me, brother, if this is all nonsense, then why do you never speak about what's going on in the palace? When you are home, we eat together and we talk about many things, but never once have you said a single word about what's going on in the king's palace!'

'That's because what's going on in the king's palace is no one's business, and even if I wanted to speak about it, I have sworn by the Quran that I never would.'

Samir shakes his head. 'What about the newspapers? Can you speak about them? Is it not true that the king built a completely useless highway in order to transfer large amounts of money to Lord Ismat and Lord Raslan so that they would support him in his effort to drive God out of our society?'

'That is the most ridiculous thing I have ever heard!'

'Of course you would say that. You live in a house that was paid for by that money!'

Abdullah snorts. 'Do you think that the Raslans need money? They are the richest family in Beledar. They have been the richest family since long before Beledar even was Beledar! Tell me, brother, why would they do something like that?'

'You are forgetting that old Lord Raslan has a hundred grand-children and great-grandchildren. When money is split in so many ways, you need all the cash you can get your hands on if you want to remain the richest family.'

Abdullah stares at his brother. This is how Samir repays him. After all of his generosity, after taking him into his house, his brother accuses his family of being an ordinary bunch of thieves.

He ought to be screaming at his brother, but he does not have the energy. He will send him out of his house, but not tonight. Tomorrow is better.

'You see, you do not deny it,' Samir says, apparently interpreting his silence as an acknowledgement of guilt. 'We are not asking you to give up your job, or your house for that matter. All we are asking for is information. You are an important man in the palace; you can get your hands on proof of the corruption. That is all we need. We had a man who was working on that. He was very close to the king too, but he . . .' His brother pauses a second. 'He became indisposed.'

Abdullah stares at his brother again, and after some time he asks, 'What was this man's name?'

'I don't really remember; I was not his contact. I think it was Hafiz, or perhaps it was Haidar.'

Haidar. Haidar had been giving information to the Muslim Brotherhood, and that is why Lord Tali'a murdered him and his family. It is all clear now, and he knows what he must do. He stands up, point at the door, and hisses.

'Get out.'

'What?' Clearly he has caught Samir off guard.

'In the name of God, get out of my house,' he says a little louder.

'Are you being serious?'

'Get out! Out!' He picks up the plate of dates and throws it against the wall. Upstairs, he hears his little son crying, but he does not care. 'GET! OUT!'

Samir looks seriously scared but does not say anything as he starts to walk toward the door. He opens it and then he pauses. 'If you ever . . .'

'OUT!'

And his brother is gone, and Abdullah sits down, puts his face in his hands, and starts to cry. Samir is not completely wrong, he knows it, and he also knows that he was harsh, but what if Lord Tali'a has a secret hallway next to his house too? His wife and son are not going to be next.

He picks up a date from the floor, recomposes himself, and makes his way to the bedroom, where Muhammad is silent again. *God is praised.*

He turns on the light and starts to undress.

'The queen's brother is dead; jumped off the Eiffel Tower,' his wife says in a voice that betrays she has been awake for quite some time. 'Wasn't he at the palace a couple of weeks ago?'

'How do you know that the queen's brother is dead?' he grunts.

'I read it in a newspaper.'

That's strange. He did not hear anyone in the palace talk about it. 'What newspaper?'

'*Le Monde.* The French newspaper.'

'And where did you read a French newspaper?'

'At the bookstore.'

'The bookstore?' He makes an effort not to start screaming again. 'Why would you go to the bookstore? Why would you go outside? We have a servant for that!'

'You are being ridiculous,' she says. 'I am not going to let Barzah buy books for me. She can't even read!'

Is he being ridiculous? Maybe he is, but if it is true about the queen's brother, at least it is a good thing that he sent his brother away. If Lord Tali'a's arm reaches all the way to Paris, Dhamar is much too close to even think about treason.

Sergeant Khalid Khan
Camp Nardin

Month of Pregnancy 2-4, 1372 A.H. (14-16 June 1953 A.D.)

The jeep comes rushing into the camp at full speed, leaving large clouds of dust in its tracks, and it hasn't even come to a full stop when a man jumps out and shouts at Khalid, 'You there, I need to speak to your commander. Now!'

The crossed swords on the man's shoulders indicate that he is a captain and Khalid salutes before replying. 'Certainly, sir. Who may I say is calling?'

'That's none of your business.'

Khalid is not some private, and even for a general it would be rude to speak to a sergeant like this, yet he knows better than to argue with a superior officer and hides his irritation as he answers. 'Follow me, if God wants it.'

When, half a minute later, he knocks on the piece of wood that is hanging next to the open canvas, the commander looks up from his desk and motions with his hand that they can enter. After Khalid salutes, he says, 'Colonel Issa, I have a captain with me.'

'And does this captain have a name, Sergeant?' the commander asks.

'I am sure he does, sir, but the captain will not tell it to me.'

The captain coughs obtrusively.

'Bless you, Captain,' Colonel Issa says, and the captain looks annoyed at Khalid. It is clear that the man wants him to go away, but without permission from the commander he cannot go anywhere.

After an awkward silence, the captain decides to put his desire into words. 'In the name of God, perhaps the sergeant can give us some privacy, sir.'

'I am sorry, Captain, but that is not possible. As you can see, my sergeant major is not here, so Sergeant Khan will have to stand in for him. I never receive anyone from outside the battalion alone. What's more, I think it is most peculiar that you have not introduced yourself.'

The captain, completely ignoring the last remark, says, 'Don't worry, I am not here to make you any dishonourable proposition. I am here with a message, directly from the king, marked for your eyes only.'

'Well, you'd better give it to me then. I will decide how much the sergeant needs to know.' When the captain hesitates, the commander continues. 'Come now, dear man, don't worry too much about the sergeant; he cannot read through the paper. Besides, you seem to come here in great haste. I will not have read your message any sooner if you insist on holding it back until the sergeant leaves.'

The captain presents Khalid with a final angry stare, but then he walks forward and hands the commander the envelope. Colonel Issa stares at him for a moment before turning his attention to the letter. As the commander had observed, Khalid cannot read it through the paper, but he can see that it is not a long message. Nonetheless, Colonel Issa rereads it at least three times.

'Is everything okay, sir?' Khalid asks.

Colonel Issa does not respond. Instead he directs his gaze at the captain again. 'Do you know what's in here?'

'No, sir. As I said, I am just the messenger.'

The commander shakes his head. 'Sometimes I wonder how the minds of those people in the palace work.'

He hands the letter to Khalid, and he, pleased by the vexed look from the captain, accepts it with a smile. 'Out loud, if God wants it. Perhaps it will sound different when we hear it.'

'Sir,' the captain begins, 'I must protest. This is a private message.'

'Don't worry, Captain. Within a couple of hours, the whole world will know what is in it anyway.'

Khalid looks at the short letter and immediately he understands why.

'Iraqi army to arrive at our border in forty-eight hours. The Queen's Brigade is coming to the Malayer province to assist you, as is the Fourth Armoured Division. You are hereby promoted to brigadier general and in charge of both the Queen's Brigade and the Fourth. May God help you. King Jalal, First King of Beledar, Commander-in-Chief, etc., etc.'

Khalid reads it again for himself. He can hardly believe that Iraq, a fellow Muslim country, is going to attack them. Finally, he can become a real hero!

'What do we do, General?' he asks, proud that *he* is the first man who may address the commander with his new title.

The commander shakes his head again. 'Going to war on the eve of summer . . . Idiots. Find my officers. Tell them all leave is cancelled, and all men must return immediately from wherever they are; this war will be over within two weeks.'

'Yes, sir.'

The brigadier does not seem scared or intimidated by the prospect of war, merely annoyed.

'And Sergeant . . .'

'Sir?'

'In the name of God, keep the news to yourself for now. We don't want soldiers thinking that since they have already filled their pockets, they might as well leave the actual fighting to others.'

'Yes, sir.'

Khalid is almost out of the tent when the commander calls him back.

'And Sergeant, send someone to the Forbidden Chambers and spread the word that until further notice, if God wills it, I will personally relieve any man I find there of his manhood.'

'Yes, sir!'

As the brigadier predicted, it takes only a couple hours for the news to spread, and fortunately by then the first trucks with supplies have arrived, which gives them something to do. Two of the trucks are fully stacked with mines, the other two with burlap sacks.

Khalid remembers the sacks from the war manual they received back at the training camp—useful for those recruits who could read, but a waste of paper for the other ninety percent—and it soon becomes clear that he is one of the few men in the camp who have actually read it.

'Can you believe it?' Lieutenant Fakeih is fuming. 'The Iraqis are preparing their tanks and warplanes, and the king sends us burlap sacks! What, in the name of the Prophet, are we going to do with burlap sacks?'

Thinking it is a rhetorical question, Khalid does not answer until the lieutenant addresses him directly.

'Well, Sergeant?'

He gives Fakeih the most dignified look he can muster and replies, 'According to Lord al-Maseeh's *Manual for the Modern Soldier,* we fill them with sand and use them to build walls and bunkers.'

'Lord al-Maseeh,' the sergeant spits. 'He was a Christian.'

Clearly this is enough for Fakeih to discredit him completely, but personally Khalid is more troubled by the fact that the 'modern' manual is, in fact, almost thirty years old.

When Captain Madani comes to check in on the men, Lieutenant Fakeih decides to make use of the moment and repeat his question for the captain; he appears genuinely surprised when he receives the same answer.

'You are truly telling me that you want us to fill bags and hide behind them?'

'Trust me, you fill enough of those bags and then you stack them high enough, God willing, not even a grenade from a tank will penetrate them.'

'Are you sure it is not a joke?' the lieutenant asks. 'Like, we are in the desert anyway, so why not let the sand protect us from tanks and bullets?'

'Please don't take shelter for my sake, Lieutenant. If you want to fight the Iraqis from out in the open, you are more than welcome to.'

'That is their strategy . . .' The lieutenant sighs after the captain has gone. He spits on the ground again. 'We are all going to die.'

Khalid thinks back to what Sergeant Shamil said to him when he had first arrived at the camp, almost two years ago. *When the Iraqis come, take one of the M38s, come find me, and ride off as quickly as possible.*

The work they have done during the last few months has not been in vain, and the camp is much stronger than when he arrived, yet the sooner the Fourth Armoured Division arrives, the better he will feel.

The sun starts to set, and Captain Madani calls together his lieu-tenants and sergeants to prepare them for what is to come. To Khalid's surprise, the captain appears very knowledgeable and confident.

'Listen up,' he says to the men sitting around him in a trench. 'They will start by shooting artillery at us, and we are not going to shoot back until the commander orders us to return fire. Howitzer shells do not come cheap, and, more importantly, they are very scarce at our camp. We do not want to waste our ammo before we are certain we are going to hit them. The first day, the general expects only long-distance fighting, and each platoon will protect a howitzer. Whatever happens, do not leave the trenches once the enemy artillery starts shelling us; if you die outside the trench, you die because of your own stupidity.'

Protect the howitzers from what? How are they possibly going to protect them against artillery shells? Khalid shakes his head but holds his tongue.

'After the shells, the airplanes will come. The Iraqis have old British warplanes, Hurricanes and Spitfires, and they have many of them, but we own American jet planes, Shooting Stars and Sabre jets. Our planes are better, more agile and faster. They are also extremely difficult to shoot down from the ground, so we have an advantage there.'

Khalid looks around and sees relief in the eyes of some of his colleagues, but he doubts this is justified. Their planes may be better, but they cannot be everywhere at the same time, and if the Iraqis really have more planes, the Beledarians are going to need all of God's help.

'Before the real attack begins, the Iraqi warplanes and artillery will try to blow up Satan's Playground'—this refers to the carefully constructed minefield on the border—'but we are confident that the mines are laid too deep for them to succeed.

'That's when they will send the infantry, followed closely by their engineers. The engineers will try to defuse the mines, and here we must do all we can to stop them from succeeding. The mines, some hundreds of yards away from each other, are connected. If we manage to get their tanks trapped in a jam on the playground, it will leave them sitting ducks, and our tanks will destroy them without even breaking a sweat.'

So much for the theory.

He has longed for war; he has spent years preparing for it; he has excelled in every strategy game; in training, he has fought numerous opponents fearlessly with his bare hands, and against the odds he has won the respect of his men. Nonetheless, nothing has prepared Khalid for the sensation that incoming artillery shells send through his body, even when they are literally missing him by miles.

Without knowing what the time is or how he has ended up there, he finds himself sitting with his back against a wall in a trench, waiting while the explosions gradually get closer.

They are also getting and louder and louder, and then there is a deafening impact. For minutes, he cannot hear anything, and once his ears are functioning again, he hears men screaming in the distance. They've been hit!

And again!

From his position in the trench, he can see the smoke and dust coming up. This one was not more than two dozen yards in front of him, and suddenly he realises how insignificant he is with his rifle. The Iraqis are miles and miles away, yet two dozen yards just made the difference between life and death!

'Where is my sergeant?' It is the voice of Lieutenant Fakeih. He has not seen Fakeih since the previous evening, and he had started to think that once the attack really began, he was going to have to lead the platoon by himself. How wrong could he have been! 'Sergeant!'

The lieutenant is standing in front of him, and he has no choice but to get to his feet and salute him.

'Thank you, Sergeant, but now is not really the moment for your etiquette. If God wants it, we are going to shoot back at those bastards! Get the men!'

'Yes, sir.'

He has no idea where the men are, but he tries to sound as confident as he can.

'Namdar!' he calls. The corporal is sitting casually on the ground and appears to be reading a letter while waiting for someone to give him an order. 'Get your squad and have them bring the platoon together, if God wants it. Meet us at the howitzer!'

'God wants it, my friend!' Namdar salutes and winks at him at the same time.

He is deeply impressed by his friend's cool attitude, but as he follows Lieutenant Fakeih, he notices that the trenches are filled with men who are handling the shelling even worse than he was. There are men sitting in ditches, their heads in their hands, yelling that they are going to die. Others are simply running around like headless chickens, bereft of all purpose.

Normally they could reach the howitzer through the trenches, but part of the way is temporarily blocked by a group of men helping a soldier who has been hit by shrapnel. Instead of asking them to move aside, though, Fakeih climbs out of the trench.

'Sergeant!' Lieutenant Fakeih calls.

Khalid hesitates; he remembers the words from Captain Madani very clearly. *If you die outside the trench, you will die because of your own stupidity!*

But the lieutenant has not been listening. 'Come on, Sergeant Khan! You can't stay in that trench for the rest of the war, anyway. The longer you wait, the more dangerous it will be!'

He doesn't have a choice; he throws his rifle on the sand above him and pulls himself out of the trench. All around him there is only dust in the air, and he can see no further than twenty yards.

'What are you waiting for?'

The lieutenant is right. Why is he standing there, completely in the open? He rushes after the commander, completing the fifty-yard sprint in the open in less than seven seconds.

At the howitzer they meet the sergeant major, who looks slightly troubled when he sees them jumping in the trench from above but chooses to ignore it.

'In the name of God, are you from Alif company?' the sergeant major barks.

'Yes, sir!' Khalid answers.

'Why the holdup? Were you not commanded to come here the moment the shooting started?'

'They have been shooting at us all morning. No one appears to be giving any commands at all!' Lieutenant Fakeih shouts back.

Khalid adds, 'It was a little chaotic, sir.'

'I'm sure it was. War is a chaotic business. Where is the rest of your company?'

'They will be here shortly,' Lieutenant Fakeih growls. 'What about those tanks we were promised?'

'Do you see any tanks, Lieutenant?'

Fakeih spits on the ground and says, 'If I saw them, I would not be asking.'

'Well, since you can't see them, they're probably not here.'

'No problem.' There is a strange kind of enthusiasm in the lieutenant's tone that is not lost on Khalid. 'Let's just load up one of those bad boys, and, if God wants it, start doing a little shooting ourselves.'

'God does not want it,' the sergeant major growls. 'You are to wait until the planes have told us how far and in what exact direction we have to shoot. In the name of God, or of the general, whichever one you like, there will not be any haphazard shooting in this brigade.'

Lieutenant Fakeih takes a step toward the sergeant major. 'Are you telling me that we're just going to let them shoot at us without doing anything?'

'That's exactly what I'm telling you.'

'Do you know that you are really annoying me today? I feel like you are forgetting that I am your superior officer. Perhaps it is time that you started calling me *sir*.'

The lieutenant takes another step forward; now their noses are almost touching.

But the sergeant major does not move back. Instead he raises an eyebrow and counters, 'Not going to happen. I fought in Syria and Iraq with the brigadier and the king. I know exactly who my superiors are, and, in the name of God, you are not one of them.'

Now Fakeih takes a step back and pulls his gun. The battle around them appears to have completely disappeared, and Fakeih hisses, 'Or I should shoot you right here for insubordination!'

The sergeant major sniffs, and then in one fluid movement he pulls the gun out of the lieutenant's hand and points it at Fakeih's head.

'And perhaps I should shoot you for being drunk.'

Fakeih grins. 'There is no law against being drunk in our country, thanks to our infidel king, and there is definitely no law against being drunk in the army.'

Crack!

The shot has come completely unexpectedly, and instinctively, Khalid takes took two steps back, almost tripping over his own feet. Meanwhile, the sergeant major looks at the lieutenant lying on the floor.

'There is a law against being drunk on duty, dumb idiot, and it is punishable by death by execution—hereby administered.' He turns to Khalid and holds out Fakeih's gun. A little shaken by what just happened, Khalid only stares at it.

'In the name of God, take your officer's gun, Acting Lieutenant Khan, and tell me, where are your men?'

At that moment a whole score of men from Alif company come running from behind the sergeant major; Namdar is in front of them. Khalid lets out a sigh of relief. He could not have come up with a better timing himself and shyly points at Namdar.

'Corporal, where is Captain Madani?'

'He's been hit by shrapnel, sir. He wanted to come anyway, said it didn't hurt much, but the medic won't let him go anywhere until he has taken everything out.'

'The rest of the officers?'

'I could not find them, sir.'

The sergeant major shakes his head and turns back to Khalid. 'Well, Acting Lieutenant, you appear to be in charge. Remember, until our fighters are in the air, I want you nowhere near those howitzers!'

'Yes, sir.'

As the sergeant major turns away, Khalid hears him mumble, 'Dumb greens.'

'What happened to him?' Namdar asks, pointing at Fakeih.

'Apparently this is the punishment for being drunk during a battle, *Sergeant.*'

CHAPTER EIGHT

ABDULLAH SAÍD
Mayasin

Month of Pregnancy 5, 1372 A.H. (17 June 1953 A.D.)

Abdullah has been in bed for less than an hour when the alarms go off, but he is immediately awake. 'Kalima, get up. Take Muhammad and run downstairs!'

He continues to his sisters' room. They are nowhere near as alert as his wife was and appear annoyed to be woken. 'Amala! Azalia! Wake up and follow Kalima!'

'Why all this noise?' Azalia asks sleepily.

'Bombs, girl! The Iraqis are bombing the city!' That should do the trick, and before he has reached the stairs to his mother's room, his sisters are standing next to their beds.

He did offer to set up a room downstairs for his mother when she became rheumatic and climbing stairs became exceedingly demanding, but she was so offended that he didn't dare to suggest it again. He realises now how stupid it is that they have allowed the least mobile person in the house to sleep the farthest from safety.

'Mother,' he shouts while he swings open her door. She is awake, but she has not left her bed. 'Mother, let me carry you down!'

'Carry me? Boy, you go down, and, if God wants it, I will be with you presently.'

That is not acceptable. It generally takes her about a quarter of an hour to get down the stairs, and at the moment she does not look like she has any intention of getting out of bed at all. 'Mother, in the name of God, there are planes coming that are going to drop bombs on the city; perhaps even on our house!'

'Boy, if they drop a bomb on our house, I'll be in Paradise quicker from up here than from down there.'

'Mother, listen to me. I am the boss in this house, and you will come down with me!'

He takes a step closer, but his mother picks up her walking stick from next to her bed. 'Boy, if you come near me, I will hit you!'

She means it. He knows it.

He stares at her. He has no idea how old she is, but she is definitely not old enough to die up here in the attic. On the other hand, she is his mother, and he cannot force her to come down with him. Or can he?

'What's taking so long?' He turns around and finds his sister Azalia standing behind him.

'Why are you not downstairs?' he barks at her.

'I *was* downstairs! Why are *you* not downstairs?'

He gestures at his mother. 'She doesn't want to come. She wants to stay here and die!'

'In the name of God, that is ridiculous!' Azalia turns to their mother, who is looking ready to fight.

'You see?' Abdullah says.

'Mother,' Azalia says angrily and takes a step forward.

Their mother swings her walking stick at her, but Azalia catches it and pulls it from the woman's hand without much difficulty.

'Mother, if God wants it, Abdullah is going to pick you up and carry you downstairs. It's not up for discussion.'

To his surprise, his mother just nods, and when his sister turns back to him and says, 'Go on,' he does not realise that he has taken an order from his little sister until they are halfway down the stairs.

They do not have a real shelter or basement, but there is a little crawlspace under the house, and although it is very uncomfortable, Abdullah figures this is the safest place to be when the bombs start to fall. Of course, if the Iraqis have a bomb like the Americans used to end the War of the West, no shelter in the city will be safe, but according to Mr Petrakis, only the United States, Britain, and the Soviet Union have bombs like that.

Please God, let the infidel be right about that.

Other bombs are not too pleasant either, and during the last few weeks Abdullah has had nightmares of his beautiful house collapsing above them, yet somehow he feels that since there are so many people in city who really have nowhere to go, he is relatively safe.

'I don't hear explosions,' Amala says.

'You mean God is praised, I don't hear explosions,' Azalia answers.

'Yes, that is what I mean.'

There isn't a hint of sarcasm in Amala's voice, and when the 'all clear' sounds an hour later, they still have not heard a single bomb.

'That must be thanks to our warplanes,' Abdullah says to his family. 'We have the most modern air force in the region!'

To God he says something else. *Thank you God, from now on I will live better. Better than I have until this day; I will do all I can to honour You.*

Before they go to bed again, it is decided that the next morning the servant will set up a bed for Mother downstairs.

When Abdullah makes his way to the palace that morning, it does not take him long to discover why there were not any explosions that night. The Iraqis did not drop bombs on the city; they dropped flyers. He picks one up and starts to read.

In the name of God, the Most Gracious, the Most Merciful.

People of Beledar,
It is with the utmost regret that we must inform you that your so-called king is a pretender. King Jalal pays tribute to his corrupt lords, not to God. He has abolished the courts of divine law so that he can hold orgies without fear of punishment. He hides a harem of Jewish girls in his palace, and his henchman, Lord Tali'a, kills whoever dares to protest.

Queen Aisha is a fraud. Her real name is Anna Christina, and inside the walls of her palace she does not even pretend to be a Muslim. Back in France, she was famous for the number of men she had seduced, and we do not believe it unlikely that it is she who has led your king away from the path of the Prophet—May God bless him and protect his soul.

People of Beledar,
Over 1,400 years ago God sent His Messenger to His people to save them from themselves and to lead them to Paradise. He wanted to unite all the Arabs under one ruler; to build a world where men could submit to Him without constant seductions; a world where His word was law and where men were prepared for Paradise.

We still want to build that world, and in the name of God we ask
you, the good Muslims of Beledar, to stand up to the evil pretender
and his whore. And I swear by the Quran, that you have the support
of every man, every gun, and every tank at my command!
Faisal II, King of Iraq

This is where Abdullah's brother got his ideas about what's going on in the palace: Iraqi propaganda. But is it all propaganda? Abdullah knows what is going on in the palace, and while there may not be orgies, the king and his wife are by no means paragons of virtue.

He has a long day ahead of him, and he should make straight for the palace, but his feet lead him to the Green Mosque, and when he pushes against the doors, they open without the slightest resistance.

'Son of Saíd, I must say that I am surprised to see you here. I would think that at the moment they need every man they have in the palace,' the scholar says after spotting him.

Abdullah takes a deep breath. 'Mr al-Rubaie, may I speak freely?'

'Young friend, if you cannot speak freely in the house of God, then where could you? If God wants it, share your mind.'

Abdullah takes another deep breath, and he looks around to see if there is anyone who might overhear them, but apart from himself and the reverend, the mosque is deserted.

'Mr al-Rubaie, years ago you taught me that the Prophet told the people to beware of inherited power and that his first Successors were therefore chosen by an assembly of wise men. When I look at our country today, it appears that all power is in the hands of a king, who has inherited his position. And while these flyers the Iraqis dropped last night may not be true, neither can we call the king a defender of our faith.'

'That depends,' the scholar replies. 'The king defends peace, and he defends the rights of all people. Why can we not call him a defender of our faith?'

'For one, he has abolished the courts of divine law. You acted as a judge there; were you not angered?'

Mr al-Rubaie shrugs. 'Son of Saíd, these things are not always as easy as they look. I do not believe that Muslims should kill other people, yet as a judge I sometimes had to condemn men and women to death. Not one day has gone by this year where I haven't thanked God that the king has lifted this responsibility from me.'

Abdullah can hardly believe what he is hearing. 'But what about the fourteen hundred years of Islamic jurisprudence and interpretations about the life of Muhammad—may God bless him and protect his soul—that the king has just thrown away? Shouldn't this form the foundation of our state and our legal system?'

Still calm, the scholar places a hand on his shoulder. 'Abdullah, I have lived in this city my whole life, and even though it is now almost ten times as big as when I was born, there are fewer murders in the street, and there is more food. The king is building schools, hospitals, and roads, and I have it on the best authority that he is working tirelessly to make our country a better place every day. He is certainly not perfect, but it is better to live thirty years under an imperfect king than thirty days under an ineffective one.'

'And so we should just let him do whatever he feels like?'

The scholar shakes his head. 'No. But we should not be deceived by our enemies into thinking that helping them is the equivalent of helping God . . .'

'I didn't mean that,' Abdullah interrupts the scholar, who silences him by raising a finger.

'Nor should we become fools to believe that a chosen king, president, or successor will make God's word resonate stronger in our society. It is true that in an ideal world we would have wise men choose our leader, and we would all follow that man, yet I will find you a three-headed donkey before you can find me ten men as wise as King Jalal to choose that man.'

CHAPTER NINE

ACTING LIEUTENANT KHALID KHAN
Nardin

Month of Pregnancy 4-6, 1372 A.H. (16-18 June 1953 A.D.)

The chaos in the battalion does not last long. At the end of the
first day, Khalid's platoon is almost complete. At the end of the
second day, almost all men move securely in the trenches. A
couple of men are removed from the front due to shell shock, and
there are about four dozen actual casualties, but overall, most of
the men recover quickly from the shock of the first attack.
Moreover, it soon becomes clear that the Iraqis have terrible aim.

The only problem is the tanks. At the end of the first day, the
Fourth Armoured Division has not yet arrived at Nardin, and
throughout the second day, there's still no sign of them. But then,
just as he has given up hope, out of nowhere they appear. Khalid
watches them through his binoculars, counting twenty-four war
machines rolling through the desert. What a magnificent sight
they make! He has no idea how many tanks there are at the other
side of the border, but the sight of the Beledarians fills his heart
with joy, and when he points them out, he can see how his men
straighten their backs and start working their duties with a new
sense of purpose.

'Lieutenant Khan!' The young man who sticks his head out of the biggest tank and salutes him is more than a little familiar, and Khalid can hardly believe his eyes. Not only has the Fourth Armoured Division finally arrived, almost three days late, but his brother is with them!

The silver stripes on his arm mean Aadhil has been promoted as well, though not as high as Khalid, which gives him quite a satisfying feeling, too, even though at the same time he feels a little guilty about it, and it is with a big smile that he returns the salute.

'Sergeant Khan!'

His brother jumps from the tank, and he hugs and kisses him.

'Lieutenant, eh?' Aadhil says. 'Did all the real officers die?'

'Jealous, brother?'

'Not really,' Aadhil replies. 'See that?' He motions with his head to the tank behind them. 'My machine. Mine!'

'Not bad.' Khalid laughs. 'Not too bad at all.'

'Not bad? It's America's greatest achievement! Just look at my tank and look at the tanks around it. What do you see?'

Khalid does not know anything about tanks, but one thing is obvious. 'Yours is bigger.'

'Not just bigger!' Aadhil exclaims. 'Faster too! See that?'

He points to one of the other tanks.

'M4 Sherman, second-hand, may have even visited Germany before coming here. It's a decent machine for sure, but you don't want to be inside it when the Iraqis hit you with a 90mm shell. And that,' he points to another one, 'M26 Pershing; there are thousands of them in Korea right now, yet it still isn't nearly as fast as mine.'

'If your tank is that fast, why did it take you so long to get here?'

Aadhil frowns. 'Didn't they tell you? The Fourth Division met a whole score of Iraqi aircraft on the way here. Only three got out in one piece. We are an improvised division; basically they took a handful of tanks from all the other divisions and sent them here.'

'Where were our own planes?' As he asks the question, Khalid also realises the answer. It is as he feared: a simple matter of mathematics.

Aadhil shrugs. 'No idea, but listen up, little brother: you are lucky! I have brought you the best tank God has given mankind. Most modern technology in the world: four-inch armour, 90mm gun, destructive range of a mile, and a top speed of forty miles per hour, imagine that! Just as fast as a camel at top speed, except that this baby can keep it up for hours!'

Khalid still has no idea what his brother's specifications mean, but he tries to look impressed, and feigning interest, he points at a tank that looks odd and asks, 'What about that one?'

'That's not really a tank; that's a tank destroyer. Will take out any one of those Iraqi tanks from a mile away, if God wants it.'

'If he can see it.'

'Trust me, little brother, the men in that machine can see much farther than you, and if they can see it, they will destroy it.'

Khalid nods and realises the fact that Aadhil is with him again gives him more confidence than all the tanks in the world.

'So, how come you've got the best one?'

Aadhil grins. 'I bet the owner that if I could fix it, it would be mine.'

'Betting is a sin,' Khalid says gravely, and Aadhil's grin grows wider.

'So is leaving a machine like that behind in the desert.'

The next morning, they are woken by a bombardment that is fiercer than the previous two mornings' bombardments combined, and this time the Iraqi warplanes have joined the fighting too.

What is more, all the shells appear to be going more or less in the same direction, most of them falling about two hundred to fifty yards in front of the line. It doesn't take long before Khalid can no longer see anything, but he knows exactly what is going on: the Iraqis are trying to blow up Satan's Playground. He prays that Captain Madani was right about the mines being too deep.

When the explosions stop, Khalid is standing at the front line, watching the dust form a thick mist. His heart is racing. This is the decisive moment in the battle to come. Chances are that the Iraqis have a lot more than twenty-four tanks, meaning that it's crucial to stop the engineers.

Khalid looks to his side through the binoculars. Thirty yards from him, he sees Brigadier General Issa at the edge of what is going to be the battlefield, and the sergeant major is right next to him.

'Ba Company, ready?' he hears the sergeant major call in the distance. 'In the name of God!'

'God! Is! Great!' echoes all through Ba Company, and Khalid watches the men climb out of the trench. They run into the sandy mist, and within seconds the fog has swallowed them. *May God protect them.*

He wishes he was on the field too, though, instead of waiting here for an order that may not come. He looks back into the mist, but there is nothing to see and nothing to hear. He turns. Around him are his men, and for a moment he catches Namdar's eyes; his friend nods at him, and he knows the sergeant will follow him without thinking.

Somewhere behind him is his brother in a tank. If they can trap the enemy tanks, it will be up to Aadhil to finish the job. If God wants it, in his giant iron war machine his brother can take out at least a dozen enemy tanks by himself.

Suddenly he hears explosions, and through the dust he sees them too, and then the mist starts to intensify again. Men are screaming in the distance. The Iraqis must have known that the brigadier would send out infantry once they stopped their bombardment; they only paused to trap them!

'Officers!' he hears the commander call. 'No man gets back in!'

He observes how Brigadier Issa and the sergeant major climb out of the trench, both with their handgun drawn; on the other side of him, Captain Madani is doing the same. Then he realises that he is a senior officer now too, and he knows what is expected of him: he must shoot every man that retreats!

'Get back, in the name of God!' The deep voice of the sergeant major is so loud that even the Iraqis must be able to hear it. Khalid looks through his binoculars again, but the mist is too thick, and he cannot see what is going on. A couple of seconds later, he hears the cracks of a handgun nearby.

Abruptly, the shelling stops again and only the sound of machine guns remains. Two hundred yards away? Five hundred yards? The dust mutes the sound, and he cannot tell. He realises that he has unconsciously climbed out of the trench too, and he has his gun in his hand. He looks down; there is Namdar, and behind his friend are the men from his platoon, all waiting for an order.

On his left is still Captain Madani. He stands there completely straight, his gun pointed at the blinding dust. It feels weird to watch the shabby captain, who normally spends his time complaining, standing there, a relentless officer made even more impressive by his size.

Khalid turns forward again. There is a man. A man! He cannot see if the man is Beledarian or Iraqi, but surely the Iraqis cannot be this close yet.

'Get back!' he calls. 'In the name of God, get back!'

The man does not. He does not raise his weapon either, though perhaps he does not have one. This is the moment; Khalid is an officer! He is going to have to shoot one of his own men. There is no other option.

Or is there?

He really doesn't have time to think, and he hears himself mumbling, 'We belong to God, and to him shall we return.'

Then he shouts as loud as he can, 'In the name of God! In the name of God!'

He puts his gun back in his holster, takes his rifle, and starts to run.

'GOD! IS! GREAT!'

In three steps he reaches the man, and with the butt of his rifle he knocks him to the ground. He does not believe that the man will be getting up anytime soon, but he does not wait to check. He looks over his shoulder and sees Namdar climbing out of the trench too. Using all the air that his lungs can filter through the dust, he calls 'Second platoon! In the name of God! To me!'

In front of him more men are coming. They are retreating, that is obvious.

'GOD! IS! GREAT!' he calls again, and he runs to the closest man and knocks him down too.

Another one, but he cannot stop them all. Helplessly he looks around, and then he realises that the retreating men are not getting far.

'God! Is! Great!' he hears men calling everywhere. But Namdar and the rest of his men aren't knocking the men down; they are simply stopping them and turning them around with their numbers and enthusiasm!

The sound of shots draws his attention forward again, and he starts to run toward the sound. Perhaps he has not fulfilled his duty in the way he was supposed to, but at least he is going to make the commander and the king proud and die an honourable death here today.

'GOD! IS! GREAT!' he calls again.

The mist of sand starts to choke him, and he does not see anything any more, no allies, no enemies. There is only dust and the sound of distant shooting. For a second he pauses to bind his scarf in front of his face. Then he sees small, obscured flashes; he hears them too. Iraqi machine guns! They are shooting haphazardly into the mist. He crouches and aims his rifle at the flashes, but when he pulls the trigger nothing happens.

Sand.

He considers using Fakeih's handgun, but he knows he will never hit anything with that, and for a moment he hesitates, while at the same time he realises that he has been taught never to hesitate on a battlefield. What other options are there? He looks around. Not far from him he sees the body of a man. Is he alive?

He runs over and shakes the body. There is no reaction. Where is his gun? He crawls through the sand, and when he finds the M1 carbine a couple yards away, he thanks God. He picks it up, points it to where the enemy may or may not be and pulls the trigger.

It works. Again he praises God. He still hears shooting in the distance, yet he cannot see flashes now. He goes forward, or at least he moves toward the sound; he is not one hundred percent sure if that really is forward.

After twenty yards, he comes across more bodies. He studies one and sees a small Iraqi flag on his arm; he is going the right way.

'In the name of God, help me!' a man nearby grunts, albeit weakly. 'Water.'

Khalid takes his goatskin and pours a little water over the man's mouth. He is bleeding heavily from his stomach. A little more water, and Khalid goes on.

His platoon must be somewhere in front of him by now, and he does not want stay behind. When this is over, no one should be able to say that he has not pulled his weight.

All sense of time is gone. He can't have been on the battlefield more than minutes, but it feels like hours, days even.

He bumps into a man in a crouched position, firing his gun in the direction of the Iraqis. Startled, the man turns around and points his rifle at Khalid.

'Wait!' Khalid calls, and thanks to God, the man recognises him.

'Lieutenant,' the soldier acknowledges him. It is Ayden. Never had he thought there would come a moment when he would be pleased to see the face of Ayden, but here it is. Finally, he is no longer alone.

'What are you shooting at, Private?'

Ayden points in the distance. 'There were Iraqis, sir; I swear it by the Prophet.'

'Well, they're not there now. Let's go.' He runs on, and Ayden follows him. On the way they come across more bodies, and the number of casualties keeps on increasing the deeper they enter the battlefield. Some are dead, others are moving. He sees a man without legs using his arms to creep to safety, wherever that may be. He hears men groan and he hears men scream, but he has no time for them; they will have to wait for help until the battle is over.

In the distance he sees flashes again, and he runs toward them until he figures he is close enough to hit them. He throws himself to the ground and takes aim. Next to him, Ayden stops too, and they both fire their guns at the flashes. When he pauses to reload, he sees that a couple of yards away from him, other soldiers are shooting in the same direction.

'Aisha!' he shouts.

'Dunya!' comes the answer. Dunya is the name of the princess; only now does he truly appreciate the beauty of the code words that have been passed down these last three mornings.

Together with Ayden, he creeps over to them.

'What are you?'

'Third Battalion, Queen's Brigade.'

Third Battalion? On the line they had been almost a mile to the south. Where are they?

'Aargh!' One of the men starts to scream, and Khalid can see that his shoulder is bleeding. Next thing he knows there are gunshots all around, yet he has no idea where they are coming from.

And then they stop.

'Can you make it back?' he asks the injured soldier.

'Yes, sir,' the man grunts.

'All right.' To the other men he says, 'Let's go!'

And they go forward again. The sun has started to break through the mist, and he is beginning to feel exposed, when he hears Ayden shout, 'Down!'

His improvised squad is on the ground in less than a second. The Iraqis are so close by that even Khalid cannot miss them, and with his first rounds he hits one of them in the chest. He sees other men fall too, slain by the bullets from his comrades, and moments later the surviving Iraqis get up and start to run.

'In the name of God, after them!'

He gets up and his men follow him, but then, without warning, there is an enormous explosion not far from them. Has the Iraqi artillery started again? They would also be shooting at their own men; that would truly be monstrous. Then again, what else can be expected from the Iraqis?

He stops. Two of his men are down, but only one is screaming.

'Sir!' one of the men from the Queen's Brigade calls. He stops and looks at where the man is pointing, but he cannot see anything. He takes the binoculars from his pocket and then he sees it.

Finally the Iraqis have sent in their tanks!

His part of the battle is over, and he goes to check on the men. The man who is not screaming has lost half of his face. He is not dead, yet, but there is nothing that can be done for him. The other has lost his foot, and the rest of his leg does not look too good either.

'Help me!' he begs.

Ayden and the last man standing from Queen's Brigade help to throw the man over Khalid's shoulder, and he turns around.

'Back to the line!' he orders before he starts to run away from the tanks.

Running with a man over his shoulder is more difficult than it looked when he saw others do it, and he does not run very quickly, but he knows that if he stops he will die. In turns, Ayden and the man from Third Battalion stop to give covering fire, while he keeps on putting his feet in front of each other as fast as he can.

This is it: life or death.

There is an explosion not far in front of him. Had the shell been fired two seconds later, he would now be dead, and he thanks God for his good fortune as he runs through the hovering sand.

How much farther?

The man is getting heavier with every step. He needs to stop, but he cannot. *Please God, give me strength!*

Would his brother leave this man? Certainly not. Namdar? Ghulam? Even the small Ghulam would find a way to go on.

The sand around him disappears, and he is back in training camp, repeating his first run. Next to him is his tormentor. *Are you a Jew? You run like a Jew. What could the king possibly want with a soldier like you? You are a disgrace to this army!*

He inhales deeply, but the bombshells the tanks are spreading across the battlefield have made the dust return, and there is little oxygen in the air, so he clings to the thought that he is no disgrace; he is Lieutenant Khalid Khan!

God, most gracious and merciful God, give me strength. Don't let me let my friends down, he prays as he keeps on running.

There are more men running in front of him now, and he tells himself that he's almost there; no more than a hundred yards. He groans. One step, two, four, six, ten, fifteen, twenty . . .

Every breath is difficult now . . .

Thirty. *God is the greatest. Praise and glory be to You, dear God. Blessed be your name, exalted be your Majesty and Glory. There is no God but You.*

Forty. *I seek God's shelter from Satan, the condemned. In the name of God, the Most Compassionate, the Most Merciful.*

Fifty. His legs are giving up under him, but he must keep running. Left . . . Right . . . Left. Right . . .

Sixty. *Praise be to God, Lord of the Universe. The Most Merciful. Master of the Day of Judgment.*

Seventy! *Glorified is my Lord, the Great. God listens to those who praise Him. Our Lord, praise be for You only.*

He can see the line!

And he can see fire, and there is a great, invisible force, that sends Khalid flying through the air.

CHAPTER TEN

ABDULLAH SAÍD
Mayasin

Month of Pregnancy 8-10, 1372 A.H. (18-20 June 1953 A.D.)

'God is praised, sir!' A man he has never seen before hugs him. 'Our Great and Merciful God, He has blessed our country and He has blessed the king! God is praised!'

The king has given everyone in the palace the day off to celebrate their victory, but Abdullah is not in a particularly festive mood. Of course, maybe the scholar was right; maybe King Jalal is a force for good in this country, but it does not feel this way.

He thinks about Siraj's House of Dreams. The king said that if he closed a whorehouse, the next day a new one would open its doors, yet Abdullah is not so sure. If all people simply follow God's rules, there is no need for whorehouses. No need for young girls to be sold to old men. It's so simple, yet it seems that everyone prefers to stay blind to this clear logic.

As long as King Jalal is in power, this country can only drift further away from the true faith, and that should be obvious to everyone, even the people who aren't working in the palace. Nonetheless, his countrymen appear completely oblivious to this fact. Has no one read the Iraqi flyers, or does no one believe them?

His brother said that everyone in the Muslim Brotherhood knew exactly what was going on in the palace, and he wonders how many men there actually are in the Brotherhood.

Looking around, he realises that one thing is certain at the moment, though: if the people on these streets were asked to choose between the king and God today, everyone here would choose the king.

The next day, Lord Tali'a himself is standing at the front of the small gate.

'Mr Saíd, I am afraid I have some bad news.'

His heart skips a beat. He hasn't done anything, has he? Or can the commander really read minds, as some people claim? Does Lord Tali'a know that he has stopped believing in the king?

'What is it, Commander?' he asks as casually as he can muster.

'I am afraid that Mr al-Rubaie died last night. Tomorrow we will bury him, but I know he meant much to you, and I thought you might want to take the day off.'

Not knowing what to say, he just nods. Tears start to form in his eyes, but he does not want the commander to see him cry.

'Thank you, sir,' he mumbles. 'We surely belong to God, and to Him we shall return.'

'It's written.'

Abdullah looks up, but Lord Tali'a has disappeared. He takes his pocket square and wipes his eyes. Lord Tali'a is right; he is not fit to work today.

It's quiet in Pervaíz's coffee house, and he wonders how long it has been since he was last here. More than ten years, probably. Pervaíz does not recognise him, but he is exactly as cheerful as Abdullah remembers him. He orders some coffee and some rolls and sits alone at a table, staring into the void, and Abdullah does not know how long he has been sitting there when a familiar voice says, 'So you've heard.'

In front of him is his brother, accompanied by two men he has never met, who introduce themselves as Quadir and Gamal.

'Tomorrow they will bury him,' Abdullah says. 'Tomorrow, the greatest scholar of our time will rest in an unmarked grave at Mayasin cemetery.'

Samir and his friends sit down, and Abdullah's brother says, 'The world has lost a great scholar, but even if he rests in an unmarked grave, we will not forget him.'

He looks at Samir. Does his little brother mean what he says? Or is he simply trying comfort him? 'Do you know, while Mr al-Rubaie was always a great man, I believe that the scholar may have died years ago.'

'How do you mean?' Samir asks.

He shakes his head. It does not matter much now anyway. 'It feels like lately he got his priorities mixed up. He didn't object when the courts of divine law were abolished; he applauded. He didn't even object to the king's hedonism. Everything was allowed, as long as stability in the kingdom was maintained.'

Samir frowns. 'Are you saying that you do object to the king's hedonism?'

Abdullah looks around. Apart from Samir, his brother's friends, and Pervaíz, there is no one in the coffee house. 'I'm saying that the king is not leading this country in the spirit of the Prophet— may God bless him and protect his soul—and I'm saying that we might be able to do better.'

'Does that mean you will help us?'

He sighs. 'If only I could, but I can't. You want information; you want proof of corruption and hedonism, proof of Godlessness.

But if I were to provide any of those things, my family would never be safe. Lord Tali'a . . . He will send us all to Paradise.'

Samir shakes his head. 'Right now, we don't want any of those things. The king is more popular than ever, which makes those kinds of things completely useless. What we do need is to know where we are needed most. What areas in the capital is the king neglecting? Where can we spend our recourses most efficiently? Provide us with information on those kinds of matters, and I promise that in a couple of years we will have all of Mayasin behind us!'

Samir, Gamal, and Quadir are all looking like he can save their lives by doing this very simple thing. And it is simple. Not only will no one get hurt, but he will also be helping improve people's lives.

And before he has thought it through, he has sworn by the Quran that he will help them where he can.

Chapter Eleven

Acting Lieutenant Khalid Khan
Camp Nardin

Month of Pregnancy 7-15, 1372 A.H. (19-27 June 1953 A.D.)

He has been drinking again. That is why the war hammer has returned to his head with a vengeance. It does not matter; it will not be long before his mother gets here. She is going to be so angry about his drinking, about him betraying God. But it was such fun! What is more, finally the men have accepted him. God is praised.

At the moment, no one is calling him. He can sleep a little longer. Besides, if he keeps his eyes firmly closed, perhaps the pain will go away.

When he wakes again, his head still feels like there's been an explosion inside it, but this time he manages to open his eyes. Above him, heavy beige canvas is spinning, and the movements make him feel sick. He has to report to his sergeant; he has to report that he killed Omar. He does not want to, but he has to come clean.

But it will have to wait; he is too tired. He is also terribly thirsty. Is there any water? He tries to raise himself on his arms, but his body is too heavy to lift.

He turns his head to his side; there is another bed about a yard away, and someone is in there.

'Hey,' he tries to say, but there is no sound coming from his mouth.

He tries again, and while this time there is definitely sound, it is no louder than a whisper, and the man does not hear him.

'Water!' he calls as loud as he can; it is a hoarse sound that leaves his mouth.

'Look who is awake.' His sister Shiya is standing at the end of his bed. She is a doctor. He feels terribly proud that she has made it, and he is amazed by how rapidly she managed it.

'Water!' he repeats.

'Certainly, Lieutenant, I'll get your water.'

It seemed like she was talking to him, but that cannot be right. He is no lieutenant. He wants to look around to see who she was talking to, but he can only turn his head left and right, and he can't see other men.

There she is again, this time holding a small cup. He should ask her who she was talking to earlier, but his mouth is too dry. Perhaps a little sip first.

She lifts his head, and he notices that she isn't Shiya; that is a shame. Carefully, she puts the cup to his mouth, and he manages to take a couple of small sips. Then he decides to close his eyes again, if only for a little bit.

He will report to Sergeant Shamil later, after he has rested some more. He will tell him that everything is all wrong and that women do not belong in the army.

All around him there are explosions, and men are running from them. They are approaching him, but they are not the enemy; they are the men from his own platoon, and he has to shoot them, even though he has no weapon. Wait, he does have a weapon. He has Lieutenant Fakeih's handgun, and suddenly he notices that the lieutenant is standing in front of him.

'You would not dare to shoot me; you don't have the stomach.' There is a bottle of arak in Fakeih's hand, and he puts it to his lips. He knows that this is the moment where he is obliged to shoot Fakeih, but the lieutenant is right: he does not have the stomach for it.

Fakeih starts to laugh, and Khalid can smell his breath. It stinks. The lieutenant reads his mind and laughs even harder.

But then Fakeih turns into a boy, and the boy is not laughing— he is crying! He looks familiar, but Khalid cannot place him.

'Why did you kill me?' the boy asks.

Why had he killed him? Khalid doesn't know. He isn't even sure if he killed the boy. Maybe, a long time ago . . .

He sees bugs crawling out of the boy's eyes, and he remembers. Omar!

'It was not my fault,' he says, but he knows that he's lying. He had protested when the men from Taj al Wadi wanted to take him. He had believed that he was protecting the boy. How could he have known?

Omar disappears and Lieutenant Fakeih returns, but Fakeih cannot be here. Lieutenant Fakeih is dead. There is no Fakeih, and Khalid does not have a gun in his hand. In fact, he is in a bed. He feels the mattress beneath him and the sheet on top of him. He opens his eyes, and there is his brother's grinning face.

'Apparently God prefers to see you alive, little brother.'

'Where am I?' Khalid asks.

'Nardin camp, second hospital tent. Officers' section; praise be unto God!'

'What happened?'

'Well, once again your brother had to sweep in to save the day. It wasn't easy, but we've demolished those Iraqi bastards; praise be unto God.'

Iraqi bastards? That does not ring any bell.

'How did I get here?'

'It seems that you ran about a mile with some half-dead private who had got his leg shot off over your shoulder, and then, when you were close enough to crawl back to the trenches, you almost managed to get yourself blown up. A man named Ayden picked you up and carried you the rest of the way.'

Slowly it returns to Khalid: the sandstorm, the shelling, the dying Iraqi, and the men from Queen's Brigade.

'It was fortunate half his leg was gone. If it still had been on, I would never have been able to carry him that far.'

They both laugh, which hurts terribly.

'What happened to him?'

Aadhil looks down, and his grin transforms into a grimace. 'Died on the operating table, may God protect his soul.'

'May God protect his soul,' Khalid repeats. Then he closes his eyes. The run had been hell, and it had all been for nothing. He silently thanks God for his own survival before opening his eyes again.

'How long have I been out?'

'You came here eight days ago. First two days they did not know if you were going to make it, but thanks to God you opened your eyes and asked for water. By then they figured you'd probably make it, but they were not sure if you'd ever be your old self.

'The last couple of days you woke a number of times, but you only talked utter nonsense. You called every nurse Shiya; you've been talking about shooting some guy named Fakeih, and something with your sergeant major.

317

'I told them they did not have to worry, of course. With half your brain gone, you'd still be smarter than most men, and I went looking for your sergeant major. It seems that in the very last minute of the battle, he got himself blown up too. God bless his soul.'

'God bless his soul. What about Namdar?'

'You mean Acting Second Lieutenant Namdar?'

'Acting Second Lieutenant?'

Aadhil nods. 'While you were sleeping, the battle raged on for two more days. Even though we had already destroyed the majority of the Iraqi tanks, they kept on coming. We've lost hundreds of men; maybe thousands. My tank,' his brother looks down, 'I won't be able to fix it this time.'

'I am sorry.'

Aadhil shrugs. 'Let's just say I've thanked God many times for giving me that tank. You should have seen what happened to my old one; it took a direct hit. The men inside were fried, God bless their souls.'

Khalid feels a cold shiver going through his body. At least he was outside in the field. He would not have liked to be blown up in a tank. What's more, it would be impossible to receive a proper burial after that.

From the corner of his eye he can see men coming in, and suddenly his brother is standing at attention.

'At ease, Sergeant.'

It's Brigadier General Issa. Khalid tries to salute, too, but his arm hurts too much. The commander smiles.

'Lieutenant Khan,' the small man with the big moustache says, 'it seems that you are a man of many surprises. I still remember how you came into my tent not so long ago, too young to be a corporal.'

Khalid remembers it too, and he tries to smile.

'When I praised Major Madani for choosing the exact right moment to get his company into the battle, he told me that he only went because your platoon was running into the field, and he didn't want to stay behind.'

Khalid sees the former captain standing behind the brigadier, looking just as indifferent as always. Somehow, he is not surprised that Madani has survived the battle.

'I will not say that you saved the day, Lieutenant, but your actions were important, and you have certainly done your family proud—not unlike your brother, I can tell you. Nevertheless, if I were you, next time I wouldn't run a mile with a dead guy over my shoulder, but I'll put that down to youthful enthusiasm.

'I would promote you too, were it not that my sergeant major apparently saw fit to promote you before the battle even started. Please tell me: what exactly happened to Lieutenant Fakeih?'

'He shot him.'

'Sergeant major shot him, eh? Better for everyone not to let that story leave your sickbed. We'll say he died honourably on the battlefield. Wouldn't want to get an angry Lord Raslan after us.

'Anyway, when you're done lying in bed, God willing, take over Major Madani's old company as a full lieutenant.'

'Yes, sir.'

The brigadier turns and walks away while Major Madani stands there for a moment longer. 'The sergeant major shot Lieutenant Fakeih.' Slowly, he shakes his head. 'I wish I had been there.'

Then Major Madani grins and follows the commander.

'That brigadier general of yours, he is one tough bastard, you know that?' Aadhil says after the officers have left the tent. 'On the last day of the battle we had four tanks left, and he was calling the men to take bazookas to the field to assist the tanks, but everybody had seen more than once what happened if you got too close to a tank and how difficult it is to destroy one. What's more, a couple of bazookas had blown up while our soldiers were using them.

'So, to set an example, he and that sergeant major took a bazooka and ran onto the field themselves. Of course, nobody could stay back after that.'

Khalid closes his eyes. He remembers how the brigadier had pointed his gun at the men who were running from the Iraqi bombs. *No man is allowed to turn back.*

'I wasn't lying when I said God loves you, you know that? If that sergeant major had not promoted you, you would certainly be dead. This place,' Aadhil gestures to the tent around him, 'it is like a palace compared with where they keep the normal soldiers.'

Khalid doesn't hear these last words; dreams of home and the battle have overtaken him.

INTERMISSION:

KING JALAL
Mayasin

Month of Pregnancy 16, 1375 A.H. (26 May 1956 A.D.)

Jalal throws open the door to his wife's sitting room and storms in. He takes one look at the ladies-in-waiting, points at the door, and shouts, 'Out!'

Immediately, they drop what they are doing and make their way to the door; a couple are already in tears.

'What is it? Anna Christina asks.

'They've killed him,' he growls.

'Who killed whom?'

'Lord Tali'a. Shot. By a boy in front of the Green Mosque."

'A boy?'

Jalal makes a dismissive gesture. 'We found him six blocks from the mosque; two bullets in his forehead. He was a pawn, and the real killers didn't have the balls to leave a note.'

Anna Christina walks over to the side table, where she pours herself a glass of port and her husband a whisky. 'Well,' she asks, 'what now?'

'Well . . .' Jalal answers. 'Since it appears that my cabinet members are all fleeing town, I have decided to dissolve the government. Do you know what Lord Raslan, our esteemed secretary of state, said to me?'

She shakes her head. 'He said that he will not return until we have rooted out the communists and the Muslim Brotherhood. He even suggested that we should bring his brother, General Raslan, and the First Division into the city.'

Anna Christina frowns. 'General Raslan? Isn't he stationed at the border of Saudi Arabia?'

He nods and raises his eyebrows. 'I told him that if we were going to be bringing any army into the city, we would order General al-Dahabi here, considering he's stationed just twenty miles outside. But Raslan said he didn't think al-Dahabi had the strategic insight for an operation like this.'

'I suppose any army in the city will be a disaster, but at least al-Dahabi is loyal. If you allow General Raslan to march his army into the city, he will never leave again.'

'You don't have to tell me,' Jalal says, more cruelly than he intended, and he softens his tone as he continues, 'I wouldn't even put it past the Raslans to be behind the assassination, exactly for this purpose.'

'Do you think they are?'

Jalal shrugs. 'I have no idea. Normally I would ask Lord Tali'a. However, I cannot speak to dead men.'

'Is there a new Lord Tali'a?'

'Salem al-Sabah. As Lord Tali'a's second-in-command, I believe he is most qualified.'

'I've never heard of him,' Anne Christina says. 'But if Lord Tali'a trusted him, that's good enough for me.'

He stares at her; she is not going to be happy with what he is about to say, but he decides he should not let that stop him. 'I think it would be best if you went away. Take the children. Take Hussein. Go to Paris.'

'No.' Her hazel eyes are staring straight into his own and look more beautiful than ever.

'You must. If something happens to Hussein . . .'

'No.'

'It would only be for a little while . . .'

'Jalal, I agreed to come with you to Beledar because you promised me that we were going to change the country together. I'm not going to be the queen who's only by her husband's side when the sun is shining.'

He lights a cigarette and sits down on one of the sofas. She follows his example, and one of her cats jumps up next to her.

'Do you know, just two weeks ago we sent orders to Brigadier Issa and General al-Dahabi to promote their best and most loyal men and spread them over the army? I wonder if Lord Tali'a's murder has anything to do with that,' he says.

'Does it really matter?' A good question, and a very small smile appears on Jalal's face. No matter what the historians will write, marrying Anna Christina was the best decision of his life.

'I suppose not.'

'I think you should do exactly what Lord Raslan has asked you. Root out the communists and the Muslim Brotherhood; hang them all.'

'To be quite straight with you, they are at the bottom of my list of suspects. I know that they wouldn't like anything better than to see me gone, but according to Lord Tali'a, a week ago we had little to fear from them.'

'That doesn't matter,' she counters. 'It's not like you'll be hanging innocent men; they are definitely preparing for a coup, which makes everyone associated with them traitors.'

'I suppose . . .' But she does not let him finish his sentence.

'We make the lords feel safe and comfortable, and we give them a couple more years while we start to prepare the officers we can trust and then . . .' She moves her long nail across her neck, 'off with their heads.'

Exactly at that moment, the cat jumps from the sofa under the table, showing only its head, and Jalal grins and points at it. 'It does not have a body; from what shall I cut off his head?'

'The cat has a head, right?' Anna Christina asks while raising her eyebrows at Jalal. 'If there is a head, it can be cut off.'

Jalal hasn't even touched the whisky, but it feels like an immense weight has been lifted from his shoulders. He stands up and bows to his wife. 'Well, I'd better go and inform Commander al-Sabah that he can start with cutting off the head of any communist and Muslim Brother he can get his hands on.'

'What do you think he'll say?'

He straightens and grins. 'Finally.'

Part V

DISRUPTION

CHAPTER ONE

ABDULLAH SAÍD
Mayasin

Month of Pregnancy 16, 1375 A.H. (26 May 1956 A.D.)

Abdullah is in his little prayer room at home, his head pressed against the floor. He has much to be grateful for: two weeks ago, his sister Azalia married Quadir. She didn't liked it very much when he told her about the match he had made for her, but Quadir is a good Muslim, and now that they are married he is sure she will come around. Nevertheless, there is one reason in particular that he has dragged himself out of bed over an hour before sunrise to make the prayer of dawn. Yesterday, God gave him a second son. Nasir.

'In the name of God, the Most Gracious and Most Merciful . . .'

There is a knock at his door. Whoever is knocking will have to wait.

'In the name of God, the Most Gracious and Most Merciful . . .'

Another knock, more violent this time, and he can hear someone shouting his name. He'd better get it. If they wake Kalima, she will not be pleased. He walks downstairs and finds two Royal Guards outside, but they are not wearing the customary dark blue ceremonial uniforms; these men are dressed in grey and black camouflage outfits, even helmets. What's going on?

'Abdullah Saíd?' one of them asks.

'You have found him,' he answers.

'You need to come with us.'

'Why?'

'Commander's orders.'

He takes a step back. Has Lord Tali'a discovered that he has been sharing government information with the Muslim Brotherhood?

'Am I under arrest?' he asks.

'If you were, we would not have knocked,' the man answers.

His relief is greater than he dares to admit to himself, but he does realise that he should really reconsider the work he is doing for the Brotherhood. Of course, he has never shared anything that's really sensitive, but still. He has two sons now; he does not want them to grow up like he did, especially now that there is no longer a Mr al-Rubaie to take care of them.

'I need to change,' he says.

'No, you don't,' the man answers. 'You look presentable enough. Now get in the car.'

The guards lead him through the main entrance of the palace to the great conference room, which is normally reserved for cabinet meetings but seems to have been remodelled overnight. Where there used to be a large table with a big chair for the king in the middle, there are now about a dozen smaller tables, all covered in stacks of paper. Some of the tables are occupied. Rashid and the king's other two private secretaries are behind three, and even Taaraz is there, the guard, his nose in a pile of papers.

A man he has never seen before walks into the room and makes straight for him. 'Abdullah Saíd?'

'That's me, and who are you and what is all this?'

'I am Salem al-Sabah, the new commander of the Royal Guard. Yesterday Lord Tali'a was murdered. Last night, we have arrested every known communist and every known member of the Muslim Brotherhood we could find. This,' the new commander gestures at the tables around him, 'is where we process the information we have found in their homes and businesses . . .'

'Wait . . . Lord Tali'a was murdered?' He does not quite know what to think. Lord Tali'a was the most dangerous man in Mayasin, but he was also a pious Muslim. Mostly, though, Abdullah can hardly believe it is true; he had believed the commander of the Royal Guard to be immortal.

'Shot in front of the Green Mosque.'

'We surely belong to God, and to Him we shall return,' Abdullah says solemnly.

'Thank you, Mr Saíd. As for the matter at hand, I want to know who these people wrote to, I want to know who owed them money, and I want to know to whom they owed money. I want to know what they wrote in their diaries, I want to know what kind of information they had, and I want to know where they got it from. I want to know everything that's in these papers.

'Now, these men here report to you as senior clerk, and you report to me. At the end of the day, I want fifty new names. There are no members of any of the great families working on this, so we hope these men are all to be trusted. However, if you see anything suspicious, or if any link between the men we have arrested and the lords is found, I expect you to report it to me immediately. Do you understand?'

'Where is Mr Petrakis in all this?' he asks while he is considering the implications of what this man has just told him. If they have found the documents he copied, could those documents lead them to him? There were notes in his handwriting . . .

'Mr Petrakis is needed by the king,' Commander al-Sabah answers.

He nods. 'And what about the men you arrested last night? What is going to happen to them?'

The commander narrows his eyes. 'We will have a friendly little talk with them, and after they have given us all of their comrades and brothers, we are going to hang them all. No one is going to walk out of that prison alive!'

'But what if they are not guilty? What about the king's justice? The law?'

Commander al-Sabah shrugs. 'They should have thought about the king's justice and the law before they joined these groups. The Muslim Brotherhood and the communists, we have ample evidence that they are conspiring to achieve a revolution, which makes them all guilty of treason. How's that for justice?'

'Mr Saíd, look what I have found!'

He walks over to the boy, who cannot be much older than he was when he started work in the back office. 'What is it?'

'It is the diary of Gamal son of Awad,' the young man says. 'He is one of the members of the Muslim Brotherhood who was arrested last night, or at least his diary was at the location of an arrest. It's full of names . . .'

Abdullah tries to sound as casual as he can when he says, 'Give it to me.'

The boy instantly obeys, and he stares at it. He has worried about his brother, who he supposes has been arrested, talking and about the documents he smuggled out of the palace being found. But a diary . . . *Gamal, you son of a donkey!*

He opens it and starts to browse. It is not so much a diary as it is a logbook with short references to the Muslim Brotherhood and Gamal's own affairs. The boy is right: this book is a goldmine. Then his eyes catch his own name, and his heart stops.

Month of Pregnancy 10, 1372

Mr al-Rubaie has died. He is a great loss to our world, but he will live on in our hearts. Also positive news. We met Samir's brother Abdullah. He works in the palace as private clerk for the king and has agreed to help us with information. God is praised.

'Mr Said?'

He looks back at the boy. 'I think I'd better take this book to Commander al-Sabah immediately.'

'Sir, if you want I can make a list with all the names that are used in relation to the Brotherhood. It shouldn't cost me more than an hour.'

Abdullah shakes his head. 'No, this is too important. I want the commander to have this right now. Tell me, what is your name?'

'Salah al-Din, sir.'

'Well, Salah, I will make sure that by the end of the day the king will know it!' The boy glows with pride. 'By the way, do you have any more papers here that were found at the house of this Son of Awad?'

The boy shakes his head. 'The guards, when they brought all this stuff in, just threw it randomly on tables. I have papers from communists mixed with papers from the Brotherhood, but most of what I have seen so far is insignificant, or it does not appear to be related to either.'

Abdullah can see the regret in his eyes. Of course, if he had been in this boy's position, he too would have loved to write down as many names by the end of the day as he could. He gives the boy a little pat on the back and walks out of the conference room with the diary in his hand.

'Mr Saíd! I was just on my way to find you.' Mr Petrakis is approaching him. Why should he run into the infidel at exactly this moment? 'What have you got there?'

'This?' He looks at the little book in his hands. 'It's nothing; in fact, it's my wife's diary. I was reading it this morning when the guards came to get me. I haven't been out of the conference room since I entered the palace. Now that everything's up and running, I thought I'd put it in my office.'

'How are things in there?' The king's secretary nods his head toward the conference room.

'Tense. I think everyone is a little shocked by what has happened. The younger ones, though,' he smiles, 'I think they might be intrigued. How are things with the king?'

The infidel shrugs. 'Mr Saíd, I think we should take a little walk to the garden; I will enlighten you there.'

Abdullah nods. Mr Petrakis doesn't say it, but it's clear that the king's secretary doesn't want them to be overheard, and in silence they walk to the garden. Only when they are surrounded by grass and the violet jacarandas does the infidel drop his bomb.

'Mr Saíd, what do you think is going to happen when Commander al-Sabah discovers that you work for the Muslim Brotherhood?'

'What do you mean?' He tries to sound as innocent as he can, yet he can tell by Mr Petrakis's tone that the infidel knows.

'You don't have to pretend with me, Mr Saíd. Or do you want to hand over that little book you're holding so near?' Abdullah does not respond. 'Didn't think so. You are lucky that Lord Tali'a never wrote anything down, otherwise Commander al-Sabah would have had you in chains the moment you walked in here this morning. As it is, the new commander asked me for advice on whom we should put in charge of that little operation, you or Rashid, and I told him that you weren't senior clerk for nothing!

'What Salem al-Sabah also does not know is that he arrested your little brother last night. That's right, Samir is in Mayasin prison, and if you have any idea about what's going on there, you know that sooner rather than later he is going to give you up, and your sons will be lucky to end up as orphans in Kobajjeb.'

'Lord Tali'a knew?'

Mr Petrakis laughs. 'If I figured it out, you can be sure that he knew too. Unfortunately for him, the Muslim Brotherhood was never very high on his list of priorities.'

'Why are you telling me this and not Commander al-Sabah?'

'Because, Mr Saíd, lately I have been worried about the king, and now I fear that he has gone mad. Or perhaps, even worse, that he has become paranoid. He has dissolved the government, and this witch hunt he has started . . .

'Mr Saíd, I know my history, and here's what happens when monarchs become paranoid: they destroy all that they have built and end up murdering everyone in their vicinity. Now, I don't know about you, but I have no intention of ending up that way.'

Abdullah looks at Mr Petrakis. Unlike the infidel, he has done few things that endanger his path to Paradise, and those things happened a long time ago. However, he does have a responsibility to his family, especially to his two little boys.

'What do you want me to do?'

Abdullah is staring at the list lying on his desk. Tawfiq al-Rabiah sells cloths in the market of Juban. He is old and by no means wealthy, yet every week he donates a proportion of his income to the Brotherhood. Ibrahim al-Nardini, a clever young man who could make an excellent living at any of the companies in the business district but instead spends his days teaching the poorest children in Mayasin to read in exchange for a handout. Abdullah has left them on the list because they do not have families to feed, and he needs fifty names; if all goes well, perhaps they will be out again in the morning.

'Mr Saíd.' The commander is standing in his doorway. 'Do you have my list?'

'Right here, Commander. Do you plan on visiting all these men tonight?'

'We'll see how far we get. I see that you have sent your team home.' Abdullah recognises a reproachful undertone in the commander's voice. 'Commander, those men started before sunrise. It is now almost ten o'clock in the evening, and the next few days won't be getting any shorter. I figured it would be better to have them well rested for the morrow.'

Some of the men, like Salah al-Din and Taaraz, wanted to continue working, but he has business to attend to. If another diary is found, he wants to be at the palace to intercept it.

The commander nods and says, 'Better take that advice to heart yourself as well.'

There is nothing Abdullah would like better, but twenty minutes later he is knocking at the door of the safe house. Quadir opens it. At least they have not got to his sister's husband yet. After he steps inside, he asks, 'Is it true?'

Quadir nods. 'Samir, Gamal, Muhammad, Omar, and a couple of dozen more.'

'And there will be more tonight,' Abdullah says. 'Fifty, Brotherhood and communists.'

His sister's husband shakes his head. 'Bloody communists. May God curse all their children!'

'Are you sure it was them?'

'Of course. The communists are monsters; they have no God. In the Soviet Union God is forbidden, and now they want to ban God here. But why is the king punishing us for their actions?'

Abdullah sits down and shrugs. 'It appears that the king sees enemies everywhere nowadays. He does not see the difference between communists and good Muslims, and he is arresting everyone he can get his hands on.'

There is a pot of tea on the table, and Quadir pours him a small cup, asking, 'But what evidence is there?'

'Evidence?' Abdullah laughs sarcastically. 'The prisoners are being questioned by the Royal Guard, men trained by Lord Tali'a. My brother will betray me. Gamal will confess, the rest of our leaders will confess, and so will the communists.'

Quadir sits down opposite him. 'Do you know what they are doing there?'

He nods. 'They pull out nails and teeth, they cut off fingers and toes, and eventually even men's genitals, using blunt knifes. Sometimes they stop after a confession; often they don't.'

'We have to leave, my friend.' Quadir is looking straight into his eyes. 'Take your wife and children and go to Saudi Arabia. The Brotherhood is well connected there; we will be welcomed and taken care of.'

Abdullah snorts. 'And what then? Everything I have worked for is in my house. And everything we have worked for is in Mayasin as well. The schools, the medical centre, what will happen to them?'

'In the name of God, your house won't do you much good when you're dead, and you won't be much good to your family. Make no mistake: they will find you. It's a miracle that the Royal Guard hasn't shown up here yet. As for the schools, a couple of years from now other men will come to take over.'

'What if we break them out?'

Quadir frowns. 'Are you saying you want to storm the prison?'

'My brother is in there, and more importantly, I'm never going to be able to smuggle my wife and children into Saudi Arabia. Nasir was born yesterday afternoon. He is much too weak for such a journey. Besides, unless we do something they'll have a thousand people in that prison before the month is over.'

Quadir stares at him and then says, 'The communists have weapons.'

Abdullah, completely taken aback by this statement, almost chokes. When he is recovered, he asks, 'Are you saying you want to work with the communists? You just told me they are monsters!'

'Your brother is in that prison, and so is Gamal. If I were there, I think I would want you to rescue me too. You know, I wouldn't last a day.'

After a long silence, Abdullah nods. His plan is working even better than expected. 'The communists it is then; may God forgive us.'

It isn't difficult for Quadir and Abdullah to find the communists' headquarters. Many people in Mayasin depend on the Brotherhood, and all these people are eager to tell them what they know and to offer shelter—just in case they need it.

Thus, just before midnight they find the men at an old warehouse in the Kobajjeb quarter. Inside it's a terrible mess; there is glass on the floor, desks are overturned and chairs are lying everywhere, many of them broken, and Abdullah wonders if it is very smart or very stupid to reconvene at a place that has already been raided.

There are about a dozen people, some carrying brooms, others large garbage bags. Unlike at the headquarters of the Brotherhood, here, men and women are working together, and the women are dressed indecently; Abdullah notices that not one of them wears a headscarf, while one is actually wearing trousers.

It's a terrible sight, and he is not surprised when Quadir turns to him. 'The women . . .'

He solemnly shakes his head. 'I know. God wants us to be strong.'

A few of the people stop cleaning to study the intruders.

'May peace be upon you,' Quadir says.

'And may peace be with you too,' one of them answers. He is very young, probably not a day older than twenty-one.

'We are looking for the men who share everything,' Quadir says.

'Who is looking for the men who share everything?'

'My friend Abdullah Saíd and myself, Quadir al-Hassani.'

'Are you working for the king?' one of the women asks suspiciously.

'It looks like the Royal Guard has already been here,' Abdullah says.

'If the king did not send you, then who did?' the woman counters.

'We are members of the Muslim Brotherhood, and we come to you in peace,' Quadir replies.

The mention of the Muslim Brotherhood clearly hits a note, and it's definitely not a good one. The communists turn to each other and start to debate, and he does not quite hear what they are saying, but he does catch a few words: 'Enemies. Allies. Barbarians. Murder. Treacherous.'

He looks at Quadir, who raises his eyebrows but says nothing.

It takes about three minutes for the communists to decide how they will respond to the intruders, and after the group opens up, once again it is the young man who speaks. 'My name is Lenin. What do you want?'

Quadir gives Abdullah a small smile before turning to the boy. 'Yesterday, the Royal Guard raided the houses of our leaders. They killed seven of them and took twenty-seven prisoners. We want to free these men.'

'If you want to free your men, we will not stop you.'

Quadir spreads his arms and then points to the mess in the hall. 'We thought we might find allies here. How many of yours did they take?'

'Thirty-two,' the woman replies, and the boy places his hand on her shoulder.

'The Muslim Brotherhood has supporters all throughout the city. Even without your leaders you could still raise a thousand men easily. Why are you here?' asks an older man who has been standing unobtrusively at the back.

'We could raise the men, that is true, but we do not have the weapons,' Quadir answers.

'And what makes you think we do?' Lenin is speaking again.

Quadir smiles. 'As your friend pointed out, we have supporters all throughout the city. We know that the Soviets have been smuggling weapons into the city; if these weapons are not in your hands, then where are they?'

'How do we know we can trust you?' It is the woman in trousers again. 'You murdered Lord Tali'a!'

Abdullah cannot believe it. Is she really accusing them of the assassination that led to the arrest of his brother? What's more, an assassination on Gathering Day, straight after the afternoon prayer?

'You mean *you* murdered him!'

'Do you really think we're that stupid? Murdering the commander of the Royal Guard while we're still a year away from being ready for any kind of confrontation? Only Muslims can be that stupid!' It looks like she is going to physically attack him, but two of the men restrain her. 'Son of a donkey! Father of whores!'

One of them also puts his hand over her mouth, pulling her away so she cannot insult him further, and Lenin says, 'You will have to forgive my friend. Her boyfriend is dead.'

'We understand,' Quadir replies diplomatically. 'They took his brother and my best friend, too, and many others. However, if you did not kill Lord Tali'a, who did?'

The boy shakes his head. 'We were convinced it was you. We thought you wanted to provoke a war before we were ready.'

'Well, you were wrong. We do not have the weapons for a war, and while Lord Tali'a was a problem, he was also a pious Muslim. Trust me, if we were selecting targets in the administration of the king, we would have chosen one of the infidels; there are enough of them,' Quadir replies.

There is a moment of silence as the communists consider this, but Abdullah is confused as well. If they have not killed Lord Tali'a and the communists haven't done it either, then who did?

'Maybe it was the king himself,' the older man offers. 'Maybe the king killed him so that he would have an excuse to strike against the communists and the Brotherhood at the same time.'

The king himself? It's not impossible. What was it Mr Petrakis said? *Paranoid kings will kill everyone in their vicinity.* The murder of Lord Tali'a would be an example of the king killing a man in his vicinity, and it would also be a great excuse for more murders.

'Forget it. We cannot trust them!' the woman calls as she draws a revolver and takes a step toward Abdullah. 'Even if they are with us, if we give the Brotherhood guns, they will end up using them against us!'

Abdullah takes a step back and lifts his hands in the air, partly to show that he is unarmed and partly because it seems very bad-mannered to shoot someone who has his hands in the air.

'Wait,' he says. 'Everyone in that prison will be tortured until he has given the Royal Guard every name he can think of, and the

Royal Guard will not stop until every new name they learn is six feet under.

'Perhaps you do not trust us with weapons, but I hope that you will trust me on this: tonight, fifty people will be arrested, tomorrow it will be seventy-five, and the day after tomorrow it will be one hundred. Unless we stop it. Unless we go to that prison and get our friends out!'

'My boyfriend is already dead,' she growls, but she lowers her gun as she says it.

In less than four hours they have managed to assemble almost two hundred men. Abdullah is not surprised by this. While the king's policies may have worked for people with money, these men have been dependent on the Brotherhood for years. Their children will grow up in even worse circumstances than his own if not for men like Quadir, Gamal, Samir, and himself, he is proud to say.

He looks at the machine guns that are coming from the wooden crates. There are also handguns, grenades, and many things that he's never seen.

The plan was for him to go home while the men around him attack the prison, but when someone hands him a rifle, he accepts it, takes a deep breath, and closes his eyes. Although he knows it is going to be a very dangerous mission, it would be too cowardly to let other men do the fighting.

There is a hand on his arm; next to him is Quadir. 'In the name of God, give me the gun.'

'Why?' he asks.

'I know you want to go, but you can't.'

'Why not? My brother is in there too.'

'My friend,' Quadir says, 'we've talked about this. You are our man inside the palace, which makes you too great an asset to lose.'

'I know, but I'm not scared. If God wants it, I will fight His battle,' he replies fiercely, and Quadir smiles.

'My friend, I know that you are not scared. In fact, you are one of the bravest men I know, but you are not a soldier. Look around you. There is an abundance of men here; men who can be missed. Each of them can carry a gun, while none of them can open the doors to the palace.'

It is true, and suddenly he feels his weariness. He has been awake for almost twenty-four hours, and he knows that he will not get many chances to rest during the days that are to come. He nods, and Quadir bows to him and kisses him on the cheek.

'I will bring back Samir and Gamal, and we will meet tonight at Pervaíz's coffee house.'

CHAPTER TWO

CAPTAIN KHALID KHAN
Al Nawaara

Month of Pregnancy 17, 1375 A.H. (27 May 1956 A.D.)

The jeep is racing through Khalid's home province, but Khalid doesn't see the land flashing by him. Two days ago, news reached Camp Nardin that Lord Tali'a was murdered, and although most men at the camp, Khalid included, have never met the commander of the Royal Guard, it feels like the army will never be the same. Lord Tali'a held no official position in the army, yet everyone knew that when the commander of the Royal Guard gave an order, it could be interpreted as though it was coming directly from the king.

And now the commander will be buried in an unmarked grave, and Khalid will never get to know the greatest soldier who has ever lived in Beledar—something he has secretly been dreaming of ever since Mr Ensour told him about the Battle of Oyoun al Jabal, and that seemed to be within reach when he received the news of his latest promotion.

Captain Khalid Khan, in General Lord Raslan's First Division.

He remembers his first year in Nardin like it was yesterday. He was treated like a child, both by his men and by his superiors, but

342

now he is probably the youngest captain in the whole army. He is a little sorry to be leaving Brigadier Issa, but General Raslan commands the most powerful division in the Beledarian army, and Khalid will never forget the flattering words of his now former commander.

'*It's the only way we can make this army stronger, Captain Khan,*' Brigadier Issa said when he delivered the news. '*If it means that they are leaving my regiment, I would like nothing better than to promote some of those idiots—let the other generals deal with the Fakeihs of this world—but if that's how we are going to build our legions, before long we will be even weaker than the Iraqis. No, young friend, know that I choose you because it is best for the army, in spite of my own wishes.*'

'Are we almost there, sir?' Ayden asks.

Khalid looks at his corporal. Who would have thought, four years ago, that Ayden would address him as 'sir' without a hint of sarcasm? He certainly did not. He turns his eyes to the road and realises they are already in Al Nawaara.

'Just keep going straight,' he answers.

He has a little more than a week before he has to report to General Raslan at Camp Ritag, and while he spent his previous furloughs in Nardin or visiting the capital, this time he has decided he will visit his family. Perhaps it is the fact that he is now a captain, or maybe it was Brigadier Issa's words of praise, but after five years he finally has the courage to face his father again.

He isn't completely relaxed, though, sitting next to Ayden. Will his old man still be angry? And his mother, what if she hits him? He doesn't think that she would dare, considering he is a captain in the king's army, but he isn't sure. His mother was never afraid of anyone, least of all her own sons, and he left her without saying goodbye. He hadn't even dared to write. Today, that feels like a mistake, but at the time . . .

At the time he had been scared. He had been more scared of his parents than he had been of Drill Sergeant Aazim, the Iraqi artillery, and the men of the Banu Farud put together. In fact, he is still scared, and the closer they get to his family house, the faster his heart starts to beat.

'You can drop me off here, Corporal,' he says.

Ayden stops and lets him out. 'Sir, I'll be staying in Taj al Wadi. According to the men there are some interesting sights to see there. I'll be back here to pick you up two hours after sunrise on the Seventh Day.'

Khalid smiles. He knows that by 'interesting sights' Ayden means whores, but he does not care. During his first year at Nardin he wondered why Commander Issa never did anything about the Forbidden Chambers, but after the war he realised that it is the responsibility of an officer to keep his soldiers sharp and to send them into the line of fire when the time comes. If a soldier doesn't let you down on duty, an officer shouldn't interfere with his choices when he's off duty.

'That's fine, Corporal. I'll see you seven days from now.'

'Sir!' Ayden salutes and drives off, while Khalid makes his way to the house. He wonders if his father and brothers will be there. They used to be away for weeks at a time, but after his father bought a truck, they were hardly ever gone more than five days in a row.

Khalid can see the house, but it is not sharp. He pauses to take his glasses from his pocket and looks at them for a second. He has only had them for two weeks, yet he is sure they are the best invention man has ever made. He puts them on and sees a man sitting in front of the house. It is his father!

An emptiness takes hold of his stomach, and he tries to combat this by inhaling deeply. He has faced the Iraqis, he should also be able to face his father. He starts to walk again, and when he is about fifteen yards away from the house, the man looks up.

For what seems like an eternity, the two men stare at each other, but then Mr Khan says, 'Khalid?'

He nods. He can feel tears forming in his eyes, but he is not ashamed of them—even the Prophet cried from time to time—and he runs the last yards to his father, who stands up and catches him in an embrace.

'Khalid!'

'Father!'

Khalid cannot remember if his father has ever given him a hug before, yet it feels completely natural. His father kisses him on both cheeks before letting him go, and then the old man looks him up and down.

'You're an officer,' Mr Khan says.

'I am a captain, father. Captain in General Lord Raslan's First Division.'

'That sounds important,' his father says. 'God is praised! Did you fight in the war?'

'I did, Father. I even got a medal.'

His old man smiles proudly. 'We listened to the king on the radio, and Aisha read the newspaper every day, hoping to find your name.'

'Aisha? You mean Shiya?' Shiya was the one who went to school and wanted to be a doctor. He vividly remembers Aisha swearing that she never wanted to go to school and wonders if his father's mind is playing tricks.

But the old man shakes his head and repeats, 'Aisha. Come inside, son. I will make us tea.'

Khalid drops his bag next to the door and follows his father, and while Mr Khan boils the water, Khalid inspects the house. There is a table in the kitchen and chairs, and there is even a small cupboard with books. His father catches him studying the cabinet and says, 'Aisha and Shiya love books. Every time Nourad and

Saifan go away, they try to bring back a book for them. Of course, Shiya only comes home twice a year nowadays, but when she's here, all she does is read.'

Most of the books are in Arabic, but not all. Khalid picks one of them up and can't help but feel a little jealous. Books were very expensive in Nardin, and it was virtually impossible to get your hands on English books. Sometimes he brought one from Mayasin—six months earlier he had bought the *Iliad*, mostly because it was really thick—but it always felt a little sinful to spend money on words on paper, and he always read them too fast, even if he reread all his books at least three times.

'What's a hobbit?' he asks his father.

'Apparently hobbits are little English people who spend their days eating and smoking pipes. This particular hobbit is chosen by a great wizard to help a group of dwarves defeat a dragon and take back their mountain.'

It sounds like a crazy story, and Khalid puts the book back, sits down at the table, and lights a cigarette, while his father pours him tea.

'You said Shiya only comes home twice a year. Where is she?' Khalid asks.

'She's in Mayasin, where she lives with my sister and her family. A couple years ago, the king built a secondary school for girls there, and Shiya was accepted. When she's finished, if God wants it she'll keep on studying to become a doctor!'

'She's really going to be a doctor?'

'Can you believe it?' His father beams. 'It turns out that girls are very smart; perhaps even smarter than men. You know, just after I bought my second truck, Lord Tanvir's son, Lord Maher, came and confiscated one. He said I was only allowed one and that he had a friend who was going to use the new one. Shiya wrote a letter to the king for me, and two months later Lord Maher's friend came to return my truck!

'Son, you know that I can write, but Shiya . . . she writes so beautifully, and she knows exactly which words to choose! But if God wants it, Aisha will one day be just as good. According to her teacher, she's the brightest girl in her class, and she works really hard too. As a matter of fact, she is there now.'

Khalid can't believe what he is hearing. His father, who had said that God would punish them because his mother had allowed Shiya to go school, is now applauding his sisters' learning abilities! It's as though the world has turned upside down.

'I suppose Mother will be proud of them,' is all he can think of to say.

His father nods, but he can see that something is wrong.

'Where is Mother?'

'God took her two years ago.'

'We surely belong to God and to him shall we return,' Khalid says gravely, but he feels more like screaming.

His father nods again, and Khalid can see the pain in the man's eyes. 'You are right, though, she was very proud of Aisha and Shiya, but she was also very proud of you and Aadhil, and she told everyone who would listen that you were heroes. I suppose she's in Paradise, lecturing the Prophet himself.'

This image makes Khalid smile, yet it does not take away his guilt. Why has he waited five years to return home?

'What about Aadhil?' his father asks. 'Did he survive Iraq?'

He looks at his father. Clearly the man has wanted to ask this since they walked through the door, and he nods. 'He wrote me about a year ago that he was promoted to lieutenant and that he was going to lead a team of tanks. He received a medal during the war too.'

'That's good,' his father says.

Khalid has a hundred questions about his mother, but he does not dare to ask them, and his father speaks of her no more. Instead, Mr Khan speaks about Nourad and Saifan and how well they run the company, and how their wives come to bring him food every day.

They move to the front of the house, and there his father goes on to tell him that he was wrong about the king—that King Jalal has built roads that have made the life of merchants so much easier. Khalid is surprised to learn that Mr Khan doesn't mind the 'taxes' at the border at all. There has always been a fee for protection, and the roads have never been safer, whereas the fees have never been lower.

And so the hours pass until, to Khalid's surprise, a jeep approaches them. When it is quite near, he sees that it is the jeep that brought him here, and when it has come to a stop, Ayden gets out.

'Sir!'

'What is it, Corporal?'

'Sir, we were listening to the radio, and we heard that the prison in Mayasin, where they locked up the men who killed Lord Tali'a, was attacked. There was also a message for you: all officers that are off duty are required to report to their commanders as soon as possible.'

Khalid turns to his old man. 'Father, I'm afraid that means me.'

'Of course.'

'Father, I promise that this time I will be back sooner. In fact, the next weekend that I'm free, I will come to visit.'

His old man smiles and says, 'I will be waiting.'

He gives his father another hug, picks up his bag, which is still next to the door, and opens the door of the jeep.

'Wait, Khalid.' His father runs back into the house to return a minute later with a book in his hand. 'Here, in case you want to know more about hobbits.'

'Thank you, Father, but that is Shiya's book.'

'Shiya isn't here, and she has plenty, while Aisha doesn't read English books yet. I think this story about little people and dragons will be best in your hands, and you can return it the next time you come to visit.'

'Thank you, Father,' he says, and before Khalid's old man can see his tears returning, Ayden has pressed his foot down and they are on their way to Camp Ritag.

CHAPTER THREE

ABDULLAH SAÍD
Mayasin

Month of Pregnancy 17-18, 1375 A.H. (27-28 May 1956 A.D.)

'Well, Mr Saíd, I believe I must congratulate you; your friends caught the guards at the prison completely by surprise,' Mr Petrakis says when they meet in the palace garden at the end of the morning. 'The king is furious, and Commander al-Sabah's position is already in jeopardy. How's the gathering of information going?'

Abdullah shrugs. He has been so scared that the documents he copied will be found, and some of them have been, but there are so many documents that it will be at least a week before they can start any serious analysis. He still can't believe how much information the Brotherhood and the communists had and what a minor role he has actually played these last years.

'Commander al-Sabah came to me about an hour ago,' Abdullah reports. 'He no longer wants names; he wants locations of possible safe houses. I told him that he'd be better off sending his guards to Kobajjeb and Gorgan, but he's afraid they will be assassinated if he sends them out in small groups, and after tonight he wants to keep as many men as possible around the palace.'

The infidel nods. 'Smart man. Too bad he is out of his depth. If he had been given enough time, though, maybe he really could have been the next Lord Tali'a. Do you think you will get the Brotherhood and the communists to participate in the next part of our plan?'

'It's a good plan, and I have an idea to make it even better. I'm sure the Brotherhood will go for it. As for the communists . . .'

'Tell me about your idea.'

'Abdullah.'

He looks at Quadir, and then he gazes around the tables that have been put together in Perva íz's coffee house. All the men are dirty, and quite a few show injuries, yet none look as tired as he feels. If only his brother were here. His sister's husband has told him what happened at the prison. The moment they stormed in, Samir attacked a guard, who shot him. He knows his brother is in Paradise, but that does not make it hurt any less. He takes a deep breath; now is not the time to mourn.

'The next couple of days we are going to infiltrate the palace. I can provide credible invitations for three people a day, and Mr Petrakis can do the same. That means that on the night of our attack, there will be twelve of us already inside the palace, excluding the infidel and myself. Together with the men from the Brotherhood and the communists who work in the palace, we'll have twenty-four men. That should be enough to overpower the guards at the doors and at the gates . . .'

'What about weapons?' Lenin asks.

'At the moment it's impossible to smuggle weapons into the palace,' he answers. 'Until we've opened the gates, we'll have to make do with knives from the kitchen.'

'And those men who will be "infiltrating" the palace, where will they hide?'

He shakes his head and thinks about the secret hallways. Mr Petrakis has told him that only Commander Tali'a knew all of them, but apparently the infidel has discovered a few over the years himself as well. 'We'll take care of that.'

'What do you think, Sergei?' the communist asks, and all eyes turn to the inconspicuous Russian who is leaning against the wall, casually smoking a cigarette.

'I do not think it is a bad plan, but the Royal Guards will not simply roll over. If you fail to open the gates and the doors, they will hold the palace until General al-Dahabi marches his regiment in to free the king. And even when the gates are open, you have to remember that it cost you forty men to take out twenty guards when you stormed the prison. Normally these guards are spread throughout the city, but at the moment the king is keeping them all inside the palace. Imagine that you have to fight five hundred of them.'

'There won't be,' Abdullah says. 'Even the guards need sleep, and there are generally no more than three hundred on active duty. On the evening of the attack, I will tell Commander al-Sabah that we are certain we have located the most important safe houses of both the communists and the Brotherhood. I am confident that he will send large teams out to "clean them up," and that is when we will attack.'

'And this Mr Petrakis,' Sergei asks, 'do you trust him?'

It is a question Abdullah has asked himself many times these last two days. The infidel is everything he abhors, yet the man appeared genuinely afraid of the king. Besides, what is the worst thing he could do? He could warn the king about the attack, but Abdullah can't understand what the use would be of assisting in its planning in the first case.

'Ever since I arrived, Mr Petrakis has lived at the palace, and with Lord Tali'a gone there's no man as near to the king as he is. I can't say that I trust him, but I'm sure that if the king ever heard about him aiding us, he would hang him within the hour, just like he did with his uncles and cousins.'

'I suppose that is good enough for me.'

'If there are three hundred guards in the palace on active duty at any given moment, and the commander sends a hundred out, there will still be two hundred left.' Although no one has asked her opinion, the woman in trousers has started to speak. 'What if we send out a notice to everyone in the city that we will pay one hundred shillings for every guard that is killed on the streets over the next couple of days?'

'You can't do that!' Abdullah says sharply.

'Why not?'

'Because after the attack on the prison, Commander al-Sabah has already lost favour with the king. Kill a dozen guards, and I promise you that within three hours General al-Dahabi will march his army into the city, and then we will never get another chance.'

'What if we start killing some ministers? I know that the king has dissolved his government, but I'm sure that if we kill a couple of ministers, they will all start to demand protection too. Then Commander al-Sabah has to send men there, and we won't have to kill any guards,' Lenin tries.

'I don't know if you realise this, but all the ministers left the city the day after Lord Tali'a was killed. The only one who's still here is al-Rikabi Junior, and he has moved in with his father, and every policeman, even the dirty ones, is guarding his house at this very moment.'

'I'd like to get my hands on those al-Rikabis,' Quadir says grimly. 'Perhaps we should just forget about the king and get them!'

It is not meant seriously, and everyone around the table knows that, yet both the communists and the Brotherhood, including Abdullah, are seriously considering it at that moment. Lord al-Rikabi has been mayor of Mayasin for as long as Abdullah can remember, and there probably isn't a man in the room who has not been extorted by his policemen at least once. Sergei puts an end to the dream.

'You don't like policemen? Just wait until you meet the soldiers from Camp Mayasin. Within twenty-four hours you will be longing for the days when policemen guarded your streets.'

It is almost three o'clock in the morning when Abdullah arrives home. Of the past forty-eight hours, he has spent about three with his eyes closed, and he hopes to get a couple hours of sleep before he needs to be back at the palace, but just as he is opening the door a man appears.

'Abdullah Saíd?'

In front of him is a European or American man in jeans, an open shirt, and a cowboy hat. He says, 'May peace be upon you.'

'And may upon you be peace,' the man replies before continuing in English. 'My name is Jack Jones. Can I come in?'

Abdullah stares at the man. 'Do I have a choice?'

'Not if you want to keep that little operation of yours a secret.'

He nods and leads the man to the kitchen, where he starts to make some coffee and look for dates. When he can't find them, he turns to the man and asks, 'What do you want?'

'Some of that coffee would be nice. No sugar, please; I cannot understand how you can put so much sugar in your coffee.'

'Life in Beledar is bitter. Whenever we get the opportunity to sweeten things, we don't want to miss out.'

'But what about your teeth?'

'We clean them. Mr Jones, it's very late and I'm very tired. Please get to your point.'

'Are we already allowed to talk business?' the American replies with a hint of sarcasm in his voice. 'I must admit that it's quite difficult to know around here. People told me your language was difficult, but your culture is way more complex. A man never quite knows how much small talk is necessary before he can start talking business.'

Abdullah scowls at the American to make clear that there has definitely been enough small talk tonight, and Jack Jones immediately understands him. 'I work for an organisation called the Central Intelligence Agency in the United States of America. Have you ever heard of it?'

Abdullah has read about the CIA in newspaper: they work to destroy communists all over the world, which is good. However, ever since he met Mr Williams, the American ambassador, he has not been a big fan of America. What's more, the Americans support the Zionists. He folds his arms and says, 'A spy, you mean.'

Jack Jones sighs. 'Some people call us that, yes, but I simply watch things, and then I decide what is important and what is not. The important things I use or pass on, the insignificant things I forget. It's simply a business of knowing things and communicating these things to superiors. At the moment I am looking for a man called Quadir al-Hassani. He's married to your sister, and I want to meet him.'

The man takes a cigarette for himself and offers one to Abdullah, too, with the words, 'Real American tobacco.'

Abdullah shakes his head and wonders how much Jack Jones knows, but then he pushes the thought from his mind. 'If you have found me, can't you find him too?'

'I probably could—I know that he was at Pervaíz's coffee house tonight, for example—but I would rather be introduced, and I reckoned you wouldn't mind doing that.'

'What makes you think that?'

'Well, as you know, your king and my president are good friends. If we were to inform him about a certain clerk who is planning an attack on his palace, I am sure that would strengthen our friendship a great deal, yet at the same time it would mean a terrible loss for your family. However, I've decided that I won't be telling anyone that you're an associate of the Brotherhood, since you are my contact, and you are going to bring me to your friends.'

Jack Jones smiles, and Abdullah smiles back. *May pigs piss on the man's grave and Jews rape his sisters in their asses*. First Mr Petrakis and now this American. Is he walking around with some kind of sign on his back? As pleasantly as he can, he asks, 'What do you want with Quadir?'

The CIA operative sits back. 'I want to offer him my friendship as well. American friendship.'

'Really?' This sounds unlikely; the king fought once with the American ambassador, but Mr Williams was replaced, and as far as Abdullah knows, Mr Jones is not wrong about the king's friendship with the American president.

Maybe it's a trick. If the Royal Guard were to arrest him, news would spread within the hour. Quadir would relocate long before Abdullah could give up their hiding place. However, if he leads this American to them, Jack Jones won't just have one Muslim Brotherhood associate as a present for the Royal Guard; he will have the entire leadership.

'Tell me something. I know you're working with the communists right now, but do you truly believe that you're actually going to run this country together someday?'

Maybe the American is trying to get to the communists through the Brotherhood. He cannot say that he would have any objection to that. No one has yet spoken about what they are going to do with the communists once they have taken over the palace, and the Americans would make for a very powerful ally.

'Mr Jones, my enemy's enemy is my friend.'

The American smiles again. 'Don't worry, I don't judge; not so long ago, we were working with the communists too. Between you and me, we still do in some places—better not make too much noise about that, though. All I'm saying is this: have you considered what will happen when you have defeated your common enemy?'

After Abdullah remains silent for a while, the American says, 'I thought so, but listen here, you will not be betraying allies by making a plan for what comes next. You can bet your ass that they're doing the same. That's why it is in your best interest to take me to your friends.'

Abdullah sighs. 'What I must understand first is how you found me.'

Jack Jones smiles and replies, 'They trust you, and there is one thing that is of the utmost importance: you must lead me to them, without the Russians finding out.'

'That is not an answer.'

The American raises his eyebrows. 'It wasn't meant as one.'

'If you are here as a spy, should you not dress a little less conspicuously?'

'Trust me, when I come with you to meet your friends, I'll make sure I don't stand out. But for an American like me, most of the time it's easiest to hide in plain sight.' He spreads his arms and makes a stupid face. 'If anybody asks, I am simply a tourist who fell in love with your country; nothing wrong with that, right?

But don't worry, few people notice things that are staring them in their face.'

'Is that really true?' Abdullah asks.

'Hey, I have been watching you these last two nights, and you never noticed.'

'Here's the thing. I need to be sure that I can trust you. You see, I don't mind if you ordered the assassination on Lord Tali'a, but I wouldn't like it if you were lying to me,' Jack Jones says.

'Why have you brought this man here?' Gamal shouts again at Abdullah. Gamal has always had a bit of a temper, and since the Royal Guard cut off one of his ears and two of his fingers during the day he spent in the prison, it has not improved. 'Two minutes inside, and already he is accusing us of lying.'

'Calm down, Gamal!' Quadir intervenes. 'I am sure that Abdullah brought him here with the best of intentions. Although I have to agree with Gamal that his interest in the death of the Lord Commander is rather salient. Why do you think he is not secretly an agent working for King Jalal?'

Abdullah bows his head. 'I don't know. He never convinced me that he is not. I thought I would leave that question up to you. What tipped the balance for me was that nothing can stop us from sending his body in a bag to the American embassy and his head in a box to the Russians, gift-wrapped. What matters is that I believe he has touched on an important issue. What do we do once we have dealt with the king?'

'Then we will deal with the communists, if God wants it!' Gamal sneers.

'That would be ideal, definitely. However, while we might have more people at the moment, the communists still have a lot more weapons, and they have the Russians to back them. We would be wise to have a powerful ally of our own as well.'

'And so you thought you'd bring the infidel to our home?' Gamal sneers.

'Do you have a better suggestion?' He looks at Gamal and Quadir, but neither of them speaks. They must know that there is just one thing worse than living in a country that is ruled by a heretic king: living in a country where it is forbidden to surrender to God. If his boys were to grow up in a country like that, he would never forgive himself.

'Now that you ladies have stopped arguing,' the American begins again, 'perhaps we can go back to the question of who killed the commander of the Royal Guard. You see, killing Lord Tali'a was either incredibly smart or incredibly stupid— depending on who did it.'

Something that resembles a smile appears on Quadir's face. 'The infidel has spirit, I will give him that. Here we are sitting, talking about whether we should trust him or execute him, and he doesn't seem to care at all. He keeps on asking that one silly question, to which we have already given him the answer.'

'Perhaps it is a silly question to you, but it's not to me. You see, while my government would love to work together, the one thing that's worse than working with people you don't trust is working with stupid people—they're terribly unpredictable. And if the communists didn't kill Lord Tali'a and you didn't do it either, then who did?'

'How can you be sure the communists didn't do it?' Gamal asks.

The American shrugs. 'They've been collaborating with the Russians for a long time, and the Russians are definitely not stupid.'

'Actually,' Abdullah begins, 'we thought the king might have done it himself. That way he could blame us and start the arrests!'

That idea seems terribly funny to Jack Jones. 'Ha! The king? He is hardly man enough to kill his enemies; he wouldn't dream of killing Lord Tali'a. What's more, Tali'a was probably the only man he trusted in that snakehole he calls his palace. No, he is pretty much the only man I do not suspect.'

'Well, you can speculate all you like, but one thing is certain: we did not do it,' Gamal says, still aggressive. 'And we do not know who did, either!'

'All right, all right,' the American replies. 'I am sure that one day the truth will find its way, but for now let us look at more urgent matters. What is your plan?'

'If God wants it, we will remove the pretender from power, and after that we will get rid of the communists,' Gamal says. 'We have much more support in the city, and they won't be able to resist us.'

Jack Jones nods. 'If God wants it, and I am sure He does, but you should never underestimate communists. We have done that on a number of occasions, and it's always a mistake. They are a clandestine kind of people and meticulous planners. Trust me when I say they have a plan to get rid of you.'

They stare at the American and wait for him to continue, but Jack Jones lets this sink in first and lights a cigarette, offering one to each of the other men as well. They silently accept them. Only after Gamal and Quadir have some American tobacco in their lungs does he speak again. 'The fundamental question is this: what kind of support do you have in the army?'

'We mean to surprise the king,' Quadir answers. 'In the city, there's only the Royal guard and the rats, and we plan to overwhelm them. The army will never be here in time to make any kind of difference.'

'Really?' Mr Jones says. 'Camp Mayasin is only twenty miles from the capital. You'll have to be very quick. In a worst-case scenario, the first soldiers will arrive at the palace half an hour from the moment news gets out; tanks will be there within two. I do not doubt your superior numbers, but the Royal Guard is an old, well-trained and very loyal regiment, even without Lord Tali'a. If they are still standing when the tanks arrive, your cause is lost.'

Gamal snorts. 'We will destroy the telephone lines.'

The American smiles. 'Smart. Telephones are an untrustworthy way of communicating, but how will you stop radio signals? Or dispatches carried by men who are not afraid to die?'

'What do you suggest?' Quadir's tone is friendlier now. Any critiques to the plan that can help the cause are clearly welcome.

'Radios can be sabotaged through interference; Morse code can easily be misread; messengers can be stopped by placing snipers at strategic positions.'

'And you can arrange this?' Gamal's tone still has not changed.

The American takes another long drag from his cigarette to build up tension. 'I would suggest you discuss this part of the operation with the communists. As I said, they are meticulous planners, and operations like these are very dangerous.'

For a moment this idea even brings a smile to Gamal's face, but then he realises that he could have come up with it himself, and the smile disappears again. 'So what would we need you for?'

'Good point. With the king gone, the army will be divided. There will be three options for the lords and the generals: Kalaldeh, Raslan, or Moscow and the communists. If you want to control the country, you need to give them another. You will need me to pay the generals and make sure that the lords know it is in their best interests to follow your cause as well.'

'And what about you?' Abdullah asks. 'The Americans do not believe in our cause. Why should we trust you?'

'Well,' Jack Jones looks at him, 'that depends how you'd define your cause. In the United States we believe in self-determination. We believe that all people are free to believe what they want to believe and that they should be free to organise their own society according to their own principles; at this moment your king is clearly preventing that. We believe you should be free, just like we believed the Europeans should be free when we supported them in their war against Herr Hitler.'

Satisfied, Abdullah and Gamal nod approvingly, but Quadir is not yet convinced. 'Are you really telling me that you are willing to offer money and support with nothing in return?'

'Well, not nothing. For nothing you get the sun every morning, not much else. However, you are in a very good position, for there are just a couple of very small things we want.'

'And what are those small things, Mr Jones?' Quadir asks.

'Apart from that, we want to trade with you, and we want a small army base in the Baylasan province, near the borders of Iraq and Saudi Arabia. Nothing big, but just large enough that we can keep an eye on our interests in the region and on the communists. We want to prevent Beledar from falling in their arms at all cost.'

'That does not sound at all unreasonable, Mr Jones.' Quadir stands up and extends his hand.

Jack Jones stands up too and takes it. 'I will meet with you before you and the communists assemble. Remember, they cannot know that we are working together.'

'Excellent,' Quadir replies. 'Don't go anywhere; I am just going to show my friend out, and then we can work out details. I don't think he can remember the last time he has slept.'

Actually, Abdullah can. This morning he had shut the door to his office for an hour to close his eyes, but he is still grateful that tonight he is going to be in bed before midnight. When they reach the door, Quadir says, 'You were right in bringing him here, Abdullah.'

'Are we really going to allow him to build an American army base here?'

Now it is his friend's turn to smile. 'Of course not, but for now we need his help. When the communists are gone . . .' He shrugs. 'America is a long way from here.'

Chapter Four

Captain Khalid Khan
Camp Ritag

Month of Pregnancy 18-19 1375 A.H. (28-29 May 1956 A.D.

When Khalid arrived at Camp Ritag, the sun had already set. A master sergeant showed him to a private room and told him that the general's adjutant, Major al-Hashimi, would receive him in the morning, after which he discovered warm showers and cleaned himself up. He took his dinner alone in the officer's mess, said his prayers, and went to his new bed, where thoughts of his mother and his failure as a son kept him awake through most of the night. Nonetheless, when he opens his eyes the sun is brightening his room, and he realises that at some point he has fallen asleep.

Camp Ritag is nothing like Camp Nardin, and it's obvious that this is the home base of an important general. In fact, it's more like a village than an army camp. The barracks are home to more than a thousand soldiers, and there are no tents. Three dozen tanks are stationed behind the barracks, while there are more jeeps and lorries than Khalid has ever seen together. But the best thing is the hot water, and he has just returned from another shower when the master sergeant finds him again.

'Captain Khan, Major al-Hashimi will see you now.'

'Show me the way, Sergeant,' he answers, and the sergeant leads him to a small palace that makes him realise just how insignificant Brigadier Issa is compared with General Raslan. As a matter of fact, it's by far the most beautiful building Khalid has ever set foot in.

'Here we are,' the sergeant says when they reach a door in front of which two other men are sitting. 'I'll go and see if he's ready for you.'

Khalid nods at the men and sees that one is a colonel and the other a major. Are they waiting to see the general's adjutant too?

He doesn't have to wait long for an answer, as the sergeant instantly comes back out of the office and says, 'He'll see you now,' both officers stand up.

'Colonel Hussein; Major Hammoud; Captain Khan,' Major al-Hashimi says as he shakes their hands. 'Gentleman, welcome to Camp Ritag. Please allow me to apologise for not receiving you upon your arrival yesterday, but the king has ordered the entire army to prepare for war, and, as our division is responsible for the defence of our borders with both Saudi Arabia and Jordan, I hope you understand that yesterday was rather chaotic.

'Not that today will be any better, but I wanted to make some time to give you a proper welcome. How do you like your quarters?'

Khalid wants to say that they are the best he has ever seen but waits for the senior officers to speak first, and when Colonel Hussein calls them 'adequate,' he just nods in agreement.

'Excellent,' the major says. 'Now, yesterday the king ordered all officers off duty to report, but I'm afraid that in your case this has caused a complicated situation. You see, we did not expect you until next week, and we haven't transferred our own officers yet. Since the king has also ordered us to mobilise our division, presently it didn't seem wise to replace the officers who have been here for years. This means that we cannot yet place you with your respective battalion or company.'

For a brief second Khalid wonders why the general's adjutant mentioned him before Major Hammoud, but then Major al-Hashimi's gaze turns to the other major and he adds, 'Nor do we want to send away our senior liaisons officer.'

'Perfectly understandable,' Colonel Hussein answers.

'Of course, you must understand that since you're here, you'll have all the privileges that are due your respective ranks, including the salary,' Major al-Hashimi continues. 'But until we've sorted this business out, we don't have much for you to do.'

'Major,' Colonel Hussein says, 'I grew up in Mayasin, and I served in the Emir's Guard before I went to serve under General al-Dahabi. Since you don't have anything to do for me at this moment, I would like to request the general's permission to go to Mayasin and find out what exactly is going on. Naturally, I will report all my findings to the general.'

'Thank you, Colonel,' Major al-Hashimi answers. 'I will transfer your request to General Raslan, and I'll let you know what the general has decided as soon as possible. Do you have any other requests?'

The other two men remain silent, and Khalid can feel the adjutant's eyes upon him. He takes a deep breath and says, 'Sir, I would like to accompany the colonel.'

'Me too, sir,' Major Hammoud adds.

'Thank you, Captain, Major. I will forward your requests as well. Anything else?'

'No, Major,' the colonel says.

'Then you're all dismissed.'

Khalid looks at the colonel, but if the man next to him is bemused by the fact that he is being dismissed by a lower-classed officer, he does not show it. 'Thank you, Major,' Colonel Hussein drily says, after which Khalid and Major Hammoud salute and take their leave.

Once they're outside the palace, the colonel turns to Khalid and says, 'Captain Khan, you've come from Camp Nardin. Tell me, how is Brigadier Issa?'

'You know Brigadier Issa, sir?' Khalid asks.

'We served together in the Emir's Guard and in the army,' the colonel replies.

'Then you'll be pleased to hear that he was doing very well, even though he was very upset about the murder of Lord Tali'a.

Colonel Hussein snorts. 'He's not alone.'

'It's an absolute disgrace!' Major Hammoud growls and offers them a cigarette. 'I heard they had a boy murdering him, and then they murdered the boy. They call themselves Muslims, but I call them cowards!'

'Wasn't it a cooperative action between the Muslim Brotherhood and the communists?' Khalid asks.

'You're right,' Major Hammoud says, 'but at least the communists don't call themselves Muslims.'

'Don't worry, Major,' Colonel Hussein says grimly. 'The king has named Salem al-Sabah as Lord Tali'a's successor, and if I know Salem, he won't rest until the last rebel is hanging outside the prison.'

A silence falls, and Khalid looks at the colonel. The man is tall, broad-shouldered, and handsome, in every sense the picture of the perfect soldier. 'Do you know many men in the Royal Guard, Colonel?'

'I know all the men with whom I've served,' Colonel Hussein answers. 'When I was a guard, Lord Tali'a forced us to learn the name, face, and position of every man who worked in the palace; naturally, this included the other guards.'

367

Khalid tries to think of the guards he knows so that he can relate to the man, but he can't come up with many. 'A friend of mine had a cousin who was a guard. Do you know a man named Zahaar?'

The colonel shakes his head. 'There was never a guard named Zahaar when I was there.'

That's strange, but maybe Zahaar came after the colonel left. 'What about Mr al-Yaziji?'

'Saddam?' the colonel exclaims delightedly. 'Yes, I know him very well. He has a little coffeehouse in Juban now, hasn't he?'

Khalid beams. 'He does, and I always go there when I'm in the capital. He can tell the greatest stories about the War of the West and his days as a guard.'

'Well, next time you're there tell him Ali sends his regards, unless, of course, the general decides to send us to the capital. Then we can go there together. As for now, gentlemen, I wish you a good day. I had planned to spend this week with my family, and my children were seriously displeased when I told them I was going to Camp Ritag to report for duty. Since I have nothing better to do, the least I can do is write them a letter.'

'So, Captain Khan, the colonel served with al-Dahabi before coming here,' Major Hammoud says when they are alone. 'And you were promoted by Brigadier Issa?'

'I was, sir.'

'The self-made generals of the Beledarian army,' the major says and offers Khalid another cigarette. 'You know, I knew Issa during the War of the West. He was a lieutenant in my company; a hero like they don't make anymore.'

Khalid smiles. In a way, a compliment for his former commander also feels like a compliment for himself, and he spends the rest of the afternoon talking to the major about past wars—the major served in all three of them—and the current situation with the rebels. It is almost time for dinner when the general's adjutant comes to inform them that General Raslan has denied their request to go to Mayasin.

'But why?' Major Hammoud asks.

'It's illegal to send soldiers on duty into the capital, except as messengers, and the general doesn't believe it befits your positions to be used as errand boys.'

Khalid sighs. He understands it, but he doesn't like it. Major Hammoud is interesting company, yet he is not made to sit around and wait. He'd rather the general use him as an errand boy, and after the general's adjutant is gone, the major admits to feeling the same.

Khalid is in the shower when he hears the shots, and together with half a dozen other officers, he grabs his towel and his gun and runs out of the bathhouse.

'I think they came from the head office,' one of the men next to him says.

He nods and starts to run toward the small palace, but at the doors guards stop him. 'What was that?' he barks at them.

'We don't know, but no one is allowed inside,' a guard answers.

'You mean no one is allowed inside, *Captain.*'

'Beg your pardon, *sir*, but I didn't see any crossed swords on your shoulders, and there's just the one hanging between your legs.'

Khalid snorts and wraps the towel that's still in his hand around his waist.

'What's going on?' asks a man next to him, also naked.

'He doesn't know, and apparently we're not allowed inside,' Khalid replies.

'I'll take care of that,' the man says before turning to the guards. 'Step aside, Privates.'

'Sorry, sir, but we can't do that.'

'Do you know who I am?'

'Yes, sir. You're Lieutenant Colonel Ismat, but the general has personally ordered us not to let anyone in. Until he tells us differently, no one's getting in.'

'Then if God wants it, we'll wait here until that time comes or until someone comes to tell us what's going on.'

Khalid looks around. There are at least twenty men standing around them now, and although he feels rather stupid with nothing but a towel wrapped around his hips and a pistol in his hand, he decides that if the lieutenant colonel isn't going anywhere, he's not going anywhere either.

They wait for nearly half an hour, their numbers only growing, but then the general's adjutant appears behind the guards.

'What's going on, Major?' Lieutenant Colonel Ismat growls.

'Gentlemen,' Major al-Hashimi says calmly, 'thirty minutes ago, while General Lord Raslan was in a private meeting with Colonel Hussein, who was transferred here yesterday from Camp Mayasin, a member of the Muslim Brotherhood broke into his office and tried to shoot the general. Unfortunately for him and Colonel Hussein, he hit the colonel instead, and this provided the general with the opportunity to kill the rebel.

'Gentlemen, I am sorry to inform you that Colonel Hussein has not made it. But surely we belong to God and to him we shall return, and I know that this goes double for our colonel, who we will bury on the morrow. We have searched the entire building, and we are certain that there are no more rebels inside, while we have also doubled the guards around our camp.

'Now, gentlemen, I believe that you all have battalions, companies, and platoons to lead, so I suggest you all start attending to your duties instead of standing here naked like a band of Roman slaves at an auction.'

Khalid does not have any duties to attend to, yet he joins the other men as they make their way back to their barracks. He wishes he had something to do, something to keep himself occupied, but for now he'll have to make do with his sister's book about little English people and a dragon.

CHAPTER FIVE

ABDULLAH SAÍD
Mayasin

Month of Pregnancy 19-20, 1375 A.H. (29-30 May 1956 A.D.)

He is sitting in his office, trying his best to look busy, when Salah al-Din knocks on his door. He looks at his watch. It's almost seven o'clock. The boy is exactly on time!

'What is it, Salah?'

'Mr Saíd, I think I may have found something.'

He narrows his eyes. 'You may have found something, or you *have* found something?'

'I'm not sure, sir, but look at this.'

'I see a list of addresses. What is important about it?' he asks.

'Well, yesterday you gave us all a list of places that were already raided and all these addresses were on that list, except for this one. I thought that if all the other addresses were safe houses, this one would be too.'

The boy points at an address at the edge of the city, where the Brotherhood has agreed to prepare a little welcome for the Royal Guard. Abdullah smiles. He has thought long and hard about how to direct the Royal Guard to the fake safe house, and he is pleased that the boy has figured out the meaning of the list he wrote this morning.

'God is praised!' he exclaims. 'That is fantastic news. God is praised!'

'God is praised,' the boy repeats, again glowing with pride.

'Come on,' Abdullah says, 'I think the commander is with the king. If God wants it, let's go show it to them.'

'Are you sure, sir? Do you want me to come?'

'Of course.'

'Who's this?' Jafar asks when they reach the king's office.

'This is Salah al-Din, and he has made a very important discovery. Who's in there?'

'The king, Commander al-Sabah, and Mr Petrakis. I suppose you want to join them?'

He nods, and the under butler knocks on the door and opens it without waiting for any reply. 'Mr Abdullah Saíd and Mr Salah al-Din.'

Jafar steps back and gestures that they can enter. Salah hesitates, but Abdullah pats him on the back before giving him a little push.

'Gentlemen,' the king welcomes them. 'Please tell me that you have good news.'

'Majesty, I believe we do,' Abdullah answers. 'Salah al-Din here has found the location to the safe house of the leadership of the Muslim Brotherhood.'

'Are you sure?' the king asks, but before he can answer, Commander al-Sabah has pulled the list from the boy's hand, and Abdullah decides to let the commander make his own judgment.

'God is praised!' the commander exclaims before turning to the king. 'Majesty, I believe Mr Saíd is right!'

The king sighs deeply, looks at the four men in the room and walks over to the whisky tray. 'Drink, anyone?'

'No, thank you, Majesty,' all four men answer, and Abdullah tries not to show his disapproval when the king pours himself a glass.

'Well, gentlemen. I suppose that is it, then.' The king looks at Abdullah and Salah and explains, 'Just thirty minutes ago, we received a tip from the Americans about the communist safe house. I suppose they want to get them just as badly as we do. Tonight at eleven o'clock Commander al-Sabah will send out a squad, or actually two squads now, to take them all out.'

He raises his glass and finishes, 'If God wants it, it ends tonight!'

'Majesty,' Abdullah says, 'I suppose you won't mind if I send Salah, the clerks, and the other men who have been helping us home early tonight. I am not sure if they still remember what their beds feel like.'

'Of course not!' the king answers. 'Get them out of here and give them all tomorrow off too. And the day after. And the same goes for you!'

'Thank you, Majesty, but I still have some things that cannot wait. I won't mind staying at home tomorrow, though.'

'Let's discuss that later tonight,' Mr Petrakis says as though the king's secretary will not easily agree with that.

It's half past eleven, exactly, when Abdullah knocks on the door of Mr Petrakis's office. Inside, the group of men that they had smuggled in during the previous days and a dozen servants have already assembled. He nods at Mr Petrakis and asks, 'Do you have the weapons?'

A man in a chef's outfit steps forward and hands him a very big knife. 'I have sharpened them specially for tonight,' the man says with a malicious grin.

He stares at the knife. It is much too big for his jacket pocket, and there is no way he's going to put a blade like this in his trousers. Then he looks back at the man. 'Where do you think I should hide this?'

'Hmmm,' the man says, and after giving the matter some thought, he takes back the knife from Abdullah and hands him a smaller one. 'Perhaps this one is better.'

He wonders if the man is this stupid because he is a communist, but he refrains from sneering at him; tonight they are allies. He puts the knife in his jacket pocket. It still shows, but not too much, and definitely not in the dark.

The infidel says, 'All right men, remember, groups of four. If you kill a guard, dispose of him directly. You can take their rifles, but do not use them until the gate is open. If anyone raises the alarm before we have opened the gate, you can consider the mission failed. Let's go!'

Abdullah and Mr Petrakis are the first to leave the office with two men from the Brotherhood. They have decided that since they are two of the most trusted men in the palace, they will take on the most dangerous part of the mission: the opening of the gates. They have hardly left their hallway when they encounter two guards, and Abdullah's heart begins to pound. He bends a little bit forward so that the men cannot make out his knife. Just as they pass them, one of the men says, 'Wait.'

He stops and turns to them. Royal Guards never talk, not even late at night, and now they stop the king's secretary! Has someone betrayed them?'

'Who are those men?' the guard asks, gesturing at the men from the Brotherhood. 'They don't work in the palace!'

He can see the man gripping his rifle a little tighter while the other guard follows his example. How can the guard be so sure? There are hundreds of men working in the palace. Does he know every one of them?

But Mr Petrakis is not intimidated. 'Do you know what is going on tonight?'

'Of course,' the man barks, showing no respect whatsoever for the infidel.

'Well, how do you think we found those safe houses? These men are informants, and Commander al-Sabah has asked us to keep them in the palace until after the mission is well underway. Since we are both on our way home, we have offered to escort them to the gates.'

The man stares at Mr Petrakis for a second, but then he nods and says, 'Move on.'

When they are out of earshot, Abdullah mutters to the infidel, 'That was close.'

'It was. Too close.'

They walk on, and when they reach the door to the back offices, they meet two new guards. Abdullah nods at them, but before they have passed them they are stopped again.

'Who are those men?'

'These are informants,' Mr Petrakis answers confidently again. 'They have helped us locate the infidels. Since we are on our way home, we are showing them out.'

'I thought you always slept at the palace,' the guard answers. It isn't completely serious, yet it also isn't a joke.

'Normally I do,' the infidel answers. 'But I also have a family, and normally I go home for a couple of hours during the day. These last days I was rather occupied, so I thought I would join my wife in bed tonight for a change. Surprise her, so to speak.'

'Well, I hope you have a big surprise for her,' the guard answers and everyone laughs, even Abdullah. It is not a very funny joke, but laughing does calm his nerves a little.

As they start to make their way through the back offices, Mr Petrakis mutters, 'Do you know, Lord Tali'a sometimes boasted that his guards knew every man that worked in the palace. I always thought he said it to impress me, but I am beginning to think he was not lying.'

The infidel might have told him this a little earlier, but Abdullah does not answer. He can feel adrenaline shooting through his body and his heart beating like when he's in bed with Kalima, on the verge of erupting. But in those moments he is completely relaxed, while presently the stress is causing him to tremble.

On a normal night they would not encounter any more guards until they reached the door, but this is not a normal night.

'Stop! Those men don't belong here!' the guard that's holding up his hand says strictly.

'They are informants,' Mr Petrakis answers. 'We are showing them out.'

'No, they are not!' The other guard steps forward and looks at his companion. 'I let the man on the left in two days ago. I remember, because I told Ali it was very strange that I could not remember him coming out!'

The guards raise their rifles, but before they are pointed at Abdullah, he is pushed to the wall from behind, and the men from the Brotherhood have jumped the guards. Abdullah sees knives flashing, and seconds later both guards are on the ground.

'Where did you learn that?' he asks, bewildered.

'I fought in the war against the Iraqis,' one of the men answers, while the other says, 'And I have fought the Zionists. All the men that you have brought into the palace over the last two days were trained in the army; Quadir specially selected us for our military skills.'

He looks at Mr Petrakis and raises his eyebrows as he gets up. The infidel does the same. Part of him had thought that the men they had smuggled into the palace would be just as clumsy with a weapon as he knew himself to be. Thank God his sister's husband had given the matter some serious thought.

One of the men opens a random door, and they drag the bodies into an office. 'There is blood on the floor,' the other man says.

'I suppose we'll have to make haste then,' Mr Petrakis answers. 'There is no time to clean it up.'

When they reach the back door, both the guards inside and the guards outside stop them to ask about the Brotherhood men, but this time the infidel's story holds up, and before they know it, they are outside, walking to the gate.

'Remember,' Mr Petrakis says, 'there should be four guards. We wait until we all have one in reach, and do not attack until I give the signal.'

'Yes, sir,' the men from the Brotherhood answer while Abdullah just nods. He does not like the prospect that he is about to kill a man. It will not be the first time, but Rizq had earned it. Rizq. He remembers how Siraj threw him out of the whorehouse so that the rat could have his revenge. If they survive this and manage to take over control of the country, the whorehouses are the first issue he will address.

Twenty yards to go. He does not like the men from the Royal Guard, but over the years he has learned that while they may be rough, they are not corrupt, and they are never shy to lend a hand when asked. He is also reasonably sure that they are all Muslims.

And now he is going to have to kill at least one.

Five yards to go. 'Hold up!'

Two of the guards have spotted them. Where are the other two? He looks at the little house next to the gate; they are inside.

'Who are those men?'

'They are . . .' Mr Petrakis starts, but before he can say any more there is a muffled crack from inside the palace, and the guard holds up his hand to silence him.

'Wait. Was that a gunshot?'

Another crack. Both guards lift their rifles, and the man who stopped them calls, 'Ra'fit, Ibrahim, there are people shooting inside the palace, while the infidel and Abdullah Saíd are trying to smuggle strange men outside.'

In seconds, Ra'fit and Ibrahim are outside, their rifles aimed at the small group of rebels.

'I promise you, it is nothing like that,' Mr Petrakis says, but he is no longer sounding as confident as before. 'We are simply escorting the informants who provided Commander al-Sabah with the information about the safe houses outside.'

'You'll not be escorting anyone outside,' either Ra'fit or Ibrahim growls. 'Ibrahim is going to call the commander now, and if any one of you so much as moves, we will shoot you!'

They are lost; beaten by Lord Tali'a from the grave. Abdullah sees Ibrahim stepping into the little office and wonders how long it will be until the guard comes out to tell them that they are under arrest.

Crack! Crack! Crack! The shots are coming through the gate, and two of the guards go down, but Ra'fit starts to shoot and before Abdullah really understands what is happening, Mr Petrakis and one of the men from the Brotherhood are down too.

He dives for cover, and it appears that the other man from the Brotherhood is doing the same, but in fact the man is diving for one of the guards' rifles, and the moment he has it, he fires it at Ra'fit.

Abdullah lets out a sigh of relief when he sees that the man has hit the guard. He looks at his companion; there is blood coming from his shoulder. The other guard is less than a yard away from him, and he crawls toward his weapon just as Ibrahim steps out of the house again. His companion instantly shoots, but Ibrahim takes a step back, giving Abdullah time to take the rifle and aim it at the door.

However, Ibrahim doesn't step out; he rolls out, drops to one knee, and shoots Abdullah's last companion. It's all down to him now! He can see Ibrahim moving his gun toward him, but his own rifle is already pointing in the direction of the guard. All he has to do is pull the trigger.

He closes his eyes. He never knew how hard it is to keep a rifle stable when you are shooting, and he can feel it sending shocks through his body. He can also hear Ibrahim's rifle going off. Has the guard hit him? He doesn't know; he doesn't feel anything, but considering the move the guard just made, it is hard to believe that he has not.

From the palace he now clearly hears the sound of the alarm, and he opens his eyes again. Ibrahim is on the ground. He studies himself; he cannot see any gunshot wounds. *God is praised.* 'Abdullah!'

He stands up and looks at the gate. Through the spikes, Quadir's face appears. 'Abdullah, open the gate!'

Yes, he needs to open the gate. Where are the keys? He searches the guards, but he cannot find them. He goes into the little house, but he cannot see them there either. *God, please help me! God, we are so close!*

He walks outside again and feels tears in his eyes. 'I cannot find the keys!'

'Run away!' Quadir calls back. 'In the name of God, run!'

Run? He looks in the direction of the palace. The guards that were outside the door are approaching him. And not just that— they are shooting at him! On his left is the main entrance, where he'll only find more guards. On his right is the wall that shields the private garden from the rest of the estate, so he can't go too far in that direction either.

'Run!' he hears again.

Anything is better than waiting here to be shot. He runs in the direction of the wall, but before he is twenty yards away from the gate an explosion knocks him to the ground.

He's not hurt, but there's a beep in his ear that drowns out all sounds around him. Suddenly the battle appears to be far away, and in the distance he can see the men from the Brotherhood and the communists running through the opening where just a minute earlier the gate was.

But they are not getting far. The guards who were shooting at Abdullah are now shooting at them, and he watches as one man after another goes down, while the guards remain standing. *God, we are going to need a little more help.*

It's as though God has heard him. The little palace door opens, and out come men from the Brotherhood, the soldiers that he and the infidel brought into the palace like Trojan horses, and within seconds they have taken out the guards. *God is praised!*

He closes his eyes and lies down again. He has done his part. Now, Quadir, Gamal, and the communists can finish it.

Chapter Six

Captain Khalid Khan
Camp Ritag

Month of Pregnancy 21-22, 1375 A.H. (31 May–1 June 1956 A.D.)

It feels like Khalid's first days at Camp Ritag are even worse than his first days at Camp Nardin. Lieutenant Colonel Ismat greets him when they meet, and he takes his meals with Major Hammoud, but for the rest everyone is much too busy to give him any attention, while he has nothing to do. Many times he has picked up the book about the hobbit during the last three days, and by now he knows the first paragraph by heart.

'In the hole in the ground there lived a hobbit. Not a nasty, dirty, wet hole, filled with the ends of worms and an oozy smell, nor yet a dry, bare, sandy hole with nothing in it to sit down on or to eat: it was a hobbit-hole, and that means comfort.'

But that's also as far as he has been able to read. The holes make him think about his mother and Colonel Hussein, and from there his mind drifts to the man's children, who are now left without a father because the Muslim Brotherhood murdered him. And then he goes on to think about the situation in the capital, and he cannot help but feel like a coward for sitting in idleness, reading a book. It's the same every time.

Thus, he sits in the shade, where he takes apart his pistol and assembles it again, and again, and again, and again. It's a good pistol, a Beretta made in Italy, and as the years have gone by it has softened his feelings about Lieutenant Fakeih.

'Captain Khan!' He looks up and finds Major al-Hashimi standing in front of him. 'General Lord Raslan wants to see you.'

General Raslan wants to see him! He jumps up, and the pieces of his gun fall on the ground, but he ignores them and salutes the adjutant. 'Yes, sir!'

The general's adjutant stares at the pieces of the pistol. 'You may reassemble your gun first, Captain.'

It takes him less than thirty seconds, and five minutes later he is standing in General Raslan's office, which is a kind of grand hall in the palace.

'Captain,' the general says, 'You are from the Oyoun al Jabal province, are you not?'

'Yes, sir.'

'Does this mean that you are a Shi'a?'

'It does, sir.'

'And do you consider the Muslim Brotherhood, as they are Sunnis, your enemies?'

'I do consider the Muslim Brotherhood my enemies, but not because they have a different interpretation of the true faith, sir. If a man says that there is no God but God, and that Muhammad is his Prophet . . . If he prays five times a day and honours the Month of Burning . . . If he gives money to the poor and saves for his pilgrimage to Mecca, then I respect that man for honouring God. The Muslim Brotherhood are my enemies because they've murdered Lord Tali'a and Colonel Hussein.'

'Well spoken, Captain, but what about the king? There are many rumours that King Jalal does not honour God in the way that would earn your respect.'

'Sir, when it comes to the king, I do not believe that I'm in a position to judge him, and I think I'd rather leave that to God.'

The general nods approvingly. 'Captain, before he was murdered, Colonel Hussein asked for permission to go to the capital to see what was going on. As you know, I declined that request, and while this saved my life, I've given it a lot of thought over the last few days, and I've come to conclusion that it was a mistake.

'I have received no new information from the palace these last days, no updates, no orders, nothing. Messages I have sent remain unanswered, and messengers have not returned. Captain, you volunteered with the colonel to go to the capital to investigate. Are you still willing to go?'

'Yes, sir!' Finally, Khalid can do something too!

'I must warn you that this may be a very dangerous mission.'

'I'll be careful, sir. When do you want me to leave?'

It's half past six in the morning when Khalid gets on the bus from Ritag to Mayasin, just outside the city, and there isn't a single seat left. He walks to the middle and stands in the aisle as the bus rides off.

An old man in the seat next to him grins at him; there are just three teeth visible in the man's mouth. Next to the man is a young woman with a small child in her lap. The woman is looking out the window, but the kid is staring at him, and he looks away. On his other side there are two men, of whom one is holding a chicken. He wonders what business they have in the capital. In fact, he wonders what business all these people on the bus have in Mayasin.

After about twenty minutes, the bus stops to let more people on, and he moves to the back to make room for the new travellers.

There's not much room left to move in the aisle, but twenty minutes later the bus stops again to let on more people. The bus now seems completely crowded, yet at the next stop three more men and a goat enter, and Khalid realises just how lucky he is that, as a senior officer, whenever he wants to go somewhere he can use an army jeep. Today is an exception only because his mission requires secrecy, but fortunately it's still early and not very hot yet.

They've almost reached the city when the bus stops and the driver starts yelling to his passengers that everyone has to get out. Khalid tries to see what is going on, but with all the people standing in front of him he can't see much. Only when he has reached the front of the bus does he see the roadblock in front of them and the men with rifles.

'Tell me your name and your business,' one of the man commands him.

Khalid studies the man. He does not wear a uniform, and he is dirty, which means that he is neither a soldier nor a Royal Guard. He could be a policeman, but the last time Khalid was in the capital, policemen didn't carry rifles. Of course, it could have something to do with the murder of Lord Tali'a and the attack on the prison.

'I am Muhammad Hussein,' Khalid says, 'and my business is to find a job and get rich.'

In his slightly dirty tunic, Khalid doesn't look much different from the other young men who come into the capital every day looking for work, yet the man studies him intensely before saying, 'You sound like you're from Taj al Wadi. Why do you arrive in a bus from Ritag?'

'One of my brother's wives is from Ritag, and she said her uncle had work for me, but when I arrived the man had already given the job to one of his cousins.'

'If your brother has more than one wife,' the man says, 'then why doesn't your brother have work for you?'

'He does, but I have five more brothers, and I'm the youngest, so you understand my position.'

The man gives him a compassionate smile, and Khalid knows that he has chosen his story well. The capital is filled with young men with similar stories.

'Do you carry any weapons?'

'I have a pistol.'

'I am afraid I have to confiscate that,' the man says. 'The business with the prison; you probably understand.'

For a second Khalid wonders if he should play dumb to get more information from this man, but since he's even caught the word 'prison' a couple of times on the bus, he decides that if he starts asking about it, there's a good chance he'll lose the man's trust, and then he'll never get to keep his gun.

'I brought all of my savings,' he says instead. 'I'd like to keep my pistol so that I can protect them. Isn't there something we can do?'

The man gives him another inquisitive stare but then says, 'If you give me ten shillings, I suppose I could pretend to have misunderstood you when you told me you were carrying a pistol.'

'How about five?' Khalid asks. He would happily pay ten shillings to keep his weapon, but it would look really suspicious if he does not try to negotiate. 'I don't have that many savings . . .'

'I suppose I could live with five.' The man smirks.

Khalid pays the man and gets back onto the bus, where the air is now cooking and humid. The man at the roadblock may have been many things, but he was certainly no policeman. A Mayasin cop would never let him get away with a five-shilling bribe after he had told him he'd brought all of his savings. The people of Mayasin don't call their policemen rats for nothing.

General Raslan warned him not to go to the palace unless he's sure it's safe, so when the bus reaches its destination in Juban, almost five hours after he got on, he starts to make his way to the small coffeehouse of Mr al-Yaziji. The colonel said that he was a good man, and Khalid cannot think of any other man in the capital whom he can trust. He wonders if Major Hammoud, who has also been sent to the capital, albeit on a different bus, faces the same problem.

The Market of Muhammad is crowded with merchants shouting their throats out with their great offers. Women and men are doing their daily shopping, and boys try to pick his pocket, but he is too quick for them. However, there are also men in corners talking in hushed voices and other men who walk around with badly concealed rifles, while the absence of Royal Guards and normal policemen makes the situation even more conspicuous. When he finds his coffeehouse and enters, the proprietor pretends not to know him, and he does not miss the suspicious stares of the men inside.

'What's up with those control posts outside the city?' he asks when Mr al-Yaziji places a small teapot on his table.

The man looks around, bends a little closer and says in a low voice, 'Two days ago there was a big battle at the palace. Officially, the king has locked himself in, together with the entire Royal Guard, while he's hired militia to guard the roads.'

'And unofficially?' Khalid whispers back.

Mr al-Yaziji looks around again before he almost inaudibly says, 'Lieutenant, I think you should go to the back and climb the stairs. You will find your answers in the second room on the right.'

Khalid nods, and when the man leaves, he quietly drinks his tea. Once he has finished two cups, he gets up to follow Mr al-Yaziji's instructions. The second door on the right is closed, and when he knocks, there's no answer. He takes his gun and carefully opens the door.

At first sight there does not appear to be anyone in the room, but the moment he steps inside he feels the point of a pistol in his neck.

'Who are you?' an unfamiliar but authoritarian voice asks.

He knows he is at the mercy of this man, but he cannot believe that Mr al-Yaziji would ever send him to an enemy of the king, and confidently he answers, 'I am Khalid Khan, captain in General Lord Raslan's First Division.'

'Khalid!' a voice calls that he does know, and from the other side of the door a face appears that he would recognise amongst millions, if only for the scar that splits it in two parts.

'Ghulam?'

'You know him?' the man who's sticking the gun in Khalid's neck asks.

'I do,' his old friend answers, 'but last I heard he was a lieutenant at Camp Nardin.'

Khalid looks at his friend. He hasn't heard from him in four years; how does Ghulam know that he was a lieutenant at Camp Nardin?

'When were you promoted?' the man with the gun asks.

'Last week,' he answers.

The man lowers the pistol. 'I'm sorry, but you must understand that we have to take precautions. We trust Mr al-Yaziji, but if the rebels discover us, all is lost.'

'Khalid,' Ghulam adds, 'meet Salem al-Sabah, commander of the Royal Guard—or what's left of it anyway—and Monsieur Lestrade, head of a French spy agency that does not exist.'

From behind the sofa another man appears, but Khalid hardly pays him any notice and turns to Commander al-Sabah. 'How do you mean, "if the rebels find us, all is lost." '

'The rebels, the communists, and the Muslim Brotherhood have taken the palace and they're holding King Jalal prisoner,' the commander answers. 'We are the king's last hope.'

'How did the rebels take the palace?'

The commander shakes his head and gestures that he should sit down, before he starts to explain how they were betrayed by the king's secretary and one of the king's private clerks. It quickly becomes clear that matters are much worse than Khalid expected, and he wonders if things would be different if the general had sent them to the capital the moment the colonel suggested it.

'What are you doing here?' the commander asks after finishing his story.

'We couldn't reach the palace, and the two messengers General Raslan sent there never returned, so I'm here to investigate.'

'Why you?' Ghulam asks.

'I volunteered, together with Colonel Hussein and Major Hammoud. The major should also be in the city right now, but Colonel Hussein was killed when a man from the Muslim Brotherhood tried to assassinate General Raslan.'

'Him too, eh,' the commander says and exchanges a look with Ghulam before adding, 'I sent two men to General al-Dahabi to ask for support, but he was murdered on the night the rebels took the palace. I've sent another three to Brigadier Issa, but not one has returned . . .'

Commander al-Sabah pauses for a second before asking, 'What did you make of General Raslan?'

Khalid shrugs. 'I have only seen him once, but he seemed genuinely concerned about the situation. Why?'

'We're working on a plan to free the king. If we succeed, we may be able to hold the palace for a day or two, but we'll also need to take back control of the city. Most of my guards are either dead or imprisoned, while the policemen who weren't killed when the rebels stormed the palace of Major al-Rikabi are in hiding; not that they'd be of much use when it comes to actual fighting.

'Fact of the matter is we are going to need an army, and with General al-Dahabi dead and Brigadier Issa unreachable, our options are Raslan or Kalaldeh.'

The generals of the First and the Second Division and scions of the most powerful two families in Beledar. Khalid doesn't know much about politics, but he does understand that if one of them were to station an army in the capital, that man might not want the king alive at all.

'I still think we should go with Kalaldeh,' Ghulam says before turning to Khalid. 'You are not a spy, Raslan doesn't know you, and you don't know this city . . .'

'I do know this city,' Khalid interrupts.

'You've visited here a couple of times during your furloughs; that's not the same as knowing this city. If you hadn't known Mr al-Yaziji, our friend would never have sent you to us, and what would you have done then? Did you even have a plan?'

'But I did know Mr al-Yaziji,' Khalid counters. His friend's remarks hurt, mostly because they are true. His plan was to talk to the people in the streets, and once he was sure that everything was safe, to report to the palace. He had never seriously considered the scenario that the rebels would be in control of the palace. Yet he does not want say that, and he continues, 'And God told me to come here.'

Ghulam sighs. 'Sure he did, but I doubt God told Raslan to send you. The general has dozens of men who are better suited for this job.'

'That's assuming he has some plan of his own,' Commander al-Sabah counters. 'It's a dangerous mission, and if Raslan's loyalty really lies with the king, it would not be strange to send an ambitious young officer.

'In the end it all comes down to this: is it possible that General Raslan did not know what was going on in the city? Now, I know I didn't send anyone to tell him, but the Raslans have spies all over this city. On the other hand, at the moment few people outside the palace know exactly what's going on, and while getting into the city is easy, getting out is much more difficult. What's more, I don't see Mr Petrakis working for the Raslans. The infidel likes power too much, and you can be sure that if General Raslan were to take over the city, there would not be a place for the king's former secretary.'

'So what do we do?' asks the Frenchman, who hasn't said a single word yet and whose name Khalid has forgotten.

'I want to know who this man, this Achmed Hammoud,' the commander answers and, turning to Khalid, he asks, 'Are you planning to meet him?'

'At Pervaíz's coffee house at two o'clock in the afternoon.'

'Ghulam, I want you to go with your friend and find out all you can about Major Hammoud. If he works for Raslan, you can be sure that he'll be making preparations for his boss's arrival, and he must not leave the city. When you've taken care of him, try to reach Brigadier Issa, but very carefully. If you notice anything suspicious at Camp Nardin, go to Kalaldeh and inform him that the king has ordered him to lead a brigade into the capital.'

'And if Major Hammoud is clean?' asks Khalid, who likes the major and finds it hard to believe that the man is involved in some dark plot with General Raslan.

'If he's clean, you may return to Ritag and tell General Raslan that the king needs him in the city.'

'What about the palace?' Ghulam asks.

'Don't worry, my friend,' the commander nudges the Frenchman as he continues, 'while you're meeting with this Hammoud, we will rescue the king.'

CHAPTER SEVEN

ABDULLAH SAÍD
Mayasin

Month of Pregnancy 22, 1375 A.H. (1 June 1956 A.D.)

The conference room has been rebuilt back to the way it used to be when the cabinet held its meetings there, but this time Abdullah is sitting at the central table, right next to Quadir. It would be the greatest honour in the world, were it not for the fact that opposite him, the woman in trousers has taken a chair. It feels like a major insult, but if they start a war with the communists now, no one will come out victorious.

'I say we reinstate the courts of divine law again, and we let the king be the first man we put on trial,' Gamal says. They've had the king locked up for three days, and today the only point on the agenda is what they will do with him. It's not going very differently from when the real ministers were sitting at this table; so far, the same positions have gone over the table about a dozen times for the last hour.

'That is unacceptable,' the woman says. 'We must instate a special tribunal and try him for crimes against the people!'

'A special court? On what crimes shall we try him then? Leading the people away from God, that is his biggest crime, and therefore the crime he has to be convicted on!' Gamal counters, but the woman is not giving in.

'His biggest crime!? What about the corruption? What about the murders he has ordered? What bigger crimes are there?'

'You don't . . .'

But this time Quadir interrupts his friend. 'Listen, we can talk about specific crimes all day, but let us first agree on the most important thing. Is everyone agreed that the king should be executed?'

'I believe he should be exiled,' one of the communists ventures, but no one supports him.

'All right. In that case, perhaps we should skip the whole trial and move straight to the execution. Is there anyone who disagrees?'

'I second the Muslim,' Sergei says in his Russian accent, and all eyes turn to him. 'You execute him, and the sooner you do it, the better. While you've been having meetings these last three days, many soldiers have flowed into this city. I know all your people do their best to stop them, but they are not trained for things like that; in fact, they are not trained at all. Meanwhile, unrest in the city is growing, and the longer you wait, the stronger the support for the king will become.'

It's a good point, but Abdullah is mostly scared of Commander al-Sabah. The commander of the Royal Guard was not in the palace on the night of the attack, and no one has seen him since. If he were to reappear . . .

'Anyone disagree?' Quadir looks round the table. No one speaks up. 'I heard the weather will be very nice tomorrow; we'll do it in the afternoon. Now, what about the wife and the children?'

'We can kill the wife,' Abdullah says, 'but the children are not guilty of anything!'

'Maybe not,' the young man named Lenin chips in, 'but they will grow older, and what then? Will they forget that they were once princes? The son, he may marry a Jordanian princess. Will the people have forgotten him when he leads King Hussein's army into Beledar? The daughter, she is very beautiful; every prince in the world would promise her an army in exchange for her hand. We cannot risk it.'

'Anyone else in favour of letting the children live?' Quadir asks. Two members of the Brotherhood raise their hands. 'The children die too.'

'I say we kill the children first. Let the king watch them die!' Gamal calls.

'Finally, a good idea from the Muslim!' the woman confirms, and the excitement the idea brings to the table is palpable, but then Sergei speaks up again.

'Unacceptable. You forget that this man is king. What if he goes crazy and starts to attack people? People might follow him, and before you know it, some idiot with a gun in his hand is going to choose the side of the king.'

'I'm sorry?' Gamal growls and curls his hand that is missing two fingers next to his absent ear. 'I am afraid I did not hear you. It appears as though you said that we should be wary of men choosing the side of the king, yet in prison I have learned a number of things that we can do with men like that.'

'Another good point from the Muslim,' the woman says. 'The king has killed my boyfriend, and there should not be any mercy for him, nor for the men who support him!'

Abdullah considers his own two sons. If someone were to kill them before his eyes, he would go crazy. 'Friends, I think we should listen to Sergei. Even if all goes well, what will the people in the street think when they hear that we killed the king's children before his eyes? They will think us monsters! How will God judge us? He will judge us as monsters!'

'I don't care about God,' the woman barks, but Abdullah can see that most men, including the communists, agree with him.

'Clear,' Quadir says, before he starts to discuss protocol for the execution.

The execution will take place in the walled garden, and the communist named Lenin is determined that he will have the 'honour' of condemning the king. Abdullah stops listening until, more than an hour later, he suddenly feels all eyes upon him. He has to inform the king that he has been condemned to execution.

'Well, which is it? Execution, exile, or trial?' are the king's first words after the guard has opened the door and King Jalal has discovered who is visiting him.

'Majesty . . .' Abdullah pauses. Should he still address the king as Majesty? He supposes he should; the man is still wearing a suit, and even though it's dirty and his tie is loose, he looks much too regal to be called Jalal. 'I have brought you a bottle of whisky.'

The king nods. 'Execution it is, then.'

'Tomorrow afternoon.' He hands over the bottle and steps into the cell, even though he does not have much more to say.

The king shrugs. 'Very thoughtful to bring me a bottle of my own whisky. Will you drink with me?'

Abdullah shakes his head. He doesn't even know if he was right in bringing in the whisky, yet he hadn't dared come empty-handed with his news.

'I supposed you wouldn't. You know, I thought it would be Mr Petrakis who would tell me about my fate.'

'The infidel is dead,' Abdullah answers.

'That's too bad; I was going to call him Brute. Can't very well call you Brute. You wouldn't understand, and it would not make much sense if you did.' The king is right. Abdullah doesn't understand. 'Do you like irony, Mr Saíd?'

He does not answer, and the king continues. 'You have locked me up in the same cell Lord Tali'a used when he locked up my uncle Sharif fourteen years ago. It's ten feet long and six feet wide. I know, because I have walked it up and down about a thousand times during the last few days.'

Abdullah doesn't know what to say, and before he can think of anything, the king asks, 'What about my family?'

He shakes his head. 'I am sorry, Majesty.'

'Bastards!' The king opens the bottle and takes a swig before asking, 'And Lord Tali'a, was that you or the communists?'

'Neither, Majesty.'

'Neither?' The king shakes his head. 'Petrakis, you backstabbing old man.'

'Majesty, Mr Petrakis did not become involved until after the commander was murdered.'

The king raises his right eyebrow. 'You have much to learn, young Saíd, especially about politics. How are things going with the communists? Are you ready for the next war?'

He stares at the king. How can the man know all this? The guards have been ordered not to talk to him, yet King Jalal seems to know exactly what is going on. Is the man right about Mr Petrakis too, or was that the paranoia talking? What if the infidel was working with the American? Perhaps they killed Lord Tali'a. But if that was so, then why did the American keep on hassling them about whether or not they killed the commander? It does not make sense.

Still, was it a coincidence that Mr Petrakis knew about the secret hallways, or had he been looking for them because he knew that he was going to need them?

'We work well together,' he says as casually as he can.

'Ha! I suppose that is why there is not going to be a trial.'

It's uncanny, and Abdullah would love to run out the door, but the king isn't finished with him yet. 'So tell me, are you Muslim Brotherhood all the way, or is your wife involved too?'

He frowns. 'My wife does not participate in politics.'

The king laughs. 'I think you underestimate her, perhaps because she is a woman. But if you are married to a real Raslan, she is always involved.'

Abdullah ignores the king and asks, 'Do you wish to me to send a reverend to help you make peace with God?'

'God?' The king takes another swig from his bottle. 'If there is a God, He is a cruel God, and I don't need to be friends with Him for eternity. After all, what kind of God creates a species as short-sighted, self-centred and treacherous as humankind? I am many things, Mr Saíd, but not a hypocrite; I will find my God at the bottom of my bottle.'

Abdullah shakes his head and walks out without another word. It is preposterous that the king says things like this on Gathering Day, and he feels dirty just listening to the man. Mr Petrakis was right: King Jalal truly is mad. He wonders how he could have missed that all those years.

CHAPTER EIGHT

CAPTAIN KHALID KHAN
Mayasin

Month of Pregnancy 23, 1375 A.H. (2 June 1956 A.D.)

After the conversation with Ghulam, the commander, and the Frenchman, Khalid spent the rest of the day waiting in Mr al-Yaziji's bedroom while his friends were making plans for the assault on the palace. Commander al-Sabah said that it was better if Khalid wasn't involved, so he could not betray them if he was apprehended by the rebels, but apparently no such caution was required when it came to Ghulam.

He slept on the floor, and since the Commander al-Sabah had ordered him not to show his face outside until Ghulam came to get him, he also spent his morning waiting and praying in solitude. He thought about his mother and the king, and he could not understand why the rebels had staged their coup. The king was a good man; even his father had come around and told him so when Khalid visited him. He had defeated the Iraqis; he built schools, hospitals and roads. Why did the rebels want him gone?

The sun has almost reached its highest point when his friend knocks on the door to tell him it's time. He looks at his watch and says, 'My meeting with Major Hammoud isn't until two o'clock.'

'We want to get there early,' Ghulam answers. 'We don't know what time he will arrive, and I want you to point him out to me.'

Khalid nods and follows his friend.

'This whole town is crowded with soldiers,' Ghulam says when they're outside.

'How can you tell?'

'Did you see those two guys we just passed?'

Khalid looks over his shoulder, and he can see two guys in private conversation. However, apart from badly hidden weapons, which could mean many things, he doesn't see anything indicating that they are soldiers. 'I have now.'

'And did you look at their footwear?'

'I did not.'

Ghulam stands still and says, 'Look again.'

The men are wearing heavy black boots, and even though they are covered in dust, there is no mistaking them. 'Army boots.'

'Very good.' Ghulam starts to walk again, and Khalid follows, but two hundred yards farther his friend stops again. 'Check out the three men over there.'

Khalid follows Ghulam's eyes and sees three men in white tunics standing next to a small table in front of a small coffee-house not far from them. He looks at their feet; they are wearing sandals, as is usual with their outfit. 'I see them, but I don't see what you see.'

'Really? Don't you see how ill-fitting their tunics are?'

'Do I look like a tailor?'

'Well, if you did see it, you would ask yourself how it's possible that three men can be wearing clean white tunics in such a bad size. After all, if they have women in their life to wash their tunics for them, those women would also make sure they were made into the right size.'

It makes perfect sense, and Khalid realises what Ghulam meant when his friend said that he was no spy; he might as well be blind compared with Ghulam. 'How long have you been here?'

'Two days. I was in Egypt when Lord Tali'a was murdered, but I returned immediately after hearing the news.'

'Egypt?'

'Lord Tali'a had heard that Othman Raslan, General Raslan's youngest brother, was going there, and he sent me to investigate. We thought he might be meeting with representatives of the Egyptian government, but he wasn't. He did meet an Englishman, though, a Lord Richard Rockingham, but before I was able to discover if Lord Rockingham was just another businessman or an English spy, news found me of the commander's murder, and I figured I'd be of more value here.'

'Lord Tali'a made you a spy . . .' Khalid observes, slightly jealous that his friend has such a cool position, but also slightly surprised. There's no question that Ghulam has the brains to be a spook, but spies are supposed to work incognito. With that scar on his face, a man only needs to meet Ghulam once, and he'll never again forget his face.

'There's actually nothing in the records about me being in the Security Agency, and officially I am a major in the First Armoured Division. Can you believe that? I have never even been inside a tank! Ha.

'But there's also no mention of the agency itself, and even Commander al-Sabah did not know of its existence. It took me quite some effort to convince the new commander that he could trust me after I tracked him down, but of course, he didn't have much choice.'

Khalid looks at his friend, who seems rather excited about everything that's going on and not at all concerned with the well-being of the king, and he decides to change the subject.

'If there really are this many soldiers in town, why don't we simply gather them to take back control of the city?'

Ghulam sighs. 'The soldiers, they are not here to save to the king—or at least most of them are not—nor to take back control of the city. They are here to see if there are possibilities for advancements for their generals and lords and to support whoever will come out of this crisis victorious. No one knows exactly what's going to happen, and no one wants to show his hand too early.'

'What if we were to gather support from the people? Demonstrate?'

His friend shakes his head. 'There are many supporters of the king in the city, but we dare not trust anyone. Any man can secretly be a communist or a member of the Brotherhood. You know I don't believe in God, but it really is a miracle that you walked into our coffeehouse and that Mr al-Yaziji thought you were trustworthy enough to send you upstairs. You don't want to know what would have happened to you if one of the rebels suspected you to be a supporter of the king.'

'Why? What would have happened?'

Ghulam shrugs. 'You'd have ended up in the graveyard within twenty-four hours, but not before you had learned something about Russian torture machines.'

Khalid stops and turns to his friend. 'How do you know all this?'

'I grew up here, remember? What's more, I've been gathering information for almost four years now, often in very unfriendly places.'

They have arrived at Pervaíz's coffeehouse, and Ghulam sits down against the wall opposite the entrance. Khalid follows his example and puts on his glasses.

'Put those away,' his friend says.

'Why? I can't see the major approaching without them.'

'You'll have to. If anyone asks what we're doing here, we are porters waiting for our boss to come out of that coffeehouse, and I've never seen a porter wear glasses.'

Khalid sighs and puts the glasses back in his tunic. If he narrows his eyes, he can make out the faces of the men who are walking across the street when they're about ten yards from the entrance, but it costs him a lot of energy, and he can't do it constantly.

For almost an hour, Khalid can't see anyone he recognises, and he's starting to get nervous. 'What if they don't believe we're porters?' he asks.

'Then they'll take us for informants for either the Brotherhood or the communists, and they will not dare to make trouble.'

Clearly, his friend has planned everything. He looks back at the road. No Major Hammoud. Then he turns his head to the other side.

There is the major, but he is too late; the man is already turning toward the entrance. He pokes Ghulam and hisses, 'That's him!'

'Why do you tell me only now?' his friend grunts. 'How can I figure out if he is who he says he is if I can only see his back?'

'I told you, I should have worn glasses!'

Ghulam shakes his head. 'It's okay. I'll spot him when he comes back out. Try to let him leave first. If that does not work, when you leave, go right and wait for me behind the second corner on your left hand. Got it?'

Khalid nods.

'All right.' Ghulam puts a hand on his shoulder. 'Good luck.'

He nods again, gets up, and makes his way to the coffeehouse, his heart pounding. If Ghulam is right, he is about to meet with a traitor. Yet he also can't shake the feeling that it's strange that Ghulam knows all those things and that apparently his friend is some really important spy, even though Ghulam is younger than himself and recognisable a mile away.

The coffeehouse is about half full, and Major Hammoud is sitting at a table in the back. Khalid starts to walk over to him, but a man stops him.

'I don't believe we've met,' the man says. 'I am Pervaíz, and this is my coffeehouse. What would you like to drink?'

'Coffee, please.'

The man bows a little and asks, 'Perhaps you would also like something to eat. I have some very nice sweet rolls with fresh cream cheese.'

'Sure, bring me two,' he answers, and the man shows him a broad grin.

He sits down next to the major, and until Pervaíz has brought him his coffee and the rolls, they talk about the weather and ciga-rette brands, but the moment their host is out of earshot, the major whispers, 'Do you know?'

Khalid nods and says softly, 'The rebels have taken the palace.'

He picks up one of the rolls, which really is very tasty, and Major Hammoud says, 'I have heard the royal family is locked up in the dungeons, and the Royal Guard almost completely destroyed, but that Commander al-Sabah may still be alive.'

'I've heard that too,' Khalid says. He would love to tell the major that he has actually met the commander and that there is a plan to rescue the king, but he has sworn that he will not disclose anything important. So instead, he continues, 'I've also heard that it was the king's secretary and a private clerk who betrayed the king.'

'Really? Good work! You know, you'd make an excellent spy,' Major Hammoud says. 'Where did you learn that?'

Khalid feels heartened by the compliment and realises that even though he has not done much, he has learned a lot. 'A matter of walking into the right people, I suppose. Unfortunately, I didn't learn much more.'

'You know,' Major Hammoud says, 'I was scared that maybe you wouldn't make it here. The rebels are very suspicious of everything and everyone at the moment—each other included. But I have learned something else.'

The man is talking really softly now, and Khalid brings his head a little closer so that he won't miss anything.

'I have learned that it was neither the Muslim Brotherhood nor the communists who murdered Lord Tali'a. It was Lord Kalaldeh.'

Khalid's eyes grow wide, and he remembers yesterday's conversation. '*Our options are Raslan or Kalaldeh,*' the commander said, to which Ghulam answered, '*I think we should go with Kalaldeh.*' If Kalaldeh murdered Lord Tali'a, it's clear whose army they should bring into the city.

'How did he do it?' Khalid whispers.

'Apparently, one of his men trained the boy who shot the commander, and this man shot the boy when the deed was done to cover up his actions.'

'And how did you learn this?' he asks.

The major shrugs and modestly answers, 'Luck, I suppose. I ran into an old friend who knew a man who had seen the boy go into a warehouse regularly in the days prior to the murder. This morning I went to the business district to discover who owned the warehouse, and from there it was all very easy to figure out.'

'Lord Kalaldeh owned the warehouse . . .' Khalid says.

'Lord Zubi, actually, but he is a crony of Kalaldeh and would never do anything without the permission of the governor of Nareng; especially not something like this!'

'What do we do?'

'Do you think Brigadier Issa trusts you?'

He looks at the man and remembers the words his former commander spoke to him before he left. 'I think he does, yes.'

'Excellent. I've arranged transport for the both of us, and I think it would be best if you were to go to Brigadier Issa. Communicate to him what we've learned and ask him to join forces with General Raslan. I don't think that Kalaldeh will dare to march on the city after he learns that a complete brigade has left him, and even if he does, he will not stand a chance.'

Khalid nods. That's probably even smarter than Commander al-Sabah's plan. 'You know . . .'

He hesitates, and Major Hammoud asks, 'I know what?'

Khalid wanted to tell the major about Ghulam's distrust of Lord Raslan and the commander's plan, but his oath weighs heavily on him, and he knows that if he spills the beans, he'll only be doing it to make his own efforts look even more successful. Thus, he says, 'I don't think it's wise if we leave together.'

'I agree,' the major says. 'You finish your roll and meet me in two hours in front of the Great Mosque.'

'Yes, sir.'

Major Hammoud gets up, but before the man walks away, he whispers, 'And Captain, please, don't get caught. I've heard the rebels have Russian torture machines and use them on every man they suspect supports the king.'

'I've heard that too, sir,' Khalid answers and starts to work on the other roll as he watches the man leave.

Suddenly, he feels like everything is going to work out fine. If Commander al-Sabah takes back the palace and Brigadier Issa aligns his brigade with General Raslan's division, the Brotherhood, communists, and Lord Kalaldeh together will not be able to challenge them. And who knows, he may even get another promotion, or at least another medal!

He has finished his roll and his coffee, and he pays Pervaíz before walking out of the coffee shop. Ghulam is now standing opposite the street, and when he turns to the right, his friend joins him.

'I suppose we have our answer,' Ghulam says.

'I suppose we do,' he replies, but then he looks at his friend and realises that Ghulam can't have any idea what they spoke about. 'What do you mean?'

'The man you met, that was not Major Hammoud. That man was Othman Raslan, the same Raslan brother I saw in Egypt.'

Khalid shakes his head. 'That can't be so.'

'Just wait and see,' Ghulam answers. 'The rats will pick him up, and then we'll question him.'

'How can the policemen pick him up? I thought they were all in hiding.'

'Trust me, if there's one thing that gets a rat out of hiding, it's a nice big piece of cheese, and by cheese I mean gold,' his friend says grimly.

'But I'm supposed to meet him in front of the Great Mosque in two hours.'

'And meet him you shall, just not in front of the Great Mosque,' Ghulam replies. 'Oh, and he will be bound to a chair.'

Chapter Nine

Abdullah Saíd
Mayasin

Month of Pregnancy 23, 1375 A.H. (2 June 1956 A.D.)

The guards have taken the king's suit from him, and the king makes his way to the scaffold in rags. He is dirty and barefoot, he has a five-day beard and untidy hair and his hands and feet are chained together. Nevertheless, King Jalal holds his head up high, and even now there is an arrogant look on his face.

When the king passes his wife, he stops. This is definitely not the protocol that was agreed upon after an hour of discussion. Abdullah wishes the king would get a move on and looks to his side at Quadir, but his sister's husband looks back a little helplessly and shrugs. Apart from the voices of the royal couple, whom nobody dares to interrupt, there is complete silence in the courtyard.

Abdullah remembers Sergei. *He is still the king.* During the meeting, he had not really understood the words of the Russian; now he does. Just as he understands why the guards do not motion the king to keep on walking like they were ordered to and instead allow him time to talk to his wife.

The words the king speaks make the queen smile, but while Abdullah can hear them, he cannot understand them. The king smiles, too, although neither he nor his wife has any reason to be happy. They are about to die, and even in death there will not be any mercy for them. Now the queen, who is not constrained, throws her arms around her husband and kisses him. There are no tears.

Their embrace seems to last forever, and Abdullah turns his eyes away; the people around him do the same. Somehow to watch feels like to intrude on a private moment between a loving husband and wife, and this makes the king and the queen more human than any of the spectators like.

But then there is a short rattling of the king's chains, and Abdullah looks up again. The queen has let him go, and the king is now standing in front of his son. He tries to lay his hand on the boy's forehead, but the chains constrain him too much. King Jalal turns to the guards, holds his hands up and stares severely at them.

One of them steps forward and unlocks one of the king's hands; the other is still bound to his feet. Had there been more sounds, even whispers, surely one of the communist or Brotherhood leaders would call out to stop the man, yet still nobody dares to break the silence, and the king gives the guard a short, sarcastic smile—probably ungrateful, because the guard has freed only one of his hands—and turns back to his son.

King Jalal lays his free hand on his son's head. This time he speaks in English, and even though he speaks softly, Abdullah can hear the words. 'Be strong, dear prince. Do not fear the man with the sword, for you are the greater man, and, like a snake, he is the one who is truly scared. Do not despair because of the darkness that is to come, for in every darkness one day there will be light, and if any man can find it, you are that man. Do not mourn that your life was short; no matter how long you are here, it will never be long enough.'

They are good words, and Abdullah wonders what he would say to Muhammad and Nasir if it were him standing there. If he can honestly say that he has tried to improve the world they will be living in, he supposes that will be enough.

'Father.' It is all the boy can muster, and even though his voice breaks as he says it, the boy does not cry. The king pulls his son toward him with his free arm and gives him a hug. It is a short one, though; ashamed by the spectators, the boy pulls away and puts on his sturdiest face. The king grins, winks at the boy, and moves on to his daughter.

Again, he chooses English as the language to say his goodbyes. 'Princess, I am sorry I did not send you away. I have failed you.'

'You could never fail me, father.'

'Have they done anything to you?'

'They would not dare.' She spits on the ground. 'Even though they are animals.'

'Are you scared?'

'No, Father. I was scared, some time ago, but I fixed that.'

'Really?'

'When they came into the palace, I was afraid that they would kill me and Muhammad would give me to one of the animals to pleasure him for all eternity, so I took a man from the Royal Guard and made sure that Muhammad thought I would no longer be worthy of that "honour."'

The king winks at his daughter, before pulling her close and kissing her on the cheek. 'You were always the smartest.' She throws both her arms around him, and Abdullah hears him softly say, 'I am very proud of you.'

He cannot believe that the king isn't angry. Minutes before he is going to die, his daughter tells him that she has thrown away her family's honour, and all the king says is that he is proud of her! If his own daughter had made a confession like this, he would have strangled her with his free hand; even at a moment like this and even if he'd had only one free hand.

In fact, though this isn't his own daughter, he still feels a strong urge to run over to her and strangle her himself. The princess is a beautiful girl, yet she is clearly a demon to do something like this, to let her body go to waste in such a manner. She ought to have been proud of the honours Muhammad would do her in the afterlife. So beautiful and a princess too, she would surely have been given to a great fighter. Instead, she has chosen eternal damnation.

He looks around to see if anybody else has understood. It is obvious that none of the members of the Brotherhood has, but he sees a small smile on the face of the communist girl who wears trousers. He is going to remember her on the day the future government of Beledar is decided. Then his eyes turn to Sergei, who must have understood too, but the Russian agent is simply staring into the void.

King Jalal lets his daughter go and starts to walk again. The guard leads him up to the small platform, which has been built specially for the occasion, and there he waits. Lenin climbs the platform too, and although the youthful communist leader is trying to look confident, Abdullah can see that his hands are trembling.

'King Jalal!' the young man begins, his voice much too loud for the small group of spectators. He appears to startle himself a little as well, and in a normal voice he starts over.

'King Jalal. For ignoring the will of the people, we have found that you are not truly the king of Beledar, and therefore you are an imposter. For this treachery, the people of Beledar have condemned you to death. Do you have any last words?'

The king turns his head toward the young man and stares straight into his eyes. For a brief moment Lenin stares back, but then the communist looks down. Satisfied, the king now turns towards the spectators.

'*Subjects.*' It comes out just as it is meant: degrading. Abdullah cannot help but feel small, and he will be glad when it is all over. Presently, though, he is forced to listen.

'I am pleased that you have come to attend this historic occasion. I would have expected there to be more of you, but I suppose your leaders feared that if too many people were here, some of them might just try to free me.' The king now stares at the communist leaders, who are standing together. It hurts Abdullah that he is right.

'If this was a tragedy written by William Shakespeare, what you are about to witness would be the conclusion of the second act. Yet I hope that when the chroniclers of Beledar write about this day, they will make a bit more of a show of it. An imposter? Really? You are embarrassing.

'My father was the man who united our country and defeated the Turks; I am the man who broke the English chains and gave you freedom. And make no mistake, the blood of the Prophet is flowing through my veins, and I strongly doubt that he will look favourably on those men who kill his descendants.'

Suddenly the king's eyes are on Abdullah. He is not to blame; he knows it. It is King Jalal's own fault that he is standing here today, yet the king's eyes burn into his soul, and he looks down too.

'Since I suppose very few of you know any Shakespearean plays, I will disclose to you that they generally have five acts. Thus, while you might think that you are advancing toward the conclusion of this drama, in fact you are not even halfway. As a matter of fact, I could also be wrong, for I am not completely sure whether we are in a drama or a comedy.'

Abdullah has no idea what the king is talking about. He has heard of the name Shakespeare and knows that he was some kind of heathen poet, but no more than that. He looks around him. Clearly he isn't the only one who does not understand.

Then he sees Sergei. The eyes of the Russian have turned dark, and very slowly and silently he moves in the direction of the entrance of the courtyard. Is the Russian spy leaving? Does the king know something he doesn't?

Three more acts after the king is dead. If Mr Petrakis and the American didn't kill Lord Tali'a, whoever did is still out there, waiting to make his move. And if Jack Jones truly was plotting with the infidel, perhaps there are more conspirators. It is not impossible; after all, he is the man paying the generals. On the other hand, Lord Tali'a had many enemies, and he may also really have been killed by some boy on the streets.

'I am condemned to death by men who tell the people that they are going to bring redemption to this country, yet in reality all you bring the people will be war and repression,' the king continues. 'Turn to your side and look at the men who want to make our country a Soviet colony, who want to enslave the people and exchange God for Karl Marx. Now turn to your other side and look at the men who believe that fourteen hundred years of learning should be ignored because God gave a man named Muhammad infinite wisdom. And let me tell you something, if *my* ancestor was here today, he would despise all of you and all of your ideas.

'Thus, fake scholars and Moscow puppet boys, you do what you have to do, but I do not acknowledge your jurisdiction. I am the sole representative of the people and the descendant of the Prophet, while you are nothing but servants of Satan.'

Quadir and Gamal look like they are going to explode, and Abdullah knows exactly how they are feeling. But before they can intervene, Lenin, whose face has become bright red, as the English officers used to be after a couple of days in the city, shouts, 'Enough! Executioner, do your work!'

A smug smile appears on the king's face, and even when the executioner takes his head by the hair and pulls it down to the scaffold, he is still grinning.

The executioner raises his sword, but Abdullah does not look. Instead, he observes the king's children. There is not a hint of emotion in their eyes as they stare at the execution of their father.

Why do they not cry? Or beg? He closes his eyes. The king deserves to die. He is the man responsible for the corruption on the streets. He is the man responsible for breaking up families, for the fact that his brother is dead and for the fact that Gamal is missing an ear and two fingers.

He is also the man responsible for the corrupt policemen and for what happened to Abdullah outside of Siraj's House of Dreams, all those years ago—if only for the reason that he allowed the House of Dreams to exist.

Abdullah opens his eyes again, and looks at the executioner, who is still standing there with his sword raised in the air. Why is it taking so long? Both the communists and the Brothers did not want to use an executioner who had previously served the government, yet it was immensely difficult to find a man willing to execute the king. Even the men who were locked up and tortured by the Royal Guard politely refused.

There had been talk of putting the king in front of a firing squad so that nobody could know who had actually done the deed, but they all felt that this would not be dramatic enough. Eventually, after they offered a hefty reward, one of the men from the Brotherhood volunteered.

Abdullah feels an urge to shout to the man that he should get on with it, but he doesn't dare to break what feels like a holy silence. He looks at the king's daughter again. In a way she reminds him of the girl who served him his brandy at Siraj's House of Dreams. What was her name again? It is actually a disgrace that while the king is being punished for his sins, Siraj may still be out there, committing more and worse crimes.

His eyes move to the king's son. The king created a world filled with debauchery and hedonism for the boy, but Abdullah now has the chance to build something better for his own boys.

He hears the sword come down, and there is a grunt from the king. That is a good sound; finally, a sign of weakness. He looks at the scaffold and sees the king breathing heavily while using all of his energy to keep his mouth closed so that he does not scream. Meanwhile, the executioner is pulling the sword from the king's shoulder. The king screams, but just for a second and then he controls himself again.

Even now, there is no reaction from the king's family.

On the podium, the executioner is leaning on his sword for a moment. The man's face is hidden under a black scarf, and Abdullah can only see his eyes, but he can feel how nervous the man is. He doesn't blame him. After today, he will be the man who has killed a descendant of Muhammad.

Slowly, the executioner lifts his sword again.

Abdullah holds his breath as the executioner reaches the point where his hands are over his head and the sword is behind him. This is it. With a big swing the man brings the sword down into the skull of the king, killing him but not decapitating him. The executioner looks a bit helplessly at Lenin, but the young communist says, 'Finish it.'

Quadir and Gamal are leaving, and Abdullah decides to follow their example. Minutes ago he could hardly wait for the execution of the king's daughter, yet he cannot watch this spectacle any longer.

This day was supposed to be gratifying! It was supposed to be about justice! But while the man who had been leading the people away from God is dead, he does not feel like any justice is done at all. Instead, as he walks through the palace hallways, he feels defeated. Not even the sight of a group of women in black burkas, something that would have been impossible in this palace just three weeks ago, can cheer him up. He also does not notice that they are in rather a hurry.

Abdullah spits on the ground of the palace floors. The king has disgraced them all with his performance. It is good that there was not a trial or a large crowd; nobody needed to know. He encounters a group of men from the Brotherhood standing in the hallway. They are armed, and he realises that even if they have failed to bring justice to Beledar in the garden, that does not mean this day has to go to waste. He can still make the world a better place today. It is his duty, both to God and to his little boys.

'Come with me,' he orders the men, and he smiles to himself. Siraj is not going to know what hit him.

CHAPTER TEN

CAPTAIN KHALID KHAN
Mayasin

Month of Pregnancy 23, 1375 A.H. (2 June 1956 A.D.)

'Where are we going?' Khalid asks as Ghulam is leading him through a string of alleys. Thirty minutes ago, he knew everything was going to be all right, but now he doesn't even know what 'all right' exactly means.

'We are going to question your Major Hammoud,' Ghulam answers.

'Is he much farther?'

'Not really. Five minutes.'

Khalid follows his friend through the alleys for a lot longer than five minutes, and he wonders if he's doing the right thing. He has enough cash to arrange transport for himself, and perhaps he should abandon Ghulam and find himself a ride to General Raslan. But he doesn't know where he is, and both his friend and Major Hammoud warned him about the people on the streets. When they finally arrive at a small house with windows that are closed from the outside world with heavy curtains, he realises that by not making any decision, he has let Ghulam decide for him.

'Here we are,' his friend says as he walks to the door and knocks four times.

'Who is it?' a voice from the other side asks.

'Ghulam.'

A man in an expensive-looking suit opens the door. 'Ghulam? Ghulam!' The man steps forward and kisses him. 'How is my favourite little vagrant?'

Khalid frowns. His friend had always claimed to be the son of an important officer. What's this business about him being a vagrant?

'I am very well, Siraj, you old crook. How are you?'

'Ah! God has been very good to me. Today I welcome you to the Palace of Dreams.'

'Not for long, I suppose. You must know what is going on in the real palace.'

'Few men in the city know better what's going on in the palace than me. The men who are there now, they come to me too—even though they despise me in public—but politics, Ghulam, they do not affect me.

'Once there were the Turks, and they said that what I did was illegal, yet their civil servants came here, and they always made sure I was well-protected. Then came the English. Many of them believed what they read in *Thousand and One Nights,* and since they could not find the women in the streets to act out their fantasies, Siraj found them for them.

'The king, he does not like my business either, but he never did anything to stop me, and many of the lords and men from his parliament came here to find my girls. Men will always be men, Ghulam, and they will always want beautiful girls. So don't you worry about me; old Siraj will be all right.'

'That's good to hear.' Khalid notices that Ghulam does not sound very confident.

'Who is your friend?' Siraj asks.

'He's good people.'

'God is praised. Tell me, have you and your friend come for a girl?'

'As a matter of fact, we have come for a man,' Ghulam replies.

Khalid sees Siraj's face grow darker. 'There is a man here. Nadir brought him, and I told him that I am not in that kind of business, but he would not listen. He did not tell me that you arranged it, though, but still, why did you have that man brought here?'

'Siraj, the city is crowded with men from the Brotherhood, and I figured this would be the safest place. I promise you that he'll gone before dark. Now, where is he?'

'If God wants it, follow me.'

They step into a room with pink tapestry on the wall. Three scantily dressed girls are sitting on two sofas. The moment they see them, the girls get up, but Siraj motions that they can remain where they are, and with a slightly bored look they gaze at the visitors.

Khalid lingers to look at them. He has never seen girls wearing so few clothes, and he wonders what it would be like to touch them. Then he notices that a woman is singing English or American songs, and in the corner of a room he spots a gramophone. Khalid has seen this device a couple of times before, but he has never heard music like this. If he gets out of all this alive, he is going to buy a machine like that for himself.

'Come, my friend,' Siraj says, and Khalid realises that he has stopped moving. 'I don't want this man in my house any longer than necessary.'

They leave the room and enter a hallway. Here, from behind closed doors Khalid can hear a man and a woman grunting. On the walls are paintings of naked ladies, and he recognises the 'Judgment of Paris,' where the Trojan prince decides which one of the Greek goddesses is the most beautiful. It's exactly as he imagined it when he read the *Iliad*.

He thinks about the Forbidden House in Nardin, and suddenly he feels sorry that he never visited it during his time there. Was it something like this? Even if there weren't any girls, he understands now why men like Ayden are so keen to visit these kinds of places.

The hustler opens a door and they enter a second sitting room, where a giant oak bookcase attracts Khalid's attention.

'A great part of his youth Ghulam spent in this room,' Siraj says. 'I taught him to read the Latin script myself, and many days and nights he did nothing else.'

Ghulam is now actually looking a little uncomfortable, but Khalid tries to act like there is nothing weird about an officer's son spending his youth in a whorehouse and asks the pimp, 'How did you get these books?'

'They came with the house, just like this.' With a smile and a grand gesture, Siraj lifts a small statue, and suddenly the fireplace moves. Behind it, a new room appears, and in the middle of the room, gagged and bound to a chair, is Major Hammoud.

'Nadir promised me there would be money,' Siraj says to Ghulam.

'I have gold.'

The hustler's face lights up for a second, but then it grows darker again. 'Remember, gone before sunset.'

His friend nods and lays a hand on the Siraj's shoulder while Khalid turns his attention to the major, who is not only gagged but also blindfolded. He knows he should not be here, but it's too late to leave now.

Ghulam closes the door and takes off the man's blindfold. The major's fury radiates from his eyes, and when Ghulam pulls the gag out of his mouth, Major Hammoud tries to spit at him. He misses, but he does receive Ghulam's fist on his nose as punishment.

It starts to bleed, and the major spits on the ground. 'In the name of God, do you know who I am?'

'According to the man next to me, you are Major Achmed Hammoud. Am I not right?'

The major now turns his head toward Khalid, and he can see the surprise in the major's eyes. 'Captain Khan, who is this man?'

'The question isn't who am I,' Ghulam answers for him, 'but who are you? Because you and I both know that even if there is a Major Hammoud, you are not him.'

'Captain,' the major is still looking at him, 'we need to get to General Raslan. The king's life, the entire kingdom is at stake. Remember?'

'General Raslan?' Ghulam says. 'Why don't you just call him brother?'

'Captain Khan, what is this man talking about?'

Khalid looks at the major and then at Ghulam. He remembers how he suspected his friend had lied to him about having a cousin named Zahaar in the Emir's Guard, after Colonel Hussein stated that he had not known a guard by that name. But now that this Siraj told him that Ghulam spent most of his nights and days in this whorehouse as a kid, he is certain that his friend lied to him when he said that his father was an officer. And everything that's about to happen right now is based on the testimony of a liar.

'So that's how you want to play it,' Ghulam says, and he unsheathes a dagger from his belt. Khalid stares at it, surprised that he hasn't noticed it earlier, for he has never before seen a dagger like this one. On the top of the hilt there is a black and gold snakehead, and the black and gold continues throughout the blade, representing the skin of the snake, as though it is the tail that is lethal. 'Let's play.'

'Captain Khan, you need to put an end to this right now!'

But Khalid is nailed to the floor and lost for words.

'This was a present from a man who was very dear to me,' Ghulam continues without even looking at Khalid. 'A man for whom I held great respect. Notice how I am speaking in the past tense? It is because he is dead.'

'So? What have I got to do with that?' Major Hammoud asks.

'Maybe not much, maybe a lot. You see, nobody appears to have killed this man. Communists haven't; the Brotherhood hasn't; urban aristocrats haven't. Some people even believe that he was killed by a little street kid. Do you see where I am going with this?'

'Are you talking about Lord Tali'a?' the major says. 'Because I know who killed him, and I have told your friend. He was killed by Lord Kalaldeh!'

'Of course you'd say that. Blame it all on Lord Kalaldeh so that you and your brother can bring an army into the city and crown your father king of Beledar. You know what I wonder? Have you already decided which of your brothers will succeed your father after he dies?'

'Captain Khan, I don't know where you've found this man, but I swear by the holy Quran that he is either crazy or working for Lord Kalaldeh. Remember, if he kills me, it will be Kalaldeh who takes control of this city. The villain will be rewarded for Lord Tali'a's murder!'

Khalid wants to say something, but Ghulam winks at him, and he decides to wait a little longer to see what will happen.

'You know,' Ghulam says as he touches the sergeant's ear with his dagger, 'I saw you in Egypt with the English lord. Do you want to enlighten us about what you were discussing?'

'I've never been to Egypt,' Major Hammoud replies.

'Really? Are you calling the man with a dagger next to your ear a liar?' Ghulam hisses in the sergeant's ear before he grabs it and starts to cut it.

Khalid looks away; he has never felt more like a coward, but he just doesn't know what to do. The major starts to scream, and he is transported back thirteen years, and it's the boy, Omar, who is screaming.

It is over quickly, and when he directs his gaze back at his friend and the major, there is blood coming out of the side of the man's head, while Ghulam is showing him his own ear. In his friend's eyes there is a sadistic happiness, and it is clear that Ghulam is enjoying this, like his brother Nourad enjoyed force-feeding Omar.

'Do you know how many body parts you have that we can cut off before you die? We can either make this a very long night or a very short one,' Ghulam says calmly.

For the first time since the blindfold was removed, Khalid sees actual fear in the man's eyes. He wonders if that is because Ghulam is right or because the major really believes his friend has only just begun. If it's the latter, the man is probably correct, and he realises that if it were him in the major's stead, he'd be pretty scared by now.

'Captain Khan, I swear by the Quran, I am not who this man says I am.'

'It's your funeral,' Ghulam replies, and he walks around the chair and squats behind the sergeant, who starts to scream again. 'Did you know that fingers make for great meat? A long time ago, during the War of the West, there were cannibals in this city. I sold them dead people, and they roasted them. They told me that a man's finger tasted like the best parts of a chicken.'

'You're a demon!' Major Hammoud grunts as he looks at the finger Ghulam is waving in front of his eyes.

'What shall we take next, Khalid? An eye?' Ghulam throws the finger on the ground and puts his knife against the major's face. Now Khalid sees real terror in the man's eyes. His friend starts to press his dagger against the major's right eyelid, and slowly, drops of blood start flowing down.

'Wait! If God wants it, wait!' Major Hammoud shouts before directing his gaze at Khalid again. 'It's true. I am Othman Raslan, but I only pretended to be someone I wasn't because my brother did not trust the situation. With the murder of Lord Tali'a, he wanted to know what kind of men were sent to him!'

Khalid wonders if it's guilt or disappointment that he reads in the man's eyes, but before he can decide, Ghulam beams at him. 'You see, I was right! I told you that he was a liar, and now I'm going to prove to you that he is also behind the murder of Lord Tali'a.'

'No, you're not,' Khalid says as he pulls his pistol and points it at his friend. 'You're going to step away from the prisoner.'

'What? But I just proved to you that I was right!'

'No, you haven't. You've proven that a man will confess anything under torture, and before that you have proven that you are a liar. Or can you explain to me why the son of an important officer spent his childhood in a whorehouse?'

'Khalid,' Ghulam says as he steps away from the prisoner. 'You don't want to do this. You don't want to hand over the keys of the kingdom to Lord Raslan.'

'You don't have to,' the prisoner says. 'Lock up this madman somewhere and drive to Issa. Don't tell him to join forces with Raslan; just tell him to get his brigade to the capital as soon as possible.'

'I can live with that,' Ghulam says a little too quickly. 'Anyone but Raslan and I'll give you my blessing. I'll even allow you to lock me up.'

His friend will 'allow him to lock him up?' When Khalid is the one with the gun? He snorts, but he knows that he must keep his cool, and he looks from Ghulam to the prisoner. If both men are okay with him going to Issa, then he either won't make it to the camp or he won't find Issa alive, and then he will still have to choose between Kalaldeh and Raslan.

Khalid has to choose between the two mightiest generals in the country, and whichever he leads to the capital will decide the fate of the kingdom. It's insane; he has been a captain for about a week, and now he has to make one of the most important decisions in the history of Beledar.

Gracious and Merciful God, please give me the strength and the wisdom to decide what is right!

Major Hammoud—or is it Othman Raslan?—was his only friend at Camp Ritag. Had his friendship been part of a bigger plan? But Raslan didn't have to send Khalid to Mayasin. In fact, Raslan didn't have to send anyone. He could have simply taken his army and marched on the city.

On the other side, Commander al-Sabah trusts Ghulam, and even if Khalid does not, he must take into account the opinion of the commander of the Royal Guard before making his decision. Or does he? Lord Tali'a outranked General Lord Raslan, but that was because he was Lord Tali'a, not because he was the commander of the Royal Guard.

Or are the two connected? The commander of the Royal Guard deals with the personal protection of the king, and if he were king, he would appoint as its commander the man he trusted most.

'Why did you lie to me?' he hisses at Ghulam. His friend shakes his head, which makes him furious and he screams, 'Why did you lie to me?'

'What do you want to hear?' Ghulam snarls. 'That I was one of a thousand kids in Mayasin who grew up on the streets and had nothing? That I spent my days on the streets, where I sold whatever I could get my hands on? Arak, girls, once even a dead girl? That my father left me before I was born and my mother died before I had my first erection?

'Do you want to hear that I dreamed of a successful dad and a cousin at the Royal Guard and that when I told other people about those dreams, they became so real to me that I could almost touch them?

'You're right, I'm a liar, and that's probably why Lord Tali'a decided I would make a good spy. But Lord Tali'a gave me a purpose and made me important. You, and Aadhil and Namdar, you promised to be my brothers, and I may have lied about the little things, but I would never, ever, betray you!

'Now, shoot me if you want to shoot me, but I swear by the vow we made back in Camp Mayasin that this man is a traitor and that we should kill him and drive to Issa or Kalaldeh and make sure that Raslan isn't going to take over this country!'

Khalid's eyes are getting wet, and he can feel his arm going down. *One for all, and all for one.*

'Wait, Captain Khan,' Hammoud/Raslan says. 'He's trying to fool you. I know liars like that, and they can sound extraordinarily sincere when they need to; it's written. But before you know it, they will stab you in the back!'

'I believe you,' he says, his gun now pointed at the prisoner. 'I believe that you are so familiar with liars that you can spot them a mile away. In fact . . .'

Crack.

He is interrupted by a gunshot in the distance, and he turns to the door, which slowly opens. He catches a glimpse of Siraj just as there's another, louder gunshot.

'That wasn't me,' Khalid says as he moves to the side of the room, while Ghulam mirrors his movements.

Crack!

The door is now completely open, and Siraj takes a step toward them before falling to the ground. The back of his shirt is red with blood. And then there are more gunshots and Khalid can see little explosions of blood on the stomach of their prisoner, before his chair falls over.

He looks at Ghulam. 'To God we belong, and to Him we shall return.'

His friend, his dagger back in his belt and a gun in both hands, tilts his head to Khalid and grins. 'You may be right, but not yet.'

CHAPTER ELEVEN

ABDULLAH SAID
Mayasin

Month of Pregnancy 23, 1375 A.H. (2 June 1956 A.D.)

The last bullet has come from his own gun, and pulling the trigger has satisfied a hunger that has lived inside him ever since he was thrown out of this house almost fifteen years ago. What's more, after the debacle in the courtyard, he really needed this.

The Brothers he has ordered to accompany him keep on firing, though, and in the room where he once sawed a girl into pieces, a man in a chair falls backwards.

There are more gunshots, and now a Brother goes down. Quickly, he follows the five men that are still standing in their retreat to the door, away from the enemy gunfire.

'What's the plan?' one of them asks once they are out of the line of fire.

What is the plan? He has the revenge he came for, but knowing Siraj, the men in the other room can only be rats. Perhaps Nadir is even among them. Any dead rat is a good rat, but Abdullah still has a special grudge against the rat who took so much of his money when he was a boy.

'How many do you think there are?'

'Two.' Six against two; even without the element of surprise that should be an easy victory.

'What about Rasoul?' He gestures at the man who is lying on the floor.

'He won't last till the evening, may God bless his soul.'

Crack! Crack!

Next to him, another man screams: Mourat. Now it is two against five, and they retreat to the next room.

'Surrender yourselves now and you will be spared!' a voice calls from the previous room.

'You surrender!' he counters. 'You're under arrest by order of the Muslim Brotherhood.'

'We don't take orders from the Muslim Brotherhood,' the voice comes back. 'We only take orders from the king.'

'The king is dead!'

Silence.

He looks to the remaining men at his side. 'We can take them.'

'They are soldiers,' says a man whose name he does not know. 'We only came here for the whoremonger.'

What are soldiers doing inside of Siraj's secret room? He calls, 'What regiment are you?'

The past week he has learned all the names of the regimental commanders, and he knows exactly who is working for the Brotherhood and who is working for the communists.

There is no answer. The man whose name he doesn't know looks at him questioningly, yet Abdullah isn't ready to call the retreat. 'We need to know who sent them. Try to keep at least one alive!'

'Yes, sir.' Carefully, the man moves his rifle around the corner of the door, but the moment his head follows there is another gunshot, and the man falls down. Abdullah sees the bullet hole in the middle of his forehead.

Next to him two more of his men crouch down, their rifles ready to fire, but they too are dead on the ground before they can use them.

'God is great! God is great!'

And then one of the soldiers is right in front of him. Abdullah wants to shoot him, but there is a fist on his nose, and blood clouds his vision. The man puts his foot on his kneecap, and his leg splits in two like a twig.

He screams. It hurts like nothing he has ever felt before.

There is the flash of a dagger, and he can only watch as his last two men go down too. He should have run the moment they killed Siraj, or perhaps he should never have come here in the first place.

The other man kneels down next to him. A terrifying face, split by a scar and with blood running down it. The man puts the dagger to his throat and brings his face so close to Abdullah's that he can smell the soldier's breath.

'What did you mean when you said that the king is dead?' the man asks in a hoarse voice.

'The communists killed him this morning.'

'Liar!' The man grabs his broken knee and pinches it. Abdullah screams in terror.

'It's true! On the Prophet, I swear it is true!' he says as quickly as he can.

'Liar!' the man repeats, and again he squeezes his knee.

He never knew that pain like this existed. If only the soldier would just kill him, it will all be over and he can go to Paradise.

But the man does not and hisses, 'You killed him together, didn't you?'

'No! No! I swear by the Prophet. The Muslim Brotherhood never wanted the king to die. We wanted to send him away, exile him. The communists, they demanded his death; they could not be stopped!'

'Liar!'

'No!' This time the soldier slams his gun into Abdullah's knee. The pain goes through his entire body.

'Tell me the truth!'

'Please!' He has agreed with Quadir and Jack Jones that they will never tell anyone the full truth, but it hurts too bad. 'All right! All right!'

'Now!' More pain.

The man snorts, and suddenly there is a bloody knife in his hand. With his other hand the man grabs Abdullah's chin and turns his face toward him. 'Look at me.'

Abdullah closes his eyes.

'Look at me!'

He opens them again, and as he looks into the eyes of his attacker, he realises that all the demons that haunt his dreams are united in this man. He wants to scream, but terror has taken his breath.

'I am sick of you forsaken liars! First I am going to cut out your tongue. Then I am going to cut off your nose. And finally, I will cut off your penis and leave you here to die.'

'Ghulam, is that really necessary?' Abdullah doesn't know where the voice is coming from. In fact, he has been so terrified that he has completely forgotten about the man who broke his knee.

'Of course it is. You just heard him, he murdered the king!'

Ghulam. Ghulam. Could it be? Of course, that scar!

'Wait, Ghulam, it's me.' But his voice is weak, and his attacker cannot hear him.

He feels the dagger pressing against his throat, and he tries again. 'Wait, in the name of God, Ghulam.' His voice is a little stronger now. 'It's me! Wait!'

He has the demon's attention, but there is no sign of recognition in his eyes. 'It's Abdullah,' he cries. 'Abdullah.'

The man pulls the knife back a little. 'Abdullah?'

'Abdullah, from Mr Darwish. Abdullah, four shillings up front. Abdullah.'

Now Ghulam is getting up.

'Who is Abdullah?' the other man asks.

'He is a traitor, yet I cannot kill him, or at least not today. You may do what you like, though.'

And with that Ghulam turns around. He walks out of the room and does not look at him again. The man who broke Abdullah's knee comes closer and towers over him.

'In the name of God,' Abdullah pleads, 'I swear by the Prophet, it wasn't me.'

'Be silent. What you say is of no importance, for I do not know you, and you may well be a liar; only God knows your precise role. Retribution for an injury is an equal injury, and the king is dead . . .'

The man pauses and stares deep into his eyes, but Abdullah daren't say more. The man is young; he can't be past twenty-five. He looks at the dark, cold eyes. They are the eyes of death. He will never see his sons again, but at least he will leave behind a slightly better world. The man lifts his hand, and now Abdullah is staring into the barrel of a gun.

'Retribution for an injury is an equal injury,' the man repeats, but then he lowers his gun again and continues. 'However, those who forgive an injury and make reconciliation will be rewarded by God. Abdullah-four-shillings-up-front, God's words save your life today.'

The man gives him one last look, and Abdullah feels the eyes of the king burning into his soul again.

Then Captain Khalid Khan turns around and follows Ghulam out the door.

Epilogue:

Henry Wilson
Brooklyn

10-11 February 1992 A.D.

The phone wakes me, and I open my eyes; it's still light outside. I am lying on the floor of my Brooklyn apartment, and while I have no idea why my previous night ended on the floor, I don't really care. I have woken up in weirder places. The phone rings again. It's not very annoying, though, and I want to go back to sleep, but then I realise it might be my daughter, and I jump up and sprint the four paces to get to the phone.

'Hello?'

'Harry, it's Gerald.' My former editor; he's an asshole. 'How's life on the other side of the river?'

Only now do I realise how sick I'm feeling, and I'm definitely not in the mood to talk to Gerald Fisher. Without another word I hang up and make my way to the sofa, where I plop down and close my eyes again. Once more the phone starts to ring, but this time I decide to let my answering machine handle it. I am back to sleep before it has stopped ringing.

*   *   *

433

When I wake it is dark, and a glance at my watch tells me it's one thirty at night. I feel pretty good, but I am dead thirsty. I get up from the sofa and walk over to the fridge, where I find a bottle of Coke. To my surprise the light on my answering machine is blinking, and I wonder who's called me. Could it have been my daughter? I press the button, and the mechanical voice of the woman on the machine tells me I have one new message. For a second, my heart starts beating faster.

'Listen up, Harry, I've got you an offer that's so good, it will make you wanna suck my dick. Call me back!' Gerald Fisher.

The moment I hear his voice, I remember that I have already been awake this afternoon. I have absolutely no intention of calling him back and delete the message. After finishing the whole bottle of Coke, I move over to my desk and sit down in front of my typewriter, where I start reading what I wrote last night. It's shit, but since it's going to be book number twenty-three of the *True Love Series* and I will never sign my name to it, that doesn't matter.

I have no idea who reads these books, but I also wrote number eleven, and that may have been even crappier, but it sold just fine. It was a story about a girl and a boy who fall in love but can't ever be together because of the enmity between their families. A bit like *Romeo and Juliet* in terrible prose—and in my version the protagonists live happily ever after. If Shakespeare weren't already dead, he'd probably kill himself after reading it.

The next day I am woken by the doorbell. I am in bed, quite hungry. I look at my watch: six thirty. There's the doorbell again. Reluctantly, I get out of bed, cover myself with the bathrobe I pick up from the floor and walk to the door. I open it and find a fat man named Gerald grinning at me.

'Harry!'

I try to slam the door in his ugly red face, but he uses his foot to block it.

'Harry, wait!'

I sigh, and since I can't close the door, I open it again so at least my former editor can see how annoyed I am by his appearance. 'What do you want, Gerald?'

'Like I told your answering machine, I've gotten you the opportunity of a lifetime! Do you know that I've left you, like, ten messages today?'

'I don't care.'

'Oh yes you do. This is your chance to get back in the game.'

I need a drink, and since I know Gerald isn't going to give up easily, I turn around and walk to my kitchen/living room, where I pour myself a large glass of Jack. Gerald has followed me, and although I see him glancing at the bottle, I have no intention of offering him one too. Instead I look him straight in the eyes and say, 'All right; spit it out.'

'Khalid Khan.' He speaks the words slowly, as though he's trying to seduce me with the name of a Middle Eastern dictator.

'What about him?'

'What do you know 'bout him?'

I shrug. 'Not much. He's the president of Beledar and ten years ago he killed about 30,000 people. He tortures prisoners and political opponents, and he supports terrorism in Israel. Pretty much your average Arab tyrant.

Gerald grins. 'I suppose that's enough, for now. We're going to publish a biography about him, and the boss wants you to write it.'

'You mean the prick who buried my last book?' I still sometimes dream about killing him.

The fat man shrugs. 'You know, circumstances were different. The things you were claiming about Saddam and the CIA . . .

your book would have made us look unpatriotic, and you know you are working in a business that depends on the favour of the public.'

'Fuck you,' I answer. 'You're a coward and he's an asshole!'

'And yet here we are, doing you a favour!'

'Why? Off the top of my head, I can think of at least a dozen people who are better suited to write this biography than me. Did they all refuse you?'

'Actually, the boss wants a gonzo book about the Beledarian president, Henry Wilson style. Can you still give me a dozen names? Because in that case, I'll be out your door in thirty seconds.'

Gerald is not wrong; there are few people who speak Arab and can write a book Henry Wilson style. If it didn't mean I'd be working for Gerald and the dickhead, I'd probably jump at the chance. As it is, I grunt, 'Not interested.'

'I don't think you understand. This story is awesome. There's a former queen they say was once the most beautiful in the world, waiting to tell her story. There's . . .'

'I said I wasn't interested,' I interrupt him.

'You haven't heard our offer yet.'

'I don't have to, and I think it's time to leave.'

'I will, but just look at this.' He reaches inside his jacket and pulls out a note. I look at it. It's a cheque for $10,000 and it's got my name on it.

'What's this?'

'That's your first advance, but there'll be four more cheques like that coming before the book is finished. What's more, everything you need will be paid for. Plane tickets, hotels, food while you're abroad. Hell, you can even send us your bar tabs!'

I wonder if I'm dreaming. I haven't seen Gerald in three years, and suddenly he turns up at my door with an offer that's too good to be true. 'What's the catch?'

Gerald shakes his head. 'You get access to the president, you decide what's going to be in the book, and we have got, like, a giant marketing budget ready for you when it's done. There's no catch, just the opportunity of a lifetime.'

I slide the cheque back across the table. 'I don't believe you, and now it really is time to leave.'

'Hey, if you wanna keep on writing about junior baseball and lost cats, don't let me stop you.' He stands up and starts walking toward the door. After he's opened it, he turns back to me. 'Between you and me, my wife loved your version of Romeo and Juliet.'

'How did you know I wrote that?'

He shrugs. 'I am in the book business. Anyhow, my offer is good until Friday. You wanna play with the big boys again, you know where to find me.'

ACKNOWLEDGEMENTS

Writing a book is a solitary process, but after you've spent one-and-a-half years behind a computer, there comes a time when you have to face up to your friends and family. My brother was the first person to read the book, and I am grateful to him for encouraging me to continue. The next draft was read by my friends, Vetter, Freek, and Patrick. Their enthusiasm gave me the strength to sit down yet again, and improve the story.

After the third version my mother read my book for the first time, while my brother took the time to go through it a second time. They made me feel good about myself, which made it easier to accept the constructive critiques from Kylie and Katy. Without them the book would have been at least two hundred pages longer, and I believe the book has become a much easier read thanks to their intervention.

Andrew made my Word document into this book and remained completely relaxed despite the countless last minute changes I wanted. Ruth met with me at the London Book Fair, and took a lot of time to explain the printing process to me. I want to thank Teis for designing the beautiful cover of this book, and Vincent for sponsoring it. A special thanks to Majd, from whose mind sprung the names of the cities and villages that you've read about in this novel.

I wrote my book in English because I wanted to tell the story of how a man turns into a dictator. I didn't just want to tell it to the people in The Netherlands, I wanted to tell it to as many people as possible, and English is the lingua franca of our time. I learned as I went along, but I am much indebted to Katy, Allister, Radhiah and Parisa, for their feedback and corrections.

While writing a story may be a solitary journey, publishing a book requires a team. *Revolution* would have never seen the light of day without a very special group of people who were crazy enough to invest in a publishing company that was founded with the sole purpose of publishing the story of Khalid Khan. Some of them hadn't even read the book yet, but they believed in the story and in me.

Sjakie came up with the idea to invest in the book, Ernst seconded it and instantly put his money where his mouth was. Freek and Patrick, were next to join, and then my brother and my father came aboard.

Together with Vetter, who put an incredible amount of his time in our project, we studied the publishing industry and spent many evenings in meetings to craft a plan. Once it was good enough, we railed in Aad, Albert, Michael, Myriam, and Tom, and we founded Xowox Publishing BV.

Lady and Gentlemen, I have learned much from all of you, and your support makes me very proud.

Last but certainly not least, I want to thank you for taking the time to read this book. Words on paper are meaningless if no one reads them, and I hope that you feel like your time was well spent. Obviously, the story of Khalid Khan is not yet finished, and I also hope that you're looking forward to his return.

Piet Hein Wokke